Summer at Hope Meadows

LUCY DANIELS

HODDER

First published in Great Britain in 2017 by Hodder & Stoughton
An Hachette UK company

1

Copyright © Working Partners Limited 2017
Series created by Working Partners Limited

A CIP catalogue record for this title is available from the British Library

B Format ISBN 978 1 473 65387 0
Ebook ISBN 978 1 473 65388 7

Typeset in Plantin Light by
Palimpsest Book Production Ltd, Falkirk, Stirlingshire

Printed and bound by CPI Group (UK) Ltd, Croydon, CRO 4YY

Hodder & Stoughton policy is to use papers that are natural, renewable
and recyclable products and made from wood grown in sustainable
forests. The logging and manufacturing processes are expected to
conform to the environmental regulations of the country of origin.

Hodder & Stoughton Ltd
Carmelite House
50 Victoria Embankment
London EC4Y 0DZ

www.hodder.co.uk

Special thanks to
Dr Sarah McGurk BVM&S, MRCVS

To the staff at Heaven's Gate Animal Rescue Centre,
Langport, Somerset, with thanks for
everything you do

Chapter One

Home. As the car swooped over the narrow bridge beside the woods, Mandy Hope had the feeling she was back where she belonged.

Beyond the leaf-heavy trees lining the road, she could see the smooth green curve of the beacon, high up on Norland Fell. A hawk hung in the air, riding an invisible current as it studied the ground for prey. Sheep dotted the fell, a scatter of cloudy white against the dark grass. Two walkers were hiking along the line of the dry-stone wall, and Mandy felt a stab of envy as she watched them climb over a stile and head up to the peak.

If only she could stop the car and go for a walk under the vast empty sky. Mandy took a sip of water from a plastic bottle, hoping to quell the butterflies in her stomach. She glanced across at the man beside her, his broad hands light on the steering wheel. Simon Webster, her boyfriend of just over twelve months, caught her eye and grinned. Mandy couldn't help returning his smile. Simon had only visited her home village of Welford twice before – the curse of their equally frantic schedules at the veterinary clinic in

Leeds – and she hoped he would learn to love it as much as she always had.

The giant oak tree that marked the boundary of the village flashed past.

'Cock-a-doodle-do!' Simon crowed.

Mandy raised her eyebrows, puzzled. 'What?'

'Isn't that how you wake up sleepy villages?' Simon teased.

Mandy groaned. 'Seriously, dad jokes already?'

Simon laid his hand on Mandy's thigh. His blue eyes were serious now. 'I know today is going to be tricky for you. I was just trying to help.'

Mandy placed her hand on top of his. His palm felt warm and solid through the fabric of her skirt. 'I know you were,' she said. 'And I appreciate it. Thank you.' She leaned over to kiss his cheek.

Simon steered the car into a space close to the centre of the village. He pulled on the handbrake and turned towards her. 'Ready?'

'I think so,' Mandy said. This was not just any normal homecoming. Today was far more important than that. James, wonderful James, the best friend anyone could have, was getting married and Mandy had agreed to be his best woman.

Simon was out of the car and had whisked round to help Mandy before she had a chance to gather her thoughts. The expression in his blue eyes warmed her as she pulled herself upright, and she was glad of his hand when she found herself teetering for a moment on the unfamiliar heels. Her jodhpur boots were so much more comfortable. The scent of newly cut silage greeted her and Mandy stood for a moment, transported back to the summers she and James had spent together all over Welford and the surrounding Dales.

In the distance, she could hear the burble of the river as they set off to walk up the lane that led to the village green. As they approached the crossroads, they passed the Fox and Goose.

Mandy nodded to the white-painted, slate-roofed pub. 'That's where the reception will be. There's a lovely walled garden out the back. James and I held a charity dog wash there one year.' That day had been almost as scorchingly perfect as this one. James and Mandy had finished soaked to the skin, but it had been worth it, knowing they had contributed to the *We Love Animals* campaign, one of the many wildlife charities they had raised funds for. Mandy couldn't remember spending her pocket money on anything else; recalling how she had nearly poked her eye out with the mascara this morning, she wondered if she should have used some of the cash to start practising make-up at an earlier age than twenty-seven.

She pointed to a terrace of grey stone cottages that were squeezed into a lane behind the pub. 'Up there is Ernie Bell's old cottage. He used to have a grey squirrel as a pet.' For a moment Mandy felt sad. Ernie and Sammy the squirrel were gone now, along with several of the villagers she had grown up with. Then she grinned as happier memories replaced the thoughts of what she had lost.

'That's the village hall.' She pointed to a low stone building on the far side of the road. 'We had a Christmas Eve party there once, and pets were invited, too. Susan Collins turned up with her pony, Prince.'

'Really?' Simon said. His eyebrows almost reached his fringe. 'Was there room in the hall for a pony?'

'Of course not.' Mandy laughed. 'Prince stood outside and stuck his head in through the window.' She could still remember how absurd the little bay pony had looked with his head through the narrow gap.

'So many big memories,' Simon mused, 'for such a pocket-sized village.'

Mandy turned to check her reflection in the window of the post office. Her face was only partly visible through the patchwork of small ad postcards. Her eyes fell on a card advertising a two-year-old lawnmower, economical to run and 100% reliable. At the bottom, in bold lettering, it was revealed that the 'lawnmower' was actually a goat named Cyrus.

'It's going to be great,' Mandy said. 'Coming back. Helping Mum and Dad.'

Throughout her long training, Mandy had never planned to return to Welford to work with her parents in the Animal Ark clinic. She wanted to find new challenges, carve out her own place in the world of veterinary science. Since meeting Simon at the clinic in Leeds, her future had seemed further from Welford than ever. But the new assistant Adam and Emily had recruited only a few weeks ago had unexpectedly quit. When Mandy learned of the struggle they were having to find a locum willing to take on large animal work, and with her own contract in Leeds coming to an end, it had been an obvious step to help out until her parents found a permanent replacement.

'They're very lucky to have you,' Simon commented.

Mandy frowned. 'Shula Maclean really let them down,' she said. 'I know it's tough in mixed practice, with large animal cases day and night and pet consultations as well, but she could at least have stayed until they'd had time to find someone else.'

Her boyfriend shrugged. 'True,' he said, 'but I can understand the temptation of a city job. Better money as well as every night and weekend off.'

Mandy sighed. 'I suppose so.'

'And what about you?' Simon prompted. 'Won't you miss living in Leeds? Exchanging the bright lights and twenty-four-hour shopping for Welford . . .' he looked around, '. . . pretty as it is. At least it will only be for a few months.'

Mandy, who had been about to say she didn't think she would miss the city at all, closed her mouth. They had reached the heart of Welford and the village green with its sombre grey war memorial and tranquil pond. A crowd of people stood chatting on the daisy-strewn grass. Beyond them, several rows of white seats were lined up in front of the oak tree in the centre of the green. A white-painted archway woven with flowers stood under the branches of the tree. Mandy was suddenly aware of the tightness of the navy sheath dress that James had chosen for her, and of just how tall she was in heels. The fascinator in her hair was tugging and she lifted a hand, hoping to relieve the tension, but her fingers met the smoothly pinned chignon and she didn't dare touch it.

'You look stunning.' Simon seemed to sense that she was having a moment of self-doubt and she managed a weak smile, but at that instant there came a cry from a figure standing on the edge of the neatly mown grass.

'Mandy?' Trying to ignore the sensation that everyone was staring at her, Mandy studied the dark-haired young woman who had called her name.

'Susan?' she gasped. 'It's Susan Collins. The girl with the pony I was talking about,' she explained to Simon.

Susan was smiling. 'It's great to see you,' she said. 'I heard James had chosen you as his best woman.' Her face softened as a small boy with huge brown eyes trotted towards them across the grass, clutching a handful of purple Michaelmas daisies.

'What have you got there, sweetie?' Susan asked, bending to greet him and then looking up at Mandy. 'This is my son Jack.' There was pride in her gaze.

'Nice flowers for you, Mummy,' said Jack. 'From over there.'

Mandy looked where he was pointing and wanted to laugh. The other half of the bouquet remained on the plinth at the base of the cenotaph.

Susan put her hand over her mouth, trying to hide a broad grin. 'They're very nice,' she said. 'But they don't belong to us. Shall we put them back?' She took Jack's hand and led him towards the monument.

'Mandy!' There was another exclamation.

'Gran!' Forgetting the dress and the hair and the heels, Mandy made a rush across the grass and hugged Dorothy Hope. 'You're looking wonderful,' she said, stepping back to admire her grandmother's clear skin and sparkling blue eyes. 'Where's Grandad?' Before Dorothy could reply, Tom Hope emerged from the group of guests that were gathered near the roadside and Mandy hugged him as well.

'It's so lovely to see you,' Dorothy said. Her blue eyes were a little more clouded than Mandy remembered, and she made a mental note to check whether her grand-mother was due to see the cataract specialist again.

'What a splendid dress!' her grandfather exclaimed. 'You look so grown up!'

'And you're so elegant and tall,' her grandmother added.

Mandy wondered if Dorothy had genuinely forgotten that she was almost a head shorter than her grand-daughter. She bent down and kissed her grandmother's smooth powdered cheek. 'You look stunning,' she told Dorothy. 'That shade of green really suits you.'

Dorothy smoothed her pistachio-coloured jacket. 'Your grandad told me I looked like a giant leaf.'

'But I like leaves!' Tom Hope protested.

'You remember Simon?' Mandy turned and pulled her boyfriend to her side.

'Of course!' said Dorothy. She shook Simon's hand. 'You look very smart, dear.'

Behind her grandparents, Mandy could see lots of faces she recognised. Brandon Gill was there. He had been in Mandy's class at school, but now raised cattle as well as pigs on Greystones Farm where he had grown up. Brandon was looking uncomfortable; his suit seemed a little too tight. Sympathy coursed through Mandy as she saw him tug surreptitiously at his collar. She felt the same about her dress.

'Hello, Brandon,' she called and he flushed bright red.

'Mandy,' he said with a nod, meeting her eyes for a nanosecond.

Mandy could also see Jean Knox, Animal Ark's former receptionist. On her retirement, Jean had moved away from Welford to be closer to her family. Mandy was delighted to see she had returned for the occasion. 'Hello there, young lady!' Jean reached up to kiss Mandy's cheek. She was looking very elegant in a sapphire blue suit. Despite Mandy's regular visits to Welford, she and Jean never seemed to be there at the same time.

'Hello!' Mandy grinned. 'It's great to see you. Are you just back for the day or will you be staying a bit longer?'

'Just for today, I'm afraid,' Jean said. 'I'm baby-sitting tomorrow but I was so pleased when James invited me.'

'How are the twins?' Mandy knew that Jean looked after her grandchildren regularly now she lived nearer to them.

'They're very well, thank goodness. A handful of trouble, but growing up so fast!'

Mandy caught sight of a thickset woman walking up the road towards the green, wearing a broad-brimmed hat and firmly clutching a fat Pekinese to her bosom. 'Look who it is,' she whispered to Jean.

'You mean Mrs Ponsonby?' Jean looked surprised. 'Did James invite her to the wedding?'

'I don't think so.' Mandy shook her head. 'There wasn't room at the reception to invite everyone from the village, or I suspect he would have done! I suppose she couldn't resist coming to take a look at us all,' she added. 'But that can't be . . .'

'It's not Pandora.' Mandy turned to see that Susan had returned, carrying Jack, whose eyes were fixed on the dog. Mandy had already realised that it couldn't be the same pampered Pekinese she remembered so well from her childhood, but the likeness was uncanny.

'She's called Fancy and she's a distant relative of Pandora's. Third cousin twice removed, I think,' Susan continued. 'Give Mrs P a few days and she could probably tell you their ancestry, right back to the time when their great-great-great-grandmother was panting her way around the Forbidden City.'

Mandy laughed, but smothered it quickly as Mrs Ponsonby approached.

'Good morning, Amanda,' she said as she walked past. Coming to a halt, she lowered her eyes to admire the raised flower bed that lay close to the pond, but Mandy could see the older woman was unable to resist a series of long glances at the wedding guests. She felt a surge of affection for the timeless pillar of Welford's community. Life in the village would have been very different without Amelia Ponsonby.

Simon touched her elbow. 'Your parents are here,' he told her.

Mandy turned to see her mother and father coming up the lane.

'How beautiful you look.' Emily Hope put her arms around Mandy and kissed her cheek.

'Indeed you do,' said her father Adam, giving her a lopsided grin. 'I wasn't sure whether James would convince you to wear something different. I half expected to find you here with your jeans and boots on.'

Mandy regarded him affectionately. 'I could say the same to you,' she teased. 'Maybe you should have come in your waterproofs and wellies.' Instead her father was looking handsome in a charcoal grey suit. There were a few more lines on his brow these days, and his dark hair had faded, but his laughing brown eyes were just the same.

'And how lovely to see you again, Simon.' Mandy was pleased to hear the warmth in her mother's voice. After all, they had barely met the man who was already such a huge part of Mandy's life. But she felt a stir of concern as she studied Emily more closely. Unlike her father, who seemed full of life, her mum was looking tireder than usual. Her skin, usually fair, seemed stretched around the eyes and there was precious little colour in her cheeks. Mandy knew better than to ask if everything was okay. Her adoptive mother had always prided herself on her stamina and, despite her compassion for others, tended to view illness in herself as a weakness. Simon had started telling Adam about the drive up from Leeds and impulsively, Mandy gave her mum's hand a squeeze.

'It's lovely to be back,' she said, with a rush of gratitude for her precious parents, who had always been so proud of everything she had done. No wonder her mother was looking tired. Without an assistant, they must be snowed under. In a couple of weeks, she would be able to help them properly, Mandy reminded herself. Thank goodness the locum contract in Leeds was finishing just at the right time. Her mum and dad might even be able to take a holiday. She was sure she could manage on her own for a few days.

The rumble of a vintage car engine broke through the chatter and everyone turned to look. It was James arriving in typical style, and Mandy found herself grinning as he pulled up on the edge of the grass and climbed out of the driver's seat. How dashing he looked in his pale blue suit. The old round glasses – the ones that had made him a dead-ringer for Harry Potter throughout their school days – had been replaced with a smart rimless pair, and he no longer wore them halfway down his nose. But his hair still flopped forwards onto his forehead, resistant to any hairbrush or styling gel.

James's face lit up when he saw Mandy waiting for

him. 'Hello,' he said and then pretended to wince as she threw herself at him and hugged him tight.

'I've missed you,' she said, 'but you're looking fantastic and it's a lovely day and . . . oh I can't believe the day has actually arrived and you're getting married.' She stopped, realising she was talking too much, but James laughed.

'It does seem a bit unreal,' he admitted and regarded her fondly. 'But what about you? You look amazing.'

Self-conscious again under his gaze, Mandy said, 'At least you had the sense to choose navy blue. Can you imagine me as a six-foot bridesmaid in lilac chiffon?'

'Not really.' James shook his head. 'But even if you were dressed in a doily, nobody has ever had a more wonderful best woman, I'm sure of it.'

Best woman. Even though Mandy had been overjoyed when James asked, the title sounded clumsy. 'I'll do everything I can to make it a good day,' Mandy said. Despite herself, she felt a sudden prickling behind her eyes. She lowered them, hoping James wouldn't notice, but he grasped her arms, suddenly fierce.

'You promised you wouldn't cry, remember?' Loosening his grip, he gazed at her. The pleading in his eyes made Mandy wince. Taking a deep breath and blinking away the unshed tears, she nodded.

'Mum! Dad!' James's parents arrived and to Mandy's relief, he turned his attention to his mother, who started to fuss over his suit, straightening the white flower pinned to his lapel and brushing invisible dust from his sleeve.

Mrs Hunter looked amazing, Mandy thought. She was wearing a long cream coat with gold brocade over a linen dress in a subtle shade of bronze. Her hair, which had always been the same shade of brown as James's, had turned white, but it was tied back in an elegant bun, and her blue eyes were full of concern as she regarded her son.

'Look at your hair!' she exclaimed, tipping her head back to see him better. 'I said you should get it cut.'

'I had better things to think about, Mum.' James shook his head, but his voice was affectionate.

'Do you have a comb?' Mrs Hunter asked and when James shrugged, she turned to her husband. 'Gavin, do you have a comb? Just look at his hair.'

Mr Hunter was regarding his son quietly. 'He looks fine to me,' he said, 'and I think it's time for us to go and find our seats.' With an apologetic wave, he guided his wife towards the rapidly filling chairs.

'I hope Paul gets here soon. Lily and Seamus are coming with him.' James glanced at his watch. Lily and Seamus were James's much-loved dogs and Mandy knew they were going to play a very special part in the ceremony.

'Maybe they've got cold feet – or paws – about their big role?' she said, trying to distract him as he looked down at his wrist again.

James managed a smile. 'I couldn't leave them out of the ceremony, not with . . .' but his words tailed off as another classic car drew up alongside his Bentley. 'Here they are.'

Mandy heard the relief in his voice. There were two people in the car, but Mandy only had eyes for the passenger, a handsome man with a shaven head, who smiled and waved as the car drew up. He climbed out, opened the rear door, and unclipped the harnesses of the two wriggling animals in the back seat. One black, one brindle, both whippet thin, the two mixed-breed dogs bounded towards James and Mandy, their sleek coats gleaming. James bent briefly and hugged them both and a moment later, they were hurling themselves at Mandy. She laughingly fended them off as Lily, the smaller of the two, scrabbled at her bare legs and Seamus, slightly taller, threatened to plant both feet on the front of her dress.

'They haven't forgotten the rings,' Mandy said, catching sight of the tiny leather boxes that James had attached to the dogs' collars. She stood up as the passenger from the car approached.

'Paul,' she said and reached up to kiss him on the cheek. 'You're looking great.'

'Thank you,' he replied, but James stepped between them with a mock-frown.

'Hey,' he said to Mandy. 'It's my job to tell him that!' Mandy moved aside as James smiled at Paul. 'Was the journey okay?' he asked.

'Not bad,' Paul said. He looked at James with appreciation. 'You really are very handsome in those new glasses,' he said with a grin. 'Just as well your looks and personality match.'

James shook his head. 'You've always been the good-looking one,' he said and he took Paul's hand. 'Ready?' he asked.

Paul nodded. 'More than ready,' he replied and, side by side, dogs at their heels, they began the solemn walk along the pathway towards the oak tree.

Mandy turned to Simon. James might be ready, but despite her determination to honour her promise, she was finding it hard to keep herself together.

'All right?' Simon whispered, taking her hand and squeezing it. She nodded and swallowed.

'Paul looks well,' Simon commented. Mandy nodded again.

'We should go,' he said, and Mandy was glad to have him beside her when they walked up the narrow aisle between the rows of chairs. Ahead of them, Paul and James stopped in front of the registrar, a kind-eyed woman in a neat navy suit, who stood waiting under the scented canopy. Simon joined Mandy's parents and she took her place beside James.

As James and his fiancé turned to face one another in the shade of the magnificent oak, the shadows around Paul's eyes that had been camouflaged in the sunshine were thrown into sharp relief. He stood square-shouldered and smiling as if everything in his life was perfect. Mandy pressed her lips together hard. That her best friend was in love, that he had found a partner for life, should have been a source of pure joy, and yet today was exquisitely painful. Paul, who was the dearest thing in the world to

James, who had brought him so much happiness, was in the final stages of osteosarcoma. Mandy knew too much about bone cancer to be under any illusion there would be a happy ending. Her friends had to steal what time they could.

In the distance, Mandy could hear the sweet chirruping of a skylark as the registrar read out the vows. 'Paul William Franco, is it your will to have this man to be your spouse, to live together in the state of marriage? Is it your will to love him in sickness and in health; and, forsaking all others, to be faithful to him as long as you both shall live?'

How serious Paul looked as he spoke. 'I will.'

The registrar turned her gaze to James. 'James Hunter,' she said, her voice calm. 'Is it your will to have this man to be your spouse, to live together in the state of marriage? Is it your will to love him in sickness and in health; and, forsaking all others, to be faithful to him as long as you both shall live?'

'I will.'

There was a moment of stillness, the silver song of the lark clear in the distance. 'And now,' the registrar smiled, 'Reverend Hadcroft has been invited to say a few words.' Stepping aside, she made way for the vicar who had presided for many years over the parish. His hair was still black, his blue eyes still twinkled as he faced the congregation. Although he had only recently met Paul, Mandy knew he had taken time to sit down with the couple and learn about their short history.

'Thank you, my friends,' he said, 'for joining us here today, to celebrate the marriage of these two wonderful young men. I was honoured when James asked me if I would be willing to say a few words at their wedding ceremony. I would also like to invite anyone who wishes to join us for a special prayer session for Paul and James at the end of tomorrow morning's service in the church.' He paused for a long moment, smiling at James and Paul, before looking out across the rows of seats. 'It takes courage,' he said, 'to commit one's life to someone, but there is a story that James has told me that I think illustrates the strength these two wonderful young men have found in one another. And,' he smiled, casting his gaze over the crowd, 'I think anyone who has lived in this village as long as I have will agree that this tale illustrates how well suited they are. I understand these two young men met in a very unusual way. They were walking in opposite directions down a street in York when they heard howling. Both of them felt unable to ignore such a sound and on investigation, they discovered a group of boys who had trapped something,' he raised an eyebrow, 'or indeed, two somethings in a plastic bag, which they were about to throw in the river. James and Paul, despite being outnumbered, chased off the boys and retrieved the bag. Inside, to their surprise, they found two young puppies, one black and one brindle.'

Mandy couldn't take her eyes off the vicar, even though she had heard the story before. 'I think all of you know where this is going,' said the reverend, bending down to pat Seamus's head and then Lily's. 'Rather than allowing the police to take the puppies to a rescue centre, Paul and James agreed to take one each, but to keep in touch so that the tiny brother and sister would not lose one another completely. And the rest, of course, is history.' He looked around, first at Paul, then at James and finally resting his eyes on Mandy. 'Many of us can recall that in James's younger days, he and Mandy Hope, who stands here beside her friend, had lots of similar adventures. I know that she will join me and everyone here in wishing you both,' he beamed at the couple, 'the great joy of sharing your love of animals with your love for one another.'

Mandy heard a single gasping sob from somewhere behind her. Half turning, she caught sight of Gran and Grandad Hope sitting beside her dad. Catching Mandy's eye, her grandfather sent her a reassuring smile. She held her breath for a moment and dug her fingernails into the palms of her hands. If her friends could be this brave, then she must be brave for them. By the time the couple had kissed and turned towards her, she was able to smile. Unsure that she could trust her voice, she reached out. Briefly she grasped their hands, one warm and dry, one cooler, with fingers too slim. A moment later she released them and the newly married couple turned to face the congregation. Joining hands, fingers tightly intertwined, they made their way back down the aisle, the two dogs with them, one on either side.

*   *   *

Mandy finished her last spoonful of chocolate mousse and sat back. She suspected she was putting undue pressure on the seams of her dress. Simon was talking to his neighbour, James's cousin Daniel, about the significance of the 1851 classification of French wine regions. On Mandy's other side, James was holding out his hand for an elderly aunt to admire his gleaming gold ring. His free hand grasped Paul's, resting on Paul's slim thigh.

The horde of young and slightly nervous serving staff had almost finished clearing away the plates. Mandy took a deep breath and tried to smooth out the wrinkles in her dress. She stood up as Gary and Bev Parsons, the landlords of the Fox and Goose, filled the last few glasses with champagne. Mandy felt a flutter of butterflies as people stopped their conversations and turned to look at her.

James had asked her to make a speech. It had been almost impossible to decide what to say. It didn't seem appropriate to joke too much and she didn't want to dwell on Paul's illness. Mandy wasn't sure she could talk about it without breaking down anyway. She had settled on keeping her comments brief. Beside her, James lifted his eyes and smiled, and she felt courage flow into her.

'I'm not going to talk for long,' she began. 'For those who don't know me yet,' she glanced over to where Paul's family were sitting, 'I am Mandy Hope and I grew up in Welford with James. Despite being a year younger than me, I think everyone who knows us would agree he has always been the sensible one. But I always knew he loved animals as much as I did and back then, we made it our mission to save the world. Unlike Noah, who saved his animals two-by-two, we set out to rescue them one at a time.' She paused as a wave of laughter ran through the guests. 'Well, it seems my efforts have been bettered. When James and Paul met, they managed to save a pair of animals. Noah would have been proud!' Another pause for laughter and a ripple of applause. 'Paul,' Mandy looked at him directly, 'I couldn't have been dethroned by a better person.'

Paul acknowledged her words with a nod. So far, so good, Mandy thought, though the most difficult part was still to come. Taking a deep breath, keeping her voice steady, she addressed Paul again.

'Your new husband is the most gentle, generous, loyal and, crucially for me,' she paused and held up her hands, managing a grin, 'the most patient man I have ever met. If I had a magic wand and could turn him into an animal, I think he would make the most wonderful pet.' She was nearing the end now. 'Obviously, I have known Paul for a much shorter time than James, but I know they are a perfect match. Paul, you too are generous, loyal and patient. I truly believe you deserve one another.' From the corner of her eye, she saw her grandparents sitting beside her father. Dorothy was wiping a tear from her eye. Although Mandy's hand was shaking, she gripped her glass tightly and raised it in a toast.

'To James and Paul!' she said and collectively, the guests lifted their drinks and toasted the newly-weds. With a thump, Mandy sat down in her chair.

James reached his arm around her shoulder and gave her a squeeze. 'Thanks,' he whispered. 'That was lovely.'

As soon as the speeches were over, Mandy left Simon talking to her parents and escaped into the garden to cool her burning cheeks. She was inhaling the scent of a huge yellow rose when she heard her name.

'Mandy?'

She turned to see Mrs McFarlane, who had worked in the post office when Mandy and James were growing up. The elderly lady was resplendent in a blue and white floral suit and scarlet hat. Mandy felt a rush of gratitude that she had taken so much trouble to dress up for James's wedding.

'I thought of you this morning,' Mandy said, 'when I passed the post office. I was remembering all the ice creams James and I used to buy.'

'Those were the days,' Mrs McFarlane agreed. Her eyes were bright behind her glasses. 'I remember you used to come in during the holidays to post samples for your mum and dad.'

Mandy smiled. 'So we did,' she said. 'So much responsibility! I think we even argued about who got to carry the envelopes.'

'You and James were always together.' Mrs McFarlane glanced around the garden and her face softened when she caught sight of James, who was sitting on a bench in the sun with Paul beside him. 'It was such an exciting day for the village when James decided to have his wedding here. And I was so happy to hear you were coming back for the occasion as well. It's amazing how time passes. You're both so grown up.'

'We are,' said Mandy.

'What are you up to now? I've seen you around Welford a few times, but I hear you've been working in Leeds this past year.'

'That's right,' Mandy said, 'but in three weeks' time, I'm coming back here to Welford for more than a visit. I'm going to help Mum and Dad out.'

The former postmistress's face lit up. 'You'll be working at Animal Ark? That's wonderful.'

'It's not a permanent thing though, is it?' Mandy hadn't heard Simon approaching and she jumped when he spoke. Several other people had drifted into the garden by now, including Jean Knox, who was helping Susan's son Jack to pick dandelions.

Simon put his arm around her waist and smiled at Fiona and Mrs McFarlane. 'Mandy is only here until Adam and Emily find a replacement. After that, we're going to open our own clinic in Leeds. We're very interested in the recent advances in orthopaedic surgery, aren't we?'

Mandy wrinkled her nose. She wished Simon hadn't interrupted quite so condescendingly. It wasn't even entirely true, she thought. Simon was much more interested in extreme surgery than she was. She had always been fascinated by animal rehabilitation and had chosen to study animal behaviour to Masters level when she had finished her vet degree. They had talked about setting up a combined clinic and rescue centre. She didn't know what to say and was glad when Jean Knox, having heard Simon's comment, started asking him questions about progress in small animal surgery.

'I'm going to see if I can find James,' Mandy said. He and Paul had disappeared from the bench. Simon was too busy explaining the technicalities of toggling a hip joint to do more than wave at Mandy as she walked away.

She couldn't immediately see James and Paul inside. She approached the bar, where Bev Parsons, red-cheeked and wild-haired, was pulling a pint of local ale.

'Hi, Bev. Do you know where James and Paul are?' Mandy asked.

Bev pointed towards an inconspicuous doorway beside the bar. 'They're through there,' she said.

Mandy walked into a wood-panelled room where James was holding the hand of a grey-looking Paul. 'Is everything okay?' she said, feeling a stir of concern. 'Is there anything I can do?'

James smiled at her in a strained way. 'Actually, you're just the person we need,' he said. 'You know how Paul has to get injections of Fragmin to help prevent blood clots?' Mandy nodded. 'Well, we're lucky enough to live next door to a nurse, and she's been helping with the injections.'

'Okay,' said Mandy.

'The staff at the hospital showed me how to give him the injection,' James said miserably, 'but I just can't do

23

it. I'm frightened I'll hurt him or inject into the muscle by mistake.'

'And you want me to help?' Mandy guessed.

'Please.' It was Paul's turn to speak, though he sounded breathless. 'I don't want my husband to do anything on his wedding day that makes him unhappy.' James was holding Paul's hand and Mandy watched as the sick man's fingers tightened.

'Where's the injection?' said Mandy. James handed her a tiny syringe. 'Watch closely,' she said as she took a small pinch of Paul's skin between her fingers and inserted the needle. 'They maybe didn't show you this, but because Paul is so slim now, you might need to put the needle in at an angle to get properly under the skin.'

James nodded, his eyes relieved. 'Thanks, Mandy,' he said. 'I don't know how you can be a vet. I would have been much too squeamish.'

'I don't think that's true at all,' she said, looking at James. 'You are one of the most amazing people I've ever met. You could do anything you wanted. Next time you have to give the injection, you'll manage fine.'

James smiled at her. He opened his mouth to speak but his face crumpled and his eyes filled with tears.

Paul reached out and took both James's hands in his. 'Mandy's right,' he said. 'You are indeed the most amazing man in the world, and I am so happy I met you. This is, without doubt, the best day of my life.'

Mandy felt tears prickling behind her own eyes, and for the first time that day, she did nothing to stop them.

Chapter Two

'What a glorious day.' Adam Hope lowered himself into his favourite armchair. Mandy spotted a new clock on the mantelpiece, and DVDs lined the shelves where there had once been videos, but her father's wing-back chair still occupied the corner where it had always stood. 'Sit down, Simon, make yourself at home.'

'Thank you, Mr Hope.'

'I've told you before, young man. Call me Adam.' Mandy's dad beamed. 'Tell me, Simon, do you like whisky?' He reached out and took a bottle from a cabinet that was close by his seat. 'I have a wonderful malt here, ten years old . . .'

Mandy raised her eyebrows at Simon. 'Don't let him get started on his malts,' she advised, 'or you'll never hear the end of it,' but Simon was already leaning towards Adam to have a look at the bottle.

'Bladnoch,' he said, nodding appreciatively. 'Flora and fauna edition. Very appropriate.' He sat back. 'I wouldn't say no.'

Adam's eyes twinkled. 'Mandy?'

'No, thanks, Dad. You know I think whisky tastes like disinfectant.' To her relief, her mother appeared.

'I'm just going to have a look at the in-patients,' Emily said.

'I'll give you a hand.' Mandy stood up, glad to have an excuse not to get involved in the whisky discussion. Together, she and Emily made their way through to the modern veterinary unit attached to the back of the cottage.

'There are only a couple of residents,' said her mum, 'but I thought you'd like to take a peek at them.'

'Of course I would,' said Mandy.

'This is Trundle.' Emily opened the door to the first cage and gently stroked the Jack Russell terrier inside. 'She came in this morning with a huge pyo. I had to operate as soon as she arrived. That's why we only got to the wedding at the last minute.' She checked the little dog's drip-line and membranes. 'She's doing fine,' she said with satisfaction.

Mandy reached into the kennel when her mum had finished and scratched Trundle behind the ear. The brown and white dog swivelled her head to lick Mandy's hand. 'She's a lovely little thing.'

'She really is,' her mother agreed. 'Our other patient isn't quite so peaceful.'

Mandy half expected to be shown a fractious cat, so she was surprised when her mum led her into the wild-life section and closed the door carefully. Emily opened the only occupied cage and a gull with a chocolate-brown head gave a loud squawk before flapping out onto the floor. Mandy dropped to her knees to take a closer look and the bird stood still, regarding her with its ringed eye.

'It's beautiful,' she said, grinning up at her mum. 'What's it in for?'

'Seb Conway, the animal welfare officer in Walton, brought it in,' Emily said. 'Apparently, there are lots of black-headed gulls nesting near the gravel-pit. Someone reported this one because its wing was hurt.'

'Oh.' Mandy looked sadly at the bird. 'I hope it wasn't looking after any chicks.'

'Seb says he watched it for a while,' Emily told her. 'It didn't seem to be nesting and it was too badly injured to fly so he picked it up. It's been eating cat food and exercising its wings and we've set up a water bath which it uses every day. I think we should be able to release it next week.'

Mandy resisted the temptation to reach out and stroke the bird. It was better not to handle wildlife too much, though she would have loved to feel the warmth of the muscular body beneath the smooth feathers. It would be good to get the bird some fresh fish, she thought, to make a change from cat food. She hoped they would be able to let it go before she returned to Leeds. It would be great to see it fly off, back to its flock.

'Would you like something to drink before bed?' her mum asked as she used a towel to guide the bird back into the cage.

Mandy thought for a moment. 'I know it's warm,' she said, 'but would it be too much hassle to make some hot chocolate?'

'Of course not.' Emily looked pleased. 'It's lovely to have you back,' she said, reaching out to give Mandy an impulsive hug. Mandy hugged her back and tried to ignore how thin and fragile her mum felt. *I'll be able to do some of the cooking when I come back, too. She needs fattening up as much as this gull!*

Despite the hot chocolate, a few hours later Mandy found herself tossing and turning. It felt strange being home but not sleeping in her own room. She climbed out of the double bed, where Simon was snoring after his evening of whisky tasting. On tiptoes, Mandy made her way to her old bedroom at the back of the house. Everything felt comforting and familiar, though the animal posters were gone and a new sewing table had been set in the corner. She sat on the single bed, wedged the pillow behind her back, and gazed out of the window.

A faint wash of moonlight illuminated the orchard beyond the cottage's lawn and flower-filled borders. Beyond the branches, Mandy could just make out the low barn where Adam stored his tools and the dry-stone walls that climbed the fell. She would sleep in here, she decided, once Simon had gone back to Leeds.

Still restless, she decided to go downstairs to check on Trundle. She was glad she did, as the little dog had twisted herself around the drip-line and the infusion pump was beeping.

'Don't worry,' Mandy whispered. 'I'll soon have you sorted out.' For a while, she knelt beside the kennel, stroking Trundle and talking to her quietly. There was no doubt the little animal was well on the way to recovery. Mandy shifted position so that she was sitting more comfortably against the cage and rested her hand on Trundle's furry flank. Her thoughts drifted back to the wedding, and the joy and excitement that had filled the air, in spite of everything.

After a while, the sound of a cock crowing roused her. She had better get back to bed, she thought. It was starting to get light and she didn't want Simon to think she had run away. Later, they would go to the church and help James and Paul celebrate the final prayers of their wedding weekend, but for now, she should return to Simon's side.

As usual for a Monday morning, the Animal Ark appointment list was full. Mandy had waved Simon off the day before, promising to call every day. Although she would be returning to Leeds for two more weeks before moving back to Welford, she had booked a few days' holiday when James had told her his wedding date and she intended to make the most of it. Despite having accompanied her parents on farm calls in the past, she hadn't worked with large animals since qualifying and was looking forward to brushing up her skills.

Mandy was sitting at the computer admiring the photos and information on the clinic's website when the door opened. A young woman with long brown hair burst in, wrestling with a bulging leather satchel. A glossy black flatcoat retriever trotted beside her, ducking out of the way when the satchel lunged towards the floor. Mandy smiled. She recognised Helen Steer, the clinic's veterinary nurse, but she hadn't seen the retriever before.

'What a gorgeous dog!'

'She is, isn't she? She's called Lucy.' Helen kicked her satchel under the desk and patted Lucy. 'How's Trundle doing?' she asked as she pulled off her jacket. Without pausing for the answer, she dropped a plastic tub of home-made biscuits on the desk, leaned over to check the answerphone and then straightened up, heading for the kennels.

'She's doing really well.' Mandy scooted after Helen, feeling slightly breathless.

Trundle stood up in her cage and greeted them with a wagging tail and a small bark.

'She looks much better,' Helen said with satisfaction. 'I think we can take her off her drip now, and I can give her a proper pain assessment before we send her home.' Mandy watched as the girl switched off the machine that was controlling the fluid running into the vein. 'Does that sound okay?' Helen looked up at Mandy, who smiled.

'Of course,' she replied. Helen seemed to be as competent as she was confident.

'How about Kehaar?'

'Is that what you call the gull?' Mandy asked.

'Yes. After the one in . . .'

'. . . Watership Down.' Mandy finished the sentence for her.

'Exactly.' Helen's eyes were sparkling. 'Seb brought him in.'

'Him? Is he male?' Mandy was impressed. 'I didn't know it was possible to tell.'

'Seb thought so,' said Helen, 'based on the size of his beak. Not that it makes any difference to his care plan.'

The sound of the main door opening and footsteps on the tiled floor alerted them to the arrival of a customer.

'I'll go,' Mandy told Helen. She was pleasantly surprised to see Bill Ward, their postman, standing at the reception desk with a cat in a wicker basket.

'Hello, Mandy.' He seemed equally pleased to see her. 'Is that you coming back all grown up and ready to get stuck in? It seems no time at all since you were at school.'

'I'm just here for a week this time, but I'll be back for longer at the end of the month.'

Bill grinned. 'Your mum and dad must be over the moon. They talk about you all the time, you know!' He reached down and poked a finger through the wire door of the basket. Inside, a furry black shape clawed the side of the carrier and let out a hiss. 'Now then, Sable,' said Bill. 'Best behaviour for young Mandy! We're actually here to see your dad today,' he said. 'Sable's been under his care for a while.'

Mandy smiled. 'Of course,' she said. 'Dad'll be through in a minute. If you take a seat, I'll let him know you're here.'

Mandy sat back down behind the reception desk an hour and a half later, warming her hands on a mug of tea. Morning surgery was over, and at times it had felt like a *This Is Your Life*-style return to her childhood. Two of the clients had been people she hadn't met before, but there had been lots of faces she knew. Old Mrs Jackson had brought two cats to be vaccinated. She was as interested in wildlife as she had ever been, and Mandy had taken her through to see Kehaar once the cats were finished. Hannah Burgess had been in with one of her huskies, Tanika, who had hurt her front paw. Hannah had been delighted to see Mandy and introduce her to the beautiful dog. Tanika was the daughter of Aspen, who Mandy had taken care of as a puppy years ago. Mandy felt as if she had fallen into a photo album of her past life.

She took a sip of her tea and wondered if she should go and find Helen for a chat. She had been impressed by the nurse's whirlwind energy and wanted to get to know her better. Before she could make up her mind, the door to the clinic swung open again and Susan Collins rushed in carrying Jack with one hand and a cat basket with the other.

'Mandy,' she said with relief in her voice. 'I'm so glad to see you. It's my cat Marmalade. I don't know if it's an infection, but his ear has suddenly blown up. It's enormous and seems ever so sore. I know I don't have an appointment, but do you think you could take a quick look at him for me, please?'

'Of course I could,' Mandy said. 'Bring him through.' She led Susan to the consulting room and opened the door of the cat basket, waiting until Marmalade walked out of the cage before reaching out to him. The problem ear was impossible to miss, swollen to several times its usual thickness, and the diagnosis was equally unmistakeable.

'It's an aural haematoma,' Mandy told Susan. 'It happens when they shake their head or scratch their ear and a blood vessel bursts between the skin and cartilage. It's good you brought him in so quickly. It's very painful because there isn't much space for the blood.'

Susan's gaze darted from Mandy to Jack, who was peering over the edge of the table, his small fingers reaching for Marmalade. Mandy took a plastic syringe from its packet, as she had seen her mother do many times before, and handed it to the small boy to play with. Jack regarded it with awe as he pulled the plunger in and out.

'Can it be treated?' Susan looked worriedly at Mandy.

'Absolutely,' Mandy said. 'We'll need to sedate him, but we can drain it right now. I'll just give Helen a shout.' She stuck her head into the waiting-room, where she was relieved to see the nurse sitting behind the desk.

'Can you give me a hand, please?' she said. 'I've got Susan Collins's cat here with an aural haematoma.'

'Poor Marmalade!' Helen exclaimed when she saw the hugely swollen ear. She took the ginger-striped cat from Susan as Mandy drew up some sedative into a new syringe. Holding him close to her body, Helen kept him steady while Mandy gave him the injection.

'Just a few minutes and he'll be asleep,' Mandy said as Helen let Marmalade walk back into his carrier.

Once the little cat was sedated, Helen lifted him back out and placed him on a warmed towel before shaving and cleaning his ear. Mandy opened and closed several drawers before she found the instruments she would need.

'I'm going to make two small incisions in Marmalade's ear,' she explained to Susan. 'Then we'll place a small drain through so that the blood doesn't build back up. Without the drain, the blood is likely to come straight back. I'll also need to take a sample from his ear canal to see if there's any infection.'

'Thanks.' Susan stood well back, holding Jack in her arms.

'Are you sure the two of you want to stay?' Mandy nodded towards Jack, whose unblinking eyes were fixed on his pet. 'It's a bit on the messy side.'

Susan smiled. 'He'll be all right,' she said. 'He always likes to know everything that's going on.'

'Marmalade okay, Mummy?' the little boy asked.

'He's fine,' Susan told him. 'Mandy is a vet. A doctor for animals. She's going to make his sore ear better.'

Mandy sutured the drain in place and then took a swab from inside the ear canal. 'He has a fungal ear infection as well, poor chap,' she explained after peering down the microscope for a few moments. 'That's probably what caused the haematoma in the first place. Was he scratching before the swelling appeared?'

Susan nodded.

'We'll treat that with some eardrops. He'll need a bandage over the wound for a few days, so we can clean his ear and put them in when he comes in to have that changed.'

Susan looked relieved. 'I'm really grateful you were here,' she said to Mandy as Helen took Marmalade through to the recovery area.

'I'm glad you came,' said Mandy. She thought for a moment. 'Would you like some tea?' she offered. 'Marmalade will be asleep for a little while yet and if there are things you need to do, you can come back to collect him later. But if you'd like to wait here, it would be nice to get to know Jack better.'

She looked at Susan, who nodded. 'That would be lovely.'

'It's strange,' said Mandy as they sat outside in the sunshine. 'I thought of you almost as soon as I came back yesterday. I was thinking about the Christmas Eve party in the village hall. Do you remember?'

'Yes, of course!' Susan laughed. 'With Prince. He couldn't come inside, but he put his head through the window, wearing that crazy hat. It seems so long ago.' She looked at Mandy over the rim of her mug. 'And now you're a proper qualified vet, just like you always wanted to be.'

Mandy nodded. 'I've been really lucky,' she admitted. 'What about you? Do you work? Around looking after Jack, I mean,' she added, hoping she didn't sound as if she was interrogating Susan.

'I'm a nursery nurse,' Susan replied. 'I'm the assistant manager at the village nursery school.'

Mandy raised her eyebrows. 'I didn't know Welford had a nursery school.'

'My boss has converted one of the houses on the other side of the church. It's really lovely, with rooms for different age groups and loads of space to play outside.' Susan's cheeks went pink. 'Sorry, I sound like I'm trying to sign you up! I guess you're too busy for babies just yet.'

Mandy smiled. 'I am. But the nursery sounds great.'

'It is. You should come and have a look around. The older children would love to hear about what a vet does.'

Mandy watched as Jack ran around the garden chasing the butterflies that were fluttering to and from the lavender bush under the window. The scent from her father's climbing roses filled the garden. Susan showed Jack a ladybird that had landed on her arm and, boosted by her earlier success with the syringe, Mandy spoke to him.

'Do you like ladybirds?' she asked, but Jack just stared at her then turned and hid his face against his mother.

Mandy shrugged. 'I've always been better with animals,' she said.

Susan lifted her son onto her lap and he put his arms around her neck. 'I'm definitely better with children,' she said with a grin.

'Does Jack go to nursery with you?' Mandy asked.

'He comes with me two days a week,' Susan replied, glancing down at the small dark head. 'My mum has him the other two days I work.'

'Does Jack's dad work in Welford, too?'

Susan shook her head. 'He didn't stick around to see what he was missing.' She softened the words with a smile, but Mandy was glad when Adam put his head around the back door.

'Did you notice anything we need to order from Thomson's?' he asked.

'Our suppliers,' Mandy explained to Susan. She smiled at her dad. 'I opened the last box of clotrimazole ear drops this morning and I used a Penrose drain on Marmalade's ear, so that needs replacing.'

Adam Hope stepped out of the doorway as Helen zoomed past. 'Just getting some lunch,' she said without breaking speed. Adam disappeared back inside to place the order.

Jack had fallen asleep in Susan's arms. His mother

leaned down to kiss the top of his head, before looking up at Mandy. 'It's been great to catch up. It feels as if you've been here forever already,' she said.

Mandy smiled. 'It feels as if I've never been away.'

Chapter Three

'See you tomorrow,' Helen called as she closed the clinic door. Mandy watched through the window as the veterinary nurse walked down the path, Lucy trotting at her heels.

Emily stuck her head around the door that led to the kitchen. 'Everything okay?'

'Everything's fine, Mum.'

'I was just going to make a cup of tea,' Emily said. 'Would you like one?'

Mandy shook her head. 'I think I might go for a walk.' Outside the window, the evening sun bathed the fells in golden light. 'Want to come?'

Emily shook her head. 'Not tonight, love.' Despite her fondness for her mother, Mandy felt relieved. It was so long since she had been able to spend time alone on the moors. Anyway, her mum looked tired again. A cup of tea and a rest would do her more good than a hike.

'Is it okay if I take the Land Rover?' she asked. She wanted to get right up onto the fell.

'Of course. Your dad's on call but if anything comes in, he can take the Discovery.'

Minutes later, Mandy was pulling herself up into the worn driver's seat of the old Defender. Clipping herself in, she engaged the clutch and was soon climbing the steep lane that led up to the old drove road. The track petered out beside a weathered ring-feeder. Churned earth, now dried, showed where the sheep had come to eat earlier in the year, before the grass had begun to grow in earnest.

Parking on a smooth patch of grass beside the wall, Mandy opened the door and jumped out onto the clean turf. Silence washed over her after the noise of the Land Rover engine and for a moment she stood still, breathing deeply, filling her lungs as a soft breeze played across her face. It was wonderful to be back.

The drove road here was little more than a broad strip of short green grass that cut a line through the darker heather, and Mandy struck out along the ancient path, revelling in the peace. She stopped when she noticed a slim brown shape on the turf. At first she had taken it for a stick, until a tiny movement made her study it more carefully. It was an adder warming itself in the last rays of the sun, and Mandy watched until, sensing her presence, it glided off into the undergrowth.

Mandy took a deep breath and stretched her arms up to the sky, working the tension from her shoulders. In the distance a curlew called, its melancholy voice drawing her eyes upwards to the cool blue sky. Her gaze was arrested by the sight of a bird soaring high above, not the curlew's white rump and long bill she had expected, but a reddish-brown body with long wings and a forked triangular tail. Mesmerised, she halted, watching as the bird circled overhead. It was a red kite, she realised. Her father had told her a breeding pair had been sighted over the moors. From the brink of UK extinction, Mandy knew they had been reintroduced into Yorkshire in the late 1990s, spreading out from the Harewood Estate near Leeds.

Unable to resist as the bird soared eastwards, she left the smoothness of the drove road to follow a sheep path through the heather, feeling glad she was wearing sturdy boots and jeans. She deliberately made a little more noise than usual as she brushed through the brittle under-growth. It might scare away other wildlife, but disturbing an adder unexpectedly was not the end Mandy wanted for her walk.

It was slower going along the narrow path, but at least the peat was dry underfoot so she could continue to watch the sky. The kite wheeled away from the setting sun and headed down into the valley. Topping a ridge, Mandy saw a patch of woodland below her. The kite made a final curling swoop and disappeared into the trees. Mandy wondered if there was a nesting site in the copse.

Knowing that she mustn't disturb a female kite with hatchlings, Mandy picked her way down the slope. As she approached, she scanned the trees for signs of a nest. Sure enough, in the main fork of one of the tallest trees, she spotted a messy heap of twigs with the bird she had seen flying in standing over it. As she watched, the male kite turned, launched and flitted away to find more food for his brood.

Mandy knew she shouldn't go any closer to the nest, yet she felt drawn to the woodland. It was a time of day when badgers were likely to leave their setts. If she was lucky, she might see a sow teaching her young to forage in the undergrowth. She turned to her left, away from the tree with the nest, and set off through the springy heather to find a different spot to enter the trees.

A few minutes later, she had made her way around the edge of the wood and the kites' nest was out of sight. At the boundary between moorland and copse, there was an old wooden fence inside a mossy dry-stone wall. To Mandy's delight, she found a series of parallel scratch marks on one of the wooden posts that she knew must have been made by a badger. There were smudgy foot-prints, too, and a slight depression in the earth that led downhill.

Mandy followed the tracks, ducking under the low branches. It was cooler among the trees, a welcome change after her hard work trudging through the heather. She paused to look up at the tree canopy, enjoying the sight of the distant blue sky through the leaves, but her head snapped down when she heard a strange mewling bleat from lower down in the valley. What kind of animal was that? She hurried between the tree trunks in the direction of the cry.

It was a fallow deer: a doe. That much Mandy could

see through the tangle of netting that had trapped the delicate creature. Her slim legs flailed as she struggled and there were white rings of terror around the edges of her dark eyes. The deer thrashed even more as Mandy approached. She stopped with her eyes narrowed. She didn't want to scare the animal to death, but there was no way the deer could disentangle herself. She needed help, the faster the better. Mandy took three long strides to reach the deer and placed her hands on her neck and shoulder.

'It's okay, you're okay, it's okay.' Her words came out in a sing-song tone as she crouched down beside the frightened animal. The netting was made of thick grey rope, and the deer was so badly tangled that the small efforts that Mandy was able to make while holding her still barely made a difference. She couldn't reach the deer's hooves to begin to untwist the knots and, although she had her mobile in her pocket, there was no signal down here. She was going to have to go and fetch help, she thought, but the idea of walking away, leaving the creature to keep thrashing around, was awful. Not only that, Mandy thought, but from what she could see, there could be milk in the doe's udder. If she had a fawn hidden somewhere, there was a limit to how long it could wait before it needed feeding again.

With a gasp of relief, she heard and then saw a quad bike bumping towards her through the trees. Half standing up, Mandy lifted a hand and waved. The man sitting astride the vehicle slowed the engine before he approached and drew to a halt several metres away. As he dismounted, Mandy studied him. He wasn't someone she recognised from the village. Maybe around thirty, with short sandy hair and a face that looked tanned from wind and Yorkshire sun rather than foreign holidays.

As he turned towards her, his green eyes moved quickly from her face down to the stricken animal and back up again. 'You look like you could use some help.'

Mandy nodded. 'Thank goodness you were passing,' she said. 'I was about to go in search of someone.' The stranger had broad shoulders and strong-looking arms, and he walked towards her with a slow easy gait as if he didn't want to scare the deer. Mandy couldn't have conjured a more suitable rescuer if she had tried.

'I'm Jimmy,' he said and he knelt slowly down beside Mandy. 'What do you need me to do? Will you hold her while I try to get some of the ropes off?'

'I'm Mandy,' she said. 'Have you got a knife to cut through the rope? That would be quicker. I'm worried she might have a fawn.'

Jimmy looked up at her. 'Wouldn't the fawn be nearby? Wouldn't we see it?'

'Not necessarily,' Mandy replied. 'With fallow deer the fawn often hides in deep undergrowth and the mother only goes back every four hours or so to suckle it. The sooner we can get this poor thing out, the better the chances the little one won't suffer. Do you have a knife?' she asked again.

'I do,' Jimmy admitted, 'but it would be better if we

didn't have to cut the netting. If you hold her still, I'll try to get her feet free.'

He stood up and, before Mandy could stop him, he walked around behind the deer. Instantly the doe lashed out from inside the heap of rope. With a thud, her hind feet connected with his thigh and he jumped back with a cry.

'Ouch!'

'Are you okay?' Mandy was surprised. Jimmy had seemed so confident that she had assumed he would know how to handle wildlife. 'I should have told you,' she said. 'It's better to work from over here or from the front. Be careful of the head as well, though. Deer have very tough skulls. I'll try to keep her as still as I can, but she might still swing up enough to hurt you.'

Jimmy nodded. Even though he must have been bruised, he crouched down in front of the deer and started to unwind the coils around her legs.

'It isn't working,' Mandy said a few minutes later. Despite Jimmy's efforts, the netting was still wound tightly around the doe's body. 'You should just cut it. Goodness knows what all this stupid netting is doing here anyway.'

'Actually, it's mine,' said Jimmy. He was tugging at a knot and didn't look up. 'I'm building a climbing net up to a high-wire skywalk in the trees.'

Mandy frowned. 'What on earth is a high-wire skywalk? And why would you want to build one out here?'

45

Jimmy met her eyes. 'It's going to be part of an Outward Bound centre,' he explained. 'I'm renting the land from one of the local farmers.'

'Which farmer?' Mandy could feel her exasperation rising. Why would any of the locals encourage people to play childish games through this lovely woodland, with its badger tracks and nesting birds? Couldn't they do that in a field on the edge of a town?

'Sam Western,' Jimmy replied.

Mandy felt like growling. She knew Sam Western was one of their most successful landowners and that he was at the cutting edge of organic farming, but he had always been more interested in money than in the kind of countryside preservation Mandy supported. Meanwhile Jimmy was still wrestling with the ropes. He didn't seem to be making any progress at all.

'For goodness' sake!' Mandy hissed. 'Any fawn will be dead by the time you get its poor mother free. Just give me your knife, will you?'

Jimmy blinked but handed her the blade, and with efficient movements Mandy began to clip away the remaining netting. 'In my opinion,' she went on, 'Mr Western should have known better than to approve a corporate activity centre out here. Wild animals have more rights than people who want to come and climb about in trees. There are rare birds, too. I saw red kites nesting at the edge of the woodland. They're just returning after being almost extinct. Don't you think that's more important?'

'I know about the kites,' Jimmy said, his voice even. 'I'm keeping my obstacles well away from that part of the copse. But the countryside should support people as well as animals. So long as it's used the right way, there's no reason to think we're going to harm anything.'

Despite his comment about the kites, Mandy felt herself bristling. 'Will you be teaching your clients the Countryside Code?' she asked. Did he even know it? He didn't seem to have much knowledge about the deer they were saving.

'What are you? The Countryside Constabulary?' He seemed to be laughing at her. Mandy glared for a moment, but he continued to smile. Her movements became tighter as she dissected the awful netting.

However, as she cut the last of the rope from around the deer's hind foot and they helped the doe to stand up, she couldn't help but feel better. They watched in silence as the timid animal trotted away, unsteadily at first and then leaping forward to vanish among the trees.

It was beginning to get dark. Mandy glanced at the time on her mobile. It was nine thirty. The sun was already hidden behind the fell, though the sky was still bright.

'I have to get home,' she said. She would just about make it to the Land Rover before it was completely dark, but it would be tight.

'Can I give you a lift?' Jimmy inclined his head towards the quad bike. 'You could ride behind me.' Mandy could see there was a small seat attached to the back of the bike.

For a moment, she wanted to refuse, but he was looking at her steadily. It really would be better to get home.

'My car is parked up on the moor beside the old drove road,' she said. 'If you know where that is.'

'I do.' His nod was firm.

With a last glance into the trees where the doe had disappeared, Mandy followed Jimmy and climbed onto the quad behind him. He seemed to know the layout of the land surprisingly well, following a sunken track up onto the fell before dropping down to where the Land Rover was parked. He cut the engine and watched as Mandy walked over to her vehicle.

'Goodbye,' she said as she opened the door.

'Bye.' Jimmy nodded again, his green eyes unreadable in the dimming light. Mandy climbed into the Land Rover and turned to wave, but he was already driving away.

Back at Animal Ark, she found her mum and dad sitting in the lounge. Adam was reading a newspaper and Emily an iPad, her cheeks lit up from the glow of the screen. They both looked up when she walked in.

'Had a good walk?' Her dad folded his paper and set it down on the floor beside his chair.

'Interesting, to say the least,' Mandy said. 'I saw the kites you told me about.'

Adam beamed. 'Beautiful, aren't they?'

'Yes,' said Mandy. 'But when I went into the wood behind their nest site, I found a poor fallow deer all wound up in some netting. It was awful.'

'It's not still there, is it?' Adam looked alarmed. 'Do we need to go and sort it out?'

Mandy could see he was poised to jump up and she stopped him. 'It's fine, Dad. Someone was passing on a quad bike and he helped. Jimmy, he said his name was. Luckily he had a knife with him. Although,' she went on, 'it was actually his netting. He said he was setting up an Outward Bound centre on part of Sam Western's land. Have you heard anything about it?'

Her dad settled back into his chair. 'Ah yes, I know who you mean,' he said. 'I met Jimmy Marsh when I was treating a cow up at Sam's. He seemed decent enough. Used to be a park ranger up in the Lake District.'

'Really?' Mandy frowned. 'He didn't seem to know much about wildlife for a park ranger.'

Her dad shrugged. 'I've heard good things about him. We should give him a chance. Some of the locals are already winding themselves up about new types of tourism. Remember the arguments when Bert Burnley set up the caravans by the river? Those fields have been bought up by a lovely couple called Mr and Mrs Dhanjal and they've turned it into a thriving campsite with hot food and everything.' Mandy could indeed remember the fuss that had been made when Bert first allowed caravans onto his land. Her dad was probably right, but there was something about Jimmy's attitude that had rankled.

'I'm going to get a cup of tea,' she said, changing the subject. 'Can I get you anything?'

'No, thanks,' said Emily. 'I think I'm going to have an early night.'

'I'll come with you,' Adam said to Mandy and they walked together into the kitchen to put the kettle on. He reached out and gave Mandy a hug. 'Rescuing a deer on your first walk on the moors?' He winked at her. 'That's my girl. I don't know how the Welford wildlife has survived without you!'

Chapter Four

'Are you sure you won't need anything to eat on the journey?' Emily asked. She and Mandy had just finished a lunch of hummus, salad and crusty bread and were sitting at the kitchen table drinking coffee.

'I'm sure,' Mandy replied. 'Dad is driving me to York and the train takes less than half an hour. I'll be eating with Simon when I get back. If I'm held up, I can always buy something.'

'And you're back two weeks on Saturday.' Emily added a little extra milk to her mug and stirred it in. 'It's been lovely having you here.'

'It's been great for me, too, Mum,' Mandy said. She picked up her smartphone to double check the timetable. Not that there would be a problem. There were plenty of trains between York and Leeds.

Hearing a sigh, Mandy looked up. 'Is everything all right?'

There was the briefest of pauses before Emily replied. 'Yes, of course,' she said. 'I was just thinking of you and Simon.' She smiled. 'Are you sure you'll be okay with living apart for a while? It's not easy to keep a relationship going when you don't see each other so often. You know you don't have to come back here, don't you? We can manage, if you don't want . . .'

'But I do want,' Mandy insisted, tucking her hair behind her ears. 'I'm looking forward to it. Simon's fine, too. We've talked about it lots.' The phone buzzed in her hand and she looked down at the screen. It was a text from James.

'Hi Mandy,' it read. 'We're having a fantastic time here in Iseo. We have the most wonderful view of the lake from our suite and there is a gorgeous little swimming pool for when we need to cool off. The local wine is amazing – sparkling rosé. We will definitely be bringing a few bottles home. Paul has been really well, thank goodness. You'll be pleased to know that your injection tip has helped. One more week to go and we'll be back in York. I can't wait to hear all your news from Welford. It will be amazing to have you back there. You must tell me all the details. So many memories to revisit. Maybe you can find the time to visit us in York again. We are always glad to see you. I hope your last two weeks in Leeds go well. All my love, James. P.S. Paul says hello.'

When she looked up, Emily was watching her, eyebrows raised. 'Anything important?'

'A message from James,' Mandy replied. 'They're doing fine.' She was relieved to hear that the trip was going well. And how lovely it would be to visit them when they returned. She loved the little café-cum-bookshop that James ran, with its home baking, its books and artwork, and tiny corners perfect for browsing with a mug of fresh coffee. 'I just need to reply,' she told her mum.

'Okay, darling.' Emily drank the last of her coffee, pushed out her chair and stood up. 'I need to get on. There's a cat spay I want to do before you head off.' She left the room and Mandy turned back to her phone.

'Glad everything is going well,' she wrote. 'Lots to tell you when you get back! Meanwhile please look after yourself and your wonderful husband and make the most of your honeymoon. I look forward to tasting your wine when you return. Love to Paul. And you, obvs. Mandy xxx' She clicked 'send', put her mug and bowl in the dishwasher and headed upstairs to the bedroom. Most of her stuff would stay here, but there were a couple of things she needed to take back to Leeds.

An hour later, she was sitting in the car beside her dad with the window open. 'Bye, Mum!' she called, with a last glance at the house before she waved at her mother.

'See you soon!' Emily called after them.

Adam headed along the lane that led through the village, past the Fox and Goose and down to the green. As they approached the narrow bridge beside Monkton Woods, Mandy saw a tractor and trailer parked in the gateway. A large pile of timber had been emptied onto the verge and she could see a broad-shouldered man hoisting up a log. She couldn't help but admire the way he balanced the weight of the wood as he strode across and added it to the pile he had already built in the trailer.

'There's your friend Jimmy Marsh.' Her father grinned. Mandy turned to look as they passed, belatedly recognising the face beneath the cropped sandy hair.

'He's not my friend,' she said. Her eyes followed Jimmy as they pulled away, but he didn't look up at her.

The station at York was packed with cars when her dad pulled up at the drop-off point outside. 'I won't get out,' he said. 'I daren't abandon the car or it will get towed away.'

Mandy reached over and kissed him on the cheek before opening the car door. 'No problem, Dad. Thanks for the lift.' Grabbing her small case from the boot, she walked around and peered in at the open car window. 'I'll miss you.'

'It won't be long until you're back,' Adam replied. 'I hope everything goes well with your last weeks,' he said. 'If you need any help with the move, give me a shout.' He held up a hand to wave her off and put the car in gear. By the time Mandy reached the main entrance and turned to look back, he was out of sight. Walking in through the archway, she crossed the concourse and made her way over the bridge, clattering down the stairs to the platform under the arched glass roof. She was pleased to see it was only a few minutes until the next Leeds train was due.

It was an express train and as they flashed through the stations, Mandy realised how much she was looking forward to seeing Simon again. Simon had said he would cook for them both that evening and from experience, he would make something delicious. It seemed no time at all until the train was passing houses again, diving through the black brick cutting before coming out near the square clock tower of Leeds Parish Church. A moment later, they were on the viaduct and Mandy gazed down onto the rooftops of central Leeds until the train drew into the station.

Simon had offered to pick her up, but knowing how busy Leeds centre could be on a Saturday afternoon, she had told him she would get a taxi. She directed the driver past St James's Hospital and into the network of streets where Simon's house stood.

Ringing the doorbell, Mandy was only kept waiting a moment before the door swung open. 'Hello, gorgeous!' Simon held out his arms and Mandy dropped her bag inside the door to hug him tightly.

'I've missed you,' she said. His familiar sandalwood aftershave mingled with the scent of cleanly washed clothes and she buried her face in his shoulder, enjoying the warmth of his muscular body pressed against her.

'I've missed you, too.' Releasing her, Simon closed the door, lifted her case and took it upstairs. Mandy followed him and they embraced again, this time with a kiss that left Mandy feeling breathless. They drew apart and she gazed at him.

'We should go down,' he said. 'I've got some things to show you.'

'Something smells good,' she said as they made their way back downstairs.

Simon led her into the kitchen and opened the oven door with a flourish. 'Vegetable moussaka,' he said. 'It'll be ready soon. I thought we could have a chat about our clinic while it's cooking.'

'Oh.' Mandy felt an unexpected swooping sensation in her stomach. She knew they had to start planning the clinic sometime, but she had imagined a lingering, thank-goodness-you're-home dinner before a long bath and an early night. 'What did you want to discuss?' she said and then, realising that sounded even less enthusiastic than she felt, she added, 'It'll be great to look at some ideas.'

'Won't it just?' Simon grinned, crinkling the skin beside his blue eyes. 'I can't wait until it's us making all the decisions. I've been looking at specialist surgical tables,' and before Mandy could reply, he pulled a slew of technical brochures from a folder beside the microwave.

As Mandy flicked through the glossy pictures, she couldn't help feeling a bit overwhelmed. Until she had suggested returning to Welford to help her parents, there had been no set date for the opening of their clinic. She and Simon had talked about it as something for the future. But since he had known she was moving away, Simon had suggested that the natural time to open up would be when Mandy came back to Leeds. Somehow Mandy had imagined waiting longer before taking such a big step. Although she had inherited some money from Emily's mother, she knew Simon had no savings to speak of. If they wanted to open both a clinic and rescue centre at the same time, it was going to be tough to stretch their finances as well as build up a practice from scratch.

She looked down again at the raft of brochures. Simon seemed to have researched every kind of orthopaedic surgery in existence.

'I think it's really important,' he said, facing Mandy across the table with his hands on his knees, 'that we start off with the highest possible standard of treatment. There's a lot of competition, not least from Thurston's.' Thurston's was the clinic where the two of them were currently working and Mandy felt another stab of misgiving. It was one thing leaving the practice to go and work in Welford. It was quite another to set up in opposition nearby.

'I know it will take a lot of work,' Simon went on, 'but eventually I'd like to offer something really different. Not just regular orthopaedics, but specialist prosthetics and so on.' He pushed another brochure in front of her. 'This company sells all kinds of instruments for the latest types of surgery,' he said. 'I thought I might get in contact with them next week.'

Mandy wondered how much it was going to cost. For some reason, there didn't seem to be any prices included. Simon was looking expectantly at her and with determination, she managed to smile.

'It's great that you have so many ideas,' she said. And it was, really. After all, it would be exciting, as Simon had said, to be the ones making the decisions about how things were run. Although Mandy enjoyed working for Amy Thurston, there were some things she knew she would do differently. Her course in animal behaviour had taught her different ways to approach frightened animals and sometimes the way she was expected to work was more stressful than it needed to be. As well as working with her rescue patients, she wanted to help Simon when it came to pain relief. That was something else she felt was important and, in the past year, she had attended two different courses to learn how to use the medicines available more efficiently. Their skills would be complementary, she thought. Simon was interested in surgery, while she could ensure that his patients were kept pain-free and mentally stable during recovery.

'The thing I'm most looking forward to,' she said, 'is being able to treat my patients without causing them stress. I'll be able to keep them in until they're properly ready to go home. And I can work on rescue animals alongside our regular patients.'

Simon frowned. 'That's a nice idea in theory,' he said. 'But we won't have unlimited kennel space at the beginning. And you'll need to concentrate on your clinical work until we start to make a decent profit. Nursing the patients needs to be left to the nurses.'

Mandy looked at him, but he had taken back the pamphlet about the surgical table and was making a great show of examining it carefully. Did Simon expect her to put the rescue part of their venture to the side at the beginning? She had known there would have to be some compromises, but he didn't seem to be offering to make any himself.

'So what's next?' she said. 'I'm due back in Welford in a couple of weeks, of course. Should we wait and see how things go there before we make any definite plans? I know Mum and Dad have been looking, but there are precious few candidates for mixed practice nowadays. I don't want to leave them in the lurch like Shula did.'

'Of course, you must help them out for as long as necessary.' Simon stood up, returning the glossy magazines to the ring binder. 'Your parents will need your help for the summer at least. But I don't think that should stop us from making plans of our own.' He leaned on the counter, his face glowing with enthusiasm. 'I thought I might start looking at possible premises. We need to get some idea of whether it will be better to rent or if we could afford to buy straight away. We'll probably have to get some work done as well. It's not likely we'll find anything that is set up perfectly. It'll all take time.'

'I suppose it's a good idea to start looking how much everything will cost,' said Mandy. Maybe if Simon did that, he would realise they needed to wait a bit longer and build up some more savings. 'We don't have to rush into anything though, do we?'

For a moment, Simon's face fell. 'I know you have to help your parents out,' he said. 'But I want you back here as soon as possible.'

'I know,' Mandy said. 'It's just . . .' She thought for a

moment. 'I think we need to sit down together and work out exactly what we both want, before we make any firm decisions.'

'Of course we will,' Simon assured her. 'I just don't see the need to wait too long.' He grinned at her. 'Are you hungry?' he asked. 'I think dinner should be ready.'

Mandy nodded. 'Starving.' The delicious scent from the oven had been tantalising her for the past half-hour and, before Simon could say anything, she leaped up and rummaged in the cutlery drawer.

Simon looked amused. 'Hold your horses with those forks.'

Taking them from her, he dropped them back into the tray, then took her hand and led her into the lounge. In front of the bay window, which overlooked the park, he had set up a round table with a chair at either side. The table was set with dark green table mats, white napkins and bright silver knives and forks. A square plate in the centre was studded with different sized candles, each one burning with a tiny flame.

'I wanted to celebrate your return properly,' he murmured. He handed Mandy a sheet of paper with a handwritten menu and bowed, his eyes sparkling.

Mandy looked down at the menu. 'Goat's cheese and watermelon salad,' she read, 'followed by vegetarian moussaka, then home-made chocolate brownies . . .' Dropping the paper on the table, she flung her arms around Simon and hugged him tight. 'You know the way to this woman's heart!' she whispered. 'How would you feel if I suggested we take the brownies upstairs with us?'

Simon wrapped his hands around her waist and pulled her closer. 'Tonight, Amanda, your wish is my command.'

Chapter Five

It seemed very strange to walk back into the Monday morning rush at Thurston's. Though it had been busy at Animal Ark, there was an intensity in Leeds that felt almost stifling to Mandy. In place of Helen juggling reception and nursing duties, there were two dedicated receptionists on the desk all the time. Five nurses worked alongside the same number of vets. Life was conducted at high speed, both inside and out.

Mandy had called at Starbucks on her way in. The physical proximity of so many bodies in the coffee shop had felt smothering and she had been glad to escape. Rounding the end of the desk, she slid a Frappuccino into Angela's hand. The dark-eyed receptionist smiled at her through her phone conversation, setting the cup down on the desk. 'Thanks,' she mouthed. A moment later, she pressed the button to end the call.

'Any chance of a quiet morning?' Mandy asked. The waiting-room was heaving, but it was still possible if there were enough vets on duty.

'No such luck,' Angela replied, checking that the name tag on her light blue tunic was straight. 'Momal is going to a funeral and David is sitting an exam. Peter wants you to spay a cat first thing. There are two booked in. You can anaesthetise them together, then do one each. After that, he wants help anaesthetising a dog and a rabbit. Momal was meant to be assisting. Simon and Samantha are covering your consultation duties.'

Despite Angela's scepticism, the timetable didn't sound too daunting. Mandy was interested in anaesthesia. Most of the time, the nurses carried out monitoring duties once the operation was underway. It would do no harm to keep her hand in.

'What about the afternoon?'

'You've got a visit to Miss Kitty with Geoff Hayes,' Angela told her. Mandy felt a tremor of apprehension. She had visited the client known as Miss Kitty with Geoff, the local animal welfare officer, just before she had left for Welford. The state of the old woman's flat had come as a shock. Mandy knew about hoarding, but nothing had prepared her for the piles of unwashed dishes and rubbish, or the stench of excrement and urine-soaked floors. It had been all she could do to keep from gagging. But despite the surroundings, the cats themselves had looked surprisingly healthy. There was no doubt in Mandy's mind the woman loved them. Mandy and Geoff had agreed that the lack of sanitation could not continue, so they had laid down several conditions, measures for improvement, which Miss Kitty had promised to carry out. Mandy hoped, rather than expected, that she had complied.

Peter was waiting in his green scrubs and surgical cap for Mandy in the prep room. There were two cat boxes on the table beside him. 'I know it's not ideal,' he admitted, 'but if we can get them anaesthetised, we can operate at the same time.' Between them, they injected both cats and prepared them for surgery. Then, one on each table in the big theatre, they began. Twenty minutes later, both cats were back in their baskets.

'Thanks for doing that.' Peter peered in at Mandy's patient, which sported a plastic collar and a warm blanket. 'This morning was going to be a bit tight, even if Momal had been here. Have you seen the other patients?' he asked.

Mandy shook her head. Angela had mentioned two spays, a dog and a rabbit. Despite the fact that rabbit spays could be tricky, it didn't seem an excessive amount of work for one morning, even if Peter had done both cats himself. 'Why?' she said.

'Come and see.' They lifted a cat basket apiece and carried them through into the recovery area. Then Mandy followed Peter into the dog kennels.

Stopping in front of one of the upper cages, Peter made a face as he looked through the glass. 'This is our next patient, Widget,' he said.

Mandy stepped forwards. What was causing Peter so much angst?

'Her owner describes her as a Chorkie.' Peter's voice held exasperation.

On the other side of the glass stood the most minuscule

dog Mandy had ever seen. 'What on earth is a Chorkie?' she asked, frowning.

'At a guess, a Chihuahua crossed with a miniature Yorkie. Traditionally, we'd have called it a cross-breed.' Peter shook his head. 'I'm all for hybrid vigour, but if the whole aim is to produce minuscule puppies, any health benefits go right out of the window. Her pelvis is so narrow, she'd probably die if they tried to breed from her.'

Mandy looked again at the tiny dog. It couldn't weigh more than a couple of kilograms. They'd have to weigh it on the exotics scale. She rubbed her forehead as she planned the operation. Would even the smallest tube fit the trachea? 'What about fasting?' she asked. 'These tiny dogs are prone to hypoglycaemia, aren't they?'

'She hasn't eaten or drunk for four hours,' Peter told her. 'That's the longest I dare leave her without anything. Come on, let's get started.'

It was difficult getting the catheter into the vein. It was harder still, titrating the anaesthetic to effect. Peter scrubbed as Mandy made the final preparations, wrapping as much of the dog's tiny body as she could in bubble wrap to avoid heat loss. While she relished the challenge of complicated cases, no adult dog should be this small. Peter, expert surgeon that he was, struggled with the scale of trying to remove the ovaries from an incision he could barely get his fingers through.

It was a relief when he put the final suture in. Reaching

out, Mandy turned the anaesthetic off so the animal was breathing only oxygen. It was essential to keep the endotracheal tube in place as long as possible. The short starvation increased the vomiting risk.

Despite keeping the anaesthesia light, it seemed an age before Widget swallowed. As soon as Mandy had taken the tube out, the tiny dog lifted her head, looking round as if wondering where she was. Lifting the insubstantial body into her arms, Mandy stroked the miniature head. She was glad to find Jenny on duty in the recovery area. Like Peter, she was dressed in scrubs. The cat Mandy had spayed earlier was curled up looking comfortable.

'Another one for you,' she told Jenny. 'Can you keep a special eye on little Widget, please? I managed to keep her temperature up, but there's a risk of fitting due to hypoglycaemia. Use some carob syrup on her gums if you need to. I'll be in theatre with Peter if you need me.' The nurse nodded.

To her relief, Peter had already anaesthetised their next patient, which was a rabbit. 'Talk about going from the sublime to the ridiculous,' he said.

Mandy stared at the enormous furry bundle. Despite being a Flemish Giant, the rabbit was even bigger than most of its breed. As she and Peter inserted the V-gel tube into its throat, Mandy was relieved it was Peter doing the surgery and not her. As he opened into the abdomen, he could barely find the uterus among the mounds of fat. Once the spay was complete, he had a difficult time closing up, and Mandy heard him muttering to himself behind his mask.

By the time Mandy handed the rabbit to Jenny, the forty-five minutes that were allocated for her lunch were two-thirds past. Just as well she had come prepared, she thought, as she pulled open the fridge in the staff room and grabbed the sandwich she had brought. It was almost time for Geoff to arrive, but she wanted to prepare a diet sheet for the owner of the oversized rabbit. Throwing herself into a seat, she pulled a piece of paper towards her and began to write.

'What's that you've got there?'

Mandy looked up, startled. She had been so engrossed, she hadn't noticed Simon coming in.

'It's a diet sheet for the rabbit Peter and I spayed this morning.' She pulled a face. 'Poor thing, Peter could hardly bring the muscle back together, the pressure from the abdominal fat was so great.'

Simon grinned. 'Don't forget to make an outline of all the exercise you want it to do,' he said. 'Maybe some hopping on the spot.'

Mandy lifted her eyes for a moment, then dropped them and continued writing. She had always been amused by Simon's quirky sense of humour, but these days there often seemed to be a dig about the attention she gave when her patients were passed back to their owners. This had been Peter's case. In the unlikely event that Simon had been roped in to assist with the anaesthesia, he would never have considered getting involved in the post-operative care plan. Not even if it was in the best interests of the patient.

'Hey, maybe we should see it as a financial opportunity?' Simon suggested. 'We could offer liposuction when we start up on our own.'

Mandy looked up again and frowned. 'You know as well as I do that cosmetic surgery on animals is illegal in the UK.'

'Maybe we should move to the US?' Simon offered. 'That way we could make even more money.'

'Even if I wanted to move to the US,' Mandy said, 'which right now I don't, there's no reason any poor animal should suffer just because their owners have been irresponsible with their feeding.' She glared at Simon, who looked surprised.

Raising his eyebrows, he held up his hands. 'I wasn't serious,' he said. 'I thought you'd know that. I fully intend to stay right here in Leeds. Unlike yours, my vet qualification isn't even valid in the US.'

Taking a deep breath, Mandy unclenched her hands and looked down at the floor. 'I'm sorry,' she said. 'I'm just tired. It's been a stressful morning.' *And I have to go out on an awful house visit in five minutes*, she could have added.

'Ah,' he said with a wry smile. 'You're already getting used to the slower pace of life in sleepy Welford.'

Mandy felt her irritation rise again. Ever since James's wedding, Simon had been making barbed little comments about Welford. It wasn't as if Animal Ark was less busy than Thurston's. During the day, things were less intense, but Thurston's closed every evening. Nights, weekends and bank holidays were covered by an emergency clinic. Animal Ark was open twenty-four hours a day, seven days a week. Every week. Yet when she had tried to challenge Simon's comments, he'd told her he was only joking.

She was still trying to think of what to say when Saloni popped her head around the door. 'Geoff's here, Mandy,' she said. With a sigh, Mandy stood up.

'How was your visit back home?' Geoff asked fifteen minutes later, as they drove towards the estate where Miss Kitty lived. Mandy glanced over at him. He was a friendly man, grey-haired, with a smile that could charm the most truculent pet-owner. Mandy had seen him use persuasion and patience many times where others might have jumped straight to blame.

'It was great,' she said. 'The whole way of life there is so different from the city.'

Geoff took his eyes off the road for a moment to glance at her, then turned back with a sigh. 'Oh yes,' he said. 'I remember not so many years ago, most practices were smaller and much less specialised. The vets would be out calving a cow one minute, the next they could be operating on a dog with a broken leg or checking out someone's goldfish.'

'It's still like that at Animal Ark,' Mandy admitted.

'Mum and Dad do all kinds of things. I hadn't realised until I went back how much I missed the variety.'

'Well, I can't wait to get back to my alpacas,' Geoff said. 'I miss them when I'm working.' Mandy knew the welfare officer had a smallholding on the outskirts of Leeds. He had been telling her, ever since they met, just how much he was looking forward to his retirement.

They were almost there, she realised as they passed a graffiti-scarred row of shops. When they pulled up outside Miss Kitty's tower block, a dispirited-looking boy of about eleven disappeared, returning a moment later with four others. Remembering Bert Burnley and his camping holidays for city children, Mandy wished she had something to offer them. They were eyeing the van as if it were some kind of prey. She wondered how their faces would look if they were taken to Jimmy Marsh's Outward Bound trail in the woods. Would they relish the challenge? Could they learn to love the moors as she did?

Geoff Hayes was more prosaic. Climbing out of the van, he offered the tallest of the boys a large pack of mini Mars Bars. 'Could you lads look after the van while I go on a house visit?' he asked. 'Share them out between you.'

Removing two cat baskets from the back of the van, 'just in case,' as Geoff said, they headed off across the rough tarmac. Trying not to look back, Mandy followed Geoff into the entrance. The tiles underfoot were gritty, and the sound of their footsteps echoed on the stained walls. The lift stank of urine. Nobody should have to live like this, Mandy thought. Welford seemed impossibly far away. As the lift juddered to a halt on the seventeenth floor and the doors slid open, they were greeted by the stench of cats.

Geoff breathed in, then shook his head. 'They almost never comply,' he said with a grimace. 'Sometimes I wonder why we bother giving them the chance.' Stamping across the landing, he set the cat baskets out of sight against the wall and banged on Miss Kitty's door. 'Geoff Hayes here,' he called. 'Animal Welfare.' From inside the flat came the sound of two cats yowling. Even outside the door, it sounded loud.

The door opened a crack and an eye peered through. 'What do you want?' rasped a weak voice.

'Can we come in, Miss Kitty?' Geoff's voice seemed loud in the enclosed hallway. 'I'm Geoff Hayes from Animal Welfare. This is Mandy Hope from Thurston's Veterinary Practice. We were here a couple of weeks ago about the cats, remember?'

The door opened a little wider as Miss Kitty peeped out. Mandy tried not to gawk at the woman's outfit. Along with a purple nightgown, she was wearing a stripy knitted hat and a huge silk shawl. A scrawny kitten was clutched to her chest. Pulling the shawl round as if to protect the tiny creature, Miss Kitty insisted, 'I don't want you to come in. I love my cats. We don't need any help.'

'Miss Kitty.' Geoff's voice sounded tired. 'We need

to get in. We have reason to believe you are not keeping your cats in a suitable environment. If you won't allow us entry, I'll have to call the police.'

The woman hugged the kitten even more tightly to herself, her mouth set in a straight line. Her eyes were defiant, but Mandy could see fear there as well. 'That's a lovely kitten, Miss Kitty,' she said. 'I know how much you love your cats. We only want to help, but we can't do anything standing here on the doorstep. Won't you let us come in? Please?'

The silence stretched out. Miss Kitty seemed to be giving her suggestion some consideration. Mandy hoped that Geoff would give her time. Eventually, Miss Kitty spoke. 'You have kind eyes,' she said. 'You can come in. But I want him,' she indicated Geoff, 'to stay here.'

Mandy looked at the welfare officer. 'Would that be all right with you?' she murmured. 'I could see how things are going, at least.'

Geoff nodded. 'We don't want to do anything to upset Miss Kitty if we can help it. I'll be right here if you need me,' he said.

Moving forward as Miss Kitty stepped back, Mandy pushed the door wide open. 'I'll just leave this open a crack,' she told the owner. 'Mr Hayes won't come in without permission.' Stepping inside, she half closed the door and followed Miss Kitty along the hallway.

It was obvious that all their previous recommendations had been ignored. Although the hallway was relatively clear, as soon as they rounded the corner into the kitchen, they were greeted by piles of rubbish. Strewn around, amid the old newspapers and broken utensils, cat faeces lay alongside filthy food dishes. There was no sign Miss Kitty had tried to clear the floor of rubbish, or serve fresh food or water. There seemed to be cats on every available surface. Mandy felt sick. There was no way they could leave the cats here. The three she could see clearly looked thinner than those she had been shown on their last visit. She stood for a long moment, just looking, trying not to breathe the overpowering stink of ammonia.

'I'm very sorry, Miss Kitty,' she said finally, 'but we are going to have to take some of your cats away. It isn't healthy for them to live in these conditions.' To her distress, Miss Kitty put her hands over her ears and started to wail.

Over the noise, Mandy heard Geoff's voice calling to her from the front door. 'I'm going to call Ranjit,' he said. 'He'll come out and give some support.' Ranjit Singh was Miss Kitty's social worker. Mandy knew Geoff had been in touch before their visit to tell him they might have to take the cats away.

The wailing grew louder. Despite feeling uncomfortable, Mandy stepped closer and patted Miss Kitty's shoulder. She caught sight of another cat, cowering in the corner behind a large plant pot. As Mandy watched, the frightened animal opened its mouth in a silent meow. When it turned its head, Mandy saw a gaping wound on the side of its neck. Miss Kitty, seeing the direction of Mandy's gaze, fell silent.

'Daisy May,' she whispered, pointing with a trembling hand.

'Daisy May is badly injured.' Mandy tried to keep her voice soft. 'Would it be okay for me to take a closer look at her? I think she needs treatment.' Miss Kitty gave a single nervous nod.

Edging closer to the little cat, Mandy managed to lift her up. As well as the wound on her neck, there was a flap of torn skin hanging from the top of her tail. A quick look around the kitchen convinced Mandy there was no way the injuries could be treated here. 'She's going to need an anaesthetic so I can clean and stitch her wounds,' she explained. To her relief, Miss Kitty just blinked at her, and didn't start wailing again.

Mandy thought for a moment. From the yowling they heard before they came in, there must have been another cat involved. Moving slowly, she took Daisy May out to Geoff and put her in one of the cages he had brought up. 'Just as well you were prepared,' she whispered.

Geoff half smiled. 'I've been doing this for too many years,' he replied.

Returning to the foetid flat, Mandy made her way back to Miss Kitty. 'Daisy May is safe now,' she said. 'I'll take her back to the clinic for treatment, but I think there must have been another cat involved. It may be injured, too. Can you tell me where it is?' Miss Kitty didn't say anything, but her eyes widened. As Mandy watched, the older woman's gaze darted to a closed door across the hallway.

Stepping around the mess on the floor, Mandy opened the door and peered into a bathroom. Compared to the other rooms in the house, it was relatively empty, though still overwhelmingly filthy and rank smelling. As she stepped over the threshold, there was a crashing sound above her. Something huge hit the side of her head and she had an impression of fast-moving ginger fur before claws scraped across her face and down her shoulder. Needle-sharp teeth sank into the thumb on her left hand. A second later, an enormous tomcat landed in the bath, hissing up at her, its black pupils glittering in a whale-eyed gaze.

Mandy grabbed two towels from the floor and lunged forward, wrapping the material around the cat, bringing her arms together and enclosing both head and claws in a bundle she held close to her body. It was a manoeuvre she had practised many times, but it had never felt this close to a fight for survival! For the first time, the scratches on her face and the bite wound on her hand started to sting. Feeling sick, but holding the bundled cat tightly, she turned around.

To her surprise, Geoff was in the doorway, his face a picture of horror. 'I heard the commotion.' His voice sounded shaky. 'Are you okay?'

'Yes,' Mandy muttered through gritted teeth, feeling blood start to ooze down towards her wrist. 'Can you get the other basket?' Geoff darted to the front door and collected it. Without unwinding the towels, they manhandled the spitting bundle into the cage and shut the lid. Mandy straightened up, reaching into her coat pocket for a tissue to wipe up the blood on her hand.

Miss Kitty was watching them. 'Poor George,' she said. 'He isn't really dangerous. He just doesn't like strangers.'

'Or other cats,' Mandy said under her breath.

Miss Kitty's shawl had slipped off her left shoulder and Mandy could see a deep set of scratches across the woman's neck. Miss Kitty noticed her looking and pulled the shawl back into place. It was like a TV warning about domestic abuse. Mandy wanted to laugh, then cry. Her body was reacting to her injuries. Pulling herself together, she made her way to the bathroom sink. Despite being filthy, the water in the tap ran clean and there was an unopened bottle of soap lying on the floor. Lifting the soap, she washed the wounds on her hand and face, then wrapped her thumb in a clean handkerchief that Geoff handed to her. Her knees were trembling.

'I can see that George has scratched you as well, Miss Kitty.' Mandy was surprised how calm her own voice sounded. 'We'll take him away and see what we can do about rehoming him.'

A tear ran down Miss Kitty's face. 'You won't have to put him down, will you?' Her voice was pleading.

'He'll be neutered, then the rescue centre will try to rehabilitate him,' Mandy said. 'Just as they will with all the cats.'

More footsteps sounded in the hallway. 'Miss Kitty?' called a friendly voice. 'It's me, Ranjit.' To Mandy's relief, a young man with spiky black hair and warm eyes appeared behind Miss Kitty. He was wearing a leather jacket and skinny jeans tucked into unlaced DMs. Mandy felt herself close to giggling at the sight of such an unlikely social worker, and she swallowed hard.

Ranjit put his hand on Miss Kitty's arm and she allowed herself to be led away to the kitchen. 'We'll make a nice cup of tea. Mr Hayes and Miss Hope will look after your cats.'

'I'll take these two down.' Geoff lifted the crates containing Daisy May and George. 'And bring back some more.' He looked round the room. 'I think it might take more than one journey to collect them all,' he said. 'We'll just have to make a start and see how we get on.'

It took a long time to catch all the cats. None of the others were as difficult to handle as George, but many of them were clearly terrified.

'I think that's the last,' Geoff said as he closed the cage on a skin-and-bone tabby.

'Except for the one Miss Kitty is holding,' Mandy reminded him. She sighed. It seemed so cruel to take every single cat. 'Is there any chance, if I came back to check on it, that she could try to keep that one? It's a tomcat, so no worries about kittens at least. Though it would be even better if she'd let me neuter him, too.'

'Are you sure you'll want to come back and check?' Geoff's eyes studied her. 'I can't say I want to come back here any more than necessary, and it wasn't even me who got bitten.'

Ranjit appeared from the kitchen. 'She wants me to see what's going on,' he said.

'We can swap,' Mandy suggested. 'If you help Geoff to take these cat boxes down, I could have a chat with Miss Kitty about the one she's holding.' It was, as she had thought, a tomcat. 'He is lovely, Miss Kitty,' she said a few moments later. 'If you would be willing to let me take him for neutering, then I will try to convince Mr Hayes you'd be able to keep him. Does he have a name?' she asked.

'He's called Friendly,' Miss Kitty replied.

It was an apt name. When Mandy started to examine the little grey cat, he rubbed his face against her hand. Miss Kitty, who had been crying throughout the removal of the cats, had calmed down a little, though her eyes were still swollen. Leaving her clutching Friendly, Mandy, trying to keep her thumb clean, made a sweep of the kitchen, clearing away dirty food and setting out clean water. She would have to visit very soon. She would also need to promise Geoff that if anything went wrong, she would immediately be in touch, or available by phone, at least.

When Ranjit returned, she spoke to him. 'We've done our part,' she said, 'in removing the cats. You will be coming back to make sure Miss Kitty has help, won't you? Not just practical help, but someone to talk to as well. Nobody in their right mind would think it was okay to live like this.'

'I'll get in touch with one of the council officers,'

Ranjit said. 'They can come back with an order that would allow them access to clean up. I can get a doctor out as well. They'll do an assessment.'

'That would be good.' Mandy was beginning to feel shivery again.

'Speaking of doctors, we should get you to one.' Geoff was looking at her wrapped-up hand. Blood had begun to seep through the handkerchief.

Mandy shook her head. 'I promised Miss Kitty I would look after these cats,' she said. 'Someone can look at me when we get back to the clinic.'

Ranjit smiled at her, his eyes the colour of melted chocolate. 'You really do love animals more than anything elsc, don't you, Mandy? I don't know what they'd do without you!'

'You know what, Mandy?' They were almost back at Thurston's. Mandy could see the sign further up the road.

'No, Geoff,' she said. 'I don't know what.' Her thumb was throbbing and she was holding her hand against her chest.

The welfare officer glanced at her. 'I think you could be as crazy as Miss Kitty. What did you want to go in that bathroom on your own for?'

'Well, I didn't know it was a bathroom,' Mandy pointed out. 'I didn't know George was there. And I had absolutely no idea he would attack. Most nervous cats run away. George has learned to bite and scratch. Anyway,' she added as the van drew to a halt, 'better that I take George away before he hurts any other cats, or worse, Miss Kitty.'

'You were very brave,' Geoff said, 'but still mad. Far too soft.'

They climbed out of the van and walked round to the boot. Instead of opening it, Geoff stopped and looked at her. To Mandy's surprise, he reached out and gave her a hug. 'You've got the biggest heart of anyone I know,' he said. 'I'm going to miss you, Mandy Hope.'

'I'll come and visit you at your smallholding.' Mandy smiled. 'Gran is always looking for different kinds of wool. I'm sure she'd love to try alpaca.'

'You would be more than welcome.' Geoff opened the van. 'Right then. We'd better get the ill and injured cats inside.'

To Mandy's relief, Peter and Jenny appeared. 'Looks like you've got your hands full,' Peter said, but Jenny was eyeing the now-red handkerchief that was tied round Mandy's thumb.

'Come on, Mandy,' she said. 'Before you do anything else, I'm going to take a look at whatever is under that dressing.'

Mandy allowed herself to be led through to the prep room, where Jenny stripped away the makeshift bandage. The nurse cleaned the puncture wound on her thumb, as well as the scratches on her neck and arm.

'You know all about Pasteurella infections, don't you?' Jenny reminded her.

'I know.' Mandy sighed. 'If the wound on my thumb swells, or I get red streaks running up my arm, I'll see a doctor.' She knew how serious the problems could be with cat-bite wounds. It didn't do to take any chances.

Jenny looked sad as she finished bandaging Mandy's thumb. 'You really are a champion for all animals. Humans as well,' she added. 'I'm going to miss you.' For the second time that afternoon, Mandy found herself engulfed in an unexpected hug. She felt heat rising up her face, but couldn't help being warmed by Jenny's words.

She hugged Jenny back. Despite her excitement about going back to Welford, there were lots of things she was going to be sorry to leave.

'I'll miss you, too,' Mandy whispered.

Chapter Six

Putting down her knife and fork, Mandy looked around the table at the people she had come to know so well during the past year.

David raised his eyebrows at her across the table. His smooth hair hung loose around his face. 'Was it as good as usual?'

Mandy glanced at her empty plate, then back up, meeting his question with a smile. 'It was great,' she said.

Jenny, Thurston's head nurse, who had organised her night out, had booked Mandy's favourite vegetarian restaurant in Leeds. Mandy had just finished a delicious plate of lentil and vegetable pie topped with mash. She would miss this place, she thought, looking around the low-ceilinged room with muted green walls. Simon and she had eaten here so often that the waiters greeted them by name when they arrived. Not that she was going to be away forever, she reminded herself, as Simon put down his cutlery and reached out to squeeze her hand under the table.

From the far end of their group, there came a loud

'chink, chink, chink' and Mandy turned to see that Amy, the owner of Thurston's, was tapping her glass with a teaspoon. Her boss was resplendent in an unexpected scarlet dress, which offset her dark curly hair and the gold earrings that glittered in the candlelight. She waited for silence around the table before she spoke.

'We're here tonight to say goodbye to Mandy,' she announced. 'Mandy, you've been with us for a year and we've learned a lot from you, as I hope you've learned from us.' She definitely had, Mandy thought. She had arrived as a new graduate and was leaving with a year's experience. 'I'm not going to go on for too long,' Amy went on, 'but I wanted to thank you for all your hard work. Also, I wanted to say that if you feel like coming back to Leeds and returning to small animal work, I hope you'll let me know and I'll do my best to find something for you.'

Mandy felt a burst of confused emotion. It was lovely to hear Amy's praise, but it was something of a double-edged sword. She was acutely aware that the plans Simon was making would put them in direct competition with Thurston's. She found herself thinking that if they did go ahead, they should look for premises in a different part of the city.

'Thanks, Amy.' Mandy knew she had to say something. Brevity was best. 'I've enjoyed working with you, too.' Her eyes flitted around the table, taking in the shining eyes and the faces, softened and golden in the muted light. 'I've learned so much since I came here and I'll miss you all.' There were smiles and appreciative murmurs from all sides.

'I think Jenny has something for you.' Amy looked across the table at the head nurse, who had abandoned her usual jeans for a warm yellow jersey dress. Jenny reached down behind her chair and hoisted up a large plastic bag, from which she started to pull a series of oddly shaped presents.

'These first.' She handed over two distinctly boot-shaped parcels. How typical of Jen, Mandy thought with a private smile, to pack two boots separately. The paper was crazy, too: bright yellow gift-wrap printed with lime-green frogs, each wearing a crown.

With a grin, Mandy ripped open the first parcel to reveal a matt-green Huntress wellington boot. She put it on the floor beside her foot and lifted the other boot-shaped package. 'If this is another left boot, I'll know you're having a dig at my dancing skills,' she joked, but when she ripped off the paper, it was the second boot of the pair. Slipping off her shoes, she slid her feet into them. They fitted perfectly.

'We thought you should start your new job in comfort,' Salomi said.

'There's more!' Jenny pulled forth another parcel. This one was large and squashy, and Mandy was delighted to find a thick pair of socks with horses galloping around the top seam and some woollen thermal underwear.

'I'm not sure why you think I'll need thermal under-wear in Welford in August,' she said, 'but I'll store them carefully, and wherever I am when January comes, I'm sure they'll be very useful.'

But Jenny wasn't finished. 'One last thing,' she said, and pulled out a rectangular box-shaped gift with familiar dimensions. Grinning, Mandy took the parcel and opened it. She was unsurprised to find a box of the long plastic gloves she would need for her large animal cases.

'Well, thanks very much for these,' she said as everyone laughed at her expression. Pressing in the perforated section on top of the carton, Mandy extracted two gloves and pulled them on, right up to the shoulder. 'Now I'm prepared for anything,' she said. 'But in particular, I think I might be ready for some dessert.'

'Dressed like that, you'd be safe if you chose the Mississippi Mud Pie!' called Peter, his blue eyes sparkling.

'You're always so thoughtful,' Mandy shot back, making a face at her soon-to-be-ex boss. When the waiter came, she ordered the chocolate brownie with ice cream as usual. It might be the last time she had it for a while.

The next day was her last in Leeds. When her shift finished at lunchtime, she wandered slowly around the clinic. Samantha was in the dental unit, while Jenny monitored the anaesthetic. Peter was in theatre with Momal. Simon was consulting. Mandy walked to the back of the clinic to her favourite place, the kennel room. This was where all the sick patients were hospitalised and where animals were cared for after operations, once they were sufficiently awake that they didn't need constant supervision. Saloni was there, checking a bitch that had been spayed that morning.

'How's she doing?' Mandy peered past the nurse into the cage. The little dog was sitting up, though she looked sorry for herself in her giant plastic collar. A white bandage covered the wound on her abdomen.

'She's doing well,' Saloni replied. 'Her colour's good and she doesn't seem sore. Simon's going to discharge her when her owner arrives.'

Mandy watched as the nurse removed the catheter from the animal's vein, set a bowl of water in the kennel and then left. There was another dog in the clinic, which Mandy had admitted that morning for stabilisation of his diabetes. She felt sad she wouldn't be able to see the job through. She opened the kennel and leaned on the metal edge for several minutes, scratching his ear. At least Samson was in good hands, she thought. Simon had assured her he would take responsibility for his ongoing care.

She moved through into the cat kennel where a ginger tom who had come in for a tail amputation was recovering from his anaesthetic. He stood up when he saw Mandy, rubbing his face on the bars of the cage and meowing until Mandy opened the door. He crept out of the kennel and up onto her shoulder, pressing his face against hers. She closed her eyes, enjoying the caress of his soft fur against her cheek and the vibrations of his purr in her ear. A few moments later, knowing she had to get on, she disengaged his claws from her top and set him back down, shutting him in carefully. Forcing herself to turn her back on her patients for the last time, she went to look for Simon.

He was still consulting. Mandy stood outside the door, listening to his voice, wondering what the future would bring. Maybe in five years she would be standing outside the consulting room of their own practice listening to the same positive tones. Unable to put off the inevitable any longer, she went to consulting room two, where she had spent so many hours during the past year. Her Littmann stethoscope was hanging from a hook on the wall, and she took it down with a feeling of sadness. Despite Amy's kind words last night, it was unlikely she would be returning. Closing the door behind her, she walked through to the office. There were a couple of behaviour and animal handling books that she needed to collect from the shelf. With a last glance around the prep room, she exited the practice by the side door and walked across the car park to her car.

It didn't take long to drive to the flat that she had shared with Samantha for the year. Not that she had spent much time there since she and Simon had got together. She had already packed most of her things. The bedroom looked very bare. The clock her parents had given her when she left for university was missing from the bedside table. There was a space on the wall where she had taken down two paintings: one a sheep in a snowstorm, the other two ponies up on the fells. She had bought them, along with two wildlife books, from James when he had first set up his café. They would go on the walls back at home in her bedroom, she decided.

Throwing the last few things into her case, she shut the lid and carried it into the hallway. Just the kitchen to check now. Samantha had stuck a photograph to the fridge door, Mandy noticed, and she moved nearer to look. It was taken on one of their practice nights out. Mandy remembered the evening well. They had gone bowling and had a drink together afterwards and the picture showed them just as they were leaving the bar. Jenny and Amy were there, and Saloni too. Samantha was grinning widely, one arm around David and the other round Simon. She had been really dressed up that night, Mandy thought, admiring Sam's body-fitting red dress and dazzling necklace. She looked more closely at her own image. She'd shut her eyes as the flash had gone off. Not terribly flattering. Simon looked good though. He had worn a soft green shirt that night that suited him well.

Mandy smiled at the memory and, leaving the picture where it was, did a quick check of the drawers and cupboards. Nothing left that she could see. She went back into the hallway, lifted her case and hauled it down the stairs. It felt very final as she shut the front door behind her. Now all she had to do was pop over to Simon's to pick up the last of her things and she would be on her way.

She was glad to see Simon's car outside the house when she arrived. Even though the clinic didn't provide its own on-call service, there was never any guarantee you would escape at the allotted time. Mandy had been touched when she asked if she should post her key through his letterbox and Simon had told her to keep it. 'After all,' he had said, 'if you come back for the weekend and I'm not around, it will be much better if you can let yourself in. You're welcome any time. I want you to feel this is your home just as much as your parents' house.'

Mounting the front door step, it felt so natural to get out the key and slide it into the lock without having to ring the doorbell. Mandy opened the door and walked in.

'Hello again.' Simon appeared from the kitchen and gave her a kiss. He was brandishing an oven glove and once again, the wonderful scent of cooking was wafting from the kitchen.

'What are you making?' Mandy followed him along the corridor.

'Just some soup,' he said.

Mandy smiled. It was always 'just' something when Simon cooked during the week, but it inevitably tasted marvellous. 'Cream of mushroom with garlic bread,' he added, setting out bowls, plates and spoons on the table. 'I thought you should have something to eat before your journey. If you want to throw a few things into your car, there's time before it's ready.'

Mandy sighed. She was going to miss Simon so much

and she would have loved to stay and watch him cook, but she did as he suggested and rushed around the house, trying to make sure she didn't miss anything. Somehow it was hard to spot things when they were all mixed up with other stuff. 'I hope I've got everything,' she said as she arrived back in the kitchen.

Simon put his head on one side and raised his eyebrows, his eyes amused. 'It wouldn't be so bad if you forgot something, would it?' he queried. 'You can leave as much stuff as you like. You're only going to be a couple of hours away. It's not like you're moving to the moon. Anyway, you'll be back at weekends, won't you?'

'Or you could visit me,' Mandy pointed out.

'I could do that,' Simon said, 'though there are things we have to tackle that we can't organise over there. You'll need to come over one weekday as well. We must talk to the bank about a business loan.'

'I'll need to see when I can get away,' Mandy warned him. 'You will wait, won't you, before doing anything? There's a lot we still need to discuss.' Although she wanted to please Simon, she was finding it hard to see beyond the next few months. She wanted to make sure the situation at Animal Ark was properly settled before starting anything else. 'That soup smells wonderful,' she added, hoping to distract him from her non-committal reply.

'I'll just check the bread.' Simon wielded the oven gloves again and within a moment, he was pulling apart a garlic-butter-slathered baguette. 'Definitely ready,' he said and began to ladle soup into the two bowls. 'Tuck in!' With a flourish, he placed them on the table. Mandy sat down, realising she was very hungry. With all the upheaval, she had forgotten to eat any lunch. Both soup and bread tasted fantastic.

After they had eaten, Mandy wandered into the sitting room at the front of the house while Simon finished putting the leftover soup away. A stack of papers lay on the coffee table, each with the name of an estate agent at the top. Simon must have put them out when she had been upstairs. They hadn't been there earlier when she checked the room for things to pack. Picking up the top one, Mandy saw a photo of a glass-fronted shop. '2,000 sq. ft. Development opportunity,' she read.

Simon appeared in the doorway, carrying a jug of coffee and two mugs. 'Good, you've seen them,' he said, sounding excited. 'What do you think?'

Mandy, whose eyes had been glued to the enormous six-figure price at the top of the page, looked up at Simon and then back down at the papers.

'What are these?' she asked, though the answer was obvious. 'I thought we agreed we would wait?'

Simon was wearing his hurt look again. 'I know we did,' he said, 'but I couldn't resist having a look. I need something to look forward to, with you going away.'

Mandy closed her eyes for a moment, then opened them again. When they had first discussed her move to Welford, Simon had seemed fine with it. He had even seemed encouraging. But now it was becoming a reality, he appeared to be pushing for her to come back as soon as possible. Mandy couldn't help feeling frustrated. Not that she didn't want to return. She very much did. But she didn't want to rush away from her parents while they needed her. It wouldn't be forever.

Simon was holding out one of the brochures. 'This one sounds good,' he said. 'Here's the floor plan. It's two thousand square feet and I've estimated that would be around the right size. We need to have room for a large operating theatre as well as consulting rooms and a waiting area.'

Mandy tucked a strand of blonde hair behind her ear as she gazed down at the drawing. She couldn't help feeling a stir of interest. 'Where are the dividing walls?' she asked. It seemed to be just one big area.

Simon reached out and pushed the plunger down on the cafetière before answering. 'There are none on that one,' he said. 'That's one of the things I like about it. We'd have a blank canvas to work from. There are other things we'll need, as well as workrooms. We should have a toilet with wheelchair access. And I want to have a proper staff relaxation area. The one at Thurston's is too small if we all have a break at the same time.' Pausing, he poured coffee over the warmed milk and handed Mandy a mug.

Putting the development opportunity property to the bottom of the pile, she looked at the next building. This time it had internal walls. It had been a training centre and the white painted rooms with their dark tiled floors looked as if they might be suitable for a clinic. The price was one and a half times that of the first.

Simon took the paper from her. 'The good thing about this one is that we wouldn't have to do too much rebuilding.' He pointed to the central room. 'That would be the waiting area,' he said, 'and we could stock food in this recess. That could be one consulting room and this another. Prep room and theatre back here. Dental room and X-ray.' It did look good, Mandy could see that. There was parking right outside the door, too, which was important.

'There isn't much space for kennelling,' she said. 'Or a separate area for rescue animals.' It was essential to Mandy that there was space in their clinic for this. Their joint venture wasn't just going to be about looking after pampered pets belonging to wealthy owners. Mandy wanted to make sure she was able to help other Miss Kittys as well.

'I suppose not.' Simon made a dismissive motion with his hand. 'It's important we use the space to maximise the profits. There won't be room for sentimentality at the beginning.'

Mandy frowned. 'It's not sentimentality,' she objected. 'Animal rescue and rehabilitation is important to me.'

'Of course it is.' And now he had that infuriating look of condescension she had seen him use with clients he considered overemotional. 'We just have to be sensible about it. That's all.'

Putting the property details back down on the coffee table, Mandy drank the last of her coffee and pushed herself up from the sofa. She didn't feel like continuing this conversation right now. She couldn't see it heading in a helpful direction. Simon stood up, too.

'I'd better get off,' Mandy said. 'Otherwise I won't be home before midnight.'

'Have a safe journey.' Simon followed her to the door. 'Give my regards to your parents.'

'I will,' she promised, glancing back up at the house one last time before climbing into her faded blue RAV4. 'Promise you won't go ahead with any decisions without me,' she said.

'I promise,' he replied, reaching in through the open door to kiss her. By the time she had put on her seat belt, he had turned and was walking back up the steps.

Mandy opened the window and waved. 'Bye,' she called.

'Bye.' He turned and waved back at her as she put the car into gear and drove off.

Chapter Seven

It was after midnight by the time she turned into the driveway, drove under the wooden 'Animal Ark' sign, and parked the Toyota at the side of the cottage. Mandy climbed out and stretched. Feeling the muscles in her back protest, she decided to leave most of her things in the boot until tomorrow and just grabbed her overnight bag.

Opening the back door, she was pleased to see the light was still on in the kitchen.

'Hello, love.' Her dad walked in from the sitting room. 'You're very late.'

Mandy let out a long breath. 'There was an accident on the A64. I had to take a huge detour.'

'Well, you're here now.' Adam went over to the fridge, grabbed a carton of milk and waved it at Mandy. 'Hot chocolate?' he offered.

'Dad, I'm twenty-seven, not six!'

'Really?' Adam looked both crestfallen and shocked. 'Don't tell me you've gone off it after all these years.'

Mandy grinned. 'Of course I haven't,' she said. 'I just wanted to see your face when I said no. I'd love a cup.

Thanks, Dad.' She walked over and hugged him and he squeezed her with the arm that wasn't holding the milk. 'Where's Mum?' she asked. Her dad turned away to pour milk into a mug as Mandy sat down at the table and rested her head on her hand.

'She had to go to bed,' Adam told her. 'She had to replace a prolapsed uterus on a cow this afternoon. Took two hours to get it back in. She was exhausted by the time she got home.'

Mandy had never tackled a cow with a prolapse before, but she remembered watching her dad one day. He had been on his knees behind a stricken Friesian; the everted uterus had been swollen to twice its normal size. The uneven struggle to get it back in before the cow pushed it out again had been painful to watch. It was one of the most physically demanding jobs in large animal practice.

'Poor Mum!' Mandy said. 'Well, if it comes back out tomorrow, I'd really like to take over. Save her struggling again.'

Adam frowned as he set the hot chocolate on the table in front of Mandy. 'I was hoping you'd spend the day with me in the clinic,' he said. 'I want to make sure you settle in and know where everything is.'

Mandy stared at him. Her dad had spoken as if she was a brand-new vet rather than his daughter, who had spent most of her life in and out of the clinic. Adam had turned away to get his own drink and didn't seem to notice. 'I'm glad you're here,' he said more quietly and, mollified, Mandy sipped her hot chocolate. Taking out her mobile phone, she looked at the screen. There were no messages. She had half hoped Simon would have sent something, good luck or a text to tell her he was missing her, but there was nothing.

'Do you mind if I use my phone, Dad?' She looked up at her father. 'I just want to let Simon know I've arrived safely.'

'Go ahead.' Her dad nodded, his smile warm. 'Good thing it's so easy to keep in touch these days.' Mandy typed her message, then put the phone down on the table beside her.

'Everything go okay with your last week in Leeds?' Adam sat down, setting his tea in front of him. 'Was the leaving meal any good?'

Mandy straightened up. 'Lovely food,' she said. 'We went to the Talisman, you know, where I took you and Mum. I got a pair of wellington boots and a box of arm-length gloves for a present.'

Adam laughed. 'They sent you prepared, then.' He paused. 'And Simon. How was he when you left?'

'He was fine. He made some lovely soup before I drove over.' For a moment, Simon's pushiness over the clinic filled her head, but she brushed the thought aside. He would settle down once he got used to her being away.

Adam looked pleased. 'Glad to hear he's looking after you,' he said. He lifted his mug and stood up. 'I think I'll turn in,' he said. 'Big day tomorrow. Your first time officially working for Animal Ark!' He made a salute, hand to forehead, and Mandy saluted back with a grin. She watched as he strode out of the room, listened to him gallop up the stairs two at a time, and then glanced back at the mobile screen. There was still nothing from Simon. Maybe he had gone to bed. With a sigh, she finished the last of her hot chocolate, picked up her case and followed her father more slowly up the stairs.

It felt strange to be back in her old room. Although it had seemed welcoming in the darkness when she had been here for James and Paul's wedding, with the light on now it looked bare and cramped. Mandy wished she had brought in the pictures she had taken from her bedroom in Leeds. She contemplated fetching them from the car, but found herself switching off the light and going to the window. The moon was rising over the top of the fell, casting strange shadows from the trees in the orchard and the low outhouse in the field. She turned her head to listen, hoping to hear the owl again, but was struck instead by the silence. There was always something happening outside the house in Leeds: a car passing or bickering students on the way home from a bar. Here there was nothing but noiseless sheep on the hillside. Pulling the curtain on the emptiness, Mandy turned back to her case, glad a moment later when her mobile buzzed on the bedside table. She rushed to answer the call.

'Simon,' she said, sitting down on the bed and kicking off her shoes.

'Hello, you.' His voice was calm and cheerful. 'You got there safely. Are your mum and dad well?'

'They're fine,' Mandy replied, pulling the pillows from under the duvet and propping them against the headboard. 'Thanks for the soup. I was glad I'd had it. Traffic was awful.' She leaned back against the pillows, pulling her feet up underneath her. 'I miss you already.'

The words were out before she had a chance to think, and sounded more desolate than Mandy had intended. She wondered for a moment if Simon would make fun of her. She had only been away a few hours! Instead he sighed.

'Me too,' he said. 'But it'll be good experience working for another practice. And it won't be long until we see each other.'

Mandy pictured him sitting up in his bed. He would be in his dressing gown, an old-fashioned blue robe, soft and fleecy and smelling of him. Maybe next time they were together, she could persuade him to lend it to her, she mused, wishing she had thought of it earlier.

'Do you think you'll be able to get away next weekend?' Simon's voice interrupted her thoughts. 'David has arranged a night out and you're invited.'

Mandy closed her eyes for a moment. As much as she wanted to say yes, she hadn't talked to her mum and dad about the rota. She had little doubt that if she asked, they would encourage her, but she had come here to help them. She didn't want to duck out at the first temptation.

'I don't know,' she said eventually. 'I haven't discussed the out-of-hours schedule with Mum and Dad yet. I'll talk to them tomorrow and let you know.'

'See what you can do. Hopefully they'll say it's okay.' He sounded as if he was certain they would. 'Anyway, I need to go now. I'm on early tomorrow. I've got that femoral fracture to fix, so I'd better get some shut-eye. Call me any time.'

Mandy put the phone on her bedside table. There was no way she'd be able to go back to Leeds next weekend. Her parents had been managing on their own for too long. It wasn't like Mum not to have waited up; she must have been exhausted. Mandy would break it gently to Simon next time he called.

A glance at the clock told her it was one thirty. Simon wasn't the only one who should get some sleep. Sighing, she extracted her pyjamas and toothbrush from her overnight bag. She could finish unpacking tomorrow.

The sun awoke her in the morning, its rays glancing onto her face through a crack in the curtains. For a moment, Mandy lay in bed looking at the familiar walls, then footsteps sounded on the stairs: her mum going down. Throwing back the duvet, Mandy pulled on her clothes and hammered down the stairs.

'Morning, Mum!' She flung her arms around Emily, who hugged her back tightly.

'What a lovely start to the morning.' Her mother was smiling and looked so cheery and well that Mandy felt a burst of relief.

'I'll make the coffee,' she offered, seeing her mum had put the kettle on and was rooting in the cupboard. 'You sit down.'

'Okay then, I will.' Emily pulled out a chair and reached for yesterday's newspaper.

'Shall I put some toast on?' Mandy opened the lid of the bread bin and took out several slices.

'That would be lovely,' said her mum. 'There's some of Gran's marmalade in the fridge if you'd like.'

More footsteps on the stairs and Adam appeared. 'Morning all,' he said. 'Are you making toast, Mandy? Finally honing your cooking skills?'

Mandy made a face at him. 'You'd better be polite or I won't make you any,' she said, placing the coffee jug on the table and setting out mugs, plates and knives. She was just finishing when the back door opened. She turned to see Helen Steer walking in with Lucy at her heels.

'Hi, all!' Helen seemed as much at home in the kitchen as she had in the clinic, Mandy thought. The nurse caught her eye and grinned and Mandy found herself smiling back. Helen's cheerfulness was infectious.

'Would you like some coffee?' Emily stood up and took a mug from the cupboard, setting it on the table and pushing the coffee and milk towards Helen, who had sat down. Lucy flopped down on the floor with a contented grunt. Mandy wondered if she had been made to walk to the clinic at top speed.

'Is there anything special on today?' Helen asked. 'Other than it being Mandy's official first day, of course.'

Adam drummed his fingers on the table, thinking. 'I'd like you to do a stock-check today, Helen.' He looked at Mandy. 'And I'd like you to shadow her, Mandy. I want to know you're up to speed with the equipment and drugs we're using. If there's anything you think we should order, Mum and I can discuss it.'

Mandy blinked and looked down at her coffee. He'd said something similar last night, but she had hoped he would have forgotten by this morning. She wanted to help with actual patients: get out and about, not be stuck in the storage cupboards. Worse, he'd said *they* would discuss any new equipment she wanted. Wasn't she going to have any say at all?

Helen could do a stock-check standing on her head, of that Mandy was certain. Surely the nurse would be insulted. But when she turned, Helen was looking at her with that hundred-watt smile on her face. 'That would be great,' she said. 'I'd love to have your company.'

Breathing out slowly, relaxing her shoulders, Mandy managed to smile back. 'Right then.' She stood up, picking up her crockery and placing it in the dishwasher.

Helen stood, too. 'Lucy, stay!' she said, then, 'Shall we go and get started, Mandy?' and without waiting for a reply, she headed out to the clinic.

'I'm so glad you're here,' Helen said two hours later. 'Stock-taking has to be the most boring thing ever.'

Mandy was surprised. Helen tackled everything with

a kind of frenetic efficiency. As she whirled through the practice, it seemed as if everything fell into place behind her. Much as Mandy had loved Jean, she couldn't help admiring the changes Helen had wrought. There were new procedures for drug ordering and rotation, efficient patient-plan printouts for hospitalised animals, and proper anaesthetic recording sheets.

Some of the equipment had come as a disappointment. The anaesthetic circuit was adequate, but the equipment used to monitor the patients was the same as it had been when Mandy was much younger. In Leeds, the nurses could track changes in breathing and carbon dioxide, blood pressure, temperature and the electrical activity in the heart. All of it was automated and easy to record. Here Helen used an ancient pulse oximeter to show blood oxygen and pulse rate. If she wanted to know the temperature, she had to use a separate thermometer.

Worse still was the dental equipment. Although Helen had demonstrated the special sharpening stone she had ordered, Mandy was used to Samantha's dedicated dental room with elevators and luxators for every kind of tooth and root removal. Thanks to Samantha, she had learned how to use a burr for grinding and smoothing rough edges of bone. Animal Ark had the most basic ultrasonic scaler and polisher. Mandy found herself wondering in what order she should prioritise the equipment she could ask for.

'Is everything okay?' Helen was looking at her. 'You seem miles away.'

Mandy shook her head. 'I was just wondering whether I'd like to get a multi-parameter anaesthetic monitor, a drip driver and some new infusion pumps, or whether we should go for some up-to-date dental equipment first.'

Helen laughed. 'Ah,' she said. 'I see you *were* miles away. Back in Leeds?'

'You're probably right,' Mandy admitted. 'What would you order first, if it was up to you?'

'I'd love a really up-to-date monitor,' said Helen after only a moment's thought. 'I know you can gauge a lot from watching the animal, but I'd like to know if the carbon dioxide starts to rise so I can keep the heart stable. And the blood pressure. If it starts to fall, I want to know so I can adjust the drip-rate.'

Mandy started to feel a tiny bit more optimistic. It sounded as if Helen would be right behind her if she asked for new equipment.

'What about you then?' Helen looked at Mandy, her head on one side, but Mandy shook her head.

'I'll need to have a think,' she said. She had to bear in mind that she wasn't going to be here forever. When she returned to Leeds, anything that had been bought would need to be useful without her. There was no use asking for specialised equipment that only she would use.

'Have you got anything planned for this evening?' Helen said, with her head stuck in a cupboard of dressings and bandages. 'We could go out, if you'd like. The Fox and Goose is good, even on a Monday.'

'Okay,' Mandy said. It would be good to have some distraction from Leeds and Simon and her friends there.

'There's this new guy in Welford. I'm kind of hoping he'll be there,' Helen admitted as she backed out of the cupboard and made a note on the clipboard beside her.

'Oh yes?' Mandy looked at the nurse, whose face had gone rather pink.

'Sam Western has agreed to have an Outward Bound centre on his land,' Helen said. 'The new guy, Jimmy Marsh, has come to build and run it. He's gorgeous,' she added, looking down at the pen in her hands.

'Oh,' said Mandy. 'I may have already met him. Over the back of a deer, actually.' Helen looked confused, but at that moment Adam opened the door and ushered Emily in. Emily's face creased into a smile when she saw Mandy and Helen surrounded by boxes and printed stocklists.

'Everything sorted?' she asked, looking from Mandy to Helen and back again. 'We could go and chat over a cup of tea,' she suggested, and together, the four of them trooped back through the cottage door and into the kitchen. 'So how did you get on?' Emily handed mugs out and set her own on the table before sitting down. 'Was there anything you thought of that would be helpful?'

'There were a few things,' Mandy confessed. 'Mostly from the work I've done with Samantha in Leeds.'

'Is she the vet who's into dentistry?'

'Yes,' Mandy said. 'She's shown me loads of techniques

for removing teeth, but you need different sized elevators and luxators. There only seemed to be a few here.'

Emily raised her eyebrows. 'Okay,' she said. 'That sounds reasonable. I'll have a look at that tomorrow, if you can show me.'

'And for pain relief,' Mandy said. 'Back in Leeds, we used several drugs in combination. Fentanyl and ketamine and lidocaine when we're doing painful surgery, all in different bags with an infusion pump for each.'

Emily frowned. 'We use fentanyl sometimes,' she said. 'But neither your dad nor I have had training in using those combinations.'

'It's easy, Mum,' Mandy insisted. It was simple, but she remembered it had seemed daunting at the beginning. She should give her mum time. It was probably better not to suggest Helen's new monitor for now.

'Thanks for the tea.' Mandy lifted her mug and took a sip. 'I can do evening surgery tonight, if you like.'

Emily looked grateful. 'That would be great,' she said. 'I could get some sewing done. It's been ages since I've had the time.'

Remembering that she still had some unpacking to do, Mandy finished her tea and stood up. 'I need to sort out my stuff from Leeds,' she said. 'Helen and I are going to the Fox and Goose later.'

'Okay.' Emily pushed back her chair. 'We'll eat in about an hour,' she said. 'There should be time before surgery begins.'

'Thanks, Mum.' Mandy walked over and opened the door. 'See you in a little while.'

The sound of the door closing behind her was achingly familiar, and Mandy had a sudden rush of joy that she had come home. Properly home, not as a child, but as a fully qualified vet. *Animal Ark has always been where my heart is!* she thought as she ran up the stairs two at a time.

Chapter Eight

Mandy looked around the Fox and Goose as Helen went to the bar with their order. On the other side of the room, at a table beside the fireplace, she could see Tommy Pickard, who she remembered as a boy a bit younger than James. Years ago, he had worn a cub-scout uniform almost every day, but now he was smartly dressed in a shirt and chinos and sat sipping a pint of bitter. Over near the window, she was amused to see the head of a Bernese Mountain Dog peeking from under one of the larger tables. His owners, she realised, were Liz and Sam Butler, who had visited Animal Ark years ago with their dog Dylan, also a Bernese.

Catching Liz's eye, Mandy gave a small wave and Liz nodded and raised her glass. Behind the bar, Gary Parsons was pouring a pint for an old man Mandy didn't recognise. Next to Gary, Bev bent to grab two bottles from the brightly lit fridge and wielded her bottle opener over the fresh orange Helen had ordered.

The door opened and another two people walked in. One was a thickset man with a ruddy face; it was Bert

Burnley, the farmer who had opened a campsite for city kids. His crinkly hair was white now, and Mandy watched as he pulled up a stool and joined the old man at the bar. The other newcomer, a younger man with deep-set brown eyes and short hair that stood rakishly upright, walked over and stood behind Helen, who was reaching into her purse to pay for the drinks. Sitting this close to the bar, Mandy could overhear everything that was said.

'Evening, Bert,' Gary said. 'And you, Seb.'

Bert Burnley murmured a greeting, but on hearing Seb's name, Helen spun around with raised eyebrows. 'Hello!' she said to the young man with spiky hair. 'Would you like a drink?' She was regarding him, Mandy saw, with the same brisk affection she showed towards Lucy, her retriever. Helen seemed to approach everything with a calm enthusiasm that was difficult to define and Mandy found herself wondering if the nurse ever felt over-whelmed by anything.

Seb's face lit up at the offer of a drink. 'Yes, please,' he said. He glanced around the bar. 'Are you here on your own?'

'Not tonight,' Helen replied. 'I'm with Mandy Hope. Adam and Emily's daughter.' She turned and smiled at Mandy, with tacit acknowledgement that she knew she could be overheard. Behind Helen's back, Mandy thought she detected disappointment in Seb's face, but it was gone by the time his eyes met hers and he walked the few steps to their table and held out his hand.

'Hello, Mandy,' he said, taking her hand and shaking

it with a firm grip. 'I'm Seb Conway. I'm the local animal welfare officer from Walton.'

Mandy sank back into her seat. 'Mum mentioned you,' she said. 'You brought in Kehaar.'

'I did,' he replied, and he half stood as Helen arrived at their table with the drinks on a small tray, only settling back down when Helen was seated.

'Did I hear you mention Kehaar?' the nurse asked, once she was comfortably ensconced on the banquette beside Mandy. 'Crazy gull!' She shook her head.

'What did he do?' Mandy asked. She had checked with Emily on her return to Animal Ark that the bird had been safely released, and her mum had assured her he had.

'Well, we set him free,' Helen said, 'and he stood in the garden, just looking at us. We'd been careful not to handle him much, but even so, he didn't seem to want to go. We didn't want to leave him on the lawn in case one of the cats came.' The nurse glanced at Mandy and Seb before she continued. 'He did eventually fly away, with a bit of encouragement . . .'

'You mean with you flapping a towel at him?' Seb put in.

'Yes, with me flapping a towel,' Helen admitted, 'and we thought that would be an end to it. But he turned up every morning for the next week and a half, landing on top of my car and making an awful racket.'

'But that's lovely, isn't it?' Mandy said. 'He was grateful enough to come back and see you.'

'Well, it would have been . . .' Helen's mouth tightened: half grimace, half grin. 'Except that every single time he left a gift of seagull poo right down the side of my car. Always on the driver's door, too.' She let out a guffaw that was so loud people in the bar turned and glanced their way. Mandy couldn't help but laugh. The sound was infectious, easily as funny as the mental image of the gull and his daily presents.

'He was a generous bird, all right.' Seb was smiling at Helen's reaction as he watched her. Noticing the warmth in his expression, Mandy felt a stab of sadness that Simon wasn't there. She had caught him looking at her that way when he thought she wasn't watching.

When the door opened, for a moment she was caught in a surge of ridiculous hope, but instead of Simon, a short, petite-framed girl with long blonde hair appeared. Spotting Helen, her face lit up and she came and stood beside their table.

'You must be the new vet,' she said, grabbing a stool from a neighbouring table and sitting down.

'Hardly new!' Before Mandy could say anything, Helen was speaking. 'Mandy's been here way longer than us!' She turned to Mandy and said, 'This is Gemma Moss. She's been running the village store since Mrs McFarlane retired. She does the most brilliant chocolate-coated ice creams.'

'I'm sorry,' Gemma said immediately. 'Of course you're not new. Helen told me all about you. How wonderful you've come back to Welford.'

'I feel very lucky,' Mandy agreed.

'Do you like horses?' Gemma asked. 'My gelding Jarvis needs his flu vaccination soon. He'll be glad to have another female vet around. He's terribly suspicious of your dad.'

Mandy laughed. 'Quite right, too,' she said. 'And yes, I love horses.'

'That's good,' Gemma said. 'That makes two of us.' She looked up as Seb stood and motioned at the almost empty glasses.

'Anyone for another drink? What would you like, Gemma?' Having listened to the order, he strode to the bar and Gemma leaned in towards Helen.

'You'll never guess who I ran into today,' she began.

Helen took a moment to glance at Seb to make sure he wasn't listening. 'Who?'

'Jimmy Marsh!' Mandy could tell the answer was no surprise to Helen. This was an ongoing conversation. 'I was up on the bridle path that goes through Sam Western's wood and he was there, chopping logs with his shirt off!' Gemma declared.

Helen's eyes glittered as a grin spread across her face. 'Really?' she said. 'And you didn't text me to let me know?'

Mandy's phone buzzed in her pocket, and she left Helen and Gemma marvelling at the wonders of Jimmy Marsh while she headed outside to take the call.

It was Simon. 'Hello, you. How did your first day go?'

'It was fine,' Mandy said. 'I spent most of it with Helen. You know, the nurse I told you about.' Loyalty to her parents stopped her from sharing her frustrations about the lack of modern equipment, or having to do a stock-take instead of going out to see clients. 'Helen invited me out to the Fox and Goose,' she went on, wondering for a moment if Simon would be annoyed that she was out socialising, but if he was, he didn't show it.

'That's great,' he said. 'I'm glad you're making friends.'

'How's your day been?' Mandy asked.

'Oh, so-so.' She could hear him mentally shrugging. 'Lots of first opinion cases, ten vaccinations and one guinea pig which needed its teeth rasped. I was glad to hand that over to Samantha.' Mandy knew Simon's real interest lay in his surgical cases, that consultation left him bored.

'How's my diabetes case?' she checked.

'Samson's doing well. His blood glucose is under control and he's eating reliably. I think we'll be able to send him home tomorrow. His owners came in today to do their first injection.' It was normal for owners of diabetic dogs to inject their pets with insulin, and Mandy knew that Simon wouldn't let the animal home until he was sure the owners could manage.

'That's good,' she said.

'So are you able to come over at the weekend?' he prompted, and Mandy belatedly remembered their conversation from last night. She winced.

'I can't,' she confessed. 'I've only just arrived. I need to be here this weekend to give my parents a break.'

'Oh well,' Simon said. 'That's understandable, I suppose.' He sounded resigned. 'Promise me one thing though,' he went on.

'What?'

'The next weekend after that is mine. Promise me you'll come home.'

Home? Or back to Leeds? Mandy wondered. 'Yes, of course I will,' she said out loud.

'Great,' he said. 'I could line up some properties to look at, if you like.'

Mandy bit her lip. 'Let's see how things go,' she said carefully. She didn't necessarily want to spend her first weekend off trawling around industrial premises.

'Sure,' said Simon, sounding as if he was mostly sure about finding half a dozen potential clinics for her inspection.

When they ended the call, Mandy felt deflated. She missed Simon's company, but his obsession with the new clinic was starting to wear her down. She only felt she had enough energy to settle into the routine at Animal Ark. She couldn't summon up any enthusiasm for planning beyond her stay.

Before she had time to put her phone back in her pocket a vehicle approached, round headlights dazzling in the gathering dusk. It was a Jeep Wrangler, and as it drew up opposite, Mandy caught sight of an Outward Bound logo on the bonnet and branding for the new

Upper Welford Hall Centre plastered across the sides. The gaudy red font seemed out of place against the backdrop of Welford village green.

As Mandy watched, Jimmy Marsh pushed open the driver's door and dropped lightly to the ground. A peal of laughter reached her through the half-open window of the bar and Gemma's admission of spying on Jimmy topless in the woods galloped into Mandy's head.

As Jimmy strode towards her, she felt a wave of warmth spreading upwards from her neck, turning her face scarlet.

'Hello,' he said. His gaze was quizzical, as if he wondered why she was standing there. 'It's good to see you again. Welcome back to Welford.' The heat in Mandy's face seemed to shift inwards to her core, and she felt a stir of irritation. The village was her home, not his. Who was he to welcome her?

'Hello,' she managed, her mind unable to think of a retort that wouldn't sound churlish. She was relieved when he passed her and headed into the bar. Breathing out, Mandy leaned against the wall, listening to the babble of voices through the window. The idea of stepping back into the warm hubbub seemed less appealing now. She heard Helen's distinctive laugh again. Peering around the edge of the open window, she saw Seb showing something on his phone to Gemma and Helen, who were leaning against each other, their faces creased with amusement.

Mandy felt a stab of loneliness. Simon had been a

near constant presence in her life for the past year. Though they had socialised separately now and then, he had always been there to go home to. She should have been kinder to him when they talked.

Turning her back on the Fox and Goose, she made her way down Main Street, turning right into the lane that led to Animal Ark. There was a chirruping overhead and Mandy looked up. Bats were flitting in and out of the trees that lined the lane. Her eyes fixed on the darkening sky, she let her footsteps lead her by instinct under the wooden sign and into the driveway before she lowered her eyes to the house. The light was on in the front room, but right now, Mandy didn't feel like having company.

Bypassing the cottage door, she made her way into the back garden. During evening surgery, she had admitted a rabbit that had stopped eating. With Helen's help, she had managed to get a catheter into its ear vein so she could give the little animal some intravenous fluids. Peering around the garden, she managed to find what she was looking for. Despite Adam's best efforts, there were several dandelions growing near the compost heap. Picking a few, Mandy made her way back to the in-patient unit and let herself in.

The little rabbit seemed more cheerful already. Instead of lying still, he stood up when the light went on and lolloped from one side of the cage to the other. When Mandy opened the door, he didn't cower away. Perching on the edge of the kennel, Mandy offered a dandelion leaf, but after sniffing it for a moment, the rabbit turned its head away.

'Poor little Arthur,' she murmured and, reaching out, gathered him into her arms. He had a fine soft coat, blended light and dark like a wild rabbit. When she buried her face in his fur, he smelled of hay. It was essential he started eating as soon as possible. Small animals really couldn't cope with going without food for long.

Setting Arthur back on his bed, Mandy stood up and went to the dispensary. In the back of the cupboard, she had seen some sachets of small animal food replacement. Grabbing one, she picked up a food bowl and made her way to the sink. The contents of the packet were a muddy brownish colour when she stirred them with water. The mixture looked unappetising, but Mandy pulled the plunger from a syringe and spooned some of the sludge into the barrel, reassembling the syringe without losing too much of its contents. Back in the kennel, Arthur snuggled into her arms and she cuddled him for a moment, before turning his head so that she could feed him. Nudging the tip of the syringe past his upper lip, she dribbled the brown mess onto the small pink tongue, feeding cautiously as he began to swallow.

One syringeful. Then another. Arthur started to wriggle, and Mandy knew if she continued, she might choke him. Fetching some paper towel, she wiped his small face clean. Then she straightened his bedding and popped Arthur gently back into his cage before walking to the sink to wash her hands.

Her eyes wandered around the prep room, from the white coat that hung on the back of the door (though no one had worn it for years) to the new autoclave. Behind the desk, someone had hung a picture, a child's drawing of 'Vet Adam with My Dog'. There were photos, too: a proud farmer brandishing a rosette beside his prizewinning cow, a woman trotting her horse along a road. Mandy sighed. This was her place; these people her world. Despite the difficult evening, despite missing Simon, she was a part of this community.

Simon. He would be in Leeds, having a last drink before bed. Tomorrow he would go into the clinic, put on his surgical gloves and perform miracles under the theatre lights. Mandy tried to imagine him here in Welford, but it was impossible. He wouldn't be happy tending to sheep in a windswept field or coaxing reluctant bunnies to eat. Turning her back on the images, she switched off the lights and made her way back into the cottage.

Chapter Nine

'Would you like to come with me today?' Emily suggested to Mandy across the breakfast table. 'Your dad is doing the small animal surgery this morning. I thought you might like to get out and about, seeing as you were stuck inside yesterday.'

'That would be great,' Mandy said. She had always loved the farming side of the practice, and though she was looking forward to seeing patients alone, it would do no harm to start out alongside her mum. 'Where will we be going?'

'It's quiet so far,' Emily said. 'There are two cows to see at Sam Western's. One has gone off her feed and the other is lame.'

'Anything else?' The more calls Mandy could get under her belt, the better it would be when she started to tackle things herself.

'There's a rather odd one,' her mum admitted. 'Do you remember Jennifer McKay?'

'Dr McKay's wife?' Mandy said.

'That's right.' Emily nodded. 'Well, she came in first thing this morning. Apparently, she went for a walk last night through Lamb's Wood and saw a couple of sheep that didn't seem to have been shorn. She thought maybe they'd been missed, but when she went to take a closer look, she noticed one of them had overgrown feet. It was very lame, she said. She went back with her husband, but they couldn't see the sheep anywhere and by then it was late. She said she barely slept thinking about the poor animals and she wondered whether we could pop up and have a look.'

Mandy frowned. Even without the lameness, it wasn't good for sheep to keep their heavy wool coats in the hot weather. As well as heat stroke, it put them at risk for fly strike. 'Where did Jennifer think they came from?' she asked.

Emily looked down at her drink, then back up. 'She wasn't certain,' she said, 'but she and Dr McKay were worried they might belong to Robbie Grimshaw. Do you remember him? He and his ferrets helped you and James to move Lydia Fawcett's rabbits.'

'Of course I remember!' Mr Grimshaw had been old even back then. It seemed a miracle to Mandy that he could still be alive, let alone keeping animals. She and James had been sure that the old man had been halfway in love with Lydia, who had farmed goats up at High Cross Farm. He had talked of the times they had danced together, years before James and Mandy had been born.

'I think they were a bit worried about Mr Grimshaw himself,' Emily went on. 'Apparently no one in the village has seen him in months. Not that they saw him often, but he used to be down regularly to collect his pension from the post office. Lately, he hasn't been at all. I thought it wouldn't do any harm to pop up and see if everything was okay. Hopefully he'll let us look round and if there are any animals that need treatment, we can discuss it with him.'

'Sounds like a good idea.' Mandy pushed her chair back and stood up. 'Do I have time to check on Arthur before we go?'

Her mum nodded. 'Quickly, yes.'

Mandy was delighted to find that Arthur had eaten the dandelion leaves she had left with him the night before. Helen had also been in and given him more of the liquid food and she had seen him chewing some hay.

'I'll take him off the drip later this morning,' she promised. Mandy gave Arthur a cuddle and thanked Helen before grabbing her new wellingtons and jumping into the passenger seat of the Discovery.

It was only a couple of minutes in the car to Robbie Grimshaw's smallholding, deep in Lamb's Wood. Mandy felt the years roll back as the present merged with memories from the past. The ancient oak trees that formed a tunnel over the roadway still shut out the sky, and at the lower end of the lane, the ancient tarmac was mazed with cracks. Further up, they had to slow to a crawl as the deep ruts of the unmade track became overrun with grass and weeds. Mandy found it hard to believe anyone still lived here. As a child, she had thought it was wild and fairy tale-like, but now it just seemed desperately impractical.

When they arrived at the tiny farmyard, there was no sign of life. The gate, which all those years ago had swung on rusty hinges, had collapsed. The Lamb's Wood Cottage sign nailed to the fence was illegible.

'Take care,' Emily warned as Mandy slid out of the car to try and move what remained of the gate. The wood was rotten, but she managed to drag the structure far enough to the side that her mum could drive through and she watched as Emily stopped, pulled on the hand-brake and jumped out to join her.

As she walked into the yard, Mandy couldn't help wondering what they were going to find. There was no sign of human habitation. The weatherboarded cottage, once green with moss, was half submerged in a tangle of weeds and bushes. A corner of the roof had several tiles missing and one of the windows at the front was boarded up with plywood. Mandy found herself hoping that Mr Grimshaw had moved away.

'What do you think?' Emily said, stopping to look at the jungle that had once been a garden. 'It doesn't look like anyone's here.'

Mandy peered down the narrow pathway that led to the front door. 'That door doesn't look as if it's been opened for months.' She rubbed her forehead. 'Maybe the sheep are neglected because there's no one left to look after them?'

A flicker in the grass caught her attention. Crouching down, Mandy saw the huge tawny eyes of a tortoiseshell cat staring back at her. A moment later it melted away, then reappeared as it jumped up to the boarded window, nudged the plywood aside and plunged through the gap. Mandy thought she saw movement through the filthy glass in the window on the other side of the front door.

'Did you see that?' she asked her mum in a low voice.

'I saw something,' Emily admitted. 'Do you think it was another cat?'

'Whatever it was, we should probably have a look inside,' Mandy decided. 'Whether or not there's anyone here, that cat looked half starved.'

'Fair enough.' Emily zipped up her coat. 'We should knock first. Just in case.'

Mandy followed as her mum pushed her way up the path between the waist-high bushes and stood in front of the blistered front door. Raising her hand, she knocked twice on the cracked and faded wood. Inside, Mandy heard a scuffling movement, but as the moments passed and the door remained shut, she began to think it might only be animals living inside.

Her mum knocked again, this time more firmly. To Mandy's surprise, it swung open a crack and an eye peered out from the shadows.

'What do you want?' The voice was rusty, as if it hadn't been used in a long time. The door opened an inch more to reveal a tiny old man, stooped and shrinking away from the sunlight.

Mandy winced as she noticed the raggedness of the man's cotton shirt, the frayed corduroy trousers and filthy jerkin. A stale smell greeted her nostrils. She recognised the face, but the piercing blue eyes were clouded and unfocussed.

'Hello, Mr Grimshaw.' If Emily was as shocked as Mandy, she did a good job of covering it up. 'We came to see if everything was all right. A neighbour thought one of your sheep might need treatment. Can we come in for a chat?'

'Who are you? What do you want?' A growl now, hostile and frightened like a wild animal.

'I'm Emily Hope. I'm a vet, Mr Grimshaw, and this is my daughter Mandy. We have met before.' The click of claws sounded in the hallway behind the old man. A dog's face appeared: a pair of dark brown eyes and a long nose with the distinctive black and white markings of a border collie. Feeling movement behind his knee, Mr Grimshaw half turned.

'Down, Shy,' he grunted. The nose disappeared, but within a moment returned on the other side of the old man's legs. 'What do you want?' Mr Grimshaw turned back to Emily and repeated the question for a third time.

Suddenly his eyes brightened. He opened the door wider and said in a clear voice, 'Everything is fine. I checked the sheep yesterday. There's nothing wrong with them.'

'Are you sure?' Emily said. 'We can just . . .'

'You can just nothing.' Mr Grimshaw's voice was final.

'I don't like busybodies. I'm fine. The animals are fine. Leave me alone.'The door slammed shut.With a worried look in her eyes, Emily ushered Mandy back down the path towards the car.

'Aren't we going to do something?' Mandy asked.

Emily shook her head. 'There's not much we can do,' she admitted. 'Not if Mr Grimshaw hasn't given us permission. The cat and dog looked slim, but there was no proof of neglect. I'll get in touch with Seb Conway, see if he can call in.'

Mandy stopped to take a last look at the grim house. Mr Grimshaw had sounded so angry. Back when she had first met him, he had seemed grumpy at first, but had proved to be a wonderful source of information. His love of animals had shone through. Now, despite the presence of Shy, he seemed very much alone. The weeds caught Mandy's feet as she picked her way back to the car. This wasn't turning out to be the fun, outdoorsy day she had hoped for. Sam Western's farm was next. She wasn't looking forward to that, either.

Her mum was looking tired again, Mandy noticed as she climbed into the Discovery and put her seat belt on. Not that she was surprised. The visit to Lamb's Wood Cottage had been depressing, to say the least. It was hard to say who had needed help more: the scrawny animals or the defiant, malnourished old man.

Chapter Ten

There was silence in the car as they drove back through the village and up the hill that led to Upper Welford Hall. It was a long time since Mandy had been to Sam Western's. They passed the Hall, drove along the side of the yew hedge and approached the main farm. Mandy was surprised to see that a section of one field had been fenced off and turned into a neatly gravelled car park. Emily drove into a parking space and turned off the engine.

'Mum?' Mandy turned to her mother. 'Would it be okay for me to tackle the cases here? See if I can manage?'

'Of course. It'll be a good way to get started.' Mandy was surprised Emily had agreed so easily. Was it because she didn't feel up to it? Why did her mother look so exhausted?

Climbing out of the car, Mandy went round to the boot. Emily watched as she collected stethoscope, thermometer, arm-length gloves and lubricant.

'Should I take the things for foot trimming, too?' Mandy asked.

'Might be as well,' Emily replied. 'I can carry some

stuff if you want.' Adding both left- and right-handed hoof knives and the heavy trimmer that would allow her to reshape feet if they were overgrown, Mandy was glad to have her mother there, though she was careful to give her the lightest bits of equipment.

Emily set off from the car park and headed through a gap that led into a yard surrounded by old stone buildings. Mandy had been in the farmyard before on visits with her parents. She recalled a grey stone hay-barn with a glorious archway and an old tractor invariably parked underneath. The byres along the sides of the yard had still been in use for young stock and the sick animals her parents had come to see. Best of all, there had been a row of calf pens, the small black and white heads of Friesian calves bawling when they heard movement in the yard.

The calf pens were still there, but in place of the byres there was now a small row of shops. Green-painted signs announced what was on sale inside, from specialised cheeses to ice cream and local crafts. Thick woollen sweaters hung on a rack in one window above a cheerful-looking toy sheep.

On the opposite side of the yard, beyond the old archway, stood a monstrosity of a building where the milking parlour had been. White, square and gleaming in the sun, Mandy couldn't imagine what the architect had been thinking. Worse still, the archway itself had been filled in with glass. Behind it, where hay had been stacked, there were tables and chairs and beyond them another window. Mandy forced herself to follow Emily across the yard, although the temptation to stop and stare was overwhelming.

A man in a blue boiler suit approached them. 'Hello.' He nodded at Emily and looked at Mandy. 'You'll be Mandy then,' he said, holding out his hand. His grip was firm, his hand work-hardened. 'I'm Graham.'

'Graham is Mr Western's dairyman,' Emily explained. 'He's been here a while now.'

Graham nodded. 'Five years.'

'Graham oversaw some of the changes,' Emily said. 'Mostly to do with the new milking parlour. Do you want to have a look?'

Graham led them through a low doorway and Mandy found herself behind the glassed archway of the old barn. The tables and chairs she had seen from outside were lined up against a massive window. From here, Mandy could see straight into the enormous new building. To her surprise, it contained a modern rotary milking parlour. It was metallic with bright blue paint and spotlessly clean.

'We can get through three hundred and sixty cows an hour,' Graham told her. 'People come for a cup of tea and a scone and to watch the cows being milked.' He grinned. 'It's a lot different from the old days.' They stood for a moment, looking through the window at the empty parlour. It was like being in a glossy brochure for twenty-first century dairies. 'We should get on.' Beckoning Mandy and Emily to follow, Graham led them through a back door to the far side of the court-yard.

Several more well-preserved outbuildings stood opposite the parlour. As Graham led them past the first two, Mandy peered inside, hoping to find animals, but instead there were piles of netting and rope, wooden frames, crates of helmets, and a whole fleet of mountain bikes.

'Jimmy Marsh's equipment,' Graham explained. 'For the Outward Bound centre.'

Mandy frowned. 'There always used to be animals in there,' she said.

'The cows are outside right now,' Graham explained. 'But when they're in, they're housed in the cubicle shed over there.' He pointed to a modern shed with well-ventilated side walls. 'There isn't room in these smaller buildings any more.' He shot Mandy a rueful grin. 'I know,' he said. 'Progress isn't pretty, is it? But it's a necessary evil. The main thing is that the stock is well cared for.'

He showed them into the third of the old stone buildings and, to Mandy's delight, this one still had old-fashioned stalls with a flagstone passageway. Thick straw lined the pens where the cows stood, each one haltered and tied to an iron ring embedded in the wall. Sunlight filtered through a window, lighting motes of dust that were floating in the air.

'This is the one that's gone off her feed.' Graham walked over and stood beside the larger of the two cows, laying his hand on her back. 'She's five weeks calved.

No sign of mastitis. I think she has acetonaemia, but I wanted to get her checked out. Make sure there's nothing underlying it.'

Standing well back, Mandy took a good look at the cow. Acetonaemia happened when cows were low in energy; five weeks after calving was peak milking time and the time they were most likely to succumb to the condition. She was a tall animal, long-legged and rangy. Her abdomen, which should have been full, had an empty look and her eyes were less bright than they should have been.

It appeared to be a straightforward case but Mandy felt a quiver of nerves. Graham seemed to know exactly what he was doing and, although in one way it made her job easier, she wanted to make a good impression. She went carefully through the routine examination. Temperature normal. No discharges. No infection in the milk. No sign of a twisted stomach. Finally, the sweet smell of ketones on the cow's breath confirmed Graham's diagnosis.

Mandy turned to Emily. 'I need to go and get her treatment,' she said.

'I'll come with you,' replied her mum, and together they set off back to the car park.

'Seeing as Sam Western's farm is organic, would it be appropriate to start just with glucose?' Mandy asked as they reached the car. Although she knew the principles of organic farming, it was good to have her mum's guidance.

'You can use whichever drugs you feel are clinically necessary,' Emily confirmed, 'but minimal use of medicines is best. You can suggest some propylene glycol to follow up,' she continued. 'Graham knows the ropes. He can dose her.'

'Thanks, Mum,' Mandy said.

'You're doing well,' Emily told her with a smile. 'Very professional.' Together they made their way back to the shed.

'I need to put this into the vein,' Mandy told Graham, and he held the cow's head while Emily pushed the hind end against the barrier. The glucose ran in easily, to Mandy's relief. It could cause irritation if it was put under the skin accidentally. Once she had finished, Mandy straightened up.

'Do you want to carry on?' Emily asked. 'Or should I tackle the lame cow?'

'I'll do it,' Mandy said. Looking at the cow, it was easy to see which foot was causing the problem. As Graham approached, when the animal turned her head to look and snuffle his scent, she barely dotted the foot to the ground. She was almost hopping as her hind end swung over.

With Graham's help, Mandy tied a rope around the affected leg.

'This is where these old buildings come into their own,' he said and, coiling the rope, he threw it over one of the wooden beams, catching the end and passing it back around the animal's hock before hauling the foot off the ground. 'We'll see if she stands still for us,' he said. 'She's a quiet old thing and her foot's painful. If she won't, we can take her to the crush, but she's finding it hard to walk, as you can see.'

Mandy set to work. The cow's foot was in good shape, though the outside cleat felt hot under her fingers. She didn't need to trim it, so she concentrated on scraping away the top layer of dirt with her hoof knife, looking for any dark areas that might indicate an abscess.

'I think it's here,' she said after a minute of careful searching. Emily gave no sign of whether she was right or wrong, and after a moment, Mandy applied the knife again, this time carving deeper, following the suspect black mark as it tracked up the side of the hoof. The cow seemed less at ease now and Mandy felt the strain on her back and arms as she struggled to hold the foot. The cow was pulling her leg away, trying to kick out backwards.

Just as Mandy lost her grip, a dark shadow passed the window, but Mandy had no time to look up. Grabbing the foot and taking a better hold, she cradled the leg against her thigh and made another cut. To her relief, a spurt of black-coloured pus emerged, under pressure at first but quickly slowing.

'Well done,' said a deep voice.

Mandy lifted her eyes and was alarmed to see that Sam Western had entered the byre and was watching. As Welford's most ruthless farmer, his bad-tempered outbursts when they were children had always frightened James more than her, but his presence was still daunting.

His hair, now white, still looked as though it had been drilled into place. The crease in the centre of his forehead was as deep as the ravine at How Stean Gorge. Unable to let go of the hoof, she paused for what felt like an age, but he nodded at her to carry on and turned to his dairyman. 'How are things, Graham?'

'Everything's fine.' The stockman began to give his boss what seemed to be a daily update on the herd. Breathing out, Mandy continued to work at the foot until she had removed enough of the side wall to ensure the hole wouldn't seal over as soon as the cow put it down. To her relief, Mr Western finished talking to Graham and disappeared as suddenly as he had arrived.

'That should be it now,' she said to Graham, and he untied the rope, allowing the cow's foot to sink back to the ground.

'Good job,' he said.

Emily agreed. 'It's not easy when the horn is as tough as that,' she said. 'It can be difficult in the summer when they harden up.'

All Mandy knew was that she was relieved the weight of the cow's foot was no longer resting on her thigh. She was sweating under her jacket and her hair felt sticky around her face, but it was worth it. Both cows were already looking better. The cow she had given the glucose was pulling at the hay in the rack in front of her and the lame animal was putting her foot down, tentatively at first, but more firmly when she realised that the pain had eased.

Graham picked up the unused trimmer and carried it to the room where the huge metal tanks cooled and stirred the milk. Mandy washed her hands, her hoof knives and the red rubber tubing of the flutter valve she had used to run the glucose into the cow's vein. Together, the three of them walked back to the car.

'Do you have some propylene glycol?' Mandy remembered she should follow up the treatment of the cow that was low on energy. Otherwise, there was every chance that she would deteriorate again.

'Yep. I'll drench her for the next couple of days and keep an eye on her,' Graham said. 'I'll make sure she's looked after.' He stretched out his hand to Mandy. 'Thanks for coming over. It's nice to have the next generation taking over at Animal Ark.'

Mandy opened her mouth to say she was only here temporarily, then shut it again. 'Thanks,' she said. 'It's good to be here.'

On the way back to the cottage, Mandy stretched out her arms and legs in the footwell of the Discovery. She was aching all over – not something she was used to even after the busiest days at Thurston's.

Emily reached out and patted her knee. 'You'll get used to it,' she promised. 'There are muscles you use in farm work that you never knew you had before. How do you feel it went?'

Mandy looked through the windscreen at the green

moors rolling past. They were already more than halfway home. 'Okay, I think,' she said. 'I was glad I managed to find the pus in that abscess. It was a shock to see Mr Western there. He moves like a ghost!'

Emily laughed. 'He's usually around somewhere,' she said. 'He doesn't work directly with the animals these days, but he likes to know what's going on.'

'He always used to scare me and James,' Mandy admitted. 'He seemed so ruthless. I thought he hated animals, but he seemed to know what he was talking about when he was discussing the farm with Graham.'

'I know,' said Emily, slowing the car as they turned into the lane. 'I'll admit that Sam can be difficult. He doesn't believe in being nice for the sake of it. I was worried when they expanded the farm quite so much because I thought the cows might just become numbers, but it was Sam who employed Graham, and he does a great job of caring for them.'

'He seems to know his stuff,' Mandy observed.

'He certainly does,' Emily said. 'He has a degree in agriculture and a Masters in dairy science. Sometimes I wonder if he needs to call us out at all, but he's very thorough.'

'What about all the shops in the farmyard?' Mandy asked.

The car drew to a halt and Emily turned off the engine. 'I haven't been up there recently,' she said, 'but Ted Forrester goes a lot with his wife. Some of the cheese and crafts come from different parts of the UK, but the ice cream and several of the food products come from local farms. Your dad and I went to see the parlour when it was first installed. The whole thing is really efficient and the cows seemed to take to it very quickly.' She thought for a moment. 'We've been lucky here in Welford. A few of the farmers sold up when the milk prices fell, but most of the families made changes and hung on. Sam Western is the most extreme version, but he brings a lot of business.'

'And now an Outward Bound centre,' Mandy said. 'I just hope they don't disturb the wildlife too much.'

'So far as I know,' Emily said, 'they want to preserve it. It's part of the Outward Bound experience. I know you didn't hit it off with Jimmy Marsh, but don't forget that he used to be a park ranger in the Lake District. Seb Conway seems to think he knows what he's doing.' She looked at her daughter. 'I'm hungry,' she said. 'I think it's time for lunch.'

As if in response, Mandy's gut growled. 'My stomach thinks you're right,' she said with a grin, and opening the car doors, the two of them made their way into the house.

Chapter Eleven

'**M**um, they're here!' Mandy called up the stairs. James and Paul had travelled back from Italy three days ago. James had called to ask whether they could visit, and Mandy had insisted they come over as soon as they'd finished unpacking.

Flinging open the door, Mandy hugged James, then Paul. 'It's great to see you,' she said. 'Did you have a good time?'

'Wonderful,' said Paul.

James held out a bottle of wine. 'For you,' he announced with a bow.

'Ca' del Bosco.' Mandy read aloud from the label. 'Is this your sparkling rosé? Thank you very much,' she said. 'I thought we'd go straight out.' She put the bottle on the side table in the hall. 'I've got some things packed up. We're going for a picnic.' She peered past the men. 'I presume you have Seamus and Lily with you?'

'Of course we do.' Paul took a sideways glance at his husband. 'You know James can't leave the house without them.'

James grinned. 'Oh yes?' he said. 'Who was it that

was so dog-sick in Italy that he had to phone Gillian every day, just to hear them scampering around her flat?'

Paul narrowed his eyes. 'You?' he suggested.

Mandy laughed. 'You can stop fighting,' she said. 'I know you're as bad as each other. I'm amazed you went anywhere you couldn't take them. You should fetch them,' she told James. 'The food's in my car. All I need is the four of you.'

'Sounds brilliant,' said Paul.

'I'll get the dogs.' James dashed off to the car. A moment later two lithe furry bodies raced towards Mandy and she crouched down to hug them as they squirmed their delight.

'Hey, you two,' she said, fending off their attempts to lick her face. Standing up again, she led them to her car. James went to the passenger side and helped Paul into the front seat, before encouraging Seamus and Lily into the back. Mandy could see that Paul had lost weight during the honeymoon. She hoped he would find something he could eat in the hamper.

Setting her gaze on the road ahead, she drove through the village and pulled up on a broad grassy verge. 'I thought we'd sit by the river,' she said, jumping out of the car. 'James, can you give me a hand?'

'Of course,' he said. Together they carried everything down the field to a sunny patch of grass by the river. Mandy felt as if every picnic in her life had taken place here, and the only thing that changed was herself.

As well as a hamper of food, Mandy had brought folding chairs and a table.

'This looks very civilised,' said Paul. He had walked across the field leaning on James's arm and was standing on the bank, shading his eyes with one hand. The river flowed slowly, its smooth surface reflecting the sky and the midsummer trees. Dragonflies flitted among the shadows. In the distance, the church clock chimed one.

'Is this somewhere you used to come together?' Paul asked. Mandy and James grinned at one another.

'All the time,' James said. Reaching out, he took a slice of bread and butter and spread it with hummus. 'Did you make this?' he said to Mandy. She shook her head.

'Sadly not,' she said. 'But I did fetch it from the supermarket with my own fair hands.' She had deliberately chosen foods that were high in calories and protein: nuts and dried fruits, cheese and eggs. She had also bought freshly made fruit salad and yogurt. It all looked as bright and appetising as she could make it.

'Remember Henry the Eighth?' said James.

'Of course I do,' Mandy replied. Reaching out, she too spread hummus on her bread, adding some slices of tomato.

Paul looked at each of them. 'I presume,' he said, 'that as well as saving lots of animals, the two of you invented time-travel when you were younger?'

Mandy laughed. 'Henry the Eighth was our class hamster,' she explained. 'James looked after him one summer and we brought him here for a picnic. He was meant to be on a diet,' she said, 'but he took a dive into the hamper and before we got to him, he stuffed his little cheek pouches full of biscuits.'

Paul grinned as he took a slice of bread, spreading it thickly with butter and honey. 'You had your hamster on a diet?'

'Yes,' said James. 'We made him exercise, too. He had to run in his wheel every day.'

'Sounds like he preferred the high jump if he managed the leap into your hamper,' Paul teased.

'Do you remember Mrs Ponsonby's scream when she saw him the next time he got into the picnic basket?' Mandy prompted.

James looked at Paul. 'She thought he was a rat,' he explained. 'It was really funny. Her face went this terrible mottled pink colour.'

'So would I, if I thought you'd let a rat loose in my food,' Paul pointed out, his eyes twinkling. 'Poor Mrs Ponsonby. And you two, you call yourselves animal lovers, but you starve the school hamster until it's so desperate it has to risk life and limb hamper-diving. Not just once but twice?' He looked down at where Lily and Seamus were sitting at his feet. 'Don't worry, you two,' he said. 'I won't let you go hungry.'

'Blackie used to carry the basket when we went on picnics, didn't he?' James said. Blackie, a Labrador, had been James's pet until he died peacefully at the age of sixteen. 'He was so helpful.'

Mandy smiled. Blackie had done more drooling than carrying. Animal lover though Mandy had always been, she'd never been too keen on slobbery sandwiches. She helped herself to fruit and yogurt and was glad to see Paul doing the same.

'Great picnic,' said James, dumping a spoonful of honey into his fruit salad.

Mandy looked around the field again. There were so many memories. On the other side of the water, a little further downstream, Bert Burnley had set up his caravan park. School children from Birmingham had been bussed in for a stay in the countryside, often for the first time in their lives. Sam Western had been against the idea, but now he was the one appealing to city dwellers with the Outward Bound centre, his dairy teashop, and his artisan boutiques.

After lunch, they moved closer to the water and rested for a while in the afternoon warmth. Lily and Seamus explored the shallows of the river and James closed his eyes. Mandy, too, felt herself drifting. She was roused when a cloud passed over the sun and she looked up. Although it was a warm day, she knew Paul felt the cold. They had better not sit still too long, she thought.

'Would you like to go to Upper Welford Hall?' she suggested.

Sitting up, James looked at her, a puzzled crease between his eyes. 'Why on earth would we want to go there?'

'Sam Western's got a new rotary milking parlour,'

Mandy explained. 'I'd like to see it working, if you two wouldn't mind?'

'But would he want all of us there?' James glanced from Mandy to Paul and back again. 'Wouldn't it be messy?'

It dawned on Mandy that he thought they would be on a private visit, probably down at udder level. 'It's not messy at all,' she said. 'There's a viewing window.'

Paul looked fascinated. 'That sounds interesting,' he said. 'I've never seen a cow being milked.'

'I suppose Sam Western won't mind?' said James. 'He was never our biggest fan.'

'True,' said Mandy, 'and we weren't his either. I don't have much choice but to get on with him now. He's an Animal Ark client.'

James raised his eyebrows. 'That doesn't sound fun,' he said.

Mandy shrugged. 'It might not be so bad. He's got a dairyman called Graham, who knows more than I do about dairy husbandry. And Sam wasn't as awful as I expected when I saw him yesterday. He seemed . . . almost human.'

'Seems like it could be a lot worse,' said James. 'I'd love to go and see the milking parlour in action.'

In a few minutes, they were all back in the car. Mandy offered Paul the picnic blanket for his knees but he shook his head, colour rising in his gaunt cheeks. Mandy blushed, too, hoping she hadn't offended him.

'We'll go and look at the farm,' she said as she buckled

her seat belt, 'but we can't stay long. Gran and Grandad have invited us round for tea at four.'

James's face lit up. 'That'll be lovely,' he said. 'Mandy's grandmother is the best baker in Welford,' he told Paul.

Paul and James seemed delighted with the changes at Upper Welford Hall. They sat in the café and watched as the cows walked one-by-one into the milking bays, circled around on the gigantic rotating floor as they gave their milk, and were decanted at the other side.

'They seem very calm,' Paul commented. 'They don't seem to mind the movement.'

'It's very steady,' said Mandy. She had been impressed by the smoothness and admired the efficient way Graham set the machines on the udders. The feed was delivered promptly to each bay and the cows stood patiently as they waited.

James disappeared to explore the shops and came back with two kinds of cheese and a woolly sweater for Paul.

'Sam Western is going to have an Outward Bound centre here,' Mandy told them. 'They're setting up climbing nets and high wires in the wood.'

'Goodness,' said James. 'That doesn't sound like the Sam Western I remember.'

'How do you mean?'

'Remember Bert Burnley and his caravans. All the fuss that he and Mrs Ponsonby made about city children running riot in Welford?' James's eyes twinkled.

'Yes,' said Mandy. 'Dad said the same thing about

Sam's change of heart. I can only imagine there's money involved,' she added dryly.

Paul raised his eyebrows. 'I never thought there would be so much going on in such a small place.' He reached out and took James's hand. 'Thank you for sharing it with me,' he glanced at Mandy, 'both of you.'

As she had at their wedding, Mandy felt a swell of unwelcome emotion. She was aware of James's eyes on her and she took a deep breath and held onto it until the threat of tears retreated.

'It's almost four,' she said as soon as she was sure her voice would be steady. 'We'd better not keep Gran and Grandad waiting.'

Despite being in their eighties, her grandparents remained remarkably fit and active, much to Mandy's delight. They had obviously been preparing for James and Paul's visit all day, and Mandy found her mouth watering as she looked at the spread they had set out.

'Cherry tomatoes,' she said, reaching over, and taking a handful. 'Your own, I presume?'

'First batch of the year,' her grandad replied.

'The sandwiches look delicious,' said Paul, watching James tuck into egg and cress in home-made crusty bread, 'but would it be okay for me to try some of your cake, please?' He pointed to the three-layer coffee cake, smothered in icing and topped with walnuts.

'Of course you can.' Gran beamed at him as he handed her his plate. She carved off a slice and handed it over.

James finished his sandwich and started on a teacake

with cheese. He took a bite and chewed before looking up at Mandy's grandmother. 'This is wonderful,' he said. 'As good as I remember! Do you think I could have the recipe, please? For the café.'

Gran looked delighted. 'Of course you can,' she said.

Paul looked up at James. 'You should get the recipe for the coffee walnut cake, too. It's divine.'

Gran bustled off to get her baking book and Grandad ushered them through into the sitting room. 'I'll just help your gran tidy up,' he told Mandy. 'It'll only take a minute.'

'You seem very much at home back in Welford,' James commented, lowering himself into a chair.

Mandy looked around the room. The old wooden clock ticked on the mantelpiece, marking time between a pair of brown and white china dogs, just as it had always done. 'I am,' she admitted. 'But I know it's not forever,' she added. 'Once Mum and Dad have found a permanent member of staff, Simon and I are thinking of starting up a clinic in Leeds. Simon wants to specialise in advanced orthopaedics.'

James frowned. 'I thought you wanted to start a rescue centre. You told me when you were doing your Masters in animal behaviour that you wanted to focus on reha-bilitation.'

Mandy shifted in her chair. 'I still want that,' she said. 'I'm just not sure how possible it's going to be to do it straight away. Simon wants to get started with the most profitable part of the business as soon as I get back from

Welford.' When she said it that way, it didn't sound so bad. 'Commercial property in Leeds costs a fortune. I'm lucky that Granny Thorpe, Mum's mum, left me a small lump sum to invest in whatever I want, but it's going to be difficult, balancing a rescue centre with what Simon wants to do. We're both going to have to compromise at the start.'

'Does it have to be in Leeds?' Paul put in. 'It'll be expensive setting up in any city.'

'Yes.' James's eyes were serious behind his glasses. 'Wouldn't it be better to set up your centre here? The field behind Animal Ark, doesn't that belong to your parents? There'd be room for buildings and space to spare for exercising the animals. You might be able to make use of the old stone shed where your dad keeps his gardening stuff. I know you'd need to extend, but still. You'll never get anywhere in Leeds with so much potential.'

'You could call it Hope Meadows!' Paul exclaimed.

Mandy turned to look at him. His face was flushed and he looked more animated than she had seen for a while. 'I can see it now,' he went on, spreading his hands as if he were unfurling a banner. '*Hope Meadows: where we never give up.*'

Mandy felt a stir of excitement. Hope Meadows was the perfect name for a rehab centre! 'But what about Simon?' she said, tucking her hands under her thighs. 'We've been planning a joint clinic for ages. He'd never agree to be based in Welford.'

James sat very still, his eyes on the empty fireplace. The clock on the mantelpiece suddenly sounded louder than before. Mandy held her breath, waiting for her best friend to answer. *I hadn't realised how much James's opinion matters*, she thought. *Why haven't I talked to him about this before?*

James took off his glasses, rubbed them on the edge of his sweater, then put them back on. 'What about York?' he said. 'It's only an hour's drive. You could have your rescue centre here and Simon could have his clinic there. There are plenty of people in the city who'd be willing to spend money on their pets. Doesn't that sound a better idea?'

Mandy couldn't stay sitting still. She jumped up and paced around the room in a small circle, almost tripping over Paul's legs. It might be possible. An hour's drive. She could help Simon with the patients there and work here part of the day as well. Both of them could sleep here. It really could work. Hope Meadows could be a reality!

'You two are brilliant,' she said and walked over and hugged Paul first and then James.

'What's all this?' Grandad opened the door and walked into the room. 'Do I get a hug as well?' he asked Mandy.

'You can have a hug any time,' Mandy told him and, walking over, she buried her face in his shoulder, holding him tightly as if she would never let go.

Chapter Twelve

'James suggested something yesterday that I wanted to talk to you about.' Mandy faced her mum and dad across the kitchen table. Both of them looked up from their plates, cutlery poised.

'Yes?' Emily prompted.

Mandy took a deep breath. 'You know I've always wanted to open a rescue centre?'

Emily nodded. Adam looked down again and seemed to be studying his food. Mandy had tried to reproduce Simon's moussaka for dinner. It hadn't been the most successful experiment. The cheese sauce had developed grey lumps and she had added too much cinnamon, giving a bitter flavour to the vegetables.

'And you know Simon and I were planning a clinic in Leeds, but it's so expensive to buy property there. It might take ages before we could save enough for the space to rescue.'

Adam was still fiddling with his dinner. Mandy knew she should have stuck with something simple, but she had wanted to impress them before she made her announcement.

'Well, James suggested that instead of Leeds, we could set up our clinic in York.'

Adam started to frown, possibly because of the moussaka. Mandy ploughed on '. . . and he thought it would be close enough that we could set up our rescue centre right here at Animal Ark.'

Silence. Emily was chewing. Adam was rolling his fork in his long fingers. Finishing hcr mouthful, Emily spoke first.

'Do you mean actually here in the clinic or . . .?'

'No.' Mandy rushed to explain. 'James suggested using the field at the back. There would be plenty of space there. Room for buildings and an exercise area, too.'

'But I thought you were leaving us soon.' Adam's frown had deepened. 'Not that I don't want you here, but we've been looking for another assistant. Have you changed your mind about that as well?'

Mandy swallowed. 'I know I said I'd only be here for a while.' She looked into her father's eyes, knowing she couldn't stop now. 'Things have changed. I've changed. Welford is home . . . If it's possible for me to be here, I don't want to go away.' She stopped for a moment, wondering at her own words, yet certain they were true. 'I'd like to stay . . . if you'll have me,' she amended. 'And if wc could open a rescue centre here . . .' She trailed off.

'It's certainly an idea.' Emily set her fork down and took a sip of water. 'There's good access, too, if you need to get horse boxes in and out, or delivery vehicles.'

Mandy felt her heart beat faster. She had been hoping, at best, they would think about it. The fact that her mum was already considering logistics had to be a good sign. She looked across at her dad. He had put down his fork, pushed away his still half-full plate, and crossed his arms.

'It is an idea,' he said slowly, 'but have you considered the practicalities?'

Mandy's mind was whirring. What practicalities exactly? They would need someone to build the centre, obviously. Living quarters for all species. Probably outhouses and storage. It didn't seem that difficult.

'Like planning permission?' her dad went on. 'It was difficult enough thirty years ago when we wanted to add the clinic onto the cottage. And for a rescue centre, you'd need charitable status. That would all need to be set up. How were you thinking of funding it? Would there be a danger of it eating too much into the practice profits? It would probably have to be a separate company.' Pulling his plate back towards him, he lifted his fork and took a mouthful, barely chewing before he swallowed and started again.

'Are you sure there's enough demand for a rescue centre here? You remember Betty Wilder used to run her sanctuary, but she had to close five years ago, because she couldn't generate enough interest. Or money,' he added.

Mandy's chest felt tight. Planning permission? Local demand? She had done stacks of fundraising before, but only on a small scale for other charities, not enough to

run one on her own. 'There's Granny Thorpe's inheritance to help with the building work.' She looked at
Emily, but it was her mum's turn to look down. Although
her inheritance would help with construction, it wouldn't
last forever. There would be ongoing costs. For a
moment, Mandy's head felt heavy. She wanted to run
from the table, slam the door and hide upstairs, but
instead, she stayed where she was and took a deep breath.
She was twenty-seven now, not sixteen.

'Mandy?' Adam's voice was gentler and she forced
herself to look at him. 'Before we can commit to anything,
you need to do a lot more research,' he said. 'Planning,
building work, charitable status, finances.' He ticked
them off on his fingers. 'You'll need to use your spare
time to work on this. You know how busy we are, but if
you need help, I'll do my best to make time for you.'

Mandy managed to smile, but the dream that had
looked so close to becoming reality a few moments ago
suddenly seemed as impossible as climbing Everest in
flip-flops. Under the table, out of Adam's sight, Emily
reached out and gave her hand a squeeze. Mandy
squeezed back, reminding herself that whatever they
said, her parents were always on her side. It was their
job to give her a reality check, however much it chafed.

Helen had invited Mandy to join her for Lucy's walk
that evening. Mandy, grateful for the excuse to get out
of the cottage, was glad she'd accepted. Although it was

late, the evening sun was warm and the breeze carried the scent of the moors.

'How long do you think you'll be here?' Helen asked, unclipping Lucy's lead and letting her zoom off across the springy grass.

'I'm not sure yet,' Mandy replied. 'Helen, what do you think of the idea of a rescue centre here in Welford?'

Helen looked startled at the sudden change in topic, but rallied quickly. 'Attached to Animal Ark, you mean?'

'Well, sort of,' Mandy said. 'Not physically attached, but in the field behind the clinic. Separate, but working together.'

'Come here, Lucy!' Helen called her dog, who came galloping over. The nurse gave her a treat before letting her race away again. 'Sounds a great idea,' she said. 'What kind of animals were you thinking of?'

'All sorts. Any animal that is unwanted or mistreated. We can find a new life for them. Paul . . . you remember Paul?' Helen nodded. 'He suggested Hope Meadows as the name.'

'That's awesome!' Helen said, adding, 'Lucy was a rescue.' Mandy watched as the shiny black dog sniffed at a harebell, leaping backwards when a bumble-bee emerged. She was surprised to hear where Lucy had come from. She was one of the most well-adjusted dogs Mandy had come across. Whatever had happened in Lucy's past, Helen had done a great job of turning her into a happy and well-trained dog.

'It would take a lot of setting up, but it would totally

be worth it,' Helen went on, sounding more enthusiastic. 'At the moment if we get any strays, we have to call Seb Conway. I know he often has trouble getting space in the council-run shelter in Walton.' She pulled a ball from her pocket and threw it, watching as Lucy hared in pursuit. 'Why don't you talk to Seb about it? He would know more about whether there's a need for a Welford-based centre.'

'That would be great,' Mandy said. Maybe she could pick his brains about other aspects of the project, too, like the regulations she'd need to follow. Side by side, with Lucy trotting ahead, they made their way across the moor with the sunset spreading out before them.

'Hello?'

Mandy's heart sank when she heard a voice in reception. She had just finished an operation and was looking forward to her lunch. Mustering a smile, she dried her hands and walked through into the waiting area.

'Seb!' Now she was smiling properly. Instead of the client she had expected, Seb Conway was standing in the middle of the room. Better still, he was clutching a paper bag from the bakery in Walton, from which a wonderful scent was rising.

'Hi, Mandy!' He looked very much at home, leaning on the desk: all white teeth and twinkling eyes. 'I hear from Helen that you're thinking of diversifying into my line of work.'

'Did you indeed?' Although she was surprised, Mandy couldn't help returning his grin. 'Did Helen tell you to come and see me?' she guessed.

'She might have done.' He winked. 'I know it's lunchtime,' he said, 'but I came armed with supplies.' He waved the bag. 'There's enough for three,' he added. 'Just in case Helen's here, too.'

Mandy swallowed her smile. Seb was so transparently keen on Helen.

'Helen?' She put her head round the door of the wildlife unit, where Helen was tending to an underweight hedgehog. 'Seb's here,' Mandy told her. 'He has lunch for us. Fancy coming out so we can chat in peace?'

'Okay!' Lifting the hedgehog back into his cage, Helen straightened up. 'I'll just wash my hands,' she said. When she appeared in the waiting-room, Seb's smile grew even wider.

'Where's the best place?' he asked. 'How about outside? The weather's lovely.' He opened the door and ushered Mandy and Helen into the garden.

Helen turned to Mandy. 'Weren't you thinking of building your rescue centre in the meadow?' she said. 'Why don't we eat there?'

Mandy closed the door behind them before responding. She didn't want her father to think she was getting carried away with her plans without doing the sensible groundwork he had pointed out.

'Yes,' she replied. 'We could sit on the other side of the wall,' *and look at the view all the rescued animals will see*, she added in her mind. People in hospitals were known to recover more quickly if they could see trees and greenery. Surely the orchard with the fells rising behind it would be as relaxing for stressed animals as it was for her. Easily better than a city with cars and lorries roaring past all day and night.

Like a picture from a child's storybook, buttercups and dandelions dotted the meadow, yellow heads in the thick green grass. The old stone barn where Adam's tools were stored stood to their left. The three of them sat with their backs to the dry-stone wall. The sun was as warm as the cheese and onion pasties Seb produced from his bag.

'So what exactly were you thinking of?' he asked, wiping his hands as he finished the last mouthful and leaning forward to look past Helen at Mandy. 'We've loads of animals coming in all the time. Finding places for them can be difficult.'

Mandy wiped her hands on the grass either side of her and sat up straight. 'I want to have space for both wildlife and domestic animals,' she explained. 'I don't know if Helen told you, but after my vet degree, I spent a year doing a Masters in animal behaviour and rehabilitation. I want to make sure the animals are healthy mentally as well as physically before we rehome them. I'd like to train new owners alongside their pet, too.' She stood up and started to pace along the wall. 'All the buildings need to be animal-friendly. They should have natural light inside and all the animals should be able to see out. They need open spaces and plenty of room for exercise.' She threw out her arms. 'What do you think?' she demanded. 'I thought we might use the old barn for a treatment and reception area.' It was just long enough to be split into two, she thought. 'Maybe a stable over here,' she took a few steps, '. . . exercise area . . .' a few more steps, '. . . separate areas for cats and dogs, at either end so they don't disturb each other. And a brand-new wildlife unit, here on the south side of the barn.' She stopped and faced them, feeling a smile stretch across her face. 'Can you imagine it?' she exclaimed. 'Hope Meadows: where we never give up.'

'Wow!' said Seb as Mandy walked back over and sat down beside them. 'You've certainly thought this through! I love the idea of the psychological approach. So many of the animals we get in have been treated so badly they've forgotten how to trust anyone.'

'It's a fantastic idea,' Helen said. 'Something I'd really like to be involved in,' but her voice was more sober than Seb's. 'Don't forget you have to discuss it all with Simon,' she said. 'From what you've said, he's all for going ahead with his plans for the clinic in Leeds.'

For a moment, Mandy felt a lurch of uncertainty, but she shoved it away. If they could build here at Animal Ark, they could get all the land they needed for the rescue centre. Most of their funds could be focussed on the clinic and Simon could have all his specialist equipment. There was no way he would fail to see how perfect this could be.

As well as the pasties, Seb had brought a bottle of cola and, pouring it into three plastic tumblers, he handed them out. 'I think we should have a toast,' he said. 'To Mandy and to Hope Meadows!'

'Absolutely.' Helen lifted her drink. 'To Hope Meadows.'

Raising her mug in return, Mandy grinned before she took a swig of her fizz. Few drinks had ever tasted better.

Chapter Thirteen

'That will be seventy-two pounds and fourteen pence,' Mandy said. Putting down the cat basket she had been clutching, Mrs Hastings began rooting in her handbag.

'Worth every penny to have peace of mind.' She handed Mandy her credit card. 'I really thought that Cara had broken her leg.'

Mandy glanced down to where Cara's small feline face was peeking out of the basket at her. The fees they charged at Animal Ark were lower than Mandy had been used to in Leeds, but asking for money was still something she found challenging. She couldn't help but feel grateful to people like Mrs Hastings, who really seemed to value the care that she tried so hard to offer.

'Thank you very much,' she said, following Welford's hairdresser to the door and opening it for her.

Evening surgery was winding towards its conclusion. It had been hectic. Adam had been called out to a horse with choke. Emily had been busy for the past forty-five minutes with a dog that had tangled itself in barbed wire and had several wounds that needed to be stitched.

Peeking into the waiting-room, Mandy was pleased to see Maureen Gill.

'Hello, Mrs Gill. Were you hoping to see Rachel? I'm afraid she's helping Mum at the moment.' Rachel Farmer, the evening receptionist, was assisting Emily with the injured dog.

'That's okay,' Mrs Gill replied. 'She'll be round later to see Brandon, I'm sure.' The receptionist was engaged to Brandon, Mrs Gill's son.

'And this must be Muffy?' Mandy had seen the dog's name on the computer screen and bent down to say hello, but as she crossed the room, the little animal bared her teeth and growled.

'She needs her vaccination,' said Mrs Gill, looking worried. 'It's a bit overdue, but I'm afraid she doesn't like coming, as you see.'

'She does look frightened,' Mandy agreed. The little terrier had stopped growling, but was hiding behind her owner's leg. All Mandy could see was a wary brown eye and a topknot of hair. Rather than call Mrs Gill through to the consulting room, Mandy walked over and sat down near the older woman. She sat close enough that they could chat without raising their voices, but far enough from Muffy so as not to seem frightening.

'Right, Mrs Gill,' she explained. 'I want to sit here and chat for a few minutes. I'm going to feed Muffy a few treats, if that's all right. I want to see if we can get her to calm down before we try to do anything with her.'

'Oh!' The client looked surprised. 'Okay. If you think it will help. Poor thing.' She reached down and stroked the tiny head. 'She does get herself so wound up.'

Mandy dropped a treat on the floor, a little in front of Muffy. Rather than staring at the dog, she continued to speak to Mrs Gill. 'We'll see if she'll take these,' she said. 'They're hickory smoke flavoured. Most dogs seem to love them, but if not, we've plenty of other things to try.' From the corner of her eye, she saw Muffy creep out from under the seat, sniff at the chew and tentatively pick it up, before scuttling back into her hiding place. Still without looking at her, Mandy reached out and dropped another piece.

'Is this a new thing?' Mrs Gill asked.

Mandy nodded, noting that once again Muffy was starting to inch forwards. 'The idea is to change a visit to the vets from frightening to fun,' she said. 'It might be difficult today because we've got to get Muffy vaccinated, but in future, you would be welcome to come in to the clinic for no reason at all. Get her used to coming in without anything bad happening.' She dropped another piece of chew and Muffy came forward more quickly this time.

'You see how she's gaining confidence already,' said Mandy. She looked around the waiting-room. 'There's nobody else due for a few minutes, so we'll continue a bit longer and then we'll take her through.' Little by little, she coaxed the tiny dog into the open.

Muffy was very pretty. Her long hair was silky smooth

and her eyes, once she had calmed down, were like glossy chocolate. Instead of cowering under the chair, she was soon sitting in front of Mandy with her ears forward.

'Does she like being carried?' Mandy asked, feeding Muffy yet another treat. 'Or would she prefer to walk?'

'I'll carry her through,' Mrs Gill said. 'It's probably easier.' She bent down and picked up her pet.

'When we go in,' Mandy stood up slowly, 'don't put her on the table. There are chairs against the wall. If you sit down and put Muffy on your knee, I can look at her there.' She followed Mrs Gill into the room, sat down beside her and handed over a few more of the treats.

'I need to get her vaccine ready,' she explained. 'If you feed her these while she's waiting, she won't have time to think about where she is.' She stood up again, selected a syringe and needle and drew up the vaccine. Changing the needle for a new one – the sharper it was, the easier it would slide through the skin – she picked up a stethoscope, walked back over and sat back down. She was pleased to see that, rather than looking nervous, Muffy was sitting on her owner's knee gazing around. When Mandy sat down, the little dog looked expectantly at her. Mandy felt in her pocket for another treat.

'There you go, sweetheart,' she murmured. She kept her left hand in front of Muffy's muzzle, letting the dog nibble at the treat, while Mandy stroked her cheek a few times before stealthily moving her free hand up to examine her eyes and ears. Everything seemed clean and in good health.

'Will you let me see your teeth?' she asked, gently lifting Muffy's lip. 'Not bad at all,' she said and quickly gave the little animal another chew. While Muffy snuffled up the snack, Mandy put her stethoscope into her ears to listen to the dog's chest. 'Her heart sounds fine,' she told Mrs Gill a moment later.

'That's wonderful,' Mrs Gill said. 'Nobody's been able to examine her properly since she was a pup. Usually I have to put a muzzle on and she struggles the whole way through until we take it off again.'

Mandy smiled. 'Just the vaccination to go,' she said. 'While I'm giving her that, Mrs Gill, I'd like you to give her another treat. Instead of letting her have it all at once, can you hold onto it and let her nibble away?'

'Like this, you mean.' The older woman held out a chew and Muffy stretched forward to reach it. While she was distracted, Mandy raised the skin on the back of Muffy's neck with her fingers and before Muffy knew what was happening, she had slid the needle through the skin and the injection was done.

'Was that it?' Mrs Gill sounded incredulous.

'That's it,' Mandy said.

'Oh, that's brilliant.' Mrs Gill was beaming. 'Good girl, Muffy, good girl.' Muffy jumped into her arms and licked her face. 'Thank you so much.'

'It was a pleasure,' Mandy told her. 'And don't forget what I said earlier. You're welcome to come in any time and let Muffy sniff around the waiting-room and get used to the place. We have treats here, or you can save up some of her daily food allowance and bring that if you prefer.'

'I'll do that.' With Muffy still in her arms, Mrs Gill stood up and Mandy opened the door.

Rachel was sitting behind the desk.

'Are you and Mum finished?' Mandy asked.

'I'm done,' Rachel replied, 'but your mum'll be a few more minutes.' She turned to her future mother-in-law and smiled. 'I'll be round later,' she said.

'I'll let Brandon know,' said Mrs Gill. 'And thanks again, Mandy. We'll see you soon.' She looked down at Muffy, who wagged her tail, and with a last wave, she walked out, closing the door behind her.

'There's just one left,' said Rachel. 'Mr and Mrs Patchett.' There was something in her voice that made Mandy glance more closely at her. She got the impression Rachel wasn't a fan of the couple, though when the clients arrived – a well-dressed couple in their fifties – the receptionist greeted them with a warm smile.

'Amanda will see you right away,' she said.

Mandy walked across the room to meet them. She had spotted her patient as soon as she entered. She was a gorgeous deerhound bitch with the typical tousled salt-and-pepper coat, heavily in pup. Mrs Patchett was gazing affectionately at the deerhound as Mandy approached. Mr Patchett had a rather insipid look, but he caught Mandy's eye and gave a tentative smile.

'This must be Isla,' said Mandy, crouching down so that her head was on a level with Isla's face. With the usual slow grace of the breed, the bitch stood up to greet Mandy, her long tail whipping from side to side as her inquisitive grey nose snuffled in Mandy's pocket. With a grin, Mandy reached in, pulled out a treat and gave it to the dog, whose tail whipped backwards and forwards a little faster. 'And you must be Mr and Mrs Patchett,' she said, looking up at Isla's owners.

To her surprise, Mrs Patchett's look was close to hostile. Mandy had no idea what she might have done.

'We're used to seeing an experienced vet.' The tone was as chilly as the eyes. 'I want to see Mr Hope.'

Mandy felt a shock run through her and belatedly stood up. For a moment, she wondered whether the woman was joking, but the frost in Mrs Patchett's eyes made it clear she was serious. Isla, oblivious to the human interaction above her, pressed her head against Mandy's thigh, inviting Mandy to rub her ear. Mandy automatically ruffled the soft furry appendage, even though her hand had begun to shake.

'Mr Hope is out on a call.' She managed to keep her voice level.

'I'll see Mrs Hope then.' The voice was relentless.

'Mrs Hope is busy with another client. You would have to wait.'

'Very well. Isla is too important to be seen by someone we don't know.' Mrs Patchett sat down and nodded to the empty chair beside her. Mute, her husband sat, too.

Isla stayed standing up, gazing at Mandy and wagging her tail hopefully.

Mandy was finding it hard to remain civil. Clenching both hands, she turned and strode back to the desk. 'If there's nothing else in, I think I'll go out for a walk,' she said. She felt better when Rachel dipped her head so the Patchetts couldn't see her and pulled a face.

'No problem. I'll let Mrs Hope know,' Rachel said.

Filled with frustration, Mandy pulled a jacket over her scrubs. She should probably change, but she just wanted to get away. As she walked up the lane, her mind buzzed with indignation. It had been a long time since she had been turned down in a professional situation. In Leeds she had already begun to have her own clients, who knew and trusted her. Of course, the customers there were used to younger vets coming in. But there was still anger pulsing through her brain. She had a whole year of qualified experience. She had seen more small animal patients on a normal day in Leeds than she saw in the course of a week here at Animal Ark. She had expected the large animal side to have a few doubters, but not in the small animal clinic. She wanted to growl. Or howl, she wasn't sure which.

She passed the Fox and Goose and for a moment considered going in, buying a stiff drink and downing it. She grimaced and shook her head. Even in Leeds, she wouldn't have resorted to that, and here in Welford, everyone would know about it by morning. She stalked on, bearing left onto the track that led down towards the river. The noise of the water rushing over the stones was comforting and in the distance beyond the trees, the Beacon rose, the calm bulk soothing her with its familiarity. In the river, a fish flashed silver as it leaped out of the water and disappeared upstream. Overhead, swallows chased flies across the sky, darting on soundless wings.

Mandy dug her hands into her pockets and kept walking. There was a bench halfway along the track and, reaching it, she sat down. The air was still.

'Simba! Zoe!' A deep voice broke the quiet evening. 'Come now!' It was a warm voice, Mandy thought. Lucky Simba and Zoe. Turning, she scanned the pathway. A man was walking towards her, two dogs trotting at his heels.

'Simba!' he said again and the dog on his left, a glorious German Shepherd, looked up at him, touched her nose to his hand and was rewarded with a treat. 'Zoe!' It was the turn of the beautiful husky to perform and she too received a biscuit. Mandy looked up at the man's face. It was Jimmy Marsh.

'Mandy!' He nodded at her. The warmth was gone, replaced by politeness.

'Hello!' she said, looking up at him, hoping he would pass by. After Mrs Patchett's performance, she wasn't in the mood for chat.

To her dismay, Jimmy sat down on the bench beside her. Despite herself, Mandy couldn't help being aware of the closeness of his body. Without being told, both dogs settled at Jimmy's feet. Looking straight ahead, he spoke. 'There are sand martins over there, did you know?' He pointed. 'Their nest-burrows are in that steep section of riverbank.'

Mandy's eyes followed his finger. She half wanted to ignore him, but her gaze returned to the two gorgeous animals that lay panting at Jimmy's feet and she couldn't resist. 'I didn't know you had dogs,' she said.

Jimmy clicked his fingers and the dogs sat up, ears pricked and tails scraping the grass. 'This is Simba.' He rested his hand on the German Shepherd's handsome domed head. 'She was a member of the mountain rescue team up in the Lake District when I worked there as a ranger,' he said. 'And this is Zoe, my new addition. She's in training for mountain rescue, too.'

Mandy's heart melted momentarily. Not only were these two lovely animals pets, but they were working dogs as well, training to save lives. No wonder Jimmy Marsh seemed so proud of them. 'They are gorgeous,' she said. 'Is it all right if I stroke them? It won't put them off their training?'

Jimmy smiled. 'You won't disturb them right this minute,' he said. 'They can have a rest while we do.'

Mandy reached over and stroked first the silky black and tan cheek of Simba, then fondled Zoe's ear as the husky leaned into her. Her fur was so soft, Mandy could hardly feel it. The panting face grinned up at her.

'I didn't know we had a mountain rescue team here

in Welford,' she said, pulling herself back up onto the bench.

'Until recently, we didn't,' Jimmy explained. 'Three of us have got together to start one off. Jack Harper brings his golden retriever Max, and Jared Boone is training one of the farm collies. We're looking for other people, though, if you know anyone?'

Helen and Lucy popped into Mandy's mind, but she needed to check with Helen first. She might find him awkward, but she suspected the nurse might jump at any opportunity to spend more time in Jimmy's presence.

'Speaking of rescues,' Jimmy went on, 'I keep a very good eye on my netting since the incident with the deer. There haven't been any further problems up there.'

'That's good,' replied Mandy. She recalled the report about neglected sheep in Lamb's Wood. Should she tell Jimmy? He was often out in that direction on his quad. Could she ask him to keep his eyes open? For a moment, she tussled with her conscience. Would it be breaking confidentiality to mention them? Surely not, if she didn't mention Robbie Grimshaw's name. Anyway, there was no proof the sheep had even been his. It couldn't do any harm to mention them.

'We've had a report about some possible neglected sheep.' She studied the field and the river in front of them as if a lonely ewe might appear at that very moment. 'Do you think you could let me know if you see any livestock that doesn't look right?'

Jimmy was looking at her with open interest. 'Would those be the ones seen up in Lamb's Wood?'

Mandy felt her ears grow warm. 'Someone called the clinic,' she said evasively.

'Are you still policing the countryside?' She remembered his laughter the first time they had met. What had he called her? *Countryside Constabulary*. She stared straight ahead, but his voice continued. 'I did hear that you were once involved in rescuing a whole warren full of rabbits.'

Mandy's whole face was burning now. She hoped that it wasn't too obvious in the evening light.

She didn't have to look at Jimmy to know that he was grinning. 'If you ever need any help rescuing any bunnies with their little paws trapped in a cattle grid, I'm your man!' he declared.

For the second time in as many days, Mandy forced herself to sit still when she wanted to flee. Yesterday her father, today this man beside her. She barely even knew him. Why couldn't anyone in this place treat her like an adult?

'I'll be sure to let you know.' The chill in her voice reminded her of Mrs Patchett. What a horrible evening this was turning out to be.

Jimmy didn't reply and Mandy risked a glance at him. His green eyes scanned her face and she had a strange feeling that he was delving into her mind.

'Sorry if I overstepped the mark,' he said. 'It was meant to be a joke.'

Mandy shrugged. 'It doesn't matter,' she said. She glanced up at the darkening sky. 'I should be getting home.' Standing up, she took a final regretful look at Simba and Zoe. She would love to have a dog of her own, but it was hardly the kind of thing she could raise with her parents just now. They had always had strict rules about rehoming the animals she had rescued and for now, work had to be her single focus. With a sigh, she turned and walked back over the field. She had better go and see what her mum had to say about Mrs Patchett.

As she reached the driveway, she found herself hoping the clients had gone. It had been awkward enough before. She was relieved to see that the windows in the veterinary unit were dark. Evening surgery must be over, though her father's car was still not back.

Mandy opened the door of the cottage. Emily wasn't in the kitchen, so Mandy went through to the sitting room. Her mum was on the couch, an embroidery ring in one hand and a needle in the other. It was a cross-stitch picture of a Yorkshire scene: a farmhouse by a river.

Emily looked up and smiled. 'Had a nice walk?' she asked.

Mandy shrugged with one shoulder. 'So-so.' She sat down opposite her mother. There was no point putting off the inevitable. 'How did you get on with Mrs Patchett?' she asked. 'What did she want that was so difficult I couldn't have tackled it?'

'Uh!' Her mum made a disparaging sound. 'Rude woman. I think,' she said, looking at Mandy, 'that we should continue this particular discussion over some tea, don't you?'

She stood up and Mandy followed. Emily filled the kettle and switched it on before turning to Mandy. 'Honestly,' she said, 'it was a storm in a teacup. Thea Patchett has always been a bit of a strange one. She was rude to Helen and Rachel as well, until I put a stop to it.' She sighed. 'She got herself wound up because you gave her dog a treat. You should have asked permission first, apparently. I told her she was welcome to opt out on behalf of her pet, but that we were starting a programme that would encourage them to see the vet practice as a pleasant place to go instead of somewhere awful. I told her you were a behavioural expert and that we were very lucky to have you.'

Mandy felt breathless. In Leeds when there had been complaints, Amy tended to judge first and ask questions when she was prompted, but it sounded as if her mum had defended her to the hilt. She felt tears begin to rise and she blinked them back.

'Thanks, Mum.' After a moment, she walked across to her mother and gave her a hug.

'We're very proud of you,' her mum murmured against Mandy's ear. 'You do know that, don't you?'

Mandy pressed her teeth tightly together and took a deep breath before stepping back.

'I'll make the tea,' she managed. 'You sit down, Mum.'

Emily reached up and rested her hand against Mandy's cheek. 'I really couldn't ask for a better daughter,' she said.

Chapter Fourteen

'So, from what we discussed, this old stone barn would be split into two parts, half to be a reception, half a treatment unit.'

'That's what I thought,' Mandy told the tall, angular man beside her. Maurice Frederick was an architect, and more importantly, a friend of Paul's from York who'd agreed to give Mandy a free consultation about plans for the rescue centre.

Side by side, they peered in through the wooden door of the old shed where Adam kept his ride-on mower and larger gardening tools. There was no natural light at the moment, but there was a large wooden door on one side that could be glassed in, like the archway at Upper Welford Hall, and small windows higher up that were currently boarded over.

'We could use frosted glass to partition the building,' Maurice suggested. 'That way we could maximise the light without having to alter the structure.'

Mandy clicked off the light, pushed the door shut and they took a few steps back.

'The rest would be free-standing wooden structures,

is that right?' Maurice went on. 'The stables here, the kennels over there. The cattery would be at the far end and there would be a smaller wildlife and bird unit on the south side of the barn, all the sections to be separate?'

'If that's the best way to keep the costs down,' Mandy replied.

Taking out an electronic measuring device, Maurice began to move around the field, checking distances and studying the contours of the ground.

'I thought we could use the lean-to that's attached to the barn for small furries,' Mandy said. Together they went over for a closer look. For the moment, it contained only ancient hay, but the wood looked solid enough.

Maurice made a note on his phone. 'There's electricity in the barn already, but you'd need a water supply, of course.'

'There's a trough over there.' Mandy pointed. 'It's connected to the water mains so it wouldn't be far to extend.'

Maurice strode across to the stone trough and plied his measuring device once more. 'Well, it should all be perfectly possible.' Returning to Mandy's side, Maurice took a last look around. 'You've got plenty of room. If you wanted, I could draw up some plans after the weekend and we can take it from there. I think you could make really good use of the ready-to-assemble sheds and storage units that are available.'

Mandy felt slightly breathless as she walked with Maurice back to the cottage. From a dream of rescued animals enjoying the view across the meadow, suddenly she was discussing dimensions and building materials.

'Will you come in for coffee?' she said as they crossed the back garden.

'That would be lovely,' Maurice replied, and kicking off their boots, they went inside. Mandy put some milk into the microwave to heat up and when the coffee was ready, they sat down at the kitchen table.

Maurice pulled out some brochures for ready-made outbuildings and laid them in front of Mandy. 'What sort of timescale would you be looking at?' He picked up his mug and took a sip.

Outside the window, Mandy saw Adam's car draw up. He had been out on what was hopefully the last call of the day. Mandy hoped it had gone well. 'I'm not sure yet,' she replied as the back door swung open. 'It isn't just up to me.'

Adam pulled off his boots and walked into the kitchen. He glanced from Mandy to Maurice and then at the brochures before turning his gaze back to Mandy.

'What isn't just up to you?' His voice was steady, but there was a deeper line than usual between his eyebrows that warned Mandy not to be flippant. She could feel herself going red. She hadn't said anything to her father about Maurice coming. It had been Paul who had spoken to his friend and, somehow, everything had happened faster than she had intended.

'The rescue centre,' she said. 'Dad, this is Maurice Frederick. He's a friend of Paul's from York. He's an

architect specialising in low-profile commercial properties. Paul suggested he come over and have a look
around.'

'Did he?' Adam's frown deepened. 'Well, it's very good
of you to come, Mr Frederick, but I think you might be
on a wild-goose chase. We haven't made any firm decisions as to whether there is even going to be a rescue
centre.'

'Oh.' Maurice looked from Adam to Mandy, eyebrows
raised.

'Mr Frederick, meet my father, Adam Hope,' Mandy
said, and the architect got to his feet and held out his
hand. To Mandy's relief, her dad did at least shake hands,
though his smile was perfunctory.

'I'll leave you to it,' Adam told Mandy. 'I'll be in the
sitting room. I'd like to talk to you when you've finished.'
He nodded to Maurice and stalked out of the room,
closing the door behind him.

Mandy's legs felt weak and she sank back into her
chair. When she glanced up, the architect was looking
at her sympathetically.

'Don't worry about it,' he said. 'I know everything is
still only at the planning stage. Paul told me and I didn't
make a special visit here, I was out this way already. I'll
make some preliminary plans based on what we've talked
about, and if and when you want to move on, give me
a ring, okay?' He walked round the table and patted her
on the shoulder. 'I'd better be off,' he said. 'Friday afternoon traffic.' He smiled. 'Thanks for the coffee.'

Sketching a wave, he opened the back door and stepped outside.

For a moment, Mandy was alone with her thoughts, then she stood up and walked into the sitting room. Adam was in his chair, a newspaper propped in front of him.

'Dad?' The newspaper dropped.

'Mandy?' His voice was cool.

'Why did you have to embarrass me like that?' Mandy stared at her father. 'That man was a friend of Paul's and he was doing me a favour. He already knew nothing was definite.' To her dismay, she realised her legs were trembling.

'It didn't sound like that,' her father replied. 'If I hadn't come in . . .'

'If you hadn't come in, nothing would have happened.' Mandy tried to keep her voice as expressionless as his. 'He came over as a friend. I wanted to hear what he had to say.'

'We talked about this before.' Adam's voice remained quiet, but she could hear the anger behind his words. 'You can't keep going off half-cocked. Any new venture needs to be properly planned. Not only that, your mum and I have spent many years building up Animal Ark. It belongs to all of us. Any new projects must be discussed. You can't waltz in and start making solo decisions.'

'I wasn't,' Mandy said hotly. 'And . . .' There were so many things she wanted to say. This project was so important to her. Last time she had spoken to her father about the rescue centre, he had told her she had to do some preparation. Now here she was, trying to do some, and he'd blown her off again. 'Oh, never mind,' she snapped, glaring at him, willing him to soften.

Adam shook his head. 'Just talk to us,' he said. 'That's all I ask.' He lifted his newspaper back in front of his face.

Mandy studied the rug on the floor, then with a last glance at her dad, she walked out of the room and headed upstairs.

She had been planning to go to Leeds this evening. She might as well head off now, she thought. There was no work waiting to be done. Throwing her toothbrush and some clean clothes into her overnight bag, she was soon on the road. She hadn't felt as if she had missed Leeds at all, but suddenly it felt like a refuge.

When Simon opened his front door, she clung to him. His arms reached around her and he patted her back – as if she were a troubled Labrador, she thought.

'Hello, you,' he said, sounding surprised. 'I wasn't expecting you till much later.'

Mandy hung there, wondering what to say. She could hardly tell him the truth about why she was early. She wanted to discuss her new ideas at an appropriate moment, perhaps over dinner.

'It doesn't matter, anyway.' Simon saved her from having to reply. 'Since you're early, we should be in time to catch the crowd. They were heading out to the Master Don. Would that be okay?'

The Master Don was a stylish new bar in the east end of Leeds. Mandy had been there a few times with the younger staff from Thurston's. It would be fun to see them again. There would be plenty of time to talk to Simon later.

'Sounds good,' she said. 'Just let me get changed.' Running upstairs, she pulled a new bright red shirt from her bag and slipped it on. Catching sight of herself in the mirror, she was pleased with the way it showed the curve of her waist and set off her pale blonde hair.

Simon raised his eyebrows when she came back down. 'Interesting choice,' he said. 'I certainly won't lose you in the shadows.' He paused, looking down at the bunch of keys he had grabbed from the hall table. 'Shall I drive, or should we take the bus and get a taxi home?'

'Bus and taxi, I think,' said Mandy. 'That way, we can both have a drink.' Perhaps, if everything went well, they would drink something bubbly to celebrate their new joint venture. Breathless, she reached out and hugged Simon again.

'What was that for?' he asked. 'Not that I'm complaining . . .'

'Just . . .' Mandy stopped. 'Just because,' she said.

The Master Don was filled with chat and music. Displaying his usual sixth sense, Simon led Mandy to the furthest corner from the entrance, straight to where their friends were sitting.

Momal spotted them and waved as they emerged from the scrum. 'Mandy!' she called. 'How lovely to see you.'

Jenny beckoned to them. 'Come and sit down,' she said, shuffling up the bench seat to make room. Mandy slid into the booth and Simon sat down on the far side of the table. He pulled his wallet from his pocket and looked around.

'Anyone for a drink?' he said. There were nods from everyone. Having sorted out two fresh orange and lemonades, a pint of Special and a gin and tonic, he deposited the laden tray on the table and sat back down.

'Just the four of you tonight?' he asked, looking round the table.

Saloni took a sip of her juice. 'Peter's on call,' she said. 'Samantha will be along shortly.'

Simon raised his eyebrows. 'Did she cope with rewiring that jaw?' he asked.

'She was finishing up when I left,' said Jenny. 'Not that the owners seemed grateful. They were just annoyed by how much it was going to cost. They should think themselves lucky they managed to find a vet who would tackle it at all.'

Simon nodded. 'In the old days, that cat would have been put to sleep,' he said. 'If I had my own practice . . .' he glanced at Mandy, '. . . I'd encourage all my owners to take out decent insurance for a start.' Lifting his pint, he took a long draught.

Solani made a face. 'Too many people don't think about how they're going to pay their fees when they get a pet. Especially cats. Remember that woman last week?' She looked along the table. 'The one whose Siamese had jumped from the fifth-floor balcony? "I thought there wouldn't be any vet's bills because the cat couldn't go outside," she said.'

'Yes.' Jenny pulled a face. 'Poor cat had to be euthanased. You were quite willing to try surgery on its hind legs, weren't you?' She looked at Simon.

'I was.' Simon ran one hand through his fair hair. 'It was just a young thing. Probably would have healed well.'

'I guess tower blocks aren't something I have to think about any more.' Mandy couldn't help but feel a bit out of touch. A few weeks ago, she would have been in the thick of the conversation. Now, though she was interested to hear what had been happening with her former colleagues, it no longer felt so personal.

'Hello there!' A voice sounded from a couple of feet away. Mandy turned to see Samantha approaching. 'How are you, stranger?'

'I'm fine, thanks.' To her embarrassment, Mandy noticed that Samantha was wearing the same shirt she was. Although she had been pleased with herself earlier, she couldn't help thinking it looked better on Samantha's curvy, doll-like proportions.

Samantha flicked her long black hair over her shoulder and patted Simon's arm. 'Shove up, Si.'

He grinned up at the newcomer. 'Always so polite,' he said, and shuffled along the bench to make more room. Mandy tried to suck her hips in as she squashed up against Jenny.

Samantha squeezed in, tucking her bag under the table. 'Good job I didn't eat that extra sandwich at lunch,' she joked, smoothing her slim thighs.

'How did your jaw go?' David looked at Samantha over his gin and tonic.

'So-so,' she replied, wrinkling her nose. 'It took ages to get the wire tight enough to be stable, and it was awkward getting the angle because of the root of the canine. And then it took ages to stitch the gum.' She twisted a paper napkin on the table in front of her, and Mandy felt a stab of sympathy. She knew what it was like to have a frustrating surgery where you just couldn't do your best for the animal.

'I don't know how you manage with that tiny see-through thread,' Momal said. 'I can hardly see where the stitches are by the time you've finished.'

Mandy had finished her drink. She found herself wishing that Samantha had offered to buy a round before sitting down. Apart from her, nobody seemed to have drunk much.

'Anyone want a refill?' she asked.

'Not yet.' David was only halfway through his.

Jenny smiled. 'Thanks anyway.'

'You must have been thirsty,' Samantha teased.

Mandy tried to grin but it felt like she was just baring

her teeth. Of course she was drinking faster than the others. They were all talking about things that had happened at Thurston's. She couldn't exactly chip in about Sam Western's lame cow or the possibly – but possibly not – neglected sheep in Lamb's Wood.

Across the table, Simon was deep in conversation with Solani. Mandy looked down at her empty glass, wondering if she could go to the bar to buy a drink only for herself, but it seemed rude. Beside her, Jenny was talking to David. Her eyes wandered to the next table. Two men were sitting across from one another hand in hand. Mandy suddenly wished that James and Paul were here. They wouldn't forget to talk to her. When she looked back round, Simon was watching her and when he caught her eye, he leaned forward.

'Would you like to go somewhere quieter?' he suggested. 'I know we have a lot to talk about.'

Mandy beamed at him. 'That would be great.'

They struggled up from the crowded bench and said their goodbyes. Samantha made a big show of sliding into the space that Simon left behind. 'Just keep telling yourself it's all muscle,' she told him, reaching up to pat his waist.

Mandy raised her eyebrows. 'Simon's not fat!' she exclaimed.

Simon looked from one to the other. 'Ladies, ladies. Much as I love being fought over, even a sturdy chap like me needs to eat. Come on, Mands.' He put his hand on her back and ushered her to the door.

'Phew, that was busier than I expected,' he puffed as they emerged in the fresh air. 'Now, my long-legged girl, could I interest you in a table at the Talisman?'

Mandy frowned. 'We won't get a table,' she said. 'Not on a Friday night.'

'You underestimate me.' Simon looked pleased with himself. 'I've already booked.'

Mandy reached up and kissed his cheek. Sitting in the Master Don, she had been wondering if they would be stuck there all night, but for once, he had surprised her. And in a few minutes, she would be able to surprise him.

'To us!' Simon held up his glass. He had chosen an expensive Sancerre, which Mandy privately thought tasted like elderflower cordial. They had decided against starters and Mandy had ordered salad with a red onion and goats' cheese tart for her main course. Unlike Samantha, she had had several sandwiches for lunch.

Mandy raised her own glass, then took a sip. 'To us,' she said and took a deep breath. There would never be a better time than now. 'I've been thinking,' she said, 'about your clinic and my animal rescue centre.'

'Oh yes?' Simon smiled. His eyes were warm in the candlelight. The waitress appeared with their plates. 'Thank you,' Simon murmured as she set his meal down.

Mandy waited for the waitress to leave before ploughing on. 'You know we've been talking about property in

Leeds,' she said, 'and how expensive it's going to be . . .'
Simon looked at her expectantly. 'Well,' Mandy went on,
'I think I might have found an answer.'

Simon held his knife and fork over his chicken breast.

'How would you feel,' Mandy said, 'if I could get my
parents to donate some of the land behind Animal Ark
and I could build the rescue centre there?'

Simon blinked. 'A rescue centre at Animal Ark? But
what about our clinic? What about us? Have I done
something wrong?'

Mandy shook her head. 'Not at all,' she said. 'It's just
we . . . I hadn't realised how much a clinic in Leeds
would cost. It will take ages to get started with animal
rescue if we go ahead here, and you'll have to wait a bit
with your orthopaedics, too.'

Simon put down his knife and fork. 'But we've been
planning this for ages.' There was a cold light in his eyes.
'What has made you change your mind?'

Mandy grasped the stem of her glass with a hand that
was shaking slightly. She hadn't changed her mind. It
was he who had been pushing forward with his ideas,
never giving her a chance to tell him what she wanted
to do.

'My mind hasn't changed,' she said. 'I know we talked
about working together in Leeds, but when we started
discussing it, it was all way in the future. When I moved
to Welford, you wanted to bring everything forward, but
it seemed a bit soon. I'd always thought we'd have more
time to save up.'

She could see the muscles working in Simon's jaw, but she pushed on. 'Setting up the rescue centre at Animal Ark wouldn't just save us money, either. It would mean I'd have my parents close by for support. Going back to Welford has shown me how much I love working with them, and how much it means to them for me to be close by.'

'You'd have me for support wherever we were,' Simon pointed out tightly. 'Am I supposed to take over your parents' practice for my clinic, then?'

Mandy felt herself going red. 'Of course not. Instead of Leeds, we could set up your clinic in York.'

'York?' Simon's frown deepened. 'Why would that be better than here?'

'It's close enough that we could run both projects together and live in Welford. Paul even suggested a name for my centre . . .'

'Paul?' Simon's eyes bored into her. 'What on earth has Paul got to do with this?'

There was a tight feeling in Mandy's chest. 'I was talking to him and James about the clinic,' she said, thinking back to their joyous, fizzing conversation. 'It was James who suggested if we wanted to have a rescue centre as well as a clinic, we could set up in both York and Welford.'

'Really?' Simon's voice was suddenly filled with anger. 'You'd rather talk to random people in Welford instead of coming to me if you weren't happy?'

I wasn't unhappy! And James and Paul aren't random

people! Mandy was shocked by his change in tone. 'James isn't random,' she objected. 'He's one of my best friends.'

'But I was here if you needed me. On the end of the phone. Why didn't you come to me instead of him?'

'I didn't go to him,' Mandy protested. 'I started telling him about the clinic. James wants the best for both of us. He asked me about the rescue centre and I said it was going to have to wait. He made a suggestion that would allow both of us to have what we wanted.'

'But we had talked about our plans.' Simon's voice had become quieter, though Mandy could hear the underlying chill. She had to lean forward to hear him. 'I thought we wanted the same things. Are you saying that you wanted something different all along?'

'No, of course not. But I . . .' Mandy stopped. She had always wanted to open a rescue centre. She had never hidden it from him. He was twisting her words.

Simon was shaking his head. 'I don't think we should talk about it here,' he said. 'Even if you like sharing our plans with all and sundry, I don't think our fellow diners want to hear.' He picked up his knife and fork and began cutting up his chicken.

Mandy looked around. Nobody seemed interested. She looked down at her salad, but she was no longer hungry. Simon was tucking into his dinner, quaffing his wine as if nothing was wrong. Mandy reached out her hand for her glass, picked it up. The bone-dry wine caught in her throat, but she swallowed it down and took another gulp.

Simon cleared his plate as efficiently as he performed surgery. As soon as he had finished, he called to the waitress and asked for the bill.

'Was everything okay?' said the young woman, looking in concern at Mandy's plate.

Mandy felt her cheeks go scarlet. She and Simon had been in here a thousand times and had never left without having dessert. Tonight her dinner was almost untouched.

'It was absolutely fine, thank you very much.' Simon slipped the waitress a twenty-pound note. Maybe, Mandy thought mutinously, if he didn't fritter away so much money, he would have saved enough to buy a clinic on his own.

There was silence in the taxi on the way home. Several times, Mandy caught the driver's curious eyes checking them in the mirror. She wanted to speak, but if Simon hadn't wanted to talk in front of the diners, he wouldn't want to share his thoughts with the driver either. When they pulled up outside Simon's house, he climbed out, paid the driver, and waved him off in a voice that sounded so normal Mandy wondered how he could be so calm. He stalked up the path to the front door and unlocked it, ushering her inside politely and taking her coat. Maybe now they could talk, Mandy hoped. Now they had some privacy.

'Would you like me to make you a drink?' she asked. 'We could both have some tea? Or hot chocolate?' She needed something soothing. Her stomach felt both empty and sick. She took a step towards the kitchen, but when she looked back, Simon was still standing just inside the door. His face was unreadable.

'Obviously, there's a lot to talk about,' he said, 'but I'm tired. I want to go to bed. If you want to continue this discussion, it'll have to be tomorrow.'

Mandy felt her breath leave her body. How could he think about sleep? Without another word, he hung up his jacket and walked up the stairs, his footsteps slow and deliberate. Mandy toyed for a moment with the idea of following him. There was no way she wanted to leave this discussion for the morning. What was it Grandad had always told her? 'Never go to sleep on an argument.' That had been one of the mainstays of his long and blissful marriage, he had told her.

But there had been a cold certainty to Simon's words. If she went up and insisted on talking now, would he listen? Her ears strained to hear his movements. Maybe he would think better and come back.

Long moments passed. With a sigh, Mandy took herself into the kitchen and made a cup of tea. If she let him sleep on it, perhaps in the morning he would be more willing to consider what she wanted. It wasn't as if it was only for her. It was for both of them.

Picking up her mug, she carried it through to the sitting room. There was a pile of brochures for medical equipment on the table along with a fresh stack of estate agents' files. Pushing them aside, Mandy put her mug on a coaster. The blinds were open and she hadn't bothered to switch on the light. Outside, her RAV4 stood under a streetlamp, looking out of place with its mud splashes and smeared windscreen. Mandy pressed her hands into her eyes. If Hope Meadows was such a wonderful idea, why was it causing so much trouble?

Taking out her mobile, she checked her messages, but there was nothing new. Opening Google, she typed in 'Commercial Properties York'. If she could find somewhere suitable for a clinic, maybe Simon would take her suggestion more seriously. But most of the properties for sale seemed to be guesthouses or restaurants. The few shops seemed to be being sold as 'going concerns'. It would be madness to dismantle a profitable business to set up a new one. Even the prices were difficult to compare to those Simon had shown her before. Lots of them included accommodation, though that would probably be an advantage if one of them wanted to do night calls for their city clients. But would that mean they'd end up living separately, one in York and one in Welford?

What was the point, she thought? Simon hadn't given any indication he would even think about it. Why did staying in Leeds matter so much to him anyway? Giving up, Mandy drank the last of her tea and went upstairs.

Simon was snoring. How could he drift off so easily after this evening? She considered sleeping on the sofa downstairs, then pushed the thought away. She didn't need to start tomorrow by making Simon feel rejected. Maybe, if she could get some sleep, they would both wake up feeling better. Crawling into bed, she lay on her back beside him. Outside in the street a car drew up, waited a while then drove off again. In the distance a siren howled. As dawn started to colour the sky beyond the curtains, Mandy fell into an uneasy sleep.

She awoke to the scent of coffee. Opening her eyes, she saw the bed beside her was empty. Simon was already up. Getting out of bed, she dressed more carefully than usual. She left last night's shirt on the back of the chair, selecting another of her favourites from the wardrobe, a creamy white silk mix with a ruffled collar. It was dressier than she would have normally selected for a Saturday with Simon, but she wanted to make an effort. She had to give herself as much confidence as possible. Making her way downstairs, she pulled herself straight and walked into the sitting room.

Simon was sitting in an armchair, holding one of the estate agents' brochures. When Mandy appeared, he stood up and crossed the room. 'Would you like some coffee?' he asked, indicating a tray on the sideboard. He poured her a cup.

'Come and sit down.' He led her to the sofa. 'I am sorry I was too tired to talk last night,' he said. 'I was all set for a quiet evening and I'd already set up some visits to some of the properties today. I was looking forward to telling you about them. You did rather spring it on me that you were thinking about backing out.' He lowered his head slightly, then looked back up. 'I've spent a lot of time researching the properties we're seeing today.'

Mandy stared at him. 'I'm not thinking about backing out,' she insisted. 'I was trying to find a way we could both achieve what we want.'

'But we've been discussing our clinic for ages,' Simon objected. 'We've only ever talked about Leeds. We know Leeds. We've worked here together and I've already put a lot of work into our project.'

Mandy didn't know what to say.

'I've booked two appointments.' Simon picked up the pile of property details and shuffled them. 'Even if you aren't sure, wouldn't you like to go look at them? Have a read of this one.' He held out the listing, which had a photograph of a modern brick and glass building. 'It's on an industrial estate so there's plenty of parking. And then there was this one.' This time, the photo showed a more old-fashioned shop front. 'It's been used as a training centre recently,' he said, 'so there are already customer toilets and tiled floors.'

Mandy wasn't sure how to react. She was glad he no longer seemed angry and dismissive, as he had the night before, but he still didn't seem to be listening. She flipped through the brochure. It seemed to be mostly details about square footage with very few photographs. 'How do you know about the tiled floors?' she asked with a frown.

Simon held out his hand for the papers and she handed them to him. 'I've already been for a preliminary look,' he said. 'That's how we whittled it down to these two. The others weren't suitable. One was too small and the other had nowhere to park. So, what do you think?'

'Who's "we"?' Mandy asked. Presumably it had been Simon and the estate agent. Not that she knew why he had started to look anyway. Hadn't she been clear enough when she had asked him not to push on too far? Then again, she recalled with a stab of disquiet, she had been speaking to an architect about her own plans. Maybe they were both guilty of not discussing things.

'Samantha came with me.' Simon's reply jolted her back.

'Samantha?' The sick feeling from last night had returned.

'She only went in your place, Mandy.' Simon's eyes flicked onto hers. 'I wanted a second opinion. A woman's opinion, you know.'

A picture of last night leaped into Mandy's mind: Simon grinning up at Samantha, small and stylish in her blouse. *'Shove up, Si!'* Pushing herself in.

Mandy's phone rang. She pulled it out of her pocket, intending to switch it off, but it was Seb Conway's number. What on earth could Seb want?

'I need to take this,' she said, and standing up, she went into the hallway, shutting the door behind her.

'Seb?'

'Mandy!' He sounded tense. 'I know it's your weekend off, but something's come up. We've had a report about a cruelty case in Welford. Neglected animals. I need an official veterinary surgeon with me before I can carry out the inspection. We're probably going to have to enter the property without permission.'

'Okay,' said Mandy. Her heart started to beat faster. Animal cruelty in Welford? Who could it be?

Seb was speaking again. 'The police will be involved as well. I thought I'd give you a call first but if you can't come, I can take one of your parents . . .'

'I'm glad you called,' Mandy told him, 'and I will come, but I'm down in Leeds. It'll take me a couple of hours to get back.' Even as she said it, she couldn't help but feel a surge of disappointment. If Seb needed help, if there were problems in Welford, she wanted to be there. 'You probably won't have time to wait.'

'Actually, it will take about that long for us to get everything set up for the raid,' he replied. 'We need to get a warrant. It's up at Lamb's Wood. Lamb's Wood Cottage, belonging to a Mr Robbie Grimshaw. Do you know it?'

Mandy started to feel breathless. Robbie Grimshaw! 'I've been there recently,' she said. 'We had a report of some neglected sheep but couldn't find anything.'

'I know. Your mum called me about it, actually. I visited the farm but Mr Grimshaw seemed reluctant to let me look around.' Mandy could imagine the scene had not been as unemotional as Seb's words suggested. Mr Grimshaw had seemed agitated enough when she and Emily had turned up.

'I'll come as soon as I can,' she said. 'Where should I meet you?'

'We'll be in the car park below Monkton Spinney on the Welford Road. We'll expect you in two hours, okay?'

Mandy ended the call, her heart pounding. There was no time to lose, she thought. If there was traffic, if she was held up . . .

'Simon!' She burst into the sitting room.

Simon stood up quickly. 'What is it?'

'I'm really sorry,' she told him. 'I have to go back to Welford. There's an emergency. I'm sorry about the visits today.'

'What's happened?' Simon was frowning.

'It's Robbie Grimshaw,' Mandy said. 'You remember I told you Mum and I visited him? Seb Conway is organising a raid on his farm. I need to be there. Poor old man. I think he's unwell, but there are animals there, too . . .' She trailed off. 'I'm sorry,' she said again, 'but I have to go. I know we need to get this stuff sorted out. Do you want to come with me?'

'I don't see how I could help,' Simon said. 'They won't need to be over-run with vets at this stage. Do you really have to go? Couldn't someone else do it?'

Mandy couldn't help but feel guilty. A few weeks ago, Seb would have called her parents, but now she felt it was her responsibility. After all, he knew about her plans for the rescue centre. Why wouldn't she want to deal with some neglected animals when they most needed help?

'Seb probably could find another vet,' she admitted to Simon. 'But this is something I really want to do.'

She looked at him for a moment, hoping he would change his mind and come, but he just stood there, looking at her.

'I'll have to go,' she said. Her actions automatic, she reached over to give him a kiss.

Simon turned his head so that her lips brushed his cheek. 'Call me later,' he said, and without looking back, Mandy headed out and started the car.

Chapter Fifteen

Before she had reached the M1, Mandy realised she was still dressed in her city clothes, but it was too late to go back. All the same, she eased her foot off the accelerator. It wouldn't help anyone if she crashed on the way to Lamb's Wood.

The traffic wasn't too bad, only a bit slow past the main exits for York, but the journey took ten minutes over the two hours Mandy had promised. By the time she arrived in the Monkton Spinney car park, there was only one police car left. Climbing out, she jogged over. There was a female officer in the driver's seat.

'Seb Conway called me out,' Mandy explained, leaning down and speaking through the open window. 'I'm Amanda Hope, the vet.'

'I'm Ellen,' the officer said. 'I'm glad you're here. I've been asked to take you up as soon as you arrive. Things look a bit more dangerous than we expected. We believe Mr Grimshaw has a shotgun. So far, he hasn't come out of the house.'

Mandy felt the breath go out of her body. Despite the wave of fear that passed through her, she couldn't help feeling the farmer must be even more frightened. Poor old man. The Robbie Grimshaw she remembered had been gruff and wily, but he had loved his animals. This degree of hostility had to be a sign of illness. Walking to the other side of the police car, she sat in the passenger seat.

'I'll need you to put this on.' The constable handed her a bullet-proof vest. Feeling numb, Mandy slid her arms in, pulled up the zip and closed the Velcro fastening, then put her seat belt on. 'All set?'

'All set,' Mandy replied. Her heart thudded inside the rigid vest. Nothing in her training had warned her about the possibility of being shot!

Ellen spoke into her radio. 'Amanda Hope, the veterinary surgeon, has arrived. We're on our way up,' she announced.

The rutted, overgrown track through Lamb's Wood seemed longer than ever, but finally they emerged from the trees and pulled up at the farmyard gate. They were met by another officer, also wearing protective clothing.

'How are things?' Ellen asked.

'Not good,' he replied. 'Mr Grimshaw came out of the house a couple of minutes ago. Seems he exited by the back door, directly into the farmyard, where there are several animals. He has a shotgun and is threatening anyone who comes near. Chief Inspector Benn is there, but Mr Grimshaw seems to be getting more agitated.' From around the corner, Mandy could hear shouting.

'Put it down!' Then again, 'Put the gun *down*, Mr Grimshaw!'

Before Ellen could say anything, Mandy scrambled out of the car, gasping as the vest dug into her abdomen. She pushed past the broken gate and headed for the yard.

When she rounded the corner, she wasn't surprised that Robbie Grimshaw was getting wound up. He was standing foursquare in the centre of the yard, the long black barrel of his shotgun shaking in his hands. At his heels, the dog he had called Shy was showing her teeth and growling. Her ears lay flat against her head. Behind them two sheep cowered at the back of a pen. A third lay panting in the corner and an ancient-looking horse, gaunt-faced and with protruding ribs, was tied to a post. From the worn pathway around the pole, it had been tied there for a while.

Several police officers stood in a phalanx of white shirts and black flak jackets at the entrance to the yard. Two of them held riot shields, which Mandy thought was ridiculous. Were they expecting to be stampeded by sheep? There was no sign of Seb Conway.

'Amanda, wait!' Ellen panted, running up to join her. 'You can't put yourself in danger!'

'Can I talk to him?' Mandy whispered, without taking her eyes off Robbie. 'I know him. Maybe I can get through to him.'

'Better just stay back,' Ellen replied, but the old man was so obviously petrified, that Mandy could stand it no longer.

'Mr Grimshaw.' She stepped forward. 'Robbie.' For a moment, the barrel moved in her direction, but when one of the police officers stepped forward, it swung back to the group. As one, the police officers raised their hands.

'No need to shoot anyone, Mr Grimshaw,' said Chief Inspector Benn. Mandy recognised him from when he had been Sergeant Benn, a familiar face in Welford during her childhood. 'We're only here to help.'

Mandy walked closer to the farmer so she didn't have to shout. 'I don't know if you remember me, Mr Grimshaw. I'm Mandy Hope. I came here years ago. You showed me your ferrets.' There was no sign that the old man had heard. Mandy took a deep breath. 'Their names were Kirsty, Marlon and Sable. You gave me Kirsty to hold, do you remember?' Her hands were shaking, but her voice was steady. 'We went to Lydia Fawcett's to save some rabbits. You helped us.'

And now the farmer's eyes had swivelled her way.

'Lydia?' When his voice came, it sounded like a creaking door that hadn't been used for years.

'Yes, Lydia. Do you remember? You used to dance with her? You came and helped her with her rabbits. And now we want to help you, Robbie.'

'Help? They want to take my animals away!' The voice was fierce.

'We only want to help them.' Very slowly, Mandy took another step towards the old man. 'Like we helped the rabbits. Lydia's rabbits. Can you put the gun down, Robbie?' From the corner of her eye, she saw the black and white collie flit away and disappear in the direction of the house.

'Mandy Hope?' he rasped. 'Met your father once when my Kirsty was sick.'

Mandy's ears strained to hear what he was saying. If Robbie recalled her father, that had to be a positive sign. He wouldn't shoot Adam Hope's daughter, would he? She took another step. One of the policemen hissed something under his breath behind her but she ignored him.

'Can you put the gun down?' she asked. 'Please, Mr Grimshaw?'

'My Kirsty . . .' A tear fell from the old man's eye. The gun swung down until it was pointing at the cracked concrete.

'We can help you.' Mandy took the last step towards the elderly farmer. 'Can you give me the gun?'

The tears were falling faster and faster. 'My Kirsty . . .'

Very gently, Mandy reached out and grasped the shotgun. There was no struggle in the old man as he released it. Ellen darted forward and took the weapon from Mandy, gesturing to her colleagues to stay back.

Mandy touched Mr Grimshaw's arm. This close, she was startled by the lack of colour in his hollow cheeks, the feverish brightness in his eyes. 'We'll help your animals, Robbie,' she promised, 'but we need to help you, too. You're not well.'

Two paramedics, who had previously been out of

sight behind the barn, stepped forwards. 'Well done,' one of them murmured, and the other said, 'You can come with us, Mr Grimshaw. Miss Hope will take care of your animals.'

Robbie Grimshaw said nothing, just stared at the ground with tears dropping like rain. Mandy felt like crying herself. How had this once proud farmer got into such a state?

Walking on either side of the old man, supporting him between them, the paramedics led him away.

Mandy's senses seemed to have gone into overdrive. The sky above looked more blue than it had ever done before, every stone and weed in the courtyard stood out in singular detail.

On the far side of the yard, the crowd of officers began to disperse, but the chief inspector was marching in her direction. His eyes seemed as black as the flak jacket he wore. Three diamonds decorated the epaulette on each shoulder. Stopping right in front of Mandy, his face was grim. 'Mandy?'

'Yes.' Mandy straightened up and met his glare.

'I can't charge you with anything, but I'm giving you an official warning. You may have known Mr Grimshaw, but your actions today put my officers at risk as well as yourself. It's essential that if we involve members of the public in an operation of this type, that we keep them safe. That is my responsibility.'

Mandy clenched her teeth together. She wanted to ask why he thought it was appropriate to carry out a raid on an old man using riot gear and so much manpower as to terrify the most innocent of victims. Instead, she stared stonily back at him.

For a moment, the chief inspector continued to glare, then taking a deep breath, his expression appeared to soften. 'Having said that . . .' His eyes were gentler now. '. . . good work, Mandy. You haven't changed much, have you? I must ask, however, that if you attend any raids in future, you give me your word that you will not go against the instructions of any of my officers.'

Mandy swallowed. Had she got Ellen into trouble? It hadn't crossed her mind. Robbie Grimshaw had filled her thoughts from the moment she had seen him. She glanced over at the constable, who was watching. Did she look distressed? Mandy's eyes came back to Chief Inspector Benn. He seemed to be waiting for something. What had he said again? That if she wanted to be a part of any police actions in future, she had to do as she was told. The adrenaline was beginning to recede. If she didn't agree, she might never be asked again to help.

'If you need my help again,' she said, 'I'll do what I'm asked to do.'

Chief Inspector Benn seemed satisfied. He regarded her for a moment, then nodded. 'Thank you. And well done,' he said. Turning, he strode across the yard towards Ellen.

Now there was a sick feeling in Mandy's stomach. Stepping away from the centre of the yard, she walked on shaky legs to the old shed and leaned on the wall for a long moment with her eyes closed.

'Are you all right?' Mandy opened her eyes. Seb Conway was looking at her, his face filled with concern.

'I'm fine.' Mandy took a deep breath and let it out slowly. 'Is Mr Grimshaw going to be okay?'

Seb ran one hand through his hair, making it stand up. 'I think so,' he said. 'Thanks to you. Dan Jones, the sergeant from Walton, told me they'd have to charge him with illegal use of a firearm, but he'll be assessed mentally and physically. There's a good chance it'll never reach court.' Looking around, Mandy could see that the police were departing. 'Guess that's their excitement over for the day. And now it's up to us to work out what we're going to do with the animals.'

'What's the protocol?' asked Mandy. 'Obviously we'll have to assess them first, but what happens after that?' She pulled herself upright. With the welfare officer beside her, she made her way across to the pen in which the sheep were trapped. The skittish creatures watched as they approached, one of them stamping its foot. Their wool was overgrown and unkempt, clumps hanging to the ground.

'As you said,' Seb replied, 'we have to assess them. Then we have to try to find somewhere for them to stay. If we can't find anywhere, we'll have to consider whether euthanasia is the kindest option.'

Mandy felt a horrible lurching sensation in her stomach. She climbed into the pen and looked at the sheep more closely. Although they were very thin, their feet were not overgrown. An old stone trough held drinking water. She approached the other ewe, which seemed unable to get up. She was obviously in distress. Her breathing seemed laboured and she was grinding her teeth. She would need a closer examination to figure out if she was seriously ill.

Mandy climbed back out of the pen and headed towards the horse. Despite his filthy coat and skeletal frame, the old gelding nickered as Mandy walked over. Looking past the neglect, Mandy could tell he had once been a proper Shire horse. Now his craggy hind quarters and feathered feet looked too big, wildly out of proportion with his chest and abdomen. As Mandy approached, she turned sideways to appear less challenging. The horse stretched out his head, breathing into Mandy's ear so that it tickled, then nuzzling her face as she reached up to pat his neck.

'Poor old boy,' she murmured. She looked at Seb. 'Do you have a bucket or bowl so we can get him some water?'

Seb nodded. 'I do,' he said and disappeared to his car, returning a few moments later with a gleaming yellow bucket, which he dipped into the sheep's trough to fill.

'Can I offer you a spare pair of wellingtons and a waterproof jacket?' he suggested as he set the water down. He inspected Mandy's shirt, which was already grubby on both shoulders. 'I'm sorry you had to rush over,' he said. 'I hope I didn't spoil your day too much.'

Watching the horse as he took a long draught of the water, Mandy managed a smile. 'Don't apologise,' she said. 'I can't say there's nothing else I'd rather be doing, but only because it's awful that these animals need our help at all. And yes,' she continued, 'I'd appreciate some protective clothing before we investigate the outbuildings . . . and the house.' She paused. 'I guess you haven't had a chance to look at anything else yet?'

'We know there are cats in the house,' Seb said. 'The dog that was in the yard with Mr Grimshaw ran back in there. But there's an outbuilding which is padlocked and there are animals inside. We need to get to them first. We heard a cow bawling when we arrived. There were chickens, too, though they disappeared when we came. As it's summer, they're probably foraging for themselves. Goodness knows whether we'll be able to get them rounded up.' He walked back to his car and Mandy stroked the horse one last time before following.

'Hang on!' she called. 'Before we go on, would you mind giving me a lift down to collect my car, please? It'll only take a minute or two. I'll need my kit to assess the animals properly.'

'Of course.' He pulled himself into the front seat of his van. 'Jump in,' he said. Together they bumped down the pot-holed track.

Mandy looked across at him. 'Seb?'

'Mm?' He glanced back, returning his eyes to the road as the car lurched to the left.

'What you said before . . . about rehoming. What are

the chances of finding somewhere for the farm animals?' Although there had been many times in her childhood that Mandy had found places for all kinds of creatures, she had never had to rehome a cow.

Seb risked another glance at her, his eyes sombre. 'Not good, I'm afraid,' he said. 'Especially not if they're in a bad way. Farmers don't have spare cash for charity, and the only facilities we have are for dogs and cats. Sorry.' He did look genuinely regretful.

For a moment, Mandy pictured Robbie's overgrown yard strewn with bodies and she closed her eyes, but she opened them again. She couldn't get washed away in a tide of sentiment.

'Whatever happens,' she said, 'I only want to euthanase animals which can't be saved. We'll get something sorted out.'

Seb made a strange sound in his throat. 'I'm glad to have you on board,' he said. 'There's nothing I hate more than having to put animals down.'

Ten minutes later, he and Mandy stood side by side outside the ramshackle door of the old cowshed. Seb was carrying a crowbar and, as Mandy watched, he inserted it behind the padlock. 'Stand back,' he warned.

The metal lock gave way with a crack and the door swung open. Mandy ducked as bluebottles swarmed out into the daylight. Inside, the ammonia and heat hit Mandy in a wave, and for a moment she doubted there could be any animals alive in there. As her eyes adjusted, she made out several cows at the far end. They stared into the daylight, eyes wide. One of them lifted her head and bellowed as the group stirred and fidgeted.

With Seb at her side, Mandy waded through the thick layer of dung that lined the floor to take a closer look. 'Do you think we could get them outside?' she gasped. The air felt so thick it was hard to breathe. 'We can't assess them properly in here.'

Together, they made their way back to the door. Jamming it shut, they crossed the yard to where there was an ancient stone-walled pigsty. Mandy peered through the low doorway to the little shelter, but the building was empty. Seb put his hand on the wall and leaned on it, then checked the gate.

'I think it should hold,' he said. 'We could bring the cows in here for now and get a better look at them, but we'll need to find a way to get them across safely.' In the corner of one of the lean-tos, they found several pallets. Between them, they lugged them across the yard to create a makeshift passageway, binding together the wooden slats until they had a solid-looking race from the door to the sty.

'Let's have a go at getting them out.' Seb gave Mandy a tight smile. 'They might not be keen to leave the shed if they've been there for a while.'

Trying not to breathe, Mandy followed him back inside and they circled behind the cows to drive them out. It wasn't easy from the start. One of the cows, a thick-coated black Galloway, was much more nervous than the others. Several times Seb and Mandy lined the group up with the doorway, only to have the Galloway shoot back past them.

On the fourth circuit, a red and white Hereford found the exit. All six cows rushed behind her, crashing along the alley of pallets, emerging into the walled yard snorting and wide-eyed at so much light.

'We should leave them to calm down a bit,' Mandy panted as she closed the gate to the pig pen. She was struggling to swallow the lump in her throat.

All the cows were emaciated like the old Shire. One of them had an infection in one of her teats. It was hugely swollen and there was a grim-looking area on her udder that looked as if it might slough away at any moment. Another had overgrown feet and a third had a wound on her shoulder. Mandy looked longingly at her car, wondering if she could drive away and leave someone else to deal with all this. But right now, she was all these animals had. Their only Hope, literally. And they were outside, no longer walking knee deep in their own faeces or breathing the rank air in the shed.

'Let's go and check there's nothing else in there,' Seb suggested, and holding her breath again, Mandy followed him back into the shed.

In the far corner, they found another ewe. Her teeth were so loose and broken down that Mandy thought she must be very old indeed. Between them, they lifted her out and put her in the pen with the other sheep. Mandy had seen an old bucket in the corner where they had found the pallets and she fetched it. She filled it with fresh water from the spicket beside the outhouse and set it close beside the two weakest sheep. Both put their muzzles into the pail and took a long drink.

Mandy looked around. All the farm animals were out in the fresh air. All had water, though for the moment, they had no food. But at least they were safe. Whatever had led Robbie Grimshaw to neglect his once-loved animals, they would be cared for now.

Chapter Sixteen

'We should look in the house,' Mandy said, but as she spoke she heard a vehicle grinding up the overgrown lane. Looking at Seb, she asked, 'Are you expecting anyone else?'

He shook his head. 'Not that I know of.'

It was Adam and Emily in the Land Rover. As her mum climbed out, Mandy ran over to give her a hug, but Emily seemed unusually tense. 'What were you thinking?' she cried. 'Putting yourself at risk like that when he had a gun! You could have been killed!'

Mandy blinked. 'I don't really know,' she admitted. 'Robbie Grimshaw just looked so frightened.'

Adam had stopped beside Emily. 'It was very brave,' he said, 'but please, never do anything like that again.'

Mandy shook her head. 'I won't,' she said. 'Chief Inspector Benn made me promise.'

'Well, thank goodness for Chief Inspector Benn.' Emily's anger seemed to disperse in a heartbeat and Mandy found herself engulfed in a proper hug.

Adam wrapped his arms around her too. 'We are very proud of you,' he whispered.

A wave of calm ran through Mandy. 'Why are you here?' she asked. 'Did Seb call you?'

'Actually, Jimmy Marsh came by and told us. What can we do to help?' said Adam.

Jimmy Marsh? Mandy wondered what the Outward Bound instructor had to do with all this, but there were more important things to think about.

'We were just going to take a look inside the house, but Seb and I can do that.' She thought for a moment. 'There are four sheep in the yard, two of which are in a bad way. On top of that, there are six cows and one very old Shire horse.'

Together they walked around the corner and Mandy showed them. 'They've all got water,' she said, 'but they're going to need food and shelter tonight. Some of them need treatment as well. The sheep are easy. We can hold them, but the cows . . . there's nowhere safe to examine them. Dad, you've got a halter in the Land Rover, haven't you? Maybe we can tie them up some-where.' Even with the halter, she couldn't imagine how they were going to treat the wild black Galloway with the torn shoulder, but Adam looked at her and held up one hand.

'Give it a few minutes,' he said. 'Jimmy was trying to round up more people to help. In the meantime, we can see to the sheep while you and Seb check the cottage.'

Jimmy again? For a moment, Mandy felt irritated, but she brushed it aside. They needed all the help they could get. Grabbing a cat basket in each hand, she and Seb pushed through the tangled garden to the front door. It opened with a loud creak and Mandy stepped inside. The stench in the house was almost as awful as the barn. The stifling air was thick with flies, and as they walked through the entrance hall and turned right into the kitchen, Mandy couldn't help but feel a sense of horror.

On the filthy counter, alongside cereal bowls with the remains of what looked like dried cat food, there were older plates caked with unidentifiable muck. In the sink and overflowing onto the drainer, dishes and pans lay mouldering in water filled with scum. There were shutters inside the window, and Mandy made her way round an ancient oak table to tug them aside. They opened to reveal cracked windows and a thick layer of spider webs.

Mandy coughed, hiding her face in the crook of her elbow until the dust settled. When she turned again, the state of the kitchen was even more startling in daylight. Flies buzzed over an overflowing bin filled with unwashed food cans. Cupboards lay open, mostly empty, but there was a sack of potatoes strewn across the floor. Many had been trampled, some looked as though they had been chewed.

A movement caught Mandy's eye. A pair of frightened eyes peered out from under an antiquated stove. Mandy tiptoed across the kitchen, pushed aside some rotten-looking potatoes with her foot, and knelt down. She was careful not to stare at the small black cat that was hiding there. She blinked slowly, turning her gaze sideways, trying to send the message she wasn't going to hurt the little animal. In turn, the cat blinked her eyes lazily and half-turned her head.

To Mandy's amazement, in the light from the window, she could see that the cat was nursing three kittens. Their eyes were not yet open, but they were suckling, mouths intent, tiny paws kneading at their mother's teats. Stretching out her hand, Mandy managed to stroke the cheek of the mother cat, who began to explore Mandy's fingers with her little black nose.

Mandy carefully stood up and backed away. Seb, who had turned left into a different room, reappeared in the doorway, clutching one of the baskets. Inside was a painfully thin silver tabby cat.

'There's another cat under the stove,' Mandy whispered, 'but she's suckling three kittens. Could we leave her a few minutes until they're finished? She's not going anywhere.'

'Probably best,' Seb agreed. 'I've been trying to get hold of the collie, but she won't allow me anywhere near. I'm going to leave this fellow in the hallway. It's too hot to put him in the van until we're done. He's underfed, but otherwise looks healthy.'

'I've got some treats in the car the dog might like,' said Mandy. She thought back to the day she and Emily had called. 'There should be at least one more cat,' she said. 'A tortoiseshell. Oh and . . .' She looked at Seb, her head on one side. 'We need to check the rest of those sheds. When James and I came here years ago, Mr Grimshaw kept ferrets in cages.'

'Don't worry.' Seb was quick to reassure her. 'We've had a really thorough look around and there aren't any ferrets. If you want to get the treats, I'll have a look for the other cat. It's amazing there aren't more of them since none of them seem to have been spayed or neutered, but I suppose if he hasn't been feeding them, they might just have left. I've got traps in the van that we can leave in case there are any hiding outside.'

Turning, he walked along the hallway and rounded the corner to go upstairs. Mandy pushed through the front door. Once in the garden, she took a few deep breaths. She went to get the pack of dog chews from the car. Given that they didn't want to load the animals until the last minute, she decided to spend a bit of time trying to get Shy used to her.

When Mandy returned to the cottage, Seb was at the door. 'I found your other cat,' he announced. 'And another lot of kittens with her.'

Mandy peered into the cage Seb had set down on the other side of the hall from the silver tabby. The tortoiseshell cat stared back at her, eyes unblinking. Beside her lay two sick-looking kittens, one ginger and white, one tortoiseshell like her mother. Their eyes were inflamed and oozing. The ginger and white kitten could barely open its left eye. As Mandy looked, it opened its mouth in a silent meow that tugged at her heart. Poor defenceless little thing.

'We'll get those eyes cleared up soon,' Mandy promised, as much to the kitten itself as to Seb. Walking into the kitchen, she grabbed a towel that was hanging on a hook on the wall. She carried it back and laid it over the cage to give the mother and kittens a hiding place.

'The collie is upstairs,' Seb reported. 'She's lying on what I presume was Mr Grimshaw's bed.'

Mandy walked along the corridor to the back of the house. Although the tiles in the hallway were filthy, she could see that they were original Yorkshire flagstone. The narrow uncarpeted staircase led up to a tiny landing. A handrail on carved wooden spindles curved round to enclose a small hallway with a low ceiling. The bedroom on the left was empty, but when she looked inside the doorway to the right, she could see an ancient iron bedstead and twisted blankets caked in animal hair. Right in the centre, curled up in a ball, was the collie.

She lifted her head as Mandy came in, her eyes narrow and wary. With a low growl, she flitted off the bed to hide on the far side. As quietly as she could on the bare floorboards, Mandy tiptoed around the bed. As with the cats, she was careful not to approach head on. The dog was beautiful in spite of her condition. Her coat was unkempt, but her bright eyes were set in an intelligent face. Symmetrical black markings covered her muzzle and a thin white stripe ran down the centre of her nose.

When Mandy was still quite a distance from the terrified animal, she crouched down and leaned against the wall, facing sideways to the dog.

'Hello, Shy.' She tried to make her voice as warm as possible and for an instant, the ears, which had been flat against Shy's head, twitched forwards. Putting her hand into her pocket, Mandy took out some food and flicked it along the floor towards the cowering animal, then stayed very still. From the corner of her eye, she saw Shy reach forward and sniff suspiciously at the chew. With her eyes still on Mandy, she picked up the treat, nibbled it and swallowed.

As soon as it was gone, Mandy tossed another piece. Again the suspicious look, followed by movement and chewing. After a few minutes, the collie had moved several inches towards Mandy. Rather than try to catch her now, Mandy decided the dog would be safe in the house until they were finished outside. Her parents would be busy for a while. There was such a lot to do and they still had to find some kind of shelter for the animals outside as well as food. With a last glance towards the frightened-looking dog, she stood up. Backing away, she left the bedroom and walked downstairs and out of the house into the yard.

To her amazement, a large bale of hay stood in the centre of the concrete.

'Where did that come from?' Mandy asked Emily, who was holding the head of one of the sheep while Adam injected her.

'It was from Bert Burnley,' said her mum. 'Jimmy got in touch with him and he brought it along. Jimmy called Mr Hapwell from Twyford as well. He's promised to bring some concentrate for both the sheep and the cattle, enough for a day or two. And Graham from Upper Welford Hall is bringing down their crush so we can examine the cows properly.'

Mandy felt bewildered. She hadn't been expecting anything like this. It seemed that Jimmy had brought together half the farming community to help out.

Adam finished injecting and looked up. 'He's even persuaded Sam Western to donate some straw.'

Mandy stared at her mum and dad. 'Where is Jimmy now?' she asked.

'You hear that hammering?' Emily grinned as Mandy turned her head to listen. 'That's him. He's round the back of one of the empty sheds, making it safe so the animals have some shelter for the night. We thought it would be better not to move them for a day or two. If you agree, that is?'

Mandy raised an eyebrow. 'You don't need to ask me. You know that.'

Emily pressed her lips together, but her eyes were smiling. 'I know I don't need to, but I want to. This is your thing, your area of speciality. Seb and you are in charge. Your dad and I would never turn our backs on animals in need, but we're here to assist, not to lead.'

Mandy stood very still. 'Thanks, both of you,' she said eventually. 'In that case, I agree with you. I think it would be very good if the animals could stay here a couple of days. Just until they've had time to gain some strength.

In the meantime,' she squared her shoulders, 'I think I'd better go and say thank you to Jimmy Marsh.'

Following the noise of ongoing carpentry, Mandy rounded the largest of the empty sheds. Halfway up a ladder, Jimmy Marsh was fixing a plank into place, blocking up a dangerous-looking gap in the weather-boarding. His movements were skilful and Mandy stopped, mesmerised by his precision. She had always liked watching craftsmen at work.

Jimmy checked that the plank was secure and descended to the ground. Turning towards the frame where more planks were balanced, he caught sight of Mandy watching him.

'Hello,' he said.

Mandy felt herself going red. What would he think of her, staring at him like that? He always seemed to catch her at awkward moments.

'Hi,' she managed, then, 'I just wanted to say thanks for everything. I mean the straw and the feed and getting in touch with so many people.' She stuttered to a halt and he smiled.

'I'm glad to help,' he said. 'I'm just fixing this so the animals can stay here for now.'

'Oh . . . good.' There was silence. He seemed to be waiting for her to say something else, but her mind was empty. 'Is there anything I can do to help?' Mandy blurted out.

For a moment, she hoped he would refuse, but his green eyes rested on her, his expression pleased. 'You could hold some nails for me,' he said. 'I keep having to go up and down the ladder. I've nothing to hold them in.'

Mandy could feel her face flushing. Hold nails? Why didn't he put them in his pocket? It sounded like he was humouring her. It wasn't as if she didn't have enough to do, but it would be rude to walk away when he had done so much. She held out a reluctant hand for the nails and followed him as he walked back and climbed the ladder.

It was the first time since the morning that Mandy had had a moment to stand still. Perched above her, Jimmy had positioned the board and was hammering nails in with effortless efficiency. As he reached down to grab a new nail, he grinned at her.

'Why are you here?' Mandy found herself asking, then kicked herself. It sounded insulting. 'I mean, you seem to have contacted half the village and got them all to help out.'

Still not right, she thought, but he didn't seem offended. 'I wanted to help,' he began, then paused. 'I get the feeling you think I don't know much about the countryside,' he went on, 'but I spent my teenage years in the Lake District.' Mandy frowned, but Jimmy continued, 'You probably remember, a few years back, the Foot and Mouth outbreak?'

Of course she remembered it. For the whole of the summer, Mandy had barely been allowed out. Hillwalking and cycling had been outlawed. When she had been able to accompany her parents on visits, she could remember scrubbing the car wheels, dipping her boots in disinfectant at every farm. Nobody wanted to call out the vet unless it was essential. Paranoia had hung over Welford for months on end.

'It devastated the area around my village,' Jimmy said. 'Most of my friends at school grew up on farms.' His voice was grim. For the first time, he stopped working and gazed down at Mandy. 'I can still remember their faces. They were family farms and my friends had grown up there. They had to watch their animals burn.' For a moment, he clenched his teeth together, then he took a deep breath. 'The community spirit carried them through. People helped one another. My best friend's father lost his whole herd of pedigree shorthorns. Farmers from all over the UK sent him pedigree cattle to restock.'

He was silent for several moments, apparently wrestling with his memories. Then shaking his head, he lifted his hammer and sent another nail into the board. Examining his handiwork, seemingly satisfied, he climbed down the ladder and stood looking at Mandy. 'I want to give something back to the communities I work in,' he said. 'I know how important it is for people to pull together.' He paused, a look of contemplation on his face. When he spoke again, his voice had fallen so low, Mandy had to strain her ears to hear. 'And I wanted to help the old man. My dad suffered from Alzheimer's. I wanted to help Robbie Grimshaw by helping his animals.'

Silence stretched between them. Mandy had asked her question in the most casual way. His reply had been intensely personal.

'Thanks for telling me,' she managed eventually. She had the sudden urge to reach out and hug him, but they stood there for what seemed an age, before Jimmy broke the silence.

'It was a long time ago,' he said. 'I hope I haven't upset you.'

Mandy shook her head. The man standing in front of her seemed very different from the arrogant incomer who had teased her about her protectiveness of the countryside. She wanted to tell him how touched she was, but there were no words that seemed to cover it. 'Thanks again for everything you've done,' she said. Hearing the sound of a tractor, she was glad of an excuse to get away. 'I'd better go and see who that is,' she said, and before he could reply, she turned and hurried off.

The tractor was being driven by Graham, and a gleaming metal cattle crush was attached to the back. Seb appeared from the house and he and Graham manoeuvred the crush into position at the end of the race they had made with the pallets.

Once it was set up, the stockman climbed over the wall into the old pigsty. 'Which do you want in first?' he asked. 'Not that I can give you a guarantee of your first choice,' he added, eyeing the wild-looking Galloway.

'Ideally the cut shoulder.' That was the most urgent,

Mandy thought. It would need a fair few stitches. 'Though if necessary, we'll deal with them in the order they come.' She watched, hardly daring to breathe as the cows circled their small pen. There wasn't much space; if one of the beasts kicked out at Graham, it could be serious. But within moments, he had sent the correct cow up the chute and the animal was racing towards the self-locking yoke at the far end of the crush. Seconds later, her head was trapped.

'I'm going to need some clean water,' Mandy said, as she examined the wound more closely. It looked recent and clear of dirt, which meant the chances of healing were good, but she would still need to bathe it. As Seb headed towards the cottage, she made her way to her car. Opening the boot, she selected Hibiscrub for cleaning, as well as local anaesthetic and a suture kit. Fetching an old milk crate, she turned it upside down, spread out a sterilised tea towel, and set her kit on top.

The local anaesthetic was painful so close to the open wound, and as Mandy injected, the cow shifted and bellowed. But as soon as the local began to work, the animal settled. Mandy put in sutures, first the muscle layer, then under the skin, to bring everything together neatly. Finally, she wielded the sturdy needle that was needed to penetrate the thick hide of the cow. Standing back a few minutes later, she was pleased with the job she had done. The edges of the cut were well aligned; the stitches evenly spaced.

'I'm just going to check her over,' she announced to

Seb, who was watching. Working round the cow, she assessed her condition score and general health. Apart from being thin, she seemed in good shape. 'I'll check if she's in calf,' Mandy commented. As the welfare officer looked on, she shimmied up and over the pallet nearest the crate. Pulling on one of the long gloves she had received from her friends in Leeds, she lubricated her arm and inserted it into the cow's rectum. As always, she was struck by the heat of the cow's body through the thin glove. Extending her arm carefully so as not to damage the thin lining of the gut, she felt for evidence that the cow was in calf. To her surprise, she felt a small hoof under her hand.

'She's quite well on,' Mandy said. 'More than five months. Probably a good bit more.'

Seb raised his eyebrows. 'I can't believe she's kept it in those conditions.'

Mandy nodded as she withdrew her arm and peeled off the glove. She scratched the cow's tail-head. 'We'll look after both of you, sweetheart.'

One by one, they put the rest of the cows through the crush, checked, treated and assessed. All six were in calf. Mandy couldn't help feeling pleased. It would make it easier to rehome them than if they had been barren.

Jimmy had completed his repairs by the time they finished. Adam and he had rolled out the bale of straw to make luscious, knee-deep bedding, and Emily and Seb had filled the mangers with hay and the troughs with sheep and cattle feed. Graham had returned to

Upper Welford to milk. So it was just the five of them
who stood leaning on the top rail of the newly mended
pen, looking at the animals. The horse, his feet trimmed,
had made his way more steadily into the barn than
Mandy had hoped. The cows looked much better
standing in fresh straw, munching hay. It was only the
two oldest sheep that still looked in a sorry state.

'The one with the white spots on her face is the worst,'
said Adam. It was the ancient sheep with the awful teeth.
Mandy gazed at her. Despite her father and mother's
best efforts, the ewe still couldn't stand. Although they
had set two pails close to her with food and water, and
a pile of hay beside her, she didn't seem interested. The
other, another Swaledale but with more regular markings,
was at least chewing hay.

'We'll have to see how they get on,' she said. If the
old ewe continued to be as bad, they would have to
consider euthanasia. Crossing her fingers, Mandy tried
not to be pessimistic, but the poor creature really did
look sorry for herself.

'There's just the dog in the house now.' Seb turned
to Mandy. 'Jimmy's going to board the house up once
you've got her out. There are no other animals inside.
I've checked thoroughly.'

'Thanks, Seb.' Mandy hadn't forgotten Shy. The
little collie had been flitting in and out of her mind
the whole time Mandy had been working with the
cows. She went back to the boot of her car and took
out a rope lead. There was no space in the boot of

her car for the dog. Walking back round to the yard, she approached Adam.

'Dad,' she said, and he looked round. 'There's no room in my car for the dog,' she said. 'Would you be able to take mine back down and leave me the Land Rover, please?'

'Of course,' her dad replied.

Making sure her pockets were full of treats, Mandy made her way back up to the dimly lit bedroom. As she entered, she saw the slim black and white body dart from the centre of the bed, back down against the far wall. She heard a low growl as she walked across the bedroom, but when she rounded the corner and Shy's eyes met hers, the growling stopped.

'Not going to growl, now you know it's me?' she asked the collie as she slid down the wall into a crouching position. Again, she made her voice warm. The wary brown eyes watched her. 'Now, how are we going to get this leash onto you?' Mandy said, thinking aloud. If she climbed onto the bed, Shy might feel Mandy was invading her personal space. Even with the treats, Mandy had not managed to persuade the dog far enough out from the corner that she could get near her head. She didn't want to move the bed either. Anything that would scare Shy would make things worse.

She eyed the metal bed frame. Like so many old beds, the frame was tall. Perhaps she could crawl underneath it and approach that way. If she stayed far enough in front of the collie, she could use the treats again to entice her forwards. She would be less threatening crawling underneath than if she just appeared above Shy's head.

It looked as though there was ten years of dust under the bed. With a rueful glance at her good trousers, Mandy knelt down and started to crawl. Trying not to think about what might be under her hands, she made her way across, aiming towards the foot of the bed. She hoped Shy would not feel the need to make a run for it. Though the dog's eyes followed her every move, she remained still.

'I'm guessing you think I'm crazy,' Mandy muttered. Once again there was that all-too-brief forward movement of the black ears. With her curled-up body, frightened eyes and ears that were flattened against her skull, Shy's body language was screaming that she was afraid.

Mandy paused and pushed her hand into her pocket to retrieve a handful of food. One at a time, she tossed the treats in front of Shy. Inch by inch, stopping each time to throw treats until Shy had relaxed, Mandy crept forwards until she was within arm's reach of the collie's attractive little face. Pulling out the quick-release leash, she made the rope into a large loop. Holding it out, she allowed Shy to sniff the rope. Edging it along and at the same time encouraging Shy forwards with the food, Mandy was able to get it round the collie's neck and tighten it.

Once it was on, Mandy couldn't help letting out a sigh of relief. Gripping the handle, she crawled backwards and, by dint of encouragement and gentle pressure, Shy followed her until they reached the far side of the bed.

It was time to stand up, thought Mandy, but again it was essential she didn't spook the little collie. Any change in position could make her seem like a threat again.

'Just as well you're hungry,' she said to Shy. Dropping treats, she stood up in stages, first to her knees, then crouching, finally upright. All the time, she kept her body from facing Shy directly and avoided leaning over her.

Although the collie didn't look delighted to have the collar around her neck, she wasn't pulling away. When Mandy began to walk forwards, she trotted alongside. Down the stairs they went and along the hallway. They kept up the brisk pace until they reached the front door. In the front garden, Shy lay down and refused to go any further.

Mandy crouched down and began again with the treats. Eventually, with encouragement and patience, Mandy managed to get the little animal close to the car, but when Shy saw the Land Rover, she began to pant. She lay down again, her eyes white-ringed and her fluffy black ears pressed against her skull.

'What's wrong, Shy? Don't you like the car?' Mandy said in a low voice. Rather than drag the collie, they retreated a few feet. Leaving the little animal lying on the ground, Mandy moved right to the end of the lead and, with both arms outstretched, was able to open the back door of the Land Rover. Digging yet again into her pocket, she threw treats into the vehicle and moved back to where Shy was sitting. The temptation to kneel down and try to pat Shy was enormous, but Mandy knew how much that could frighten her. They had got this far. It was important not to do anything that might cause fear. So far, the collie had shown no sign she might bite, but collie dogs were more likely than many other breeds to do so. Remembering the growls at the police earlier, and the reaction that had greeted her when she entered the bedroom, Mandy kept her hands away.

'The last thing I want is to scare you,' she promised, but Shy didn't look up. Being near the car was more stressful than being talked to in the bedroom, Mandy thought.

Step by tiny step, Shy moved nearer to the vehicle, sniffing it first, backing off, then approaching again. Using the treats, Mandy encouraged the dog to explore. She watched in silence as the collie put her feet up on the sill of the doorway, sneaking her nose forward to grab the food, retreating and approaching. When she finally made a leap into the back of the car, Mandy didn't move. If she closed the door right away, this experience could become terrifying. Instead, she encouraged Shy to jump in and out freely.

Once she was leaping in and out in her own time, Mandy slowly closed the door. Through the window, she saw Shy sniff at the now closed door and then start to sniff out the last of the chews. She didn't look delighted to be in the car, but nor did she look petrified. It was the best Mandy could hope for right now.

Walking back into the yard, Mandy found Seb making a last check on the animals. She leaned her elbows on the wall of the pigsty. 'Everything okay?' she asked.

'So far so good,' he replied. 'Did you manage to catch the collie? She seemed a nervous little thing.'

Mandy half smiled. 'She's certainly that,' she said. 'But yes, we managed.' It was going to be a challenge to get her ready for a new home, she thought, but the image of the sweet little face with the terrified eyes was burned across Mandy's brain. Shy would be a wonderful dog if Mandy could take away that fear.

If.

Mandy had never wanted to help an animal more.

Chapter Seventeen

Pulling the duvet closer around her chin, Mandy felt herself relax for the first time that day. She had driven the Land Rover the short distance to Animal Ark with Shy in the back. By the end of the journey, the little collie had been cowering in a corner and shaking. When Adam had come out to greet them, she had growled, ears back and hackles raised.

'Is she likely to bite?' Adam asked, and Mandy admitted it was possible. When an animal was that scared, there was a high risk they could become vicious if pushed. Mandy was determined that wouldn't happen.

It had taken another half-hour to get Shy out of the Land Rover and into one of the kennels in the wildlife unit, which had been taken over by Robbie Grimshaw's animals for now. The cats and kittens all seemed comfortable. The little black mother had remained calm throughout the transfer and the kittens had suckled again after the move. Knowing all the animals were safe and contented, Mandy had allowed herself to fall into bed.

The phone on her bedside table rang. Jerked from her doze, Mandy banged her hand on the table as she was reaching for her phone. Pressing her lips together, she looked at the screen. It was Simon. Her toes curled under the bed covers as she pulled herself into a sitting position. *'Call me later . . .'* It had been the last thing he had said that morning. Mandy had been so caught up with the animals at Lamb's Wood that it had slipped her mind.

'Hello, Simon.' She held the mobile tentatively to her ear.

'Mandy.' The single word held reproach.

'I'm sorry I haven't phoned,' she said in a rush. 'It took all day to get everything sorted out. It was really late by the time I got back.' She closed her eyes, waiting for his reply.

'What was it you had to do that took all day? I thought you'd be back here by now. You said you'd let me know.'

Had she said that? Mandy couldn't remember her exact words. 'I'm sorry,' she said again. 'It's been a crazy day. There were so many animals at the farm and Mr Grimshaw had to be taken away by ambulance.' A picture flashed across her brain of the old man with his shotgun, Shy growling, and the crowd of police officers at the far end of the yard. Mandy couldn't face telling Simon all the details. Especially not the part where she had to wear a bulletproof vest – and still walked up to an unstable man holding a shotgun.

'There were cows and sheep and a horse as well as the cats and a dog,' she said. 'We couldn't bring them all back here. We had to gather supplies and equipment to house them where they were.'

'Oh well,' Simon said grudgingly. 'It does sound as though you had a lot to organise. Did many of the animals need treatment?'

'I had to stitch a cow,' she replied, 'and there was another with mastitis. The horse was lame. We trimmed his feet and gave pain relief, but the farrier is coming tomorrow. On top of that, there were four malnourished sheep. Two of them were in a very bad way.'

'You were definitely needed then,' Simon commented with a slight edge.

Mandy stifled a sigh. She couldn't help judging her boyfriend. There had been so many people who had helped today. Jimmy Marsh had done so much without even being asked. She couldn't help wondering whether Simon could have found a way to come with her. Then again, it might have made things more difficult if he had come. Would she have felt as able to approach Robbie Grimshaw, gun in hand, with Simon watching?

'I have to go now,' she said. It was too late tonight to tackle the subject of York vs Leeds. Today had convinced Mandy even more that Welford would be a great place to open a rescue centre. The support the animals had received from their neighbours had been beyond anything she could have hoped for. She found herself willing Simon not to raise the subject again tonight, and to her relief, he didn't.

'You should get some sleep,' he replied. 'It's after midnight.' Mandy looked at the clock. She hadn't realised it was quite so late. 'Will you be busy again tomorrow?'

Would she be busy? There were all the farm animals that would need rechecking and feeding. There was the search for new homes that would have to start. And she would have to make plans for rehabilitation. The kittens would need to be socialised, as would Shy.

'Very,' she said. 'I know there's lots to talk about, but I'll try to find time to call you, okay?'

'I guess so,' he said. They said their goodbyes and then he was gone. Feeling strangely empty and deflated, Mandy closed her eyes and tried to sleep.

Opening her eyes in the still darkened room, Mandy couldn't tell whether she had been asleep or not. Reaching out, she picked up her mobile from the bedside table. It was four a.m. She lay for a moment, ears strained to catch any hint of what might have awoken her, but there was nothing. Despite the long day behind her, she felt wide awake. Sitting up in bed, she decided to go down to see how her new inmates were coping. She crept down the staircase, across the kitchen and headed out to the residential unit.

The kittens with the black cat had obviously been suckling and now they lay in a peaceful furry tumble, their mother's body wrapped round them. To Mandy's delight, when she approached the cage with the tortoise-shell and her two kittens, the mother came forward. Mandy quietly opened the door and sat down, letting the little animal rub her face against Mandy's fingers.

Careful not to stare, she felt the cat move onto her lap. Better still, the kittens, their tummies round from milk, also crept out. Following their mother, they began to investigate. Although their eyelids were still inflamed, they seemed to be stronger already. Three sets of eyes gazed at Mandy in the dim light of the heat lamp. She couldn't help grinning to herself as she stroked the little family.

On the far side of the room, she made out Shy, curled on a blanket in her cage. With a last snuggle for each of the kittens, Mandy managed to get all of them back inside the kennel and closed the door. If she was wide awake, so was the collie. In the half-light, the bony little body looked even more anxious than before. Shy's back was hunched and her pretty face was filled with tension. Mandy had rarely seen any animal look more frightened. Tomorrow, she thought, she would need to get Shy out of the cage. Persuading her that the world was not such a scary place was going to be an uphill battle. Guessing that Shy was at least two years old, Mandy knew that the collie was long past the age where socialisation would be easy.

Mandy kept her body low, as small as possible to appear less threatening. She inched across the room until she could open Shy's door and drop some food into the cage. Leaving the door ajar, she turned away and sat with her back to the neighbouring empty kennel. Shy had seemed to like the sound of her voice yesterday. Perhaps talking to her would help. Keeping her tone light, Mandy started to tell the dog about the rescue. About Mr Grimshaw and Seb, Mum and Dad, and about Jimmy Marsh and all the people he had mustered to help.

Although the collie didn't move, Mandy saw Shy's face relax. Her eyes closed then opened again and her ears were no longer flat to her head. It was restful in the low-level lighting and warm. Halfway through a sentence, Mandy felt her own eyes becoming heavy. Leaning against the empty cage and pulling her towelling robe around her, she allowed herself to drift off.

'Good morning.' Emily, still in her dressing gown, was standing in the doorway to the wildlife unit. 'I won't come any closer,' she said. 'Shy is still a bit panicky,' and when Mandy looked round, she could see that once again the collie was cowering in the corner.

'Poor little girl.' Mandy sighed. 'She seems afraid of everything.'

Emily bent down and peered in at the tortoiseshell cat and her kittens. 'They seem well,' she commented, and Mandy, who had skooshed across the floor before she stood up, agreed.

'I was worried about them last night,' she said. 'They seemed so little and defenceless, but they've really bounced back.'

'It's often the way with young animals,' her mum said. 'If you'd like, once we've fed our new visitors, we can have some breakfast ourselves. What do you say to pancakes?'

Mandy grinned. 'That sounds marvellous,' she said.

There were only the three adult cats and Shy to feed for now. Bert Burnley had offered to call on the farm animals first thing to feed them.

Soon the litter trays had been cleaned, the kittens' eyes bathed and the animals fed and watered. Emily watched from the other side of the room as Mandy started the long process of getting close enough to Shy to get the lead around her neck. If anything, it was harder than it had been yesterday. She shouldn't be disappointed, Mandy told herself as she crouched with the lead stretched out into a huge loop. Yesterday, Shy had been on her home ground. At least Mandy had managed to get into the kennel today without making Shy growl.

Once on the leash, Shy walked outside quite readily. In the garden, she lagged behind Mandy, legs in cautious slow motion, eyes hyperactive as she squatted.

'What do you think about her?' Emily asked from the doorway as Mandy led the dog back inside. 'Seb said she looked ferocious yesterday.'

'She's not ferocious.' Mandy stepped inside and closed the door behind her. 'Just scared out of her wits. That's not to say she wouldn't bite. Quite likely she would if we pushed her too far. But that's exactly what I want to avoid. If we can work with her to change the way she sees things, desensitise her to the things she'll have to cope with, it's possible we might be able to rehome her.'

It was a long shot, Mandy knew. However attractive she was, Shy would need a special home with an owner who understood how difficult life could be when you were afraid of so many things. She walked the dog back into the kennel and removed the lead. Shy slunk into the corner and Mandy sidled out and closed the door.

Emily watched the process with interest. 'You are so good with these animals,' she said. 'I'm sorry it was difficult with your dad about your plans for a rescue centre. There are just so many things to think about at the moment.'

Mandy shrugged. 'It was my fault, too,' she admitted. 'I was so excited about the idea, I got ahead of myself. I should have talked to you and Dad before letting Maurice come over.'

'Like it or not,' Emily said with a smile, 'right now, we have a rescue centre. And before you do any more rescuing, I think you deserve some breakfast.' With a final glance at the animals, she opened the door.

Mandy followed her to the kitchen. For a moment, she toyed with talking to her mum about Simon. The row over Animal Ark and York meant that whatever happened here, it wasn't possible to make more plans before she could talk to him. But she didn't know where to start. Anyway, it seemed disloyal to Simon. He had been so angry about James and Paul and the fact she had talked to them. For now, she pushed the thought of confiding in her mother from her mind.

'Paul came up with a name for my rescue centre,' she said.

Emily, who was delving in the fridge, turned her head. 'Oh yes?'

'He suggested we call it Hope Meadows,' Mandy said. She hoped Emily wouldn't think she was getting ahead of herself again, but her mum closed the fridge and stood there clutching a carton of milk.

'Hope Meadows,' she echoed. 'What a lovely name. Giving hope to animals in need is exactly what you do.'

As her mum began to beat flour and eggs to make the pancake mixture, Mandy fetched a binder and a thick pad of paper. Leaning her head against her hand, she started to write. Ten minutes later, she looked up as the door opened and Adam walked in.

'Good morning, beautiful ladies.' He walked over and gave Emily a kiss, then turned to see what Mandy was doing. She turned the paper to show him.

'Rehabilitation plans,' she explained. 'A page for each of Robbie's animals. Identification details, medical and behavioural treatment plans for each. What do you think?'

Adam studied the notes she had made. 'Very methodical.'

Mandy looked up and was pleased to see genuine warmth in his eyes. 'This is part of what I was doing with my Masters,' she said. 'My thesis was about ways to use fear reduction alongside medical intervention. From the research I did, it seems you can use the same techniques for all kinds of animals. You just have to find out what motivates them and makes them feel better.'

Adam handed the sheets back to Mandy and smiled at her. Emily looked expectantly at him and Mandy saw her father nod.

'Mandy,' her mum began, 'your dad and I have been talking, and . . .' She paused, then went on, 'We'd like to look at the architect's plans you had drawn up.'

For a long moment, Mandy couldn't think of anything to say. Her eyes moved from Emily's smiling face to Adam's serious one.

'Do you mean . . .?'

'That we want to make your plans a reality?' Adam said. He nodded. 'We want to make the financial invest-ment, too, as it's a family venture,' he went on. 'We want you to save Granny Thorpe's money for now.'

Mandy stood up and threw her arms around her dad and then her mum. When she let go, she could see tears in her mother's eyes.

'I'll put the kettle on,' Emily said. 'I think we could all do with a congratulatory cup of tea, don't you?'

Mandy couldn't help laughing. Hope Meadows had already been toasted with cola over a meal of pasties. Now they were going to drink tea with pancakes.

'We're so proud of you,' Emily said. 'What you did yesterday. The future of Animal Ark is in the safest possible hands.' She paused as she was filling the kettle and looked at Mandy. 'As long as you promise never to confront someone holding a shotgun again, please!'

Mandy winced. 'Don't worry. I'm not in a rush to look down the wrong end of a gun barrel again.'

Emily switched on the kettle and turned to Adam. 'What do you think about the name Hope Meadows?' she asked. 'Paul suggested it.'

'Did he?' Adam raised his eyebrows. 'I like it.' He reached across the table to hold Mandy's hand. 'We talked before about how much work there would be, but we will do our best to help. Once we've looked at the architect's drawings, you could show us your plans for setting up. Not that I think we need to check up on you.' He nodded at the paperwork on the table. 'It's obvious you're very organised, but we do have experience of council inspections and legal documentation. If there's anything you need, just ask.' He smiled his twinkling smile and opened his arms again, and Mandy rushed over to be engulfed in the biggest bear hug he had given her for years.

Loosening his grip, Adam held her by the shoulders. His face was filled with love. 'We know you're going to make Hope Meadows a great success,' he said. 'And a second generation of vets at Animal Ark? You know how to make an old man very proud!'

Chapter Eighteen

Mandy stood by the door of the clinic, trying to remember if she had everything she needed. Her veterinary equipment was in the car and she had the rehabilitation plans for the farm animals in a folder. This time, she was dressed in old clothes and a sturdy pair of wellington boots. The breakfast pancakes and celebratory tea were finished. It was time to return to Lamb's Wood Cottage to see how the animals had fared overnight.

Mandy had a strong suspicion that two of the sheep would probably have to be euthanased, unless they had made significant progress overnight. Just in case, she grabbed a fork and spade. They would be useful if she had to dig a grave.

Hearing the sound of a car coming up the driveway, she walked outside and round the end of the cottage. It was James and Paul. With a feeling of dismay, she walked towards them.

'Hi, Mandy!' James called as he pulled himself upright. He stretched and then walked to the other side of the car to help Paul out.

Mandy took a deep breath. 'I'm really sorry, James,'

she said. 'It's lovely to see you both, but I'm busy. Remember Robbie Grimshaw?' She looked at James. 'Course you do. I spent most of the day at Lamb's Wood Cottage yesterday. Robbie isn't well and his animals were being neglected. We sorted them a bit, but I need to go back and carry on.'

James leaned on the car, his face amused. 'I know that, silly,' he said. 'That's why we're here. I've heard all about your escapades.'

'From whom?' Mandy stared at him and he grinned.

'Your grandmother, actually. I rang her about one of the recipes she gave me and she told me all the gory details. How you were almost shot, and then you saved hundreds of animals single-handedly . . . at least that's how she made it sound.'

Mandy shook her head, half amazed, wholly amused. She had forgotten how efficiently Welford whispers worked.

'I came over to offer my help,' James continued.

Paul had climbed out of the car with James's assistance and he stood with one hand resting on the door: tall, thin and impossibly pale. Mandy felt a rush of concern. He was in no fit state for rescue work. Despite the ghostly white aspect of his face, Paul smiled and Mandy felt the usual rush of painful affection.

'Hello, Mandy,' he said. 'It's good to see you.'

'You too, Paul,' she said, meaning it. 'Why don't you both come in? Mum and Dad are in the kitchen. We've just finished breakfast, but we can get the kettle back on.' She walked slowly, trying not to notice how much James had to help his husband.

'Mum?' She opened the back door and put her head in and Emily appeared. When she saw who it was, she rushed outside.

'James! Paul! How lovely to see you both.'

The two young men looked equally pleased to see her. James reached out for a hug. 'Hello, Emily. We came over to help Mandy,' he explained.

'How generous.' Emily looked from James to Paul. 'Why don't you go up to Lamb's Wood and help Mandy with the animals, James, while Paul stays here to keep me company? I think I overdid it yesterday and I'd love to sit down this morning.' She looked directly at Paul. 'You and I could sit in the garden,' she suggested. 'It's already lovely and warm, and I've got all the Sunday papers.'

Paul dipped his head. 'I'd be honoured to keep you company,' he said. 'Thank you, Emily.' Together they made their way to the table and chairs that stood near the climbing-rose trellis. Emily made sure Paul was sitting comfortably before vanishing indoors to fetch tea and the papers.

Mandy looked at James. 'All set?' she said.

James squared his shoulders and saluted. 'All set,' he replied.

Adam stuck his head round the back door. 'Hello, James. Have you come to help?'

'I have,' replied James with a nod.

Adam looked at Mandy. 'Would you like an extra pair

of hands? There's some paperwork I need to do today, but I could spare a couple of hours.'

'I think we can manage,' Mandy replied. 'If I can get a phone signal up there, I'll call you if we need help.'

Adam reached out and hugged her. 'We'll look after Paul,' he whispered in her ear. Straightening up, he patted James's shoulder. 'Have fun! Don't let Mandy work you too hard!'

'Why change the habit of a lifetime?' joked James as he followed Mandy to her car.

Up at Lamb's Wood Cottage, everything seemed calm. There was a new bale of hay standing in the yard, but no sign of a tractor. Bert must have finished the morning feed and gone away again, Mandy thought.

James gave a low whistle when he saw the overgrown garden and tumbledown yard. 'I can't believe anything was living there,' he said, climbing out of the SUV and walking into the farmyard.

Together they made their way to the sheep pen. Three of the sheep were standing, Mandy was pleased to see, but as they got closer, she could see no movement from the fourth.

'She's dead,' James said, climbing over the fence and bending to check more closely. The old sheep was cold and stiff.

Mandy clambered over to join him. 'I'm not surprised,' she said, crouching down beside James. She showed him inside the ewe's broken mouth. 'I could see she was in a bad way,' she admitted, 'but I wanted to give her a chance. That one there,' she pointed to the Swaledale, which yesterday had also been unable to stand, 'looked almost as bad. Dad seems to have worked one of his miracles.'

The ewe was standing beside the other sheep, staring at James with huge yellow eyes.

'Let's get this dead one out before we check the others,' Mandy said.

The old sheep's body seemed light as they lifted it between them, and Mandy felt tears prick her eyes at the thought of the animal starving slowly to death, unable to eat.

'We can bury her over there.' She nodded to an earthy patch of ground at the edge of the yard. They carried the sad bundle between them and left her underneath three silver birch trees. James bent down and stroked the ewe's ragged fleece once more.

As Mandy collected her stethoscope and thermometer from the car, they heard another vehicle approaching. It was Jimmy Marsh's Jeep. They stood and watched as the car drew up and Jimmy got out and came towards them.

'James, this is Jimmy Marsh,' Mandy said. 'He's opening an Outward Bound centre up at Welford Hall. Jimmy, this is James, the best friend anyone could have.' If Jimmy thought this was an odd introduction, he showed no sign. To Mandy's relief, he also seemed at ease, despite their discussion the day before.

James was looking at Jimmy with a puzzled expression.

'Don't I know you from somewhere?' He frowned, his head on one side.

'I'm sometimes over in York,' Jimmy replied. 'I've been in your café a few times for tea.'

James's eyes widened. 'So you have.'

'Good tea, best in Yorkshire!' Jimmy declared, and James looked pleased. 'I can't stay long,' Jimmy continued. 'I'll be back this afternoon to check over yesterday's repairs and see if there's anything else that needs doing. But Graham said he needs the crush back as soon as possible. Will you be using it this morning?'

'We'll need to check over the cows I treated yesterday,' Mandy replied. 'We'll get that done first.'

'I'll give you a hand.'

The new cattle shed could not have been more different from the distressing barn where the animals had been yesterday, Mandy thought as the three of them looked over Jimmy's hastily constructed fence. Instead of sinking into dung, the cows were standing on clean straw. Their legs had dried out and they looked calm, chewing cud, moving around and sniffing at the hay in the manger.

Working together, James and Jimmy set up the crush in a corner of the byre. It would be much easier to catch the cows if they didn't have to take them outside the pen.

'There are three we definitely need to look at,' said Mandy. 'That one there,' she pointed at the Hereford, 'had badly overgrown feet. Dad trimmed them, but there's a bandage on her left hind which we'll need to change. That one,' she nodded at one of the Angus cattle, 'she had mastitis . . . an infection in her udder,' she explained when she saw Jimmy raise his eyebrows. 'We'll need to milk out that teat as best we can and she'll need antibiotics. And that one,' she pointed to the wild Galloway, '. . . that one I stitched up yesterday.' She could see the sutures from a distance. The wound looked good, she thought, but if she could get a closer view, it would be much better. 'Other than that,' Mandy said, 'I thought it would be useful to take blood samples to check for mineral deficiencies, but it'd be better to do that tomorrow. Otherwise the samples will just sit overnight until the post office is open.'

Although the cows were not as anxious as they had been yesterday, it still took plenty of chasing to get them into the race. Mandy had plenty of experience driving cows but Jimmy and James were less expert. Several times they stood panting and laughing as the beasts crashed past them in the opposite direction.

'They can tell I'm a novice, can't they?' Jimmy bent over to catch his breath.

'They sure can.' Mandy couldn't help laughing. 'One more try!' she said. Jimmy straightened up as Mandy moved behind the cows and sent them on another circuit.

'Well, that's okay then,' James said, forty minutes later as they let the last of the cows out of the crate. The stitched wound looked clean, the foot under the bandage was less swollen than yesterday and the udder, after several minutes of milking, was soft and pain free. 'You're some vet,' he said.

'You're some friend.' Mandy patted him on the shoulder with a smile. 'And thanks very much for your help,' she said to Jimmy.

'I've enjoyed it.' He looked from Mandy to James and back again. 'I'd better get on though. Graham will be wondering where I've got to.' Between them, they manoeuvred the crate out of the cattle pen, rigged it for transportation and attached it to the tow-bar of the Jeep. Mandy hoped it would stay put along the rutted track.

Once Jimmy had ground his way over the scarred mud, the crush bouncing behind his Jeep, James looked at Mandy. 'He seems nice,' he commented.

'He did so much yesterday,' Mandy admitted. 'I didn't take to him the first time we met, but yesterday he surprised me. He pulled people in to help, I wouldn't even have considered.'

'Really?' James was looking at her, an amused look on his face. 'I thought you weren't afraid to ask anyone, if there was an animal's wellbeing at stake.'

'Would you have asked Sam Western for help?' Mandy raised her eyebrows and gave an exaggerated shrug.

James looked amazed. 'Did Jimmy do that?'

'Not only did he ask, he succeeded. It was Sam who sent the straw.'

James whistled, then grinned. 'Sounds like a good man to have around. I'll give him his tea for free, next time he comes to the café.'

Mandy smiled, then got back to business. 'Let's assess the other sheep,' she said, 'and then we can look at the horse. The farrier is coming this afternoon to the Shire. His hooves are shocking.'

She was pleased to find the ewe's temperature was normal. According to her dad, it had been sky high yesterday. 'Her lungs are clear,' Mandy announced as she slung her stethoscope back round her neck. 'We'll give her another shot of antibiotic and see how she looks tomorrow, but I think she's going to make it.'

The Shire horse was looking much more comfortable in his deep bed of straw. Mandy got James to lead him around. She laughed when the old gelding gave a hearty lick to the back of James's head, causing him to yell.

'Urgh!' he said, stepping away from the horse's head and glaring. The gelding just reached out and nuzzled in James's pocket, looking for something to eat.

'I'm sorry,' James said to him. 'I should have brought you a carrot.' The horse rested his huge head against James's shoulder as if in agreement. James stretched up and rubbed beneath his forelock. 'You're a sweetheart, aren't you?'

'I'm going to give him more pain relief,' Mandy decided. 'Hopefully once the farrier has been, he'll be better, but he still looks a bit sore.' She fetched the injection from the car and James steadied the mighty head as she pressed her thumb into the jugular furrow and raised the vein.

'That's it,' she said a moment later. 'I think he likes you,' she added as the gelding rubbed his head on James yet again, knocking him two feet to the left.

'Either that, or he has a very itchy ear,' replied James, but he was smiling.

'Dad suggested I should have a look in his mouth,' Mandy said. Holding a torch between her teeth, standing close beside the Shire and facing in the same direction as him, she put one hand over the Shire's nose and with the other, pushed her hand into the side of his mouth. Taking hold of his tongue, she turned it so it was pointing upwards and her fist was upright, holding his mouth open. Then she grabbed the torch and shone it onto the large molars at the back of his mouth.

'Aren't you worried about getting bitten?' James asked.

Mandy shook her head. 'Not really,' she said. 'There's a gap here.' She showed James the space between the incisors at the front and the molars further back. 'So long as my hand is in that opening and I have his tongue, he won't bite me.' She let go of the tongue and pulled her hand out, wiping it on her jeans as the horse moved his head to snuffle in her ear. 'His teeth look fine,' she said. 'As worn as I'd expect for a horse his age, but nothing that needs treatment.' With a last rub of his neck, they left the horse standing with his nose in the hayrack.

'We'd better go and bury the poor old ewe,' Mandy sighed, and they trudged out of the yard to the birch copse.

'A nice place to be buried,' James commented, looking around.

Mandy couldn't help thinking of Paul. She wondered if James was doing the same. Holding out the spade, she pushed the fork hard at the ground and, when the tip was embedded, put her foot in place to drive it further. She felt as if she was forcing away her gloomy thoughts. They were both hot and sweaty by the time the hole was deep enough to ensure that foxes wouldn't come and dig the sheep back up. A few minutes later, they had lowered the body into the ground and filled in the hole. Despite the sadness of the task, it felt like they had done the best they could.

'We should go back to Animal Ark,' Mandy said, looking at her watch. 'Mum will be making lunch.' They carried the tools over to her car and put them in the boot. 'I have to be back here by two for the farrier,' Mandy said. She waited to see if James would say that he would come with her, but he didn't reply.

Back at Animal Ark, the garden was deserted. Kicking off their wellies, James and Mandy washed their hands at the kitchen sink. Mandy wondered why Emily wasn't there preparing food, but when they went through to the sitting room, the reason was clear. In the space of the morning, Paul seemed to have deteriorated. Mandy was shocked by the shadows under his eyes and the way his breathing seemed to have quickened. Something in her mum's glance told her that Emily was worried too. Leaving James alone with Paul for a second, Emily and Mandy went through to the kitchen.

'Is everything okay?' Mandy whispered.

'I don't think so.' Her mother's green eyes were distressed. 'He seems so tired and breathless. I brought him indoors so he could have a more comfortable seat, but it didn't seem to make a difference.'

'Did he say anything about how he's feeling?' Mandy asked.

Emily shook her head. 'He didn't. And I didn't like to ask.' She closed her eyes for a moment, then opened them again. 'Poor Paul, poor James,' she said.

The door opened, and James came in supporting Paul on his arm. 'I think we're going to call it a day,' he said. 'Thanks for this morning, Mandy.'

'No, thank you,' she said. She walked over and hugged him, then turned to hug Paul as well. It was frightening to feel his skeletal body under the warm clothes he was wearing. 'I'll come over and see you both as soon as I get a chance.'

'Even if you don't get a chance, we'll come and see you.' Paul seemed to have rallied slightly. His face didn't look quite so deathly white. 'I hear you liked the name Hope Meadows.' His face seemed all teeth as he grinned. 'Maurice sent his regards,' he said. 'He enjoyed his visit. And I,' he paused then continued, '. . .want to help some more, so I'm going to start doing some research into your application for charitable status.' Mandy stared at him. 'Don't look so worried,' he said. 'I can do it all from the comfort of my chair. The Internet is a wonderful source of information, and failing that, there's the telephone.'

Mandy hugged him again. 'You're too good to me,' she said. 'I'll see you again soon, I promise.'

'We'll be back over before you know it,' James said.

He sounded as if this was the most ordinary goodbye in the world, and suddenly Mandy wanted to howl. James gave his head a tiny, fierce shake and Mandy pulled herself together.

'Drive safely,' she said.

Once they had driven off, Mandy made some sandwiches. Adam was out on a call and her mum seemed tired again. No wonder, Mandy thought. She'd had the easiest morning by far, working at Lamb's Wood with James. She made the sandwiches carefully, filling them with egg and cress, which she knew Emily liked. She carried them through on a tray and they ate in the sitting room.

'I'm going to have to head back to Lamb's Wood,' Mandy said as the hands of the clock on the mantelpiece approached quarter to. 'The farrier's coming for the Shire at two.'

Emily looked up at her. 'Thanks for lunch,' she said. 'That was lovely. Will you be okay going up there on your own?'

'I'll be fine, Mum. Other than trimming the horse's feet, I don't think there's much else to do until the evening feed.'

'That's good.'

Mandy looked at her mum. There was something she had been wondering about throughout lunchtime. She glanced at the clock again. She had a few minutes before she needed to leave. 'Mum, is it okay if I ask you something?'

Emily nodded. 'Of course.'

'How do you think James manages to stay so . . . so normal?' Mandy burst out. 'How is he facing up to things so well?'

Emily smoothed the seat cushion beside her, brushing the velvet nap in the same direction. 'I'm not sure he has faced up to what's happening yet,' she said. 'I get the feeling he's trying to ignore it in the hope everything will miraculously be all right.' Her eyes were steady. 'Paul was very unwell today,' she said, 'but I didn't get the impression James could see the difference. It can be hard when you're with someone every day. You don't always notice the changes.'

'Oh.' Mandy felt something heavy inside her chest. 'Did Paul seem really bad to you?'

'I'm afraid so,' Emily said. There were tears in her eyes. 'I just hope, for James's sake, that I'm wrong. At least he has you.'

Mandy was very still for a moment, then drawing in a deep breath, she stood up straight. 'I'd better get on,' she said. 'Thanks, Mum.' She leaned down and hugged Emily, then headed out of the cottage and drove back up to Lamb's Wood.

To her surprise, Seb had just arrived and was opening the back doors of his van.

'Hi, Seb,' Mandy said. 'I wasn't expecting to see you today.'

Seb looked over his shoulder. 'Hello,' he called. Reaching into the van, he pulled out a metal cage. 'I was thinking about the chickens,' he said. 'And just in case there were any other cats running around, I thought I'd set up a few of these.' He showed Mandy the cage, which had an opening with a door that could be fastened out of the way, but would close automatically when triggered by an animal entering. 'I think they should work for either,' he said.

Mandy was impressed. She remembered he had mentioned chickens yesterday, but she hadn't seen any sign of them yet. 'That's great,' she said. 'I should be able to come up here quite often to check the cages.'

'I'll be up every day too,' Seb said. 'We should keep in touch, co-ordinate our efforts.' A Land Rover drew up. 'That'll be the farrier,' Seb guessed. 'Will you deal with him while I get these sorted out?'

'Of course.' Mandy walked across to welcome the new arrival.

'Mandy Hope?' A short, stocky man jumped out of the Land Rover and pulled on a tweed cap. He held out his hand and Mandy shook it. 'I'm Mathew Morris. I understand you've got a Shire with overgrown feet,' he said. 'Sounds like a big job!'

Mandy grinned. 'It certainly is,' she said.

The Shire stood patiently while Mandy put on a headcollar and tied him to a metal ring. She watched as Mathew trimmed away the overgrown horn, cradling the massive hoof in the lap of his leather apron.

'I'd just like to see how he moves before I finish,' he said after about fifty minutes. He watched as Mandy led the old boy across the yard and back again, first at a walk and then at a slow, slightly ragged trot. In combination with the pain relief, the farrier's work seemed to have eased the horse's lameness considerably.

'I'll just take a bit more off the back to balance him,' said Mathew, pulling his trimming knife out of the pocket in his apron.

Once he was satisfied, he packed his equipment back into the Land Rover. As soon as he had pulled away down the track, another car drew up.

It was Helen. Seb arrived back from setting his cages as she was getting out of her car. Mandy watched his face carefully. Sure enough, his eyes lit up as soon as he saw the nurse.

'Hi, Mandy. Hi, Seb,' Helen said. 'Is there anything I can help with?'

'I'm almost finished,' Seb answered. 'I've had a look around all the sheds and I'm going to have a walk round the cottage to check for any sign of cats.' He paused long enough for Mandy to wonder if he was hoping Helen would offer to go with him. When she said nothing, he turned and strode off in the direction of the front door.

'How about you?' Helen asked Mandy.

'I think I'm nearly done as well.'

Helen sidled closer to her and murmured, 'Actually I was hoping to find Jimmy Marsh here.' She looked so hopeful that Mandy laughed.

'Ever the optimist!' She shook her head. 'He was here earlier, but I'm not sure when he's coming back.' As she spoke, another car appeared. 'Actually, scrub that,' she said. 'Here he is!'

She laughed as Helen started pushing her fingers through her hair and rubbing her cheeks to put colour in them.

'Hello.' Jimmy marched towards them and stopped in front of Mandy. 'I told you I'd come back to check the repairs were holding up.'

'So far as I could see, everything looks solid,' Mandy said. Seb reappeared, wading through the long grass at the side of the cottage. 'I think Seb's had a closer look,' she added as the welfare officer came towards them. 'Jimmy was wondering about the barn repairs,' she told him.

'Everything looks sound,' Seb said.

'We still need to get the animals moved elsewhere. They can't stay here with no one on site to feed them.' Mandy looked from Seb to Jimmy and back again.

'I'm doing my best to find somewhere.' Seb's expression was apologetic.

Mandy turned to Jimmy. 'What about Jared Boone?' she said. 'Do you think there's any chance he'd let us use one of the fields at Upper Welford?'

Jimmy scratched his ear. 'There's an empty paddock I'm going to be using for the Outward Bound centre,' he said. 'If you need some space, I could probably wait a month or so.' As he said it, Mandy caught sight of

Helen's face. She was gazing at Jimmy, her eyes sparkling and her cheeks flushed. Mandy raised a hand to her mouth to hide the smile that threatened to give away her thoughts.

'That would be great,' she said after a moment. 'We should be able to move the livestock tomorrow or the day after.'

'Are we all finished then?' Helen asked, stepping forwards. 'Maybe we could retire to the Fox and Goose.' She turned to Jimmy. 'What do you think?'

But Jimmy shook his head. 'I have to pick up the children. This week is the start of their summer holiday.' Mandy looked at him in surprise, but Jimmy turned and walked back to his Jeep without saying anything else.

'I didn't know he had children,' Mandy said as the Jeep disappeared down the track.

'Oh yes,' said Helen. 'Eight-year-old twins, Abigail and Max.' The nurse's eyes were bright. 'They live with his ex-wife in Manningford,' she went on, '. . . and she's married to Dan Jones, who's a police sergeant in Walton.'

'Wow!' Mandy stared at her. 'Have you been Facebook-stalking Jimmy?' She realised she had hit the nail on the head when Helen's face flushed scarlet. For a moment, there was silence, and then Seb spoke.

'I'd like to go to the pub,' he offered. 'We could all go for a drink.'

'Oh, okay.' Helen sounded startled. 'You'll come too, won't you, Mandy?'

Mandy was about to agree when her phone vibrated in her pocket. Pulling it out, she read the text in an instant. Her knees started to shake.

'It's from James,' she said. 'Paul's in hospital.'

Chapter Nineteen

For the second time in as many days, Mandy found herself concentrating on the speedometer. James hadn't explicitly asked her to come, but he had told her which hospital Paul had been taken into. Arriving at the site, she realised she didn't know where in the hospital she should look. She tried to call James, but his phone was switched off. Abandoning her car in the car park nearest to accident and emergency, Mandy jogged up the ramp and through the big sliding doors. Catching her breath, she approached the receptionist's desk.

'I hope you can help me,' she said. 'I received a message that my friend Paul Franco,' she spelled it out, 'has been admitted. I don't know if he's here or somewhere else in the hospital.' She stood there, tension knitting her shoulders together as the woman consulted her computer.

'Do you know his date of birth?'

Mandy shook her head. 'I'm sorry, no.' The receptionist sighed so loudly that Mandy felt the urge to reach through the open window and shake her. The surname Franco was hardly common. Clenching her fingers into fists, she forced herself to wait as the woman slouched in her seat, regarding the screen with apathetic eyes. Finally, she looked up.

'He's in the oncology unit.'

Mandy waited a moment for instructions, but when none were forthcoming, she turned on her heel, ran back out of A&E and round to the main entrance. There she found a sign for oncology and took the stairs two at a time to the fourth floor, knowing she'd be quicker than waiting for the lift. She burst through the double doors to the ward and walked briskly along the corridor, searching for her friends. She stopped beside a single room with PAUL FRANCO written on the whiteboard outside.

Paul lay in the bed, his face almost as white as the sheets. His eyes looked huge and he was strung up to monitors, intravenous fluids, blood and oxygen, but he still smiled when Mandy entered. James was sitting beside the bed holding Paul's hand. When he looked around, Mandy was shocked. He seemed to have aged ten years in the course of an afternoon. Walking over to the bed, she sat down, placing one hand on James's arm and the other reaching out to Paul, who took her fingers in his and gave them a squeeze.

'How is everything?' she asked. She wanted to ask what tests they had done, what they planned to do, but it didn't seem appropriate.

'I'm fine,' Paul wheezed. 'They're looking after me well. Waiting for an ultrasound.' Despite the oxygen, his breathing was rapid and Mandy could feel in his wrist that his heart was beating fast.

A nurse came in and spoke to Paul. 'We're going to take you up for your ultrasound now.' They watched while she made everything ready for moving then, as she wheeled his bed towards the door, Paul looked back at Mandy.

'Why don't you take James for a cup of coffee and something to eat?' he suggested. 'He hasn't had anything since breakfast.'

'How about it?' Mandy prompted once the bed had rolled out of sight. 'Do you think you could eat anything?'

James managed a wan smile. 'I could try,' he said, but once down in the cafeteria, he only chose a small flap-jack and pushed it around the plate before shoving it away. 'I can't,' he muttered. 'I want to go back up to the ward to wait.'

Leaving the cake and coffee on the table, he walked off so quickly that Mandy struggled to keep up. James sat back down in the chair beside the empty space where Paul's bed had been. Reaching out, he lifted something from the bedside unit. It was Paul's watch. As James turned the familiar object over in his hands, a tear suddenly dropped onto his lap and then a second.

Mandy crouched down and put a hand on his arm and James turned to her, burying his face in her shoulder. His whole body was shaking and she held him tight until the spasm passed and he pulled away. There was a box of tissues on the table and Mandy reached over, lifted it, and held them out, before taking one herself.

'I'm sorry,' James said, swallowing hard. Mandy gripped his hand tightly. 'I've been so happy these last weeks.' His voice was a whisper. 'I don't want it to end. Not now. Not so soon.' And then, sounding strangled, 'I don't know if I can do this.'

Mandy clenched her teeth together so hard it hurt. Several moments passed before she could speak. 'You can do this.' It was a fight just to say the words, but she forced herself to go on. 'Whatever you have to do to get through this, you will. There's no right or wrong way. Paul trusts you and so do I.'

James was still shivering. Mandy could feel the tension in his hands, but the raggedness of his breathing began to subside. She handed him another wad of tissues and he dried his eyes while she rubbed away her own tears. His hand was still in hers when the door opened and Paul's bed slid through, pushed by a serious-faced porter. James managed a smile and reached out his other hand to hold Paul's. All three of them watched as the nurse bustled in and reset the equipment, reattaching the wires, checking everything.

'They didn't find anything new,' Paul reported when the nurse and the porter had gone. James lifted Paul's fingers to his mouth and kissed them.

Placing a hand on her friend's shoulder, Mandy stood up. 'I need to let my parents know where I am,' she said. 'I'll come back in a minute.' She jogged down the stairs and walked outside, taking deep breaths of clear, cool air.

'Hello, Mandy.' Adam picked up on the first ring. His voice sounded so normal, so disconnected from what Mandy was experiencing, that it felt like a shock.

'I'm in York,' she told him.

'Oh yes?' He sounded interested. 'What are you doing there?'

There were tiny stones on the asphalt car park. Mandy could feel their roughness through the soles of her shoes. 'Paul's been taken into hospital,' she said. 'James is with him. I came to help.'

She heard her dad sigh. 'I'm sorry to hear that. Your mum said he didn't look well this morning.'

'Can I stay here tonight?' Mandy checked. 'Is everything under control? I'll get in touch with Seb about the animals at Robbie Grimshaw's if you can carry on with the small animals.'

'Of course. Stay as long as you need to. Your mum and I will take care of everything back here.'

Mandy felt a lump rise in her throat again. 'Thanks, Dad.'

'Look after James . . . and yourself,' he added. On the other end of the line, Mandy heard the telephone receiver go down. It had rained while she had been with James and Paul, and she found comfort in the dusky smell of the summer shower. The evening air was soft on her cheeks. With a last glance at the ranks of cars under the streetlights, Mandy made her way back inside.

Paul's eyes were closed by the time she got back. He looked so frail against the pillow amongst the banks of monitors. Mandy walked over and touched James's arm and he turned to her and stood up.

'They've given him sedatives,' he said. 'They told me he would sleep now. That I should go and get some rest.' His voice was oddly calm, fuelled by exhaustion. Mandy took his hand, intertwining her fingers in his, and led him downstairs.

'Where are you parked?' she asked.

'I came in the ambulance. I don't have the car with me.'

She helped him into her RAV4 and turned the heater up as they drove back through the quiet streets. A few minutes later, they drew up in front of the apartment James and Paul shared. When they went inside, Lily and Seamus rushed to greet them and, for a moment, everything seemed normal. James crouched down to hug them both and then stood up, taking off his jacket and hanging it on the hooks beside the door. Removing his shoes, he placed them on the rack.

'I'm going to have a shower,' he said.

Mandy understood. The scent of antiseptic had hung heavy in the heat of the car and she could feel it clinging to her hair and clothes. James returned several minutes later in his pyjamas, hair slicked back. His glasses were halfway down his nose and he pushed them up. He looked so young and vulnerable. Swallowing hard, Mandy smiled.

'Come on,' she said. 'Let's get you into bed.' She tucked him up, pulling the covers over him and sitting down on the edge. Lily and Seamus jumped onto the bed beside her. Seamus very gently licked James's hand.

'Try to get some sleep,' Mandy said. Stupid impossible advice, but he seemed comforted.

'Thanks for being here,' he murmured. She gripped his hand one last time and then stood up and made her way to the spare room. The bed was unmade so Mandy found some bedclothes in the hall cupboard. Showering, she cleaned her teeth and then fell between the crisp sheets. The dim light of the orange streetlamps cast a gentle glow on the ceiling. Closing her eyes, she allowed her mind to drift.

By the time she awoke, morning light infused the room. Climbing out of bed, she was greeted by the dogs. Mandy squatted down, enjoying the feel of the two lithe bodies pushing against her, tails wagging: the beating signal of friendship.

The bed in James's room was empty and there was a message on the kitchen table.

'Gone back to the hospital. Help yourself to breakfast.'

In typical James fashion, he had taken the time to set out breakfast things: cereals, bread for toasting, butter and marmalade. Despite the heaviness in her chest, Mandy forced herself to eat. Lily was lying under the table on her feet and, when she had finished, Seamus stood up and licked her hand. Bending down, she rubbed the soft fur beside his ear. Two pairs of bright eyes gazed up at her. She stood up, an outrageous idea scalding her brain. Calling the two dogs, she put on their halters, led them out onto the patch of ground outside the flat so they could relieve themselves, and then scooped them into the car.

Outside the hospital, Mandy's heart quailed for a moment, but she marched on, not giving herself time to think. The corridor outside Paul's room was empty and she strode the length of it accompanied by the distinctive click-click of paws on linoleum, hoping against hope that nobody would come. They reached the door of Paul's room. Peering through the glass partition, she could see Paul in the bed, James beside him on the chair. They were alone. Grabbing the door handle, Mandy pushed open the door and let the dogs go, and in an instant they were on the bed, frantic tails aloft, licking and squirming in delight.

The look on Paul's face made it worth the risk. Despite the strict hygiene rules, Mandy doubted the dogs, which until yesterday had been in constant contact with Paul, would present any additional hazard to his health. He looked at her, a grin splitting his face.

'Mandy, you are going to get me into so much trouble, but . . .' He paused and shook his head. 'Thank you. Thank you so much.' He buried his face in Lily's neck and then reached out to hug Seamus. He looked so animated that Mandy's heart was lifted. James, too, was smiling and he hugged her quickly before turning back to ruffle Lily's ears.

There was the sound of footsteps and the door opening.

'What do you think you are doing?' thundered a voice, and Mandy had to stop herself from laughing at the outrage in the woman's eyes.

'Mandy.' She looked round at Paul, who had spoken. 'This is my consultant, Mrs Puranam.' He too seemed close to laughing. 'Mrs Puranam, this is my friend Mandy.' Despite her diminutive stature, Mrs Puranam seemed determined to make her presence felt.

'Was it you who brought in these . . .' She paused a moment, and Mandy wondered what hyperbolic word would come forth, '. . . dogs . . . onto my ward?' The consultant spat the word dog as if it was an insult. 'Do you not understand the importance of hygiene?'

For a second, Mandy toyed with the idea of setting out her credentials, but with a glance at Paul, decided against it.

'I'm very sorry,' she said, trying to sound contrite. 'I'll take them out immediately. Lily, Seamus!' she called, and the two dogs bounded down from the bed. The memory of Blackie, James's badly behaved childhood Labrador, sprang into Mandy's head. Thank goodness James and Paul had trained these two so well.

Walking back down the stairs with the dogs at her heels, Mandy decided this had been thoroughly worth Mrs Puranam's wrath. She hadn't seen Paul look so . . . joyous . . . for weeks.

She took the dogs for a walk before taking them back

to the flat. The way they trotted at her heels, looking up at her, tugged at Mandy's heart. How lovely it would be to have a pet of her own. She had never been allowed to adopt any of her rescues when she was younger, and since going to university, she had moved around so often that it hadn't been possible.

Back in the flat, she wondered what else she could do to help. Everything was neat and tidy, and anyway, housework had never been her forte. Settling the dogs down, she made her way back outside and walked the few doors along to James's café. She had been there often enough to know that James's staff would welcome her help.

It was a charmingly bohemian place, filled with shelves of books for sale, tables set into little booths and original artwork on the walls, supplied by friends of James and Paul.

Sherrie, James's assistant manager, greeted her. 'Hi, Mandy,' she said. 'It's good to see you. Have you been to the hospital? Is there any news?'

'No change since last night,' Mandy reported. James had texted her after she'd left with the dogs. 'They're doing more blood tests later today,' she added. She went behind the counter, and was soon embroiled in making tea and serving brunch toasties to the eclectic clientele.

When the door swung open, she was quite unprepared to see Jimmy Marsh crossing the room. Lifting her chin from the floor, she managed a smile. He looked equally astonished to see her.

'What are you doing here?' she asked.

'I'm in York to collect some climbing equipment,' he said. 'This place serves the best Yorkshire tea. What about you? Have you suddenly given up being a vet?' His eyes were laughing, but when she explained about Paul, his expression sobered. He pressed his lips together, his green eyes serious.

'I'm sorry to hear that,' he said. He thought for a minute. 'I know there's not much I can do, but if you like, I can look after the animals at Mr Grimshaw's until you get back. Let me know, and I'll take care of them for as long as you need.' His mouth lifted at one side and his head tilted as he studied Mandy's face.

She had the sudden urge to cling to him. Instead she shook her head. 'Thanks, but I'm pretty sure I'll come back to Welford today,' she said. 'The clinic is always hectic on a Monday.'

'No problem,' said Jimmy. 'But the offer stands. Call me if you need me.' He gave her his mobile number and she sent him hers. She watched as he took his tea and sat down at a table with the York Minster magazine. For a moment Mandy was tempted to join him with a mug of coffee but then a family came in, the children clearly giddy to be on holiday from school, and Mandy was distracted by their order for milkshakes, brownies and freshly made flapjack.

Twenty minutes later, as Jimmy waved his goodbye and left, Mandy felt empty. She checked her phone, but there were no messages. She should probably contact

Simon. Not that he had called her, she thought. Could he still be annoyed about the other night? She was surprised how untroubled she felt. Their row seemed insignificant in light of Paul's illness. She texted him anyway to say that Paul was ill, hoping he would phone, but there was only a text in return, saying he was at a course all day. Letting out a breath she hadn't realised she was holding, Mandy turned to Sherrie.

'I think I'll go back to the flat,' she said. She would try to give James another call. Not that he would probably be able to answer, but he would call her back as soon as he got the chance. As she donned her jacket, she heard the door opening again and, to her surprise, James walked in. His face lit up when he saw her.

'I thought I might find you here when you weren't in the flat,' he said.

'I was just going to head up there and give you a call. Is there any news?' By the expression on James's face, things must be looking up, she thought.

Her friend smiled. 'The blood infusion made a huge difference,' he said, 'and they've started him on some new injections. They're going to continue monitoring him closely today, but he's not in immediate danger.' He held out his arms and hugged Mandy close. 'I'm so grateful for your help,' he said.

Mandy shook her head. 'I didn't do anything,' she insisted. 'Nothing you wouldn't do for me in a heartbeat.' She paused. 'I'm so glad about Paul,' she said. 'He never gives up fighting, does he?'

James shook his head. 'He doesn't.' He smiled again, searching Mandy's face. 'Do you need to go? I could tell last night that you were worried about being away from Animal Ark.'

Mandy grinned. James could read her so well. 'As long as Paul is okay, I should probably go back,' she admitted. 'I don't think Dad wants to run Hope Meadows without me. Robbie Grimshaw's animals have started everything a bit faster than we planned!'

They shared one last hug and she said goodbye to Sherrie before walking outside.

James saw her into the car. 'Drive safely,' he said.

Mandy arrived back at Animal Ark to find the list full and Rachel looking frazzled behind the desk. Both Emily and Adam had been called out to emergencies. The waiting-room was heaving. Rachel greeted her with open arms.

'Thank goodness you're here!' she gasped. 'I've told everyone your mum is expected shortly, but they'll be relieved to see you.'

Even though Emily returned half an hour later to help with the surgery, it was nine o'clock before Mandy ushered the last patient out. She was standing in the kitchen making tea for her mum, who looked as drained as Mandy felt, when she remembered she was still supposed to check on the livestock at Lamb's Wood. She closed her eyes for a moment. She was so tired. There was nothing she wanted more than to curl up in an armchair and chat to her mum for half an hour before falling into bed.

Jimmy's words from earlier swam in Mandy's head. She had been telling herself she wouldn't trouble him; it was too much to ask. But when she looked at her mother's exhausted face, she couldn't face going back out. Feeling slightly nervous, she pulled out her phone.

'I'm just going to make a call,' she told her mum. Walking outside, hands shaking – she hated asking people for favours – she pushed the buttons on the screen and held the mobile to her ear. The phone rang a long time and the temptation to call it off was strong. But it wasn't like her childhood, when you could call people untraceably. If she put the phone down, Jimmy would know she had tried to call. Her face felt hot when the ringing stopped on the other end and his calm voice came down the phone.

'Mandy,' he said. 'What can I do for you?'

She took a deep breath. 'I know it's late,' she said in a rush, 'but would you be able to check the livestock at Lamb's Wood? We've been snowed under this evening and . . .'

'Of course I can.' It was there again. That feeling of being anchored to something solid. 'I'll head up right now. I need to take the dogs out anyway.'

Mandy closed her eyes and let her head tip backwards against the wall. 'Thank you,' she said. 'I'm truly grateful.'

'You sound tired,' he said. 'Will you be able to get some rest now?'

Normally, like Emily, Mandy disliked it when anyone drew attention to anything that could be regarded as weakness, but Jimmy sounded so sympathetic it was hard to feel anything but grateful.

'I'll try,' she said.

'That's good. And don't worry about the animals. I'll make sure they're okay,' he promised.

Mandy stood for a moment, breathing in the sweet night air, before walking back inside.

Chapter Twenty

Mandy stared helplessly at the computer screen. Helen had shown her how to update the Animal Ark website, but this was the first time she had set up a new page. She needed to concentrate but her mind had never felt less able to focus.

Mandy had called James a few minutes ago. Paul had continued to stabilise, but despite the better news, it was impossible to put him out of her mind.

Hope Meadows. Even typing the name at the top of the page felt like a big step. What else did she need? What was most important? Details of the animals available for rehoming? That was obvious. But there had to be something more. Information about what they did. What they were aiming to do.

She could write about the rescue operation at Lamb's Wood, she thought. If she could list those who had given assistance, perhaps it would encourage others to do the same. Hastily she typed a brief report, leaving out names for now. She ought to check whether the people involved wanted to be identified. At the last minute, she deleted all references to Lamb's Wood. There was no way she wanted people hunting down Robbie Grimshaw. Her mother had spoken to one of the police officers yesterday and learned that Robbie was being treated in hospital for malnutrition and dementia. There was no way he would be returning to his beloved smallholding, sadly.

Finally, Mandy listed the animals that were available for rehoming. There seemed to be a lot of cats and kittens. She looked at the page she had created. Although all the data was there, it seemed too impersonal. Photographs, she thought. They would bring the whole thing to life. When she went back to the farm later, she would take some pictures. It was important people knew it was not only small animal work they would undertake. For now, she took her phone through to the kennels.

Despite their blatant cuteness, it took about fifteen attempts to take a decent picture of the kittens. Most of the time, they looked like an amorphous lump of fluff, when Mandy needed to show each individual. She didn't think people would want to rehome kittens by the kilo.

When she added the images to the page, she knew it had been worth the effort to separate the protesting kits. Who wouldn't want to look at something so adorable every day? She should link it through Facebook, she thought. Twitter too.

Momal had been responsible for the page at Thurston's. What was it she had said? Something about Facebook trying to increase the number of videos posted. Videos were better for promotion than still photos. Walking back through to the wildlife unit, Mandy looked at the kittens.

Those belonging to the black cat were too young. Their eyes and ears were not yet open, and they didn't move around much. The others were a few weeks older, ready to start being handled. Mandy scooped up the two little cats and carried them through to the cottage. Later, she could video them in different situations as she worked with them, but for now she settled on filming them investigating the kitchen.

Once the kittens had been returned to their mum and the videos uploaded, Mandy gave the page one last check. She and James had rehomed so many animals over the years but this seemed far more serious. Would it be possible to find places for so many kittens? People's lives were different now: busier, tighter for spare cash, more frantic. Mandy told herself that she had to believe it was possible. With a decisive sweep of the mouse, she moved the arrow on the screen to publish the page, then attached it to the Animal Ark Facebook page.

What next, she wondered. Emily had given her the details of the company who had produced the Animal Ark website. Hope Meadows would need an official site of its own, not just a page on the original site. Mandy drafted an e-mail to the web designer. She would need to discuss the layout and content with them. That reminded her about the building plans. Paul's architect was coming back next week to draw up an official proposal. She shot off another e-mail to him regarding the timing of his visit. Until now, her plans had seemed like castles in the air. Now they were taking shape so fast, it was almost too much, and Mandy's head was starting to spin.

Standing up, she stretched. The clock on the mantelpiece told her it was four thirty. Walking through, she found Emily in the kitchen.

'Would it be okay for me to go out to Lamb's Wood Cottage?' she asked. If she went now, she thought, she might get some good shots of the animals while the sun was still high in the sky. She could check on them and give them their evening rations.

'Of course. Dad and I will cover evening surgery. It's your night for an early finish. Yesterday evening was so busy.' Emily regarded her fondly. 'You should have something to eat before you go. Your dad and I were about to have a sandwich.'

Another hour later, Mandy drew up at the farm. As she had hoped, the evening light was glossily golden, slanting in at the open-fronted shed where the cows were housed. She filled the mangers in the cow and sheep pens with hay, and stuffed a net for the Shire. His flanks were rounding out already, Mandy noticed, and his coat was looking smoother. Helen had found some old brushes in the shed where the ferrets had once been kept. Mandy knew the nurse had been coming up before work to groom the old fellow. The first day, she had told Mandy, the yard had been blowing with hair and birds kept swooping down to take it for their nests.

Moving his hay net outside onto a hook, Mandy led the enormous horse outside. Helen had been calling him

Bill. It suited him, Mandy thought. Picking up his feet, she cleaned them first. The farrier's work seemed to be holding up well. Next, she began to groom. The huge animal seemed to enjoy the attention. He leaned into the brushes as Mandy rubbed his coat, first in circles with the rubber curry, then following the direction of the hair with a dandy brush to remove the dirt she had loosened. Mandy felt herself relaxing into the rhythm. The past few days had left tension in her shoulders and she could feel her muscles smoothing out with the gentle exercise.

By the time she finished, Bill looked very smart. His dappled grey coat gleamed, and his mane was brushed neatly on one side of his neck. Even the feathers on each leg were looking whiter. He showed no sign of lameness as Mandy put him back in the sun-filled barn. It struck her that she should have taken before and after photographs to show how far the animals had come. Had Seb taken any, she wondered, back on that first day? She made a mental note to text him about it.

Mandy let herself bask in a moment of pride as she took photographs of Bill, then the cows and sheep. They were all doing well, and several of them were unrecognisable from the state they'd been in on Saturday. The wound she had stitched was healing, the mastitis was gone. Tomorrow they were due to move the livestock to Upper Welford Hall. Mandy would be able to examine them more thoroughly once they were there and the crush was available again.

Remembering Seb's cat and chicken traps, Mandy took a wander around the overgrown property to check the cages, but they were empty. The garden was peaceful, the air only faintly stirred by buzzing bees and the trill of birdsong. When she returned to the yard, the cows were chewing their cud and the sheep were lying down. Bill stood in the evening warmth, resting a hind leg with his eyes half closed. His ear twitched forwards when he heard Mandy, but she stayed at a distance, not wanting to disturb the tranquil scene. With a bubble of happiness welling in her chest, she headed back down the track and returned to Animal Ark.

If she had expected evening surgery to be finished, she was disappointed. Rachel's face was flushed as she stood behind the desk fielding telephone enquiries and payments.

'This is the second night in a row it's been like this,' she muttered to Mandy.

'Where's Dad?' Mandy asked as Emily rushed into the waiting-room and called through the next client. Her voice, to Mandy's ears, sounded weary.

'He's in theatre,' Rachel replied. 'That old setter of Mrs Peterson's came in with a gastric torsion. He and Helen have been in there for hours.'

Mandy felt a stab of guilt. She should have been here helping. Instead, she had been out with Robbie Grimshaw's animals, ambling around in the sunshine.

Mentally rolling up her sleeves, she checked the computer screen. There wasn't much left to do, but she could at least take Emily's last client. Rushing into the second consulting room, she switched on the computer and called the history up on the screen. Ear problems mostly, from what she could see. Not difficult, but time consuming if they needed cleaning out. Opening the door to the waiting-room, she leaned her head through. There was only one person waiting: a grey-haired woman in a mustard sweater and terracotta-coloured trousers. 'Mrs Fleetwood?' she called.

She was met by a pair of widened eyes and a flustered smile. 'I'm really sorry.' Mrs Fleetwood looked down at the rough-coated terrier at her side. 'But I'd rather wait for Mrs Hope. I hope you don't mind. It's just that Lucky here is used to seeing her . . .' The voice trailed off. Mandy could feel her face becoming hot. How long would it take before people started to accept her? When she had been a child, there had been none of these problems. People had been ready to accept her help alongside her parents. She had gone away and come back qualified and, suddenly, only Mum or Dad would do.

Miserably, she walked through into the wildlife unit. Even if nobody else wanted her, there were still her rescued animals to tend. For half an hour, she played with the older kittens. Before they could be rehomed, she wanted them to be fully socialised. Later, she would introduce them to different animals, people and children, but for now, she worked with them on her own, shifting them into different positions, getting them used to being handled. Substituting tuna for medicines, she practised holding their heads as if giving them tablets, until they saw having a titbit thrust into their mouth as a fun game. Finally, she had a go at getting them used to a halter and lead. It wasn't usual to walk cats like dogs, but it could be useful if you needed to exercise a cat in difficult circumstances. Predictably, the kittens didn't love the idea, and squatted down mutinously when Mandy put pressure on the lead. But she knew it would take time, and she had plenty of that for these precious little creatures.

She had finished with the kittens and was thinking about what she was going to do with Shy when Simon clicked into her head. She hadn't updated him on Paul's progress, she realised. Or on the new plans for Hope Meadows and the rescues. Pulling her phone from her pocket, she dialled his number. The phone rang for so long she thought he wasn't going to reply, but there was a click at the other end followed by Simon's voice, rather impatient.

'Hello?'

He must know it was her, she thought. Her name would have shown up on the screen. 'It's me, Mandy,' she said.

'Mandy!' He managed to sound surprised nonetheless. There were voices in the background.

A sound like grinding or drilling and then Samantha's voice quite clearly. 'Can you hold this?' she said.

'Simon, I,' Mandy began, but he interrupted her.

'Mandy, it's really not a good time right now. Is it anything vital?' They must be in the dental unit, she realised. 'I'll call you back some other time, okay?' The phone went silent. Why had he bothered to answer, she wondered?

Sighing, she turned her attention to Shy. Despite working with the collie over the past few days, Mandy wasn't seeing the progress she had hoped for. By the end of each session, the dog seemed more relaxed, but every time Mandy went away and came back to start again, Shy was as nervous as ever.

Keeping her body position unthreatening, Mandy started to talk. 'What are we going to do with you?' she murmured through the kennel door. 'Mum made some enquiries about Robbie earlier,' she went on. 'He's going to be moved to a residential home soon. They aren't going to press charges.' As ever, when she spoke to the dog, Mandy was encouraged by a forward twitch of the ears before they returned to their fearful position.

'Shy?' Mandy made her voice as welcoming as possible. There it was again. The ear twitch, but the body still cowering, the face wary. 'It's all very well,' she told the collie, 'but just because you're called Shy doesn't mean you have to live up to your name.' Putting her hand into her pocket, she pulled out a chew before opening the kennel door. Holding her body sideways, she held out the treat, but Shy didn't respond. Only when she dropped it onto the floor of the kennel did the little animal creep forwards and take it.

'Shy,' Mandy mused. 'Do you think we could make it something less prophetic? We could change it to something positive. What do you think?' The bright eyes were watching her now. 'Sky?' Mandy called the name in the same voice. The ears twitched forwards and, with them, the collie moved an inch towards Mandy, towards the source of the food and warmth. Mandy dropped another treat on the floor and the dog moved closer, watching and waiting.

Mandy smiled. 'Sky it is, then,' she said.

By the end of the session, the collie had moved out of the cage. She could sit on command and she would allow Mandy to stroke her ear if distracted with food. Yet there was still not enough trust for Mandy to move to the next stage. Before she could try going outside, Sky and she would have to build a strong enough bond of trust that the collie would turn to Mandy if she began to panic. She had to return reliably if she managed to escape.

Mandy sat with the collie for a long time. 'One day, beautiful girl,' she whispered. 'One day.'

Chapter Twenty-One

'Okay, that's the lot.' Bert Burnley lifted the ramp of the trailer before returning to lean on the gate beside Mandy. 'They're looking a lot better than the day I came to drop off the hay.' The cows had cantered into the field at Upper Welford Hall, kicking their heels in the air like calves. 'It's like watching the herd the first time they get outside in spring,' he added.

Mandy was amazed by their energy. The sheep, too, had rushed into their new field and were cropping the grass as if they had never tasted anything so wonderful. Even Bill had trotted from the trailer, whinnying with the joys of summer. 'Thanks so much for bringing them, Bert.' She turned to Sam Western who was standing on her other side. 'And thanks for letting us use your land.'

Mr Western nodded. 'No problem,' he said briskly. 'So long as you understand it's temporary. I want the Outward Bound centre up and running by December as planned. Jimmy Marsh is in the outhouse there. You should let him know what you intend.' Pushing himself away from the gate, he nodded. 'Good day to you both,' he said and stumped off.

Bert straightened up and pulled his cap tighter on his bristling hair. 'I need to get on,' he announced.

Left alone, Mandy stood beside the field for a few minutes longer. She should do what Mr Western had said and talk to Jimmy Marsh. Not that she had firm plans for a more permanent home for Robbie's livestock, but she should make it clear she knew they couldn't stay here forever.

It was dim in the barn after the brightness outside. To her surprise, Jimmy was not alone. There were two children with him: a girl with long brown hair, and a boy, taller but with shorter hair. Their green eyes were so similar to Jimmy's, there was little doubt who they were.

'Hello,' Mandy said.

Jimmy put down the saw he had been wielding and looked up. 'Mandy! How are you?' he said. 'And how's your friend in York?' The last time she had seen him had been in James's café.

'Paul's stable for now,' she said.

The children, who had been helping Jimmy with his woodwork, had laid down their tools and were looking at her. Mandy felt a bit uncomfortable under their steady gaze.

Jimmy half turned. 'These are my children,' he said. 'This is Abi,' he indicated the girl, 'and Max.' The twins smiled: two younger versions of their father. 'Max and Abi, this is Mandy Hope, one of the vets from Animal Ark in Welford.'

As ever, when faced with children, Mandy felt out of her depth. As the adult, she ought to say something, but she never knew what. How could she guess what would interest them? 'Are you enjoying your holiday?' she said eventually.

'Yes,' said Abi, and Max nodded.

'Are you helping your dad?'

Again the nod and the one-word response. Giving up, Mandy turned back to Jimmy. 'I just wanted to say the animals are safely here,' she said. 'Mr Western said I should remind you that I'm looking for somewhere more permanent. I appreciate you finding the space for them. I hope they won't be in your way.'

Jimmy gave her the look of quiet amusement that he seemed to reserve for whenever she talked too much. 'They won't be in the way,' he assured her. 'Most of the work I'm doing is in here or out in the woods. If you need help, just let me know.' That slow, gentle voice. Nothing ever seemed to be a problem.

But when Mandy looked round, two pairs of intense green eyes were gazing at her and she felt unsettled again. 'I'll have to go now,' she said. 'Lots to do!' That much at least was true. She had invited Susan Collins to bring Jack to Animal Ark. She wanted to get the kittens used to all kinds of different people, especially children. For a second, she contemplated asking Jimmy and the twins, but she wasn't sure she could cope with that double intense gaze for long. 'Thanks, Jimmy,' she said. 'And goodbye, you two.'

'Bye.' He walked her to the door and Mandy felt his eyes follow her as she retreated to her car.

Back at Animal Ark, Susan's eyes sparkled as she watched Jack play with the kittens. Mandy had carried the two young cats into the garden wearing their halters, along with a bag of their favourite toys. If she had been worried Jack wouldn't be gentle enough, her concern had been unnecessary. Susan was a wonderful mum, she thought. She had shown her son how to play with the tufty fish-on-a-string toy. He seemed to find it hilarious each time a kitten pounced. He roared with laughter as first the tortoiseshell, and then the white and ginger kitten, grabbed the fish in its mouth and tried to run away. The kittens seemed unfazed by the child and the gurgling laughter. When not playing, they sat wide-eyed, gazing with tilted heads at the outside world, exploring the daisies on the lawn.

'Hello?' Footsteps sounded around the corner of the house and a dark-eyed woman in a teal blue hijab appeared.

Wiping her hands on her jeans, Mandy stood up. 'Hello,' she said. 'Can I help?'

The woman's face creased into a smile when she spotted the kittens. 'I think perhaps you can,' she replied. 'Hi, I'm Roo Dhanjal.' She held out her hand. Mandy reached out her own. 'I've been looking at your website about the rescued animals. I wondered if it would be possible to adopt one of the kittens,' Roo explained. She held her hand out to Susan as well. 'I see they are outside enjoying the lovely weather,' she went on. 'They looked irresistible in the photo, but the picture didn't do them justice! May I join you?' She looked at Mandy, who nodded.

'Of course you can,' she replied. 'I'm Mandy Hope, and this is Susan Collins and her son Jack. We've been working on socialising the kittens.'

'How wonderful.' Roo knelt on the floor and grinned at Jack, who was smiling right back. Much more natural with children than I am, Mandy thought. The kittens also seemed interested in the newcomer, scampering across and climbing onto her lap. 'I have two children,' Roo said. 'It would be great to get a kitten that is used to toddlers. Obviously, we'd supervise them closely until they know how to handle their new pet.'

Mandy watched as Roo lifted the kittens one by one, stroking and talking to them. It was obvious she was used to having cats.

'What would we have to do to qualify?' Roo asked. 'We would be happy to make a donation, of course . . . or is there a rehoming fee?'

A rehoming fee was a good idea. 'A donation would be very welcome,' Mandy said, kicking herself for not thinking of this before.

Roo continued to watch the kittens. 'Would it be possible to take both? It seems a shame to separate the two. Obviously, we'd get them vaccinated when it's time.'

Better and better, thought Mandy. 'It would be lovely if they could stay together. But before any of our pets are rehomed, I need to carry out an inspection of where they will be living,' she explained. 'Would it be okay for me to come and have a look round your home?'

'You'd be very welcome.' Roo was smiling again. 'We run the Moor View Campsite. You know where it is?'

'Is that the one on the road out towards Kimbleton?'

'That's the one. We have a restaurant, too, offering traditional Indian and Pakistani food. Maybe you could try some?'

'That sounds lovely.' Mandy missed her local curry house in Leeds. 'The kittens are almost weaned, but after that, it's important they are socialised while they are still with their mother. They won't be ready to leave for a few weeks yet. It's probably best if I call you nearer the time, if that's okay?'

'Of course it is.' Roo stood up. 'I'll have to be going. Josh, my husband, will be wondering where I've got to.'

'I think we'll need to go as well.' Susan pulled herself upright. 'Come on, Jack.' She lifted the little boy. 'One last wave,' she said. 'We'll come and see them another day.'

'Goog-bye kitties.' Jack leaned his head over Susan's shoulder, watching until they rounded the corner of the cottage. Mandy carried the young cats back inside and put them with their mother. Sitting outside Sky's kennel, she watched as they settled down for a nap. They were tired after their play. Mandy couldn't resist a mental high-five over Roo's visit. If the inspection went well, the first of the rescued animals would be rehomed!

Taking out her mobile, she did an internet search for stables with Bill on her mind. Six Oaks, in between Welford and Walton, had been run by Mrs Forsyth years ago, but now it had a new owner: Molly Future. Finding the number, Mandy dialled and put the mobile to her ear. The phone was answered by a woman with a cheerful voice. 'Six Oaks Stables. Molly Future speaking.'

'Hello, Molly.' Mandy's throat felt dry, but she was committed. 'My name is Amanda Hope and I work at Animal Ark, the vet clinic in Welford. I don't know if you've heard, but we've recently rescued some neglected animals. One of them was a Shire, quite an old boy. I was wondering whether you might be able to help?'

'I had indeed heard.' To Mandy's pleasure, Molly sounded enthusiastic. 'It's not often you hear of something like that here in Welford.' If only she knew, thought Mandy, remembering all the animals she had rescued over the years. 'Anyway, I would love to get involved,' the voice went on. 'What were you thinking of? If you were looking for a new home for your Shire, we could probably find space for him.'

Mandy's heart soared. She had been expecting to beg for temporary space, and Molly had offered without prompting. 'Where is he now? Does he have a name?'

'He's called Bill,' Mandy said, 'and for the moment, he's at Upper Welford Hall. Do you know it?'

'Yes of course, off the Walton Road. I'm afraid I'm

away for a day or two, but perhaps I could visit at the weekend. I'm sure we can find somewhere for him, but it would be good to get an idea of his size and requirements. Is he healthy, do you think?'

'He was very lame,' Mandy said, 'but we had the farrier out to him and he's much better. Other than that, he's eating and drinking well. There's no sign of any illness, just the usual signs of old age.'

'Excellent. In that case, I'll let you know nearer the time and I'll come and take a look. Thanks for thinking of me.'

Mandy put the phone away, feeling breathless. Another probable rehoming in one afternoon. She could do with a cup of tea to celebrate. Standing up, she left the rescue unit and walked back to the kitchen.

Emily was sitting at the table, her drawing pad in front of her and pencils scattered around. She looked up when Mandy came in.

'What are you drawing, Mum?' It was ages since her mum had done any art.

With an unexpectedly shy glance, Emily turned the paper to show Mandy. She had sketched the most gorgeous outline of one of the outhouses behind Animal Ark, complete with the silhouette of a heavy horse, a cow, a sheep, a dog and a cat. The name 'Hope Meadows' curved underneath.

'Oh, Mum. It's beautiful!' The words burst from

Mandy and she rounded the table and hugged Emily. Stepping back, she looked again at the picture. The dog even looked like a collie. It was the most perfect image.

Emily looked delighted. 'I'm so glad you like it.'

'Of course I do! Anyone would.'

Emily watched as Mandy filled the kettle. 'I've been in contact with the Charities Commission about setting up Hope Meadows. There will need to be a separate bank account, and you'll need to choose some trustees. There is documentation that needs to be in place, but they gave me details of where it can be done online. It doesn't seem too complicated.'

'You've been so busy. Thank you so much.' How lucky she was. Mandy got out two mugs and made them each a cup of tea.

'It was fun.' Mandy could see pride in her mum's smile. If she had hoped to rekindle the closeness of her childhood by coming back to Animal Ark, she needed no further proof. Mum had always been there for her, and she was still. 'It gave me the chance to sit down for the afternoon.'

A tiny nudge of concern entered Mandy's head and, for a moment, she wanted to ask whether there was anything wrong. She had wondered about her mother so often lately. Was she paler than usual? It was so subtle. Emily's fair colouring meant any time she was under the weather, she looked wan. Even a busy night without much sleep would do it. But when Mandy studied her mum again, Emily was sipping the tea she had made and was looking so happy that Mandy couldn't bear to bring it up.

'Everything seems to be happening so quickly,' she said. It was going to be all right, she thought. When Simon saw how things were progressing, he wouldn't be able to resist admitting that everything was unfolding perfectly.

'I'm just happy we're working together.' Emily stood up and took some biscuits down from a shelf, picked one and offered the rest to Mandy. 'It's lovely to have a family project,' she said. 'I know it's your baby, but I'm so glad I can help.' Mandy knew she meant every word.

Evening surgery was quiet.

'Mrs Gill's the last,' said Helen. 'She wanted to see you about Muffy's ears. She was very impressed with the way you managed last time.' This was the first time a client had asked for her since coming back to Welford, and it gave Mandy a small but definite thrill.

She took her time, waiting until Muffy was calm before leading her through to the consulting room, showing the little dog the auroscope, getting her used to having her ears touched before going ahead with the examination. The little terrier walked out of the clinic, tail high, pulling her owner behind her. Anyone would think coming to the vet had been the highlight of Muffy's day.

Mandy leaned over the reception desk and gave Helen a high-five. 'We rock!' she declared.

Helen beamed. 'If things are going this well, you should buy a lottery ticket!'

'I might just do that,' said Mandy.

'I think I'm going to go to the Fox and Goose,' Helen said. 'Do you fancy a drink?'

Why not, thought Mandy. It would be a good end to the day.

The air outside was cool on Mandy's skin as they strolled together down the lane, but the bar was packed. A wave of noise burst out when Helen pulled open the door. For a moment, Mandy thought about backing out, but then they were inside and fighting their way to the bar.

'What would you like?' Helen shouted above the din.

Mandy thought for a moment. She needed something cool. 'A glass of white wine,' she said. Turning round, she leaned on the wall at the end of the bar. Jimmy Marsh was standing by the fireplace on the far side of the room. A young woman stood beside him, her eyes fixed on his. She looked dainty next to his sturdy build, and her short red hair framed a pretty, heart-shaped face. Mandy felt an unexpected lurch of disquiet. 'Who's that with Jimmy Marsh?' she asked Helen.

A wave of interest crossed the nurse's face as she turned to look. 'That's Molly Future,' she said.

Mandy was surprised. From their conversation about rehoming Bill, she had expected someone older.

Helen was talking again. 'Molly and Jimmy dated

eighteen months ago, when Molly first moved to Welford,' she said, 'but I thought they'd split up.' Mandy waited for her to say something negative, but Helen was unexpectedly serene. 'Seb said he might be in later,' she added. Mandy sent a sharp look at Helen's face, but the nurse just lifted her glass and smiled.

They managed to find a seat and, for several minutes, Mandy sipped her drink without saying much. She tried to concentrate on what Helen was saying, but her eyes kept wandering back to Molly. Her haircut was sharp, her make-up perfect.

She couldn't help feeling relieved at the distraction when her phone rang. She pulled it from her pocket. It was James.

Leaning over, she shouted in Helen's ear, 'I just have to take this!' She pointed to the screen. 'James,' she mouthed. By the time she had made it to the door, the phone had stopped ringing, but she dialled James's number and called him back.

'James! How's it going?'

It was so long before James replied that Mandy wondered if he had been cut off. When his voice came, it sounded remote.

'Paul's dead.'

There was silence again. Mandy felt as if the street had tilted and she was clinging to the wall to stop herself falling.

'Shit, James.' She wanted to take back the words, but they were gone already. 'When?' Her voice was high.

'A few minutes ago.' How calm he sounded. 'He'd

been improving. He was so much better this morning. I just wasn't expecting it.'

Mandy found her way along the wall to the low windowsill. She needed to sit down. 'Is there anything I can do? I can come over.' Through the glass, she could still hear the inappropriate din.

'Don't come just now,' James said. 'There's nothing you can do.'

Mandy could feel her heart pulsing. Across the road, the village green had never looked more peaceful.

'I need to go now.' His voice came as if from a great distance.

'Thanks for letting me know.'

'No problem.'

The beep, beep, beep told her the call had ended. The asphalt of the pavement seemed far away, as if Mandy was seeing it through a tunnel. The hand holding the phone was shaking. Gritting her teeth, Mandy had to remind herself to breathe. She wanted to do something. Help somehow. She wanted to go to her friend, but he had said no. Hardly knowing what she was doing, she called up Simon's number. With a trembling finger, Mandy pressed the dialling button.

'This is Simon Webster's phone. Leave a message after the tone . . .'

Mandy ended the call. No way could she leave a message. The hand holding the phone dropped onto her knee. To her left, she heard the door of the bar open, then close again, and then Helen was looking down at her.

'Has something bad happened?' she asked.

Mandy took a deep breath. 'Paul's died.' She wanted to say more, but couldn't find her voice.

Helen reached out and put an arm round her. 'Poor James,' she said. 'Are you going to York?'

'He doesn't want me.' Mandy dug her fingernails into the palms of her hands.

'I'm sure that's not true,' said Helen. Her hand gripped Mandy's shoulder for a moment. 'Come back in,' she urged. 'I'll buy you another drink.'

'I can't.' Mandy found it hard to get the words out.

Paul was dead. Mandy's eyes were dry. Shouldn't there be tears?

A car drew up and Seb Conway climbed out.

'I think I'll go home,' Mandy said to Helen. She couldn't face telling anyone else just now. Seb looked surprised as she brushed past him, but she couldn't be bothered to explain. The lane that led towards Animal Ark seemed to undulate under her feet.

A few moments later, she paused at the cottage door. Mum and Dad would be there. She would have to tell them and then they would be sympathetic. She couldn't face it. Not yet. Instead, she turned and went into the wildlife unit. Without switching on the big overhead lights, she entered the kennel room. Opening the door to Sky's kennel, she leaned on the wall opposite. Her legs started to shake and Mandy slid down until she was sitting on the floor. Tears stung her eyes for the first time. Why wouldn't James let her help?

There was a scuffling noise and something cold touched her ear. It was Sky. Lifting her head, Mandy was amazed to see the little collie looking at her from barely a hand span away. With a whine, Sky stretched out her head and licked Mandy's face. Without thinking, Mandy lifted her arm and Sky moved closer, pressing her warm furry body against Mandy's cold side. Burying her face in Sky's soft coat, she let herself sob. She remembered the last time James had called and she had rushed to York to be with him. He had loved Paul so much. Why did it have to end so soon?

The phone in her pocket rang and she pulled it out. For a moment, she wondered if it was James. Maybe it had been a mistake. Paul was not gone. The thought was there and she banished it: ridiculous. The best she could hope for was that he would ask for help.

But it was Simon. 'Hello, you!' He sounded cheerful and Mandy faltered. Despite the noise of the mobile, Sky was still close against her. The wet nose nudged her ear again; the warm tongue flicked out, licking away a salty tear.

'Hi, Simon.' Speaking was difficult, but she had to tell him quickly. 'James called. Paul's died.'

There was a pause. Random voices filled Mandy's ear. 'Sorry, Mands, what was that?'

'Paul's dead.'

There was an even longer pause, clattering in the background.

Then Simon's voice again, quite different this time.

'I'm so sorry to hear that. Do you want . . .' There was a crackling noise and Mandy couldn't hear the end of his sentence.

'What was that, Simon?' Shouting in the background now, and a loud thump as if the phone had been dropped. Mandy waited to see if he would speak again, but there was only the crackle of static. 'Oh, never mind,' she said. Her voice was shaking too much; she couldn't do this right now. She pushed the button on the screen to end the call. There was silence in the dim kennel room. Tears were running down her face.

Sky lifted a paw onto her arm; a cold nose nudged her ear. The liquid brown eyes gazing into hers were filled with trust. Comforted beyond words, Mandy wrapped her arms around Sky's lithe body and for the first time, the little collie didn't pull away.

Chapter Twenty-Two

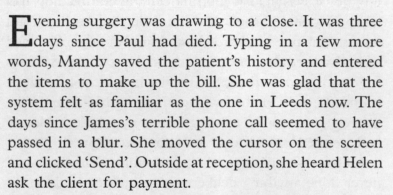

Evening surgery was drawing to a close. It was three days since Paul had died. Typing in a few more words, Mandy saved the patient's history and entered the items to make up the bill. She was glad that the system felt as familiar as the one in Leeds now. The days since James's terrible phone call seemed to have passed in a blur. She moved the cursor on the screen and clicked 'Send'. Outside at reception, she heard Helen ask the client for payment.

Several minutes later, Helen stuck her head around the door. 'That's me for tonight.' Her voice hovered between compassion and brightness. Since the night Paul had died, neither of them had referred directly to it. Despite the awkwardness, Mandy preferred it that way. Silence was better than sympathy. Even attempts to discuss the situation with Simon on the phone ended with tears and awkward snuffling pauses. She had asked him to come to the funeral, but he couldn't make it.

Now that Helen had left, the clinic seemed hollow. Usually there were signs of life, even late in the evening: an in-patient barking, the hum of the fan that changed the air in the cat kennels. But the only residents were Mandy's rescues in the wildlife unit. Neither the cats, nor Sky, made any noise at all.

Sky. Despite her pain, or perhaps because of it, Mandy felt closer than ever to the collie. She never flinched now when Mandy approached. She never objected when Mandy hugged her. Tears were licked away by a gentle tongue. Yesterday, for the first time, when Mandy had taken Sky into the garden, the little dog had not lain down, had not hidden behind Mandy's legs. She had trotted at her side, concentrating on the training exercises they had been working on. Even when a car had swept round the side of the cottage, there had been only the briefest panic in the trusting brown eyes before Mandy had stepped in with distraction and comfort.

Mandy was convinced that Robbie Grimshaw had never done anything deliberately to hurt or frighten his dog. Sky's problems came from lack of socialisation, from being shut up with a man who was scared of his own demons and lacked the strength to care for all his animals. Mandy wished she could tell Robbie that Sky was all right, that all his animals were safe and cared for now, apart from the poor old ewe with bad teeth. Perhaps she would visit him once he was settled in the residential home. If he could even recall the animals he had once loved so much . . .

Dragging her gaze from the computer screen, Mandy found herself dazzled. The sun was sinking, sending a golden shaft of light through the window. Turning back, she logged off and stood up. It was time, she thought: time to take Sky out for her first proper walk. She could walk to heel, she could be distracted from potentially scary things. Mandy would keep her on the lead. More than anything else, she wanted the little dog's company.

Walking through, she grabbed a lead from the back of the wildlife unit door. When she opened the kennel, Sky no longer cowered at the back. Instead she ran forward, round Mandy's legs and sat at her side, gazing upwards.

'How lovely to see you too.' Mandy reached down with a treat, then scratched the soft fur on the side of the collie's face. Sky leaned into her hand, eyes half closed with enjoyment.

'You're a precious, precious girl,' Mandy whispered to her. Clicking on the harness, she led Sky outside.

Up on the moor, the heather was beginning to bloom. The pale pink ling merged with the darker bell heather, creating a glorious mist of purple that would intensify into a thick carpet within days. Reaching the edge of a rise, Mandy sat down. Far below in the valley, the sound of the church bells rang out. Grandad Hope no longer rang the bells himself, but Mandy had been pleased when he told her he had organised a quarter peal in honour of Paul this evening.

The bells would toll again tomorrow for his funeral. It was to be held in Welford church. James had told

Mandy that Paul had wanted to be buried there, in the village where they had married. Had wanted to be in the place James would always call his home.

Remembering the wedding only weeks before, Mandy found her face wet with tears. There were moments when Paul's death still seemed unreal. Now and then, she was convinced it had all been a bad dream: that James and his husband would walk through the door of Animal Ark, bringing a gift of food or wine, demanding a picnic. Then the realisation would overwhelm her again.

How was James managing? It was hard enough to face the loss of a friend. For James it must seem impossible. There was fear, too. The only deaths Mandy had known so far had been of people much older. Now she looked around those she loved and found herself wondering how many more times she would see these faces.

As she had so often in the last days, Mandy clung to Sky. Burying her face in the collie's fur, she found comfort in the muscular body. Despite having left the farm weeks ago, Sky still seemed to smell of sweet hay. As if trying to give comfort, she nuzzled the back of Mandy's neck, leaning her head into the curve of her shoulder.

In the distance, the church bells ended, the calm notes lingering in the evening air. Mandy felt Sky's body stiffen and a low growl sounded in her ear. Lifting her head, she scrubbed at the tears on her cheeks. A wave of embarrassment ran through her when she spotted Jimmy walking along the path with Simba and Zoe at his heels. Her face must be a picture.

Mandy scrambled up to let them pass, but instead of carrying on, Jimmy stopped. 'Hello . . .' he began. Catching sight of her ravaged eyes, he looked away, gazing into the distance. 'Would you like me to leave you alone?' he said quietly.

Mandy almost felt like laughing. 'You're the first person this week who hasn't asked if I was okay, or what was wrong.' Her voice sounded thick and muffled, but Jimmy smiled his friendly smile and looked down at Sky. To Mandy's relief, the collie had stopped growling and was wagging her tail, sniffing at Simba and Zoe with ears forward, face relaxed.

'Nice dog,' Jimmy said. He sounded as though he meant it. Instead of bending to greet Sky, he watched with interest as the dogs moved alongside one another, nose to tail investigation. Mandy had the feeling he didn't want to interfere with their interaction.

'We're going to the top of Sowerby Fell,' he said. 'Would you like to come?'

Mandy let out a breath. 'I'd love to. If I cry any more,' she said, 'Welford will be flooded. Anyway, I promised Sky we'd walk right to the top of the fell.'

'Sky? That's a nice name. Is she the dog you rescued from Robbie Grimshaw's?'

They started out along the path at an easy pace. Simba and Zoe trotted ahead, their tails aloft, but for now, Mandy kept Sky on the lead.

'She is.' Sky glanced up as Mandy spoke, then went back to her exploration of the scents around the path. A bumble-bee emerged from the heather and for a moment she pulled on the lead, returning when she felt pressure on her halter.

'You must be good with animals. I heard she was in a terrible state. Probably terrified, poor little thing.'

Was this the same man she had scorned for his ignorance of animals when she had met him for the first time? Mandy cast a fleeting look at Jimmy's face, but he was tramping forwards, gazing out over the moor.

'There's a merlin!' His finger pointed to a distant speck in the sky, then he shot her an embarrassed grin. 'Sorry for the sudden change of subject,' he said. 'I'm a bit of a hawk nut. Merlins are one of the UK's threatened species. There are only just over a thousand breeding pairs, probably forty on the North Yorkshire Moors. I get over-excited when I see one.'

Mandy watched as the bird came closer overhead. It was a male, his white breast contrasting with his brown speckled underbelly, the long square-cut tail shifting as he navigated the wind.

'I love the way their feet tuck in so neatly underneath them,' Jimmy murmured, as if he didn't want to disturb the magnificent bird. 'Except when they strike. They sometimes catch birds almost as big as themselves!' He looked unexpectedly awkward. 'Sorry,' he said. 'You probably know all that already.'

'It's lovely to hear,' Mandy replied. She had a lot to

learn about raptors, having treated only one since qualifying. 'You used to be a park ranger in the Lake District,
is that right?'

'I was.' Despite the speed with which they were striding
up the hillside, Jimmy seemed barely out of breath. 'The
National Park Authority encourages landowners and
farmers to look after the moorland so the wildlife benefits. This area is part of a specially protected area for
merlins.' He stopped walking and, for a moment, his
eyes studied her face. 'I know you don't approve of my
Outward Bound project,' he said, 'but nothing is more
important to me than respecting the local wildlife. The
last thing I want to do is disrupt their habitat.'

Mandy felt a wave of shame run through her. 'I'm
sorry,' she managed. 'I judged you too quickly.' She gave
him a weak grin. 'It's something I've been guilty of since
I was a child, apparently.'

'Really?' Jimmy raised his eyebrows, his voice light
with humour. 'I can't imagine that.'

They were approaching the top of the fell. A hundred
yards ahead, Zoe and Simba were exploring the cairn
that marked the summit. Reaching the crest side by side,
Mandy and Jimmy turned their faces into the breeze.
The valley lay before them, its winding river silver in
the sunlight, Welford clear in the distance. The farms
that made up the practice dotted the hillsides all around,
interlocked by never-ending dry-stone walls.

Mandy breathed in. The scent of the heather was
sweet and the air caressed her face, cooling her still

warm eyes. Together they sat down, their backs to the cairn.

'I guess you've seen this view a thousand times before,' Jimmy commented.

It was true, Mandy thought. Adam and Emily had brought her up here before she could walk, they'd told her. Her dad had carried her in a backpack. And she had been on dozens of farm visits in her car-seat. How lucky she was to have been so loved. To have so many treasured memories of growing up here.

'Has Welford changed much?' Jimmy prompted, his eyes on her face instead of the scenery.

Mandy looked at him for a moment, then her gaze wandered back down the slope to the village. 'There are quite a lot of new houses since I was a child,' she said.

From here, she had a good view of the small modern housing estates that were scattered along the Walton Road. When she was down in the valley, the village seemed the same as ever, yet from this angle it was clear how much it had changed. But the hub of the village remained almost unaltered. The Fox and Goose stood where it always had. The post office. The little school Mandy had first attended when she was only four.

'Some of it is different,' she admitted, 'but it happened so gradually, I hardly noticed.' Her eyes fell on the old grey church. The bells were silent now. 'I was christened in Welford church,' she said. 'Mum and Dad were married there.' She smiled. 'There was such an awful storm that day, Mum ended up wearing wellies under her dress.' There had been other weddings too. Mandy had been a bridesmaid for Hannah Burgess, all those years ago. 'James's family have been here forever as well. His maternal grandparents are buried in the churchyard.'

'It must be comforting, having roots that run so deep.' For the first time since Mandy had met him, there was wistfulness in Jimmy's voice. 'My parents settled in the Lake District when I was twelve, but before that, we moved around a lot. There's nowhere I could really say was home. Except where my children are.' His expression softened. 'They're anchor enough for anyone.'

For a moment, Mandy felt a pang of something she couldn't quite name, and yet why should she feel that way? She had everything she wanted, didn't she?

'Do you have the children often?' she asked.

'Not as often as I would like.' His voice sounded resigned, more than resentful. 'I wanted to have them fifty per cent, but I was living in the Lake District. Belle moved here with the children and it just wasn't practical. I have them every other weekend and much more in the holidays.'

Mandy watched his face as he was speaking. 'Was that why you moved here?' she asked. 'To be closer to them?'

'Yes.' He smiled. 'I still don't see them as often as I would like, but I try to make up for it when we are together.' His eyes passed over the scenery and back to her. 'How about you?' he said. 'What made you come back?'

'Welford is my home,' she answered. 'It always will be.' Simon swam into her thoughts. Her certainty that her future lay here was at odds with what he seemed to want. It wasn't something she could push aside. She was going to have to convince him. It seemed a daunting task. Simon was always so convinced about the decisions he made. It was one of the things Mandy had first admired about him. Sighing, she shoved the thought away.

'I'm so glad I came back to Welford,' she said. 'I've always wanted to open a rescue centre, you see. I'm so fortunate, helping animals as a vet, but I want to look after the ones who have nobody else.'

Jimmy reached out towards Sky. Extending his hand, he allowed her to sniff his fingers before inching them closer to caress the soft fur underneath her ear. 'If this collie is anything to go by,' he said, 'I can't imagine there's anyone better.'

'She is gorgeous, isn't she?' Mandy looked down again into the valley, letting her gaze rest on Animal Ark and the field where the new outbuildings would be. 'We're calling the new rescue centre Hope Meadows,' she said.

'It's a lovely name.'

'It was Paul's idea,' Mandy told him. A fresh wave of grief passed through her. Paul would never get to see Hope Meadows. Her eyes filled up again and the tears overflowed. 'It's his funeral tomorrow.'

Jimmy nodded. 'I know.' He pulled a clean handkerchief from his pocket and gave it to Mandy, allowing her a moment, before he stood up and offered her his hand. 'We should head back,' he said.

His face was sympathetic, but he didn't ask any prying questions. He walked at her side, or close behind, all the way down the long slope. When they reached the lane at the edge of the village, Mandy expected him to take the turning that led to Upper Welford Hall. Instead, his footsteps steady, he walked beside her all the way back to Animal Ark. They passed under the old wooden sign, stopping in front of the cottage.

'Would you like to come in?' she asked, half hoping he would say yes.

'Not tonight.' He shook his head. 'Thank you.' His eyes searched her face. 'Will you be all right?' There was a gruff tone to his words that somehow made it easier to answer.

'I'll be okay.'

His eyes still holding hers, he reached out, put a hand on her waist, and kissed her cheek. It sent a not unwelcome shiver through Mandy. 'Look after yourself,' he said. Stepping back, he nodded and strode back down the driveway.

Mandy swallowed hard. She could still feel the place where his hand had been, the feather-light touch of his lips on her cheek. She wanted to call him back, let him comfort her again. At her heels, Sky whined.

Mandy looked down. 'You're right,' she said. 'We should go inside.'

Once she had got through Paul's funeral, she would

phone Simon. She had to make him see how important Animal Ark and Hope Meadows were to her. He would understand, wouldn't he? They had been together for so long, he must know her well enough by now.

In her pocket, her mobile phone buzzed. It was a message from Simon. How odd that he should contact her, just as she was thinking about him.

'Hope everything goes well tomorrow. I will be thinking of you.'

Mandy's eyes filled with tears again. Wiping them away, she unlocked the door of the unit and took Sky inside.

Chapter Twenty-Three

'I'm so sorry, I'll have to go. It's a calving.' Adam looked apologetic as he squeezed Mandy's hands.

She glanced away, then back with a barely perceptible nod. Her eyes, for the moment, were dry, but she felt physically drained. Emily put her arm round Adam and gave him a kiss, before he departed with a last haunted look.

Overhead the bell began to toll: first the three strokes to denote that a man had died; then the long, slow chime, twenty-nine strokes, one for each year of Paul's life. The churchyard was normally a place of serenity. Now the voices were subdued, the clothes sombre. It had become painfully solemn.

In the lane outside the church, the hearse drew up followed by two gleaming black cars. Paul's mother and father and his two sisters stepped from the second vehicle. The door of the first car remained shut. Through the darkened windows, Mandy could see James's parents talking, her friend's bent head in the centre. When the door finally swung open and James emerged, Mandy swallowed a cry of dismay. He seemed to have lost a stone in the short time since she had last seen him. She wanted to rush to him, hug him, to help somehow.

A warm hand fell on her shoulder and she turned. It was Gran and Grandad Hope.

'Hello, love.' Tom Hope was looking at her with concern.

'Hello.' Dorothy pulled Mandy towards her. For a moment, she melted into her grandmother's arms, comforted as she had been so many times over the years. When she turned back towards the funeral cars, Gran kept her hand in place behind Mandy's back.

The oak coffin had been taken from the hearse and James stood beside it, his hand resting on top. His eyes were dark against his white face. He was surrounded by people – Paul's family and the friends from York who were to carry Paul's coffin – but without Paul by his side, without Lily and Seamus, he seemed so far away: a shadow of the person he had been.

'We should go in.' Emily reached out her hand and gripped Mandy's for a second. 'Or do you want us to wait with you?' Mandy had been asked by James to follow the funeral procession into the church.

Tom Hope frowned. 'Isn't Simon coming?'

'He said he couldn't.'

Her grandfather pursed his lips, but made no further comment. Gran squeezed her arm.

'Grandad will stay with you then, won't you?' She looked up at Tom.

'Of course I will.'

Dorothy linked arms with Emily. Mandy watched them disappear into the church. She was conscious of her grandad standing beside her, stiff and starched in his black suit. She was more grateful for his company than she could say.

The coffin was on its way into the churchyard. If Mandy had hoped for a glance from James, she was disappointed. He stared straight ahead as he passed. His fingers were white as they gripped the brass handle. With Grandad Hope's hand holding her elbow, Mandy made her way into the church.

The walk up the aisle seemed so long. On either side, the pews were packed: so many faces Mandy didn't recognise. From the corner of her eye, she caught sight of Helen and Seb Conway sitting together.

The pallbearers had reached the apse and were setting the coffin down. The people in front of Mandy melted away into the seats that were reserved for family and friends. She found herself guided by Tom Hope into a seat beside Emily and Dorothy. A jolt ran through her. Jimmy Marsh was sitting in the row behind. He nodded at her, his green eyes sending warmth through her chilled body.

'We managed to save you a seat,' whispered Gran. 'There was no room, but the gentleman in the row behind moved for us.'

Mandy blinked. She couldn't help wondering why Jimmy was there. Perhaps he had met Paul in York. But James had barely recognised Jimmy when they had met at Lamb's Wood Cottage. Whatever had brought him, it felt strangely comforting to know he was there.

She sat between her grandparents as the long service unwound. Reverend Hadcroft spoke so kindly and knowledgably about Paul, that it seemed to Mandy she could have no tears left, yet they kept coming. Gran had an endless supply of paper hankies in her handbag.

James talked about Paul as well. His voice sounded so tremulous at first that Mandy thought he would break down, but with his eyes on the coffin, he seemed to steady.

Reverend Hadcroft was speaking again. 'Thank you, James,' he said. Mandy could see that his eyes, too, were bright with tears. 'Thank you for those words about your husband, a man who, during his tragically brief time on this earth, has brightened the lives of all of us here. I believe that you and Paul will meet again one day. And during the days that remain, he will continue to live on in all our hearts.'

Chrissie Hunter had her arms around James's shoulders. She had buried her own parents from this church, thought Mandy. Now she was supporting her son, as best she could, through his loss. Grandad was gripping her hand tightly on one side and Gran reached out and patted her knee. And now the pallbearers had risen and were approaching the coffin again. Three on one side, three on the other, they raised the casket to their shoulders and made their way back down the aisle.

Adam Hope was waiting outside. How like him,

Mandy thought, to come straight back but not disturb the ceremony.

'Everything go okay?' Emily whispered.

'One heifer calf, safely born.' Dad glanced her way, assessing, Mandy guessed, whether it was appropriate to say anything. But she had lived her whole life knowing there were times when her parents had to put their work before almost everything else. It didn't mean that life's events were less important to them than to other people. In fact, it made the times they did have together all the more precious.

'Good.' Mandy couldn't say any more.

They followed the coffin round to the newly dug grave on the west side of the church. The pallbearers lowered it onto the wooden struts that lay across the gaping hole. It seemed hard to believe that Paul's body was inside. That they would never see him again. Across from Mandy, on the far side of the burial site, Seb and Helen were standing together. Something about the protective way Seb was comforting the nurse told Mandy he wasn't just being kind. As she watched, Seb reached out and pulled Helen to him and they kissed, just briefly. Then they were standing side by side again, another two mourners. Mandy sighed. She was pleased for them. Seb was so kind and he was clearly devoted to Helen, just as she deserved.

At the foot of the grave, Mandy spotted Jimmy Marsh. He was looking at James, but for a moment he glanced over and met Mandy's eyes. Once again, she felt a wave of comfort that he was there.

Reverend Hadcroft was speaking, his cassock billowing in the soft breeze. 'We have but a short time to live. Like a flower we blossom and then wither; like a shadow we flee and never stay.'

How bitterly true those words were, thought Mandy. James's face was white. Paul's mother's, too. Like James, she looked a hundred years older. Mandy was gripping so hard onto her father's arm, she was amazed he didn't cry out.

'. . . in sure and certain hope of the resurrection to eternal life, through our Lord Jesus Christ, who will transform our frail bodies, that they may be conformed to his glorious body, who died, was buried, and rose again for us. To him be glory for ever.'

'Amen.' The word whispered through the people around the grave like the autumn wind through leaves.

'It breaks my heart to bury someone so young.' Gran leaned in close to Mandy. 'Poor James. I hope he'll come and see us again soon.'

'I'm sure he will,' Mandy assured her.

There seemed to be a queue of people lining up to speak to James. Helen and Seb went and shook his hand and hugged him. Mandy thought it didn't seem right to rush over yet. There was a distance in James's face, as if he wasn't really there somehow. Jimmy Marsh waited his turn in the line: approached, shook hands and backed away. For a moment, Mandy thought he had left, but then he materialised behind her. She felt his touch on her arm and she turned to find the calm green eyes studying her.

'Sorry I didn't get to speak to you before the service,' he said.

Mandy shook her head. Why should he have done so? 'It was kind of you to come,' she said.

'Oh.' For a moment he looked awkward, and then he said, 'I wanted to show my support. I had nothing but admiration for James the day we met at Robbie Grimshaw's place.'

There was a long silence.

'Will you be coming to the wake?' Mandy realised she wanted him to say yes.

'I'm afraid I can't. I have to take the twins to the dentist. Will you be okay?'

Mandy looked over to where James was still surrounded by people. Adam and Emily had moved away and were waiting with Gran and Grandad.

'I'll be fine,' she said.

Jimmy didn't take his eyes from hers. 'I'll see you again soon,' he said, and reached out to give her hand a squeeze. For an instant, Mandy wondered if he would kiss her goodbye again, but then he turned and walked away.

Twisting her fingers together, Mandy went back to her family, who had almost reached James. Joining them, she shuffled forwards, waiting her turn.

'Mandy.' For a moment, her friend looked at her with the old warmth in his eyes. 'Thanks for coming.' He must have said it a hundred times already, Mandy realised. 'You'll be coming to the Fox and Goose,' he said.

'Of course.' Mandy wanted to reach out and hug him, but there seemed such a distance between them. His movements automatic, he reached out and shook her hand.

'Thanks again,' he said. For what exactly, Mandy wondered. She couldn't remember a time when she had felt so helpless. James had moved on, was shaking hands with Gran and then Grandad, and Adam was explaining he had been called away. Mandy half expected James to ask about the animal her father had been called to, but the blank look was back in place and he merely thanked Adam for returning. A wave of exhaustion washed over her. She left the graveside with her family, and they walked from the church to the Fox and Goose.

She was surprised to find she was hungry. Bev Parsons had laid on all kinds of sandwiches and Mandy helped herself to a thick wedge of bread with cheese and tomato. The atmosphere in the Fox and Goose was less sombre than she had expected. There were so many young people there, so many people with warm and funny memories of Paul, that there were bursts of laughter and smiles dotted around the room.

Mandy found herself talking to an aunt of Paul's who had been at the wedding.

'Where's that nice young man of yours?' the older woman asked, and Mandy's mind spun for a moment, before she realised the aunt was referring to Simon.

'He couldn't come, I'm afraid.' She glanced around. It was getting noisier. Paul's friends from York were standing at the bar. They were drinking pints of the local brew as if they were determined to empty the cellar. Suddenly Mandy couldn't see anyone she knew. The villagers who had come to pay their respects had been and gone. Tom and Dorothy Hope had returned home and Emily had accompanied Adam, who had been called out yet again. Where was James, Mandy wondered? She apologised to the aunt and went to search him out.

She found him in a low seat at the side of the fireplace. His face was ashen, his eyes dry. Mandy held out her hand. 'Come on,' she said. To her relief, James stood up and followed without a word.

She steered him round the edge of the room and they made their escape through the back door. Outside, she stopped. Holding out her arms, she beckoned him to her and held him close, feeling his shoulder blades sharp under the dark suit, sensing the trembling of his body. Mandy held him until the shaking subsided and then she led him along the lanes to Animal Ark.

Together, they made their way round to the wildlife unit and into the room where the rescue animals were.

'I'm so tired.' James's voice sounded weak.

Mandy wondered whether he had eaten anything. 'Are you hungry?' she asked, but he shook his head. Still in his suit, he slid down the wall and sat on the floor. For a moment, Mandy looked at him. Then she opened Sky's kennel and the little collie crept out, timid at first, then seeing James, she made her way to him. She licked his face, nudging his arms until he was holding onto her tightly as she leaned her face against his. James closed his eyes, and when he opened them again, he smiled up at Mandy.

'She's lovely,' he said. 'So different from last time I was here. Are you going to keep her?' For the first time that day, he sounded like himself.

'I don't know,' Mandy replied. 'You know Mum and Dad's rule.' Would it still be the same, she wondered, now she was an adult?

'I hope you can.' Stiffly, James got to his feet. Looking down at his suit, he managed a grin. 'I see she's just as hairy as Seamus and Lily,' he said. 'Anyway,' he looked around, peering into the other kennels, 'there's work to be done.'

Mandy was filling up the water bowls when she heard the door open. James paused, an incongruous figure cleaning out a litter tray in his shirt and tie. Emily and Adam walked in. If they were surprised to see Mandy and James, they didn't show it.

'Might have known we would find you two in here,' Adam said. 'No, don't stop, James, I can see you've got your hands full.'

James had placed the litter tray back into the cage and was in pursuit of two of the kittens, who had escaped and were chasing each other around his legs.

'Mandy, we've got something to show you,' Adam said. 'You too, James, if you're interested.'

Shooing the kittens into the cage with their mother, James stood up and tucked in his shirt-tails. There was colour in his cheeks and his hair was sticking on end. 'Who'd have thought such tiny animals would be so much work?' he panted.

Mandy wanted to hug him. He was so brave, so strong on this grim day. No wonder Paul had loved him. She contented herself with grinning at him as they made their way to the kitchen. Emily put the kettle on as Adam took out some plates. He carved thick slices of Gran Hope's parkin and shared them out before he turned and drew some papers from a folder that was lying on top of the stove.

With a flourish, he laid them in front of Mandy and James. 'We've been working on these with Maurice Frederick,' he announced.

Mandy stared up at her dad. 'The architect?'

'He's drawn up some revised plans for Hope Meadows,' said Emily. 'Your dad and I have been in touch with the council and we made some suggestions that should make it easier for you to get planning permission.'

Mandy stared down at the papers. There it was in black and white: *Hope Meadows*. 'What have you done to the barn?' she said. 'It looks much bigger than before.' She traced her finger over the drawings. In place of the separate wooden structures she and Maurice had planned, a stone and glass construction doubled the size of the barn. Wooden extensions stood on either side, linked to the main building. Mandy turned the page and studied an image of what the completed centre would look like. Old stone was offset by stained wood. Large windows would allow natural light into all corners. The building looked graceful, classic, and functional. She couldn't have asked for anything better.

'We've already spoken to the council,' said Adam. 'As it's only one storey and it counts as an extension of the surgery, there shouldn't be a problem with planning.'

'Maurice designed it so the materials would fit with its location,' added Emily.

Jumping up, Mandy hugged her parents in turn, then sat back down beside James to gaze again at the plans.

'It's beautiful.' James ran one slender finger over the drawings. 'And you're really calling it Hope Meadows?' His voice was husky. Shaking his head, he reached out to Mandy. 'Paul would be so proud,' he said.

'I'll never forget that he named Hope Meadows,' Mandy promised. 'I'll think of Paul every single time an animal in need comes through the door.'

Chapter Twenty-Four

Putting her mug of hot chocolate on the coffee table, Mandy dropped onto the sofa, stretching out her legs. For a moment she closed her eyes, enjoying the silence. It was Friday evening; her clinic duties were over for the weekend. She only had her rescue animals to consider, and with assistance from Graham and Jimmy with the farm animals, the immediate future looked more peaceful than it had done for several weeks.

When the doorbell rang, she sighed. Pushing herself upright, she made her way round to the kitchen door. Outside, a huge bunch of flowers tucked under one arm, stood Simon.

'Surprise!' He swept inside and threw his free arm around her. For a moment, Mandy's body tensed, but as she breathed in the scent of soap and sandalwood, she relaxed.

Loosening his grip, Simon stepped back, and with a half-bow, presented her with the bouquet. As always with Simon, he had spared no expense. Gorgeous scented freesias were blended with white roses and carnations.

'They're beautiful,' said Mandy.

Simon looked pleased. 'There's something else,' he said. 'I haven't booked anything yet, but I've made enquiries and they can fit us in. How would you like a weekend in the Crossley Arms Hotel? Dinner tonight, afternoon tea tomorrow and a horse-drawn carriage ride through York in the evening?'

Mandy felt herself go hot and cold. It sounded wonderful, and perhaps it meant Simon was softening about York, but there was no way she could go off for the weekend. Mum and Dad had done so much in the past weeks. She couldn't ask them to care for all her rescue animals as well.

'What's wrong?' Simon was studying her face. 'Can't you get away?'

Mandy sighed. 'I really can't,' she confessed. 'Not this weekend. I need to stay and do some work with the rescue animals. Some of them have made amazing progress.' She pictured the two oldest kittens, who were now almost fully socialised, could sit and come when called, and would walk on a harness. And Sky, of course, who was becoming far more than a mere rehabilitation project.

Simon's face had fallen. Mandy felt a stab of remorse. There was nothing else she could do, but Simon wasn't ready to give up yet. 'Really?' he said. 'Does it have to be you? Couldn't someone else step in?'

'There isn't anyone else.' For a moment, Mandy toyed with asking Jimmy, but she couldn't ask him to do any more. Simon looked as if he was fighting back anger. Mandy felt caught between guilt and irritation. He had obviously gone to a lot of effort, but if he had asked her first, she could have told him she wouldn't be able to get away. She couldn't help but feel disappointed, too. The Crossley Arms was the hotel they had stayed in the first time they had been away, and they had promised one another they would go back for the carriage ride one day.

She looked again at the huge bouquet. It reminded her of Paul's flowers. There had been so many flowers at the funeral. It was odd, she thought, that Simon hadn't asked about it. Mandy gave herself a mental shake. Paul and James had been her friends. Perhaps it was natural he didn't want to discuss it.

'I need to put these in water.' She went over to the dresser, opened the cupboard and pulled out a vase. Once she had done that, she would make Simon a cup of tea and show him the Hope Meadows plans. Maybe, despite his disappointment, he would be able to see how neatly everything was falling into place. A pang of guilt crossed her mind as she filled the vase with water and crushed the stems of the flowers. She should have shared a lot of the details with him earlier, but it had been impossible, one way or another, to contact him, and things had moved so quickly. Putting the magnificent flowers in the centre of the scrubbed pine table, she put the kettle on.

'Would you like some tea?' She began to pull out

mugs and the proper teapot from the dresser. Simon liked leaf tea in a warmed pot. Decanting some of the hot water from the kettle, she swirled it round in the pot and emptied it in the sink before adding the tea. Two teaspoons and one extra for the pot. 'Milk or lemon?' she prompted, and to her relief, he managed to find a wan smile.

'Lemon, please.' With a sigh, he sank into a chair. Pouring the almost-boiling water onto the tea, Mandy set the pot on the table, sliced some lemon and sloshed some milk into her own mug. Grabbing the plans, she sat down beside him.

'What's this?' Simon frowned as he took the papers.

Steeling herself, Mandy explained, 'It's some plans. Architect plans for a rescue centre. I've spoken to Mum and Dad and they are happy for us to go ahead. In fact, they've been really helpful.' She stopped, aware she was talking too much. Better give Simon a chance to look at the drawings for himself. It was time to pour the tea. Her hand was shaking.

When Simon spoke, his voice was cold. 'I would have thought,' he said, 'you would have talked to me before throwing time and money at some idea we hadn't agreed on. How can you work here if we're running a clinic in Leeds?'

Mandy winced. 'It's like I told you before. If we have the rescue centre here, we can run a clinic in York. It can still work.'

He was glaring at her now. 'I know you suggested

that,' he said, 'but I told you I didn't want to. We have to be practical about how we spend our money. There's no way we can run a clinic in Welford, and York is an unknown quantity. I'm not giving up all that we've planned, least of all for some fairy-tale, pie-in-the-sky, idealistic nonsense.' Mandy blinked. 'I've spent hours visiting premises in Leeds. Samantha and I thought two of them were pretty much perfect. Have we been wasting our time completely?'

Mandy was reeling. Idealistic nonsense? Was that really what Simon thought of her rescue centre idea? And she *had* tried to talk to him. It wasn't as if he hadn't known she was considering something different. If she had pursued her ideas without telling him, so had he, dragging Samantha around to look at properties.

Since Paul's death, it felt even more important to Mandy that she was near York. James would need her in the next months. She was about to say as much before she bit the words back. The last time she had mentioned James and Paul with regard to Hope Meadows, it had escalated the row she and Simon had never quite resolved.

'If I've been wasting my time and money, then you have just as much,' she said. 'I told you about my ideas before. Why did you carry on looking at places in Leeds? And what does Samantha have to do with us?' *Samantha and I thought two of them were pretty much perfect.* 'It's none of her business what we decide.'

Simon ran both hands through his hair, making the

curls spring up. 'You're right. It isn't. But do you expect me to do everything on my own? I was honestly only thinking of us. I thought it was what you wanted.'

A wave of tiredness passed through Mandy. 'I can't cope with this right now,' she said. 'Not after the last week.'

Simon's voice was more gentle as he went on. 'I know your rescue centre means a lot to you. But other people have ambitions, too. If we want to do this together, we have to find some common ground.'

Mandy lifted her mug and took a mouthful of tea. Wasn't that what she was trying to do? She couldn't tell any more who was right and who was wrong.

'I'm sorry,' she said, fighting to keep her voice steady. How complicated this had all become. 'I should have discussed it with you before going ahead with the architect. Can we talk about it later?'

Simon sighed. 'Of course we can.' Reaching out a hand, he patted her knee. 'You do get carried away, saving your animals one by one, don't you?'

One by one. Mandy thought of the wedding. *Poor Paul. Poor James.* Compared to what he was going through, any squabbles she had with Simon were meaningless. Or perhaps – Simon didn't have as much meaning for her as he used to? Mandy swallowed. *Have we reached the end of the road?*

Chapter Twenty-Five

Simon kept his word and didn't raise the subject of Hope Meadows again that evening. Instead, he went to Upper Welford Hall with Mandy and met Bill, the sheep and the cows for the first time, then helped her do the evening rounds in the residential unit.

Mandy was amused by his fascination with the tortoiseshell's kittens, and the simple things she had taught them.

'I always thought cats were impossible to train,' he said as he watched the kittens race across the floor when Mandy called to them.

On Saturday morning, Mandy asked him to come with her to see Roo Dhanjal and check her house was suitable for cats. Simon beamed at her. 'You take this all very seriously, don't you? Of course I'll come.'

As they walked through the campsite, Mandy's heart was racing. Although she and James had rehomed so many animals before, this was the first time she had carried out an official inspection on behalf of Hope Meadows. She had a mental checklist of things she wanted to discuss, and she'd found a form online which would give the Dhanjals official responsibility for the cats.

The campsite looked much smarter than Mandy remembered. As well as an area for tents and caravans, there were wooden chalets set at polite distances along the riverbank. Mandy was pleased to see the campers were encouraged to leave their vehicles in a car park outside. Any cars that did enter were limited to walking speed, and had to give way to bicycles and pedestrians. She couldn't have asked for a safer environment for two cats.

The Dhanjals' house, like the chalets, was made of dark varnished wood. The sound of a radio drifted from an open window. Stepping onto the terrace at the front, Mandy rang the bell. As they waited for the door to open, she turned around. Almost the whole campsite was visible from here, spread out across inviting green grass.

When the door swung open, they were greeted by the warm scent of cooking spices. Roo Dhanjal stood there carrying a delectable baby in her arms. A small girl was half hidden behind her, peeking out from the folds of her mother's wide-legged trousers. Today Roo's hijab was the colour of copper beech leaves, glowing against her skin.

'Hello. Welcome.' Pulling the door wide open, Roo beckoned them into a large open-plan living area. 'This is Herbinder . . . Herbie.' She put a hand on the little girl's head. Huge brown eyes peered up at them before they disappeared again into Roo's tunic. 'And this is Kiran.' She indicated the baby. 'Is this your young man?' Her eyes twinkled at Simon.

'Sort of,' Mandy managed. 'This is Simon.'

The house was just as attractive inside. Wooden beams were supported by thick upright timber posts. Heavy terracotta pots held palm plants, their deep green fronds lending a cool feel to the room.

'They're Paradise palms.' Roo noticed Mandy stroking one of the leaves. 'They're safe for cats. I did check. And the pots are heavy enough they can't be pulled over.' She led them across the room and opened a scrubbed wooden door, which had already been fitted with a cat-flap. 'They'll have a litter tray in here.'

Mandy could see it was a sizeable cupboard, which would be nice and private.

'And there will be another in the utility room off the kitchen. They have a bed in here.' Roo led her through to the kitchen. 'We thought we could feed them and get them used to their cat basket at the same time.' She led them through to a smaller room off the kitchen, which had a sink, as well as a washing machine and tumble-drier. 'For now, everything is stored in the utility room, which is out here.'

Throughout the tour, Mandy had been ticking off the list in her head. They discussed worming, vaccinations, flea control and future veterinary care. Roo seemed to have thought of everything.

'I'll be at the end of the phone day and night if

anything crops up,' Mandy told her, 'but for now, do you have any other questions?'

Roo smiled. 'I don't think I have any questions about the kittens,' she said. 'You've been very thorough. But would you like to have some lunch? It would be lovely if you would stay a while.'

'That would be nice,' said Mandy, adding, 'I'm vegetarian, though. If it's not possible, then don't worry.'

'Come through to the kitchen.' Roo turned and led the way. 'We have plenty of dishes without meat. Sit down, please.' She pulled out two chairs and ushered Simon and Mandy into them. Placing Kiran into a pram and strapping him in, she rocked him for a moment. She lifted Herbie into a high-chair and handed her a piece of chapatti. Mandy was amazed how quiet the children were. The kittens would be more boisterous!

Roo bustled around the kitchen, taking pots and pans from a cupboard in the corner, boiling water to cook rice. As she heated up the sauces, wonderful scents hovered in the air. Mandy's mouth started watering.

'These look delicious,' she said as Roo set down the dishes on the table.

'Please help yourselves,' Roo urged. 'This is a kadala curry: a Southern Indian curry made with chickpeas. And this is our brinjal bhaji.' Mandy could hardly wait to try the food. Aubergine bhaji had long been a favourite. The chickpeas smelled wonderful as well.

Roo served Herbie some of both dishes, and more chapatti, and then turned to Simon. 'So tell me more about yourself,' she said. 'You're very lucky to have such a lovely young lady.'

'I couldn't agree more,' he said. Mandy felt her ears burn.

'How long have you been a couple?' The question was directed at Simon. Mandy took a mouthful of curry. The flavours of tomato, chilli and coconut cream sang on the fork.

'Just over a year.' Simon looked down at the food on his plate. 'This is great, thanks.'

'It's amazing.' Mandy seized the opportunity to join the conversation and hopefully steer it away from the subject of their relationship. 'What spices do you use?'

'A whole selection,' Roo replied. 'There's chilli, coriander and cumin and some of my husband Josh's special garam masala.' She looked from Simon to Mandy and back again.

'So you two . . .' Mandy's toes curled as she heard the playful tone. 'I know a year isn't considered long these days, but Josh and I got married much more quickly than that. He's a wonderful husband. I'm sure you would be, too, Simon. What do you say, Mandy?'

Mandy could feel her face going scarlet. The only proposals she'd heard from Simon had been business proposals. 'I'm sure he would,' she said. The conversation was becoming excruciating. She began to eat more quickly, swallowing down the delicious scented rice, chickpeas and aubergine. 'This really is delicious.'

'Thank you.' Roo stood up and moved to the counter.

'Would you like something sweet?' she offered. 'I have some imarti here that Josh made earlier.'

Mandy pushed her chair out. 'I couldn't eat another thing,' she said. 'And we've got another appointment,' she added. They had arranged to meet Molly Future at Upper Welford Hall. After years of seeing her parents eat on the run, it wasn't like Mandy to cut any meal short unless it was essential. But with the chat taking a direction that was torturously uncomfortable, she was glad of the excuse to escape.

'You're quite sweet enough anyway, aren't you?' Mandy tried not to cringe as Simon wrapped an arm around her waist before planting a kiss on her cheek.

'You do look lovely together.' Roo's voice was wistful. 'I remember when Josh and I met. He looked at me just like that.' Having cleaned Herbie's face with a dishcloth, she lifted the little girl down from her high chair. 'You will come back, won't you?' she said. 'See the kittens, once they're here, and try some more food?'

'I'd love to.' Mandy was telling the truth. But next time, she would come on her own. Roo was delightful, when she wasn't trying to matchmake. 'I'll be in touch in a few days,' she promised.

Waving goodbye to Kiran and Herbie, Simon and Mandy walked back to the car. Mandy tossed her paperwork into the back seat and climbed in behind the wheel. Just this visit to Sam Western's to meet Molly, to see if she could find a place for Bill. The rest of the weekend was her own. Perhaps she could take Simon up on the moors, if the weather held. He wasn't a fanatical walker, but the view from the tops was stunning. They could take Sky as well. It would be good to get her used to as many men as possible.

'You know,' Simon's voice interrupted her thoughts as she drove. 'I can't help thinking that Roo had a good point.'

Mandy frowned. Which point exactly? Something about the cats?

'Maybe we should think about getting married.'

The road was narrow here and the verges were flashing past close on either side. Mandy's hands tightened on the steering wheel. Swallowing hard, she glanced at Simon to see if he was joking, but his face was earnest.

'Are you proposing?' she asked, trying to keep the disbelief out of her voice.

'I do believe I am.' Simon sounded firm. 'I can get down on one knee if you like. Just pull over here and I'll do it.'

Mandy kept her foot on the accelerator. *Is this actually happening?*

The silence stretched.

'Is that a no then?' It was Simon's turn to sound incredulous.

Mandy risked another glance at him. Why would he spring it on her like this? If they had gone away as he had planned: a romantic weekend, a horse-drawn carriage ride, that would have been the perfect setting. Not on the edge of the Walton Road.

But even if everything had been perfect, she was not sure how she would answer.

'I just didn't imagine it happening like this.' She gripped the steering wheel tighter.

'But you did imagine it happening, right?' Simon still sounded as if he couldn't believe the way the conversation was going.

Mandy's head spun, and she blinked to keep her focus on the road. Had she imagined marrying him? Of course she had. For a whole year, they had been so close. There had been wonderful moments at the beginning when the idea of being swept into his arms had been like a dream. As time went on, they had talked about their clinic. Though there had been no hurry, their discussions had been a suggestion of a stable future, working together, comfortable in their partnership.

But they hadn't agreed on anything for weeks – not since Mandy had moved back to Welford. Simon had dismissed her plans for a rescue centre as sentimental nonsense, and had been viewing properties in Leeds with Samantha. And Mandy found herself not minding quite as much as she should, if she was honest with herself.

Meanwhile, there was Jimmy, with his gentle smile and dedication to Robbie's animals, and the way he always seemed to be around when Mandy needed him. If she truly loved Simon, would she be able to feel like that about someone else?

Simon was still looking expectantly at her.

'Thank you for your offer. I will think about it, I promise.' Mandy winced. That came out wrong.

When she glanced at Simon again, his expression was petulant.

'I want to marry you,' he said. 'I'm not offering you a second-hand car.'

Mandy couldn't think of anything else to say. She lifted her hand to touch Simon's knee, but put it back on the wheel. He wasn't a spaniel to be comforted with a quick rub on the head.

'We need to talk about the future,' she said, risking yet another glance at his angry expression. 'If we could talk about the clinic and the rescue centre . . .'

She saw Simon's head twitch sideways. 'Why would you bring that up now?' His voice was repressive, his mouth constricted.

'But we have to discuss it.' Mandy had to force herself to reply. If he couldn't see that her work was as important as his, there could be no future, but Simon's lip curled and he turned away, looking out of the window, his silent anger filling the car.

Mandy was relieved when they reached Upper Welford Hall. She steered into the car park and pulled on the handbrake. Still in silence, Simon was undoing his seat belt and opening the door. Mandy's mind was stuck, but what more could she say? There wasn't time to talk about anything now. Molly Future would be here at any moment to meet Bill. The gentle Shire horse was hanging his head over the gate, watching her approach. He gave a rumbling whicker as she held out her hand to stroke his nose. Bill's forelock reached halfway down the broad white blaze on his face, and his eyelashes were impossibly long. Mandy stretched up to rub his ears.

Simon had followed and was standing so close, she felt uneasy. She found herself wishing he had stayed in the car.

'I'll get that.' He held out his hand for the headcollar she was holding. Unable to give a reason why not, she handed it over and, once he had buckled it over Bill's enormous head, she let herself into the field to pick out Bill's hooves. The gelding lifted each foot patiently, waiting for Mandy to find her balance under the weight of the massive hoof.

As she cleaned out the last hind foot and placed it back on the grass, there was a cheerful shout from behind her.

'Hello!'

Pushing the hoof-pick into her pocket, Mandy straightened up. Molly Future, smart and perky in a short, padded vest over a bright pink polo shirt, was letting herself into the field.

'So this is Bill.' She walked over and placed her hand on Bill's neck. 'What a magnificent boy. And you are?' She looked expectantly at Simon.

'I'm Simon. Good to meet you . . .?' He held out his hand. How normal his voice sounded. So different from the cold tone he had used only moments before.

'Molly Future. I run the Six Oaks Riding Stables.'

She gave him a brisk handshake and turned back to the horse. 'Any idea how old Bill is?'

Mandy stepped out from behind Bill's rump. 'Hello, Molly.' Her voice sounded okay, she thought, though it wasn't easy to find her smile.

Molly grinned. 'Hi, Mandy. I almost didn't see you there. He's a giant, isn't he?'

'But gentle with it,' Mandy said.

In a gesture that was appealingly childlike, and quite unexpected, Molly pressed her cheek against Bill's. 'Oh yes, I can see that,' she murmured. 'What a sweetie.' She bent down and ran her hand down Bill's front legs. Lifting his left fore, she considered the massive plate-like foot. 'Your farrier has done a good job,' she remarked.

'Yes, he has.' Shutting out Simon's presence, Mandy set her mind firmly on the task in hand. Mathew Morris's work had made all the difference. 'I'm afraid it's not possible to give you an exact age for him,' Mandy admitted. When she had examined his teeth, Galvayne's groove had disappeared from all but the very end of his corner incisor. That would put him between twenty-five and thirty, but even that wasn't reliably accurate. 'I think it would be reasonable to say he's a very old boy.'

'Fair enough.' Molly stepped back for a wider look. 'Is he still lame?'

'Not really,' Mandy said. 'He's a bit stiff, but he seems quite willing to move around. He can't work any more, obviously, but he is a sweet old thing. So what do you think?' she urged. 'Could you find space for him somewhere?'

'I don't see why not.' Molly moved back in to lean her head on Bill's shoulder, wrapping her left hand under his neck. He was a magnetic horse, Mandy thought. It was impossible to resist the urge to touch him. 'I can't see that he'll be any trouble. Obviously, we'll have to see how he gets on with my lot, but even if he doesn't get on with them all, we'll find him space and company somewhere.'

'That's wonderful.' Mandy let out a long breath. She had hardly dared hope Molly would find room for Bill. It wasn't a small request, not like taking on a tiny kitten or even a cow. It was so kind of Molly. Not only that, but she could see from the way the stable owner had approached and handled the old Shire that she knew exactly what she was doing.

'Tell you what.' Mandy's rush of gratitude nudged her onwards. 'I'd be happy to pay for his food and veterinary bills. I'm so glad you can find room for him.' As she said this, she caught sight of Simon, who was holding the lead rope. He rolled his eyes at her and shook his head.

'That's very generous,' Molly said. 'Of course, I could manage without, but it would make everything easier. At his age, I would love to be able to call you without worrying it would end up costing a fortune. I'm not going to be able to get insurance for him, am I?'

Mandy's eyes were still on Simon. He hadn't said a

word, but waves of disapproval came from him. It was her money, Mandy thought mutinously. Bill's future was important. Hope Meadows might need Molly's help again.

She pulled her attention back to Molly, who seemed oblivious to the chill that had descended. Mandy wondered what she'd say if she knew that Simon had asked Mandy to marry him ten minutes ago.

'I'll get everything sorted out at the yard so I can collect him tomorrow,' Molly said. She beamed up at Bill, her pixie haircut gleaming in the sun. She was like a little doll, Mandy thought. But she loved horses, that was clear.

'I'm very happy for you to have him,' Mandy said. 'I'm sure we can keep the costs down.'

Simon's mouth was still turned down at the corners. It wasn't a good look.

With a last pat on Bill's shoulder, Molly let herself out of the field. 'See you tomorrow!'

Chapter Twenty-Six

It should have been a triumphant moment, Mandy thought. Of all the rescued animals, it was Bill who had concerned her most. He could no longer work and was so old he might easily need extra care. There weren't many people who wanted to take on such a large pet.

Simon hadn't said a word, but his silence hung heavy. Why didn't he say something? At least they might be able to clear the air. Mandy took a breath. Should she begin? But what could she say? He would probably deny he was upset. With a feeling of defiance, she unbuckled Bill's halter and slung it over her shoulder without looking at Simon.

As they reached her car, another vehicle appeared. It was Jimmy's Jeep. Pulling up alongside her RAV4, he opened the door and jumped out.

'Mandy! How's it going? Are all the cats and kittens well? I know these lot are thriving.' He nodded to Bill and the sheep and cows in the field. 'They look better every day.'

Simon was on the far side of the RAV4. Mandy waited for him to come round and meet Jimmy, but he stood there with a look of exaggerated patience on his face.

Jimmy walked round the bonnet of the car, holding out his hand. 'Sorry,' he said. 'I should have introduced myself. I'm Jimmy Marsh.'

With a chilly smile, Simon held out his own hand. 'Simon Webster. Mandy's boyfriend.' Mandy twitched.

'We've just had a meeting with one of the local stable owners,' Mandy put in. 'She's agreed to take Bill.'

'That's great news.' Jimmy walked back round the car. 'I know you were worried about him. Who's taking him?'

Mandy had been hoping he wouldn't ask. The memory of Jimmy and Molly side by side and laughing in the Fox and Goose was seared into her brain. If she mentioned Molly now, would he confirm they were seeing each other? On the other hand, why was it any of her business? She was acutely aware of Simon standing near the passenger door of her car.

'Molly Future,' she said.

'Oh Molly. I know Molly quite well.' Mandy studied Jimmy's face, but he didn't give anything away. 'She'll look after Bill as well as anyone could.' He was smiling, though whether at the thought of Molly or Bill's rehoming, Mandy couldn't tell. She glanced across the car at Simon. However angry he was, did he need to be so rude? He was acting as if Jimmy wasn't there.

Jimmy seemed to pick up on the atmosphere. 'I'd better let you go. I've just dropped the children off with their mum, and there are a few things I need to catch up on.'

'I'll see you soon,' Mandy said, opening her car door.

Jimmy sketched a wave as he strode towards the farm-yard.

It was quiet on the short drive back to Animal Ark. Mandy's mind kept skipping back and forth between Simon's proposal and the reality of where they were now. How could she agree to marry him when they hadn't reached an agreement about their clinic? Mandy bit her lip. She knew she had made things far more complicated since coming to Welford. She hadn't actively planned for Hope Meadows to happen. One tiny idea had snowballed, and with Robbie Grimshaw's animals, Paul's funeral, her physical distance from Simon and all the difficulties in communicating, she seemed to have passed the point of no return. She couldn't back out now, and unless Simon was willing to compromise, she couldn't see a way forward.

'Is it possible for us to talk more about York?' she began. 'I know I should have discussed Hope Meadows more with you, but everything has happened so fast. I really didn't want you to waste your time looking at clinics in Leeds. I'm sorry if you feel that.' Her eyes were on the road and she couldn't look at him, but she was aware of him shifting in his seat, turning to face her.

'Is that why you said no before? To us getting married?' Simon sounded hopeful.

Mandy felt a jolt of exasperation. Couldn't he leave that to one side?

But Simon was speaking again. 'Do we really need to decide right now about the clinic? I can see you'll have to keep Hope Meadows running for a while, and I've progressed so far in Leeds with these properties that it's difficult to back out, but we can still get engaged, can't we? If things go well in Leeds, maybe I can open a branch in York further down the line. Or Hope Meadows could be looked after by someone else. You could make a new rescue centre in Leeds.' He paused and laid his hand on Mandy's knee. 'We could get engaged now. Plan later.'

For a crazy moment, Mandy was tempted to say yes. How easy it would be. No difficult decisions about the future, just a confirmation that everything would be okay because they were together.

Taking her silence as consent, Simon's voice rose. 'What about it, then?' he said. 'Shall we tell your parents the good news? We could take them out for a meal to celebrate.'

Mandy frowned. Could he just let her get a word in? The road ahead was rushing towards them, trees flashing past. She took a deep breath. She couldn't face confronting Simon with a definite no, but there was no way she could give him the answer he wanted. 'There's so much going on right now. Will you give me time to think about it?' She was glad she could grip the steering wheel. It felt solid and reassuring under her fingers.

'If that's what you want.' Simon's voice was flat.

Mandy flinched. She could take away that pain. All she had to do was say yes. She pressed her lips together.

'Should I just go back to Leeds?' Simon went on. 'Do you need some space?'

Suddenly it seemed airless in the car. Reaching out, Mandy pressed the switch and lowered the window. The wind rushed in, tugging at her hair, carrying the scent of the moors.

'No, of course not. Stay for the weekend.' So long as she didn't have to go into the house and announce their engagement. She put her hand on top of Simon's. 'I like having you here,' she made herself say.

Simon just grunted.

When they drew up outside Animal Ark, both the practice cars were outside the clinic. Mandy and Simon jumped out and went round to the kitchen door.

'How did it go?' Emily looked up from her embroidery as they entered the sitting room.

'Oh, really well.' Mandy tried to remember what had happened that morning. This day seemed to be going on forever. 'The Dhanjals are going to be perfect for the tortoiseshell kittens, and Molly Future is taking Bill. Now all we have to do is find someone to take the farm animals and the other cats.' Mandy couldn't bring herself to mention Sky. Despite all their progress, the little collie would still be difficult to rehome. Mandy was also finding the idea of parting with her harder and harder to think about.

'That's great news.' Emily beamed up at her. 'Well done, you.'

'Is it okay if I go upstairs for a bit?' Simon asked. Mandy shot a glance at him but his expression was unreadable.

'Of course. I'll go out to the wildlife unit,' Mandy said. 'Check on the cats.' She had a sudden urge to hug Sky, too.

Even before Mandy could see Sky, she could hear the thumping of her tail and the frenzied claw-clicking that greeted her every time she came in now. When she opened the door, the little collie was squirming with delight. Opening the kennel door, Mandy laughed as Sky bounded out and threw herself against her legs, begging to be stroked.

Mandy sat down on the floor where she could see out of the window. Outside, the fells rose against the clear blue sky. Sky curled up beside Mandy, pressing warmly against her hip.

'Why is life so complicated?' Mandy said out loud. Sky licked her face. 'Simon's asked me to marry him.' Even saying it here, with Sky as her only witness, felt odd. 'I wish he hadn't. Paul has died and James needs me. We can't agree on where to open a clinic, yet Simon still wants to get engaged.' She sighed. Sky gazed up at her with trusting brown eyes.

'Can I just stay here with you?' Mandy whispered, pressing her cheek against Sky's face. 'Life would be so much easier.' Sky gave a little whine. 'You know the strangest thing?' A cloud crossed the sun and Mandy watched its shadow scud across the landscape, drifting up the steep fellside. 'If he'd asked me a few weeks ago, I'd have said yes. But since I've come back to Welford, everything has changed. I've changed.'

She leaned her head down and closed her eyes, feeling the warmth and softness of Sky's fur against her face. It was true, she thought. She had changed. The only problem was, Simon hadn't.

It seemed like ages since Mandy had eaten Sunday lunch at Gran and Grandad's house. Lilac Cottage had barely changed at all from her childhood. Sitting at the table, full of peach crumble and home-made custard, she could remember a time when she had sat on the same oak dining chair, swinging her legs because they were too short to reach the floor.

'So what do you think of the plans for Hope Meadows?' Tom Hope might be heading towards frailty now he was in his eighties, but the eyes that studied Simon were as shrewd as they ever had been.

'Things are certainly moving fast,' Simon replied. 'Mandy's done a brilliant job with Robbie Grimshaw's animals. I'm very proud of her.' Reaching out his hand, he patted Mandy's knee under the table. Mandy made herself smile at him, though she wished he didn't sound so condescending.

Gran put down her spoon. 'Has everyone had enough to eat?' There was a chorus of assent from around the table.

'I'll tidy up,' Mandy announced. Standing up, she began to clear the dessert plates from the table.

'And I'll give you a hand.' Tom Hope's voice brooked

no disagreement. 'Maybe you'd like to have a look round the garden,' he suggested to Simon. 'Dorothy, will you show him?'

'Of course I will.' Gran's eyes were twinkling. 'He's not as spry as he once was, and he doesn't always hear everything, but he still loves his garden,' she whispered once Tom had left the room. With a conspiratorial grin, Gran led Simon out through the back door. Sorting the glasses and cups onto a tray, Mandy followed her grandfather into the kitchen.

Tom Hope was standing at the sink. Despite the presence of an efficient dishwasher, he still liked to clean the cutlery by hand. Lifting a tea towel, Mandy walked over and stood beside him.

Looking up from the soapy water, her grandad studied her. 'How are things?'

'Fine, thanks,' Mandy lied. She was sleepless with worry about James, and the situation with Simon seemed so overwhelming she could hardly bring herself to think about it.

Tom Hope was regarding her seriously, as if he could hear her thoughts rather than her words. 'I don't know exactly what's going on,' he said, 'but I hope you're not going to rush into anything so far as that young man is concerned. Tell me you'll think carefully.'

Mandy stared at her grandad. 'What do you mean?' she said. How could he know anything? So far as she was aware, neither she nor Simon had breathed a word.

The old man shook his head. 'Nothing more than

that,' he said. 'Just don't make any hasty decisions. You have lots of time.'

For a long moment, they gazed at one another and then Mandy reached out for a hug. She had to stoop to rest her head on Grandad's shoulder now, but he could still comfort her better than anyone else. The only thing Mandy knew was absolutely right was that she was back in Welford with her family. She stayed in her grandfather's arms for a long time, not wanting to let go.

It was getting dark. Mandy and Simon stood outside Animal Ark. Simon had packed everything into the car, combing the house carefully for all his possessions. He always hated leaving anything behind, even a sock or half a tube of toothpaste.

Mandy wondered if he'd mention his proposal again before he drove away. She had asked him for time to think, and so far he seemed to be willing to do that. Holding out his arms, he smiled into her eyes. Was there sadness in his gaze? Or was it a reflection of the melancholy she was feeling herself?

'You will come and see me next weekend, won't you?' he asked.

'Of course I will.' She stretched up and kissed his cheek, hating herself for not wanting to hug him as usual.

Simon slid into the car. 'Have a good week,' he said.

He wound down the window and looked up at her. 'We are all right, aren't we?' Suddenly there was a note of doubt in his voice.

Mandy felt tears prick her eyes. This wasn't the time or place for that conversation, she told herself. She patted his shoulder. 'Everything's going to be fine,' she told him.

She watched as the car rolled up the drive. Next time she saw him, she would make him listen to her properly, show him just how far apart their plans and dreams had grown. Simon had to know that being in Welford had changed a lot for her: her priorities, her ambitions for the future. Her sense of who she wanted to have in her life.

With a sigh, Mandy turned her back on the empty driveway and walked inside.

Chapter Twenty-Seven

The whole Dhanjal family was waiting for Mandy on Monday afternoon, though Kiran was fast asleep. Mandy peered into the pram and smiled. He was almost as cute as the kittens she had brought.

'We've got everything ready,' Roo explained, her dark eyes earnest. 'I want them to stay in this room at first, until they get used to us. We'll be very careful with Herbie until the kittens are bigger.'

Mandy looked at the two-year-old. She was sitting on the floor, wide-eyed, rolling a ball and watching as first the tortoiseshell kitten and then the ginger and white batted it back and forth. Mandy had been impressed by the way Roo had talked to her little girl about the kittens. Why it was important for Herbie never to pick them up when Mummy or Daddy were not there. Not that they would be leaving her alone with them, Josh had murmured to Mandy. She felt a wave of satisfaction as she left the family with their new pets. Rehoming was one of the best parts of her job.

She glanced at her phone. It was three o'clock. Time to get back to Animal Ark. For once, Emily and Adam had agreed to go out and leave Mandy in charge. They were going to the theatre in York and had booked a table for dinner before the show. Mandy drove the short distance back to the cottage and went inside.

Adam was still reading his paper at the kitchen table. He looked up as Mandy entered. 'How did it go?'

'Perfect. It's going to be a lovely match, I think.'

'That's good to hear.' Adam folded his paper and laid it down on the table. 'We had two calls while you were out. Another prospective owner for one of the adult cats.'

That was great news, Mandy thought. That would only leave the black cat and her kittens. Mum and Dad would be pleased to get their wildlife unit back.

'The other was from the builder. He thinks he should be finishing his job in Walton a week tomorrow. After that, he'll be able to make a start on the outbuildings here.' He twinkled up at Mandy, obviously enjoying her reaction. That was even better news than the cat rehoming. She could hardly believe everything was happening so fast and so smoothly.

Adam stood up. 'I'd better go and make myself look presentable.' He grinned. 'Otherwise your mother will roll up my newspaper and chase me round the table with it.'

Mandy laughed. 'The way you run, she'd catch you easily,' she teased.

It was quiet in the clinic once her parents had left for York. Helen was in the residential unit and Mandy had opened the new Hope Meadows website to check it once more before it went live.

There was a squeal of tyres on the driveway. She looked out of the window, half expecting it to be her parents coming back for something they had forgotten, but it was a car she didn't recognise. A man jumped out of the passenger seat and ran for the surgery door. A woman climbed from the driver's seat and dashed round to the boot. With her heart in her mouth, Mandy recognised Mr and Mrs Patchett, who had made it so clear to her that they would only see her parents. Standing up, she met Mr Patchett at the door.

'It's Isla,' he panted. 'She started whelping about four hours ago, she's been straining the last half-hour and she isn't making any progress. She's really upset.'

Grabbing a pair of gloves and a bottle of lubricant, Mandy rushed out to the car. Isla stood in the back of the vehicle. She was panting heavily. Her eyes seemed to beg Mandy for help.

'I'll need to do an examination first,' Mandy said.

'You should fetch your parents.' Even though she had been expecting some kind of objection, Mandy felt her anger rise, but Mrs Patchett went on, 'This is an emergency. It needs someone with experience.'

'I'm afraid they are both out.' Mandy kept her voice calm and polite. 'I believe I'm capable of handling this, if you'll let me try.' They could, of course, refuse. There was another vet in Walton. For a moment, she thought Mrs Patchett was going to slam the boot and leave, but

Mr Patchett, who had followed Mandy out to the car, spoke firmly for the first time.

'Please go ahead,' he said. 'Isla needs your help.'

Despite Mrs Patchett's glare, Mandy didn't wait for her to say anything else. Smearing plenty of lubricant onto her fingers, she inserted them into the dog's vagina. It was obvious what was wrong.

'A puppy has got stuck,' she announced. 'There's just a tail presenting and the birth passage isn't wide enough for the pup to come through. We need to do a Caesarean.'

Mrs Patchett drew in her breath. 'Are you certain you're competent to go ahead?' she snapped. 'You understand that Scottish deerhound anaesthesia is not straightforward?'

Mandy didn't waste her time with a direct reply. 'We need to get her inside,' she said. 'I want to do a Prothrombin Test to make sure her blood is clotting normally.' Mrs Patchett looked as if she were about to speak, but Mandy held up her hand. 'It won't take any extra time,' she said. 'I'll need to place a catheter anyway. I'll run the test while the nurse gets everything set up in theatre.' She paused, then spoke again. 'I want to do routine biochemistry as well. Isla's probably dehydrated. I'll use minimal anaesthesia. I'm fully aware deerhounds don't have much body fat, so it's essential not to overdose. I'll ensure her temperature is closely monitored, too. If necessary, we'll use a high oxygen flow rate and other methods to cool her down.'

Mrs Patchett's mouth had fallen open. Mandy caught

Mr Patchett's eye. Despite the fact he was obviously worried about Isla, he sent her an encouraging smile.

'I can catheterise her in the car,' Mandy said. 'The less we stress her out, the better.' Luckily the sun was shining. It should be easy enough to see the vein. Leaving the still silent Mrs Patchett, Mandy hurried back inside.

'Can you set up in theatre, please?' she called to Helen. 'Scottish deerhound needing a Caesarean. Low dose fentanyl. And call Rachel, will you? See if she can come in and give us a hand.'

Helen shot off without comment, efficient as always. Gathering the things she would need for the blood test, Mandy ran back outside. Isla let out a low whine, her ears flat against her head.

Mandy sat down on the edge of the boot and spoke to her. 'Poor Isla,' she murmured. 'It's going to be okay.' Reaching out, she ran her hand down the side of the deerhound's neck. The dog's muscles were trembling. 'Can you sit down here and give her a cuddle?' she asked Mr Patchett, who took Mandy's place at once, holding Isla with one arm and putting her leg in the right position for the blood test.

'I'll get the test done and then I'll come straight back,' Mandy explained. 'Keep her as calm as you can.'

The clotting test was normal. Biochemistry showed that Isla was indeed dehydrated. Mandy passed the information to Helen. Taking a deep breath, she went back out to the car. 'I want to get her inside now. We're ready to go ahead.' Between them, she and Mr Patchett lifted Isla down from the boot of the car and guided her inside.

There was just the premedication to go, Mandy thought, and then she was going to have to have the most difficult part of the discussion. She had drawn up small doses of fentanyl and midazolam into syringes. With Isla still on the floor but with the stretcher table close by, she injected the fentanyl and followed with a small amount of midazolam into the vein. Helen had finished setting up in theatre.

'We're giving her additional oxygen before induction,' Mandy explained to the Patchetts as Helen turned the machine on and applied the mask to Isla's face. Though she looked confused, Isla stood still.

'She's so good.' Helen rubbed the fluffy grey ear as she held the oxygen mask in place.

'She is,' Mandy agreed. She gave a further small dose of the sedative. Girding herself up for objections, she turned again to the Patchetts.

'I'm going to give her an injection in a moment that will make her go to sleep. Then I'm going to place a tube in her trachea. Once that's done, we'll be taking her through to theatre. You can sit in here to wait. Once the puppies are breathing, we'll bring them out to you to look after.'

Mandy wasn't surprised when Mrs Patchett started to go red with fury. 'Your father has always allowed us into theatre when he was carrying out a section.' She drew herself up to her full height. 'It's essential you allow us in. Someone has to be there to revive the pups.' To Mandy's relief, she heard the door crash open.

'I'm here!' Rachel Farmer panted.

Mandy introduced her. 'Mr and Mrs Patchett, this is Rachel Farmer. She will be in theatre with me. Along with Helen, she will revive the pups.' Rachel had arrived in the nick of time, she thought. Although it was true her father allowed breeders to accompany him into theatre during Caesarean operations, it was something Mandy wasn't happy to do. If something went wrong, either with the anaesthetic or the operation, Isla's best chance of survival depended upon Mandy's ability to remain calm. Cold as it seemed, the presence of the owners was likely to increase the risk.

'I'm sorry.' Mandy was firm. 'I am happy for you to help look after the puppies in the waiting-room, but I can't allow you to come into theatre.'

Mrs Patchett began to protest, but once again Mr Patchett came to Mandy's aid. 'We need to let Amanda get on,' he said. 'For Isla's sake.'

Mandy felt weak with relief as, with bad grace, Mrs Patchett sat down. Breathing steadily, Mandy picked up the syringe with the ketamine. Attaching it to Isla's catheter, she injected the drug in increments, with Rachel and Helen helping to keep the big dog steady until she was ready for intubation. The tube slid into the trachea without incident and, between them, they lifted the stretcher onto its wheeled trolley and rolled the sleeping dog into the prep room.

Helen was so thorough that Mandy felt confident enough to leave her in charge of the ongoing anaesthesia. Rachel helped clip and scrub the area on Isla's abdomen. Once the patient was ready, they moved her to theatre. Helen began the complicated task of connecting up the anaesthetic tubing, the drip and the monitors.

'Is everything stable?' Mandy looked at Helen, who nodded. Picking up the plastic drape, Mandy laid it over Isla's abdomen, clipping it into place. Lifting the scalpel handle, she pushed the blade into place and took a deep breath. The bright theatre light shone down as she reached out to make her incision, a firm stroke along the midline.

The shining bulge of one of the uterine horns pushed its way upwards. Lifting it out, Mandy surrounded it with gauze swabs before sliding the blade along the glossy surface. As always, the uterine wall was stretched and thin. It parted easily under Mandy's blade. Reaching in, she drew forth the first pup, enveloped in its protective sac. She tore the membrane from the blunt little nose and handed the tiny body to Rachel, who was waiting with a towel. Readjusting the swabs, Mandy reached inside again. There was another pup. Working her fingers inside, she retrieved the second shining sac, splitting it open and passing the warm little bundle to her assistant. So far there had been no noise from the first pup.

Mandy forced herself to stay focussed and worked her way to the third. This was the one that was stuck.

Chances were high it wouldn't survive. As quickly as she could, she drew it forward into the light. As she had expected, the amniotic fluid had drained away, but she cleared the remaining membrane from the nostrils, and handed the pup over, this time to Helen.

A tiny squealing noise caught her ear. Turning her head, she could see Rachel rubbing away at the other two pups. A second squeal.

Rachel beamed. 'Both breathing well.'

There was a pup in the other horn. Making sure she did not cut into the placenta, Mandy made a second incision. She pulled the chunky little body out and, for the last time, broke through the membrane. A quick check showed her there were no more.

'Last one,' she said. Helen was still rubbing hard at the pup that had been stuck, so Mandy gave the final puppy to Rachel, who had put the first two in a box with a hot water bottle. 'Any joy, Helen?'

The nurse sighed. 'Sadly not,' she said. 'I've given dopram, but nothing so far. Isla's doing well though.'

Mandy nodded and turned back to her final task. It was always fiddly, suturing the uterus. With tiny, painstaking stitches, Mandy brought the edges together. As she opened the last vicryl to begin stitching the abdominal muscles, she heard a tiny snuffling squeak. Whirling round, she looked at Helen. The nurse was grinning widely, holding up the stuck puppy, which was starting to wriggle.

'Breathing!' Helen confirmed, her voice triumphant.

Still smiling, she handed the pup to Rachel, who put it with its littermates in the box.

'Soon as you think they're ready, you can take them out to Mr and Mrs Patchett,' Mandy told her. Although she loved to hear the wonderful sound the puppies made in the corner of the theatre, Isla's owners would want to help with the young litter. A few minutes later, both white line and skin were sutured. The stitches lay in a neat line along the centre of the abdomen.

'You can switch her off now,' she told Helen.

'Already done,' Helen reported. 'I'll just get her cleaned up.' Together, they wiped away the blood and mess from the skin. It was important the pups could suckle as soon as possible. Moving Isla onto the trolley table, they wheeled her back through.

Mrs Patchett rushed over, leaving her husband in charge of the puppies. 'How did it go?'

'Everything was fine,' Mandy assured her. She had half hoped the pups might have time to suckle before Isla woke, but the dog was already showing signs of waking. She coughed and lifted her head almost simultaneously. Mandy grabbed the tube, whipping it out of her mouth. To her pleasure, a moment later, the deerhound was wagging her tail and nuzzling Mandy's ear.

'Can you bring the pups over?' Mandy asked Mr Patchett. 'It looks as if she's coming round nicely.'

As soon as she heard the snuffling and squealing, Isla's ears pricked. When the pups were presented to her, she put her long nose into the box, sniffing first one pup and then another. She looked up at Mandy.

'You're right,' Mandy told her. 'They are lovely.' Picking up the smallest of the puppies, she moved round to Isla's flank. She opened the tiny jaw and manoeuvred the little head into place on one of the teats. The pup wriggled round, dropping the teat, then searching again. Mandy put out her hand and drew a tiny drop of milk. Readjusting the puppy's head, she held it in place. A moment later, the tiny creature had latched on. Mandy watched for a couple of seconds to check it wasn't going to slip off, then reached for another pup.

A few minutes later, Isla was lying calmly on her side with all four pups suckling. Giving the dog's head one last stroke, Mandy stood up and stretched. She was worn out. Operating was always exhausting.

'Would you be able to look after her for a few minutes?' she asked Helen.

'Of course.' Helen was still on her knees beside Isla, watching the new puppies take their first precious drink. Mandy found herself smiling. She would get a quick cup of tea, then relieve Helen so she could do the same before it was time to start again.

She sat at the kitchen table, feeling a wave of quiet satisfaction. Thank goodness the operation had gone well. However thorough, however careful you were, things could still go wrong. A few minutes later, she stood up and put her mug in the dishwasher.

When she returned to the waiting-room, the puppies

were asleep and Isla was just getting to her feet. She stood a moment, paws spread wide, then gaining her balance, started to walk. Rachel and Helen stayed either side of her as she followed the puppies in their box, which Mr Patchett carried out to the car.

'I wanted to say thank you. You've done a good job today.' Mrs Patchett's face showed no sign of cracking a smile, but Mandy appreciated her words. 'You'll send the bill as usual?'

'We'll do that.' Mandy nodded. Following the little procession outside, it took three of them to lift Isla's long-legged shape back into the car.

'Make sure she takes it easy for a few days,' Mandy said. 'Stitches out in ten days, please.'

'Thank you very much.' Mr Patchett closed the back door of the car. 'Don't worry,' he promised, 'we'll take good care of her.' Mandy was sure they would. With Helen and Rachel, she made her way back inside.

'I think I'll head off,' Rachel announced. It was Helen's night to help with the evening clinic. 'See you tomorrow.' She donned her coat and, pausing only to wave, she sped off.

'Has the kettle boiled?' Helen asked Mandy.

'Yes, it has. I'll make you a cup.' She would have another herself, Mandy thought.

'Thank you. That would be lovely.'

She had just poured water into the mugs when she heard a car draw up outside. Opening the cottage door, she stepped through into the waiting-room. Helen was behind the counter, talking to Jimmy Marsh. He turned as Mandy came in.

'Hello again.' He smiled at her. 'I came in for some worming tablets for the dogs. Helen's sorted me out.'

'That's good,' Mandy replied. She searched for something else to say, but her mind had gone blank. Feeling her face grow warm, she walked over and put the tea down on the counter.

'I popped in to see Bill on the way over,' Jimmy said. 'He's doing very well. Thriving under Molly's five-star care. I thought you'd like to know.' A strange feeling passed through Mandy. Though she was delighted to hear the Shire was in a good place, the thought of Jimmy popping in to see Molly left a sinking feeling in her stomach. She liked Molly, but the riding instructor's petite figure and cropped hair made her feel like a lanky Irish wolfhound in comparison. When she looked back up at Jimmy, he was watching her again.

'Thanks for letting me know,' she said.

'Any time,' he replied. 'Let me know when you want me to feed the cattle and sheep. I'm often up at the farmyard.'

'Thanks,' Mandy repeated.

Jimmy waved, put the worming tablets in his pocket, and walked out. Mandy watched him disappear around the corner. When she turned to look at Helen, she was surprised to see the nurse grinning.

'I knew Molly and Jimmy used to be a couple,' Helen

said, 'but I thought it was long over. Sounds to me as if he still likes her.'

Pulling herself together, Mandy managed a smile. 'Poor Jimmy,' she said. 'He can't do anything without all of us gossiping like chickens. We'll be as bad as Mrs McFarlane was when she worked in the post office, if we don't watch out.'

Helen grinned. 'Seb would never allow that,' she said. 'He would put duct tape over my mouth long before that could ever be the case.'

Mandy laughed. 'Maybe we should gossip about you,' she teased. 'You and Seb seemed to be all loved up, last time I saw you together.'

Helen was smiling openly now. Her eyes gleamed. 'I looked past him for ages,' she said. 'And then there he was, right under my nose.' She looked so happy.

How long was it since she had felt that way about Simon, Mandy wondered? She thought of the conversation they needed to have next weekend, and her heart sank.

Chapter Twenty-Eight

Despite the evening drizzle, Mandy was feeling jubilant. She had taken Sky out to the meadow to work, and everything had gone well. Sky came easily now whenever her name was called. She would lie down when told, and sit, and stay. Best of all, when a car drew up at the clinic, or when an occasional low-flying jet zoomed overhead, she would run to Mandy rather than anywhere else. Although she was still prone to cowering as if the sky was about to fall on her head, it was obvious she considered Mandy's side to be a place of safety.

It was only a few days until building work would start on Hope Meadows' new kennel block. Mandy looked down at Sky and smiled. Crouching beside the slim body, she ran her hand over the damp furry ear and down the side of Sky's neck.

'What do you think?' she whispered. 'We'll be able to rescue lots more dogs when the centre's up and running.' It was a wonderful thought. What about Sky, though? During her childhood, Mandy's parents had been very strict. With so many needy animals to look after, she had been allowed very few of her own pets and all rescues had been rehomed.

It was the one constraint about living back with her parents that made Mandy sad. But Sky was so special. Now she was an adult, surely the decision should be hers? The collie leaned towards Mandy, asking for a hug. Mandy was happy to oblige.

'You know what?' Sky looked at her. 'For you, I'm going to make an exception. I'm going to ask Mum and Dad if you can stay. And I'm not going to take no for an answer.' Mandy laughed as Sky stood up, wagging her tail and asking to play. 'I'm really sorry, but we have to go in now,' Mandy said, looking back towards the cottage. A car had just drawn up.

It was Brandon Gill. 'Hi, Brandon. What can I do for you?' Although farmers usually telephoned when they wanted the vet to come out, it was not uncommon for them to come to the clinic to buy supplies. It was, however, later in the day than usual.

Brandon reddened. Despite the years they had known each other, he still seemed to find communication difficult. 'Actually, I think I might be able to do something for you,' he managed. 'Rachel tells me you have some farm animals that need rehoming.'

'Come inside,' Mandy urged him. He followed her through the door, but stood on the mat, seemingly unwilling to trespass further.

'Three ewes and six cows, is that correct? At Upper Welford Hall? If you'd like, I could take them all.'

Mandy stared at him. For all his trouble speaking to people, he could certainly get to the point fast. 'Really?' she said. 'You'd take them all?'

Brandon nodded. 'I could pick them up tomorrow. Rachel will give me a hand. Would the evening suit?'

'Absolutely.' Mandy felt like doing cartwheels all around the cottage. Instead, she grinned at Brandon, who flushed red again. 'Thank you so much, Brandon. I can't imagine anyone who would give them a better home.'

'No problem.' He nodded and gave her a shy smile in return. 'Glad to help.' He turned and stepped back outside, closing the door behind him.

Behind Mandy, the door opened and Emily came into the kitchen. 'Who was that?' she asked.

'It was Brandon Gill.' Mandy still felt breathless. 'He's going to take all the farm animals. Every single one.'

She was gratified to see the astonishment in her mum's eyes. Emily shook her head. 'I don't know what it is you do to people,' she said, 'but whatever it is, it's a marvellous gift. And how lovely of Brandon. We must invite him and Rachel over for dinner one day.'

Knowing Brandon's shyness, Mandy wasn't sure dinner was something he would relish, but he might appreciate the invitation. 'That would be lovely,' she agreed. There was a beeping noise from her pocket, signifying that she had received a message. Pulling out her phone, she opened it.

'Wow. Look at these, Mum!'

Roo Dhanjal had sent her three lovely photographs.

One was an image of the tortoiseshell kitten, peering through tall grass. It reminded Mandy of the first time she had seen the kitten's mother in the overgrown garden at Lamb's Wood Cottage. 'Somia in the garden,' she read. There was one of the ginger and white kitten, lying on his back. 'Shahu playing,' Roo explained. The third picture was of both kittens fast asleep on a fluffy blanket. 'Finally some peace!' said the caption.

Mandy laughed. 'She says we can use them for the website.' She held out her mobile for her mother to see.

'That's kind of her.' Emily put her arm round Mandy's shoulder and gave her a squeeze. 'Which reminds me. I need to talk to you about charitable status. Dad and I thought we could sit down tomorrow evening. We need to get the application sorted out.'

'Oh.' With everything else going on, Mandy had almost forgotten. There were several things that needed to be researched before they could go ahead. 'Would you mind if I rang James?' she asked. 'I'd like him to be one of the trustees.'

'That would be a lovely thing to do.' Emily was as encouraging as ever. 'I can't think of anyone better qualified.' She smiled. 'Give him a ring, then let us know. We can arrange a meeting time that will suit all of us.' Mandy watched as her mum walked out and closed the door. Pulling out her mobile, she dialled James's number.

It took a long time for James to answer the phone. 'Hello, Mandy.'

Mandy felt a tightening in her chest. His voice sounded

leaden; she should have called sooner. Hopefully what she had to say would make him feel better. James had always been enthusiastic about her rescue centre and now, with the name Hope Meadows, it was inextricably associated with Paul.

She toyed for a moment with whether she should ask how he was. She took a deep breath. Probably better to get on and talk about practical things.

'Hello, James.'

'It's good of you to call.' His words were at odds with his tone.

'James, I was wondering . . .' She paused a moment, then started again. 'Mum and Dad and I are about to begin the application for Hope Meadows to become a registered charity. I want you to be involved, to be one of the trustees.'

There was silence on the other end of the phone, then a sigh. 'Mandy, I appreciate your offer. You know I do. But I'm not up to it. I can't think straight.'

She waited to see if he would say anything else, but there was nothing. 'What about if I left it a few days? I could call you back, if you need time to think.'

'There's no point. I really can't, Mandy.' His voice sounded strange. Mandy had been prepared for tears; not this alarming emptiness. 'I'm going to go now. Thanks for thinking about me.'

The line went dead. When she dialled again, the phone was switched off. Mandy stood a moment, then walked through to the sitting room.

Dad was in his chair, Mum was on the sofa. Both of them looked round. 'What did James say?' Adam prompted.

Mandy frowned. 'He didn't really give an answer,' she said. 'He sounded so odd.' She gazed at her parents. She had asked so many favours recently. But James didn't sound as if he could wait. 'Would it be okay if I went to see him?' she asked. 'I know it's asking a lot . . .'

'Of course you can.' Adam was studying her. 'Are you sure you'll be okay? You can stay there overnight, if you think that would help. Poor James.' He looked at Emily. 'I'd offer to come with you, but you know how it is.'

Mandy did. There was still evening surgery to be tackled. She felt a twinge of guilt. She had come here to help her parents, and somehow, she seemed to be making more work for them.

As if reading her mind, Emily spoke. 'Don't worry, we can manage.' She smiled at Mandy. 'James needs you more than us right now.'

'Are you sure?'

Emily nodded. 'Do what you have to do. Now that we're setting up Hope Meadows, we get to keep you here for the foreseeable future. We know how lucky we are.' Her eyes told Mandy everything would be all right. 'You know James is welcome here, too.'

With a sigh of relief, Mandy headed out to her car. She would go and see how James was, and if at all possible, she would bring him back.

The traffic on the York road was awful. It took her

an hour and a half to get into the city, but she drew up outside James's apartment as the sun was setting. Peering up at his windows, there was no sign of life. Lights were springing up everywhere, but if James was inside, he must be in darkness. When Mandy pressed the buzzer beside the door, there was no reply.

She pressed again. Could he have gone out? It was possible, of course. But he had sounded so strange on the phone. She didn't want to turn round and go without finding out if he was okay. She leaned on the jamb, gazing out over the park opposite. A man was walking his two dogs, bathed in the orange light of the newly lit streetlamps. For a moment, Mandy hoped it was James, but the dog walker came closer and it was not her friend.

Turning back, she surveyed the panel of doorbells outside the flat. The one below 'James and Paul' read 'Bradshaw'. Was that the neighbour who had looked after Seamus and Lily when James had been on his honeymoon?

Mandy pressed the buzzer. A female voice answered. 'Hello?'

Leaning close to the grille, Mandy spoke. 'Hello, Mrs Bradshaw,' she said. 'I'm sorry to disturb you. I'm looking for James Hunter. I've tried calling him and I've rung his bell, but I can't seem to get any answer.' There was a time for respecting James's privacy, Mandy thought, and this wasn't it.

'Oh.' There was a pause. 'Well, I think he's in. I heard the dogs just a little while ago. He's been very quiet lately. Understandable, of course.' Mandy waited again. 'What's your name, please?'

'It's Mandy Hope.' Would James have spoken about her to the neighbour?

'Oh, Mandy. He's often talked about you. Why don't you come up? I'll let you in and you can knock on his door.'

'Thank you very much,' Mandy said as the door buzzer went. She hoped Mrs Bradshaw heard her. James's flat was on the first floor. She ran up the stairs and banged on his door. On the far side, she heard a flurry of claws on wood and frantic whining. Lily and Seamus were in, at least.

After what seemed an age, Mandy heard the sound of a bolt being drawn back. The door swung open.

For a moment, it was as if she was seeing the ghost of Paul. The figure that stood looking at her was so thin and white. There were frightening shadows around his eyes.

'James?' she said. At her feet, Seamus and Lily were giving her their usual greeting. It seemed incongruous as James stood there in hollow silence, staring.

'Mandy.' His voice echoed in the hallway. She stepped inside and closed the door. 'Mandy,' James said again.

She opened her arms, half expecting rejection, but taking a step closer nonetheless. Wrapping her arms around him, she could feel the boniness of his spine, the stiffness of his muscles. Then the stiffness left and he was clinging to her and she was supporting him, holding him up as his whole body was wracked with grief.

Mandy hugged him tightly, surrounding him with all the warmth she could. Her eyes were closed, but tears were escaping nonetheless.

When James finally managed to speak, his breathing was so ragged she couldn't understand him.

'I'm sorry,' she whispered. 'I didn't hear what you said.'

The body in her arms was still shaking, trembling now, rather than sobbing. Mandy felt James draw breath, try to hold himself steady.

'I can't bear it,' he said. 'I can't bear life without Paul.'

Chapter Twenty-Nine

'Come with me,' Mandy said. She took James by the hand and led him into the kitchen, switching on the wall lights as she entered. As she sat him in a chair, the two dogs, who had walked through with them, made another dash for the front door. A moment later there was a knock. 'Stay here,' she told James.

On the doorstep stood a friendly-faced woman in a white polo-neck sweater. It was Mrs Bradshaw. 'Is everything okay, dear?' she asked. 'I just wanted to check.'

'Everything's going to be okay.' Mandy studied the woman's kind face and worried eyes. 'I'm going to take James home with me,' she said.

Mrs Bradshaw bent to pat Seamus, who was gambolling at her feet. 'Will you be taking the dogs with you? I looked after them before, when James and Paul were away.'

'We'll take them,' said Mandy. James would want them along and, in the circumstances, Mum and Dad wouldn't mind. She thought for a moment. 'Would you mind sitting with him while I get everything organised, please?'

'Of course,' Mrs Bradshaw said.

Mandy felt relieved as she led the older woman through to the kitchen. There were several things she would need to sort out before they could leave, and with Mrs Bradshaw keeping an eye on James, she could concentrate.

First, she had to get in touch with Sherrie. Hopefully she would be able to run the café for a few days. Mandy went through into the sitting room and picked up the phone, crossing her fingers that the number would be programmed in. Otherwise, she was going to have to ask James. Flipping through the names, she found it. 'Sherrie Home.' Mandy dialled and waited.

'Hello, James? Is everything okay?'

'It's not James, it's Mandy.' She stopped then continued. 'Sherrie, I've come to see James and he's not in a good way. I want to take him home to Welford for a few days. Is there any way you could manage on your own?'

'Poor James,' said Sherrie. 'He's been coming to work every day but it's obvious he shouldn't be there. I told him to take time off, but he wouldn't. Don't worry at all about the café. I can manage fine. I've a couple of friends I can call on if it gets busy. Tell James we'll be thinking about him.'

'I will,' Mandy assured her. 'Thanks, Sherrie.' She rang off.

Next, a suitcase. There was a cupboard in the hall. Opening the door, Mandy peered inside. There were two cases. Pulling out the one she thought most likely to be James's, she closed the door and took it through to the bedroom. Rifling through the drawers, she threw in clothes for several days, a clean pair of pyjamas and James's dressing gown and slippers. In the bathroom, she found a comb, shaving equipment and a toothbrush. What else, she thought? The clinic had plenty of equipment for Seamus and Lily, but they would probably like to have their own bed. For the sake of their stomachs, it would be better to keep them on the food they were used to.

Piling everything together in the hallway, Mandy opened the front door and began to carry luggage out to the car. Once everything was organised, she went back to the kitchen. Mrs Bradshaw had made tea, but James's mug stood untouched.

'James?'

He looked up slowly. 'You're coming with me,' Mandy ordered. 'You too Seamus, Lily!' The dogs stood up.

James looked stricken. 'I can't go anywhere.' He shook his head. 'I have to work.'

'No, you don't,' Mandy told him. 'Sherrie will look after the café. It's all organised.' She looked at Mrs Bradshaw. 'Will you be able to water the plants?'

Mrs Bradshaw glanced from Mandy to James and then back again. 'Of course I will,' she said. 'And I'll tidy up in here,' she added, her eyes on James's undrunk tea.

'So that's everything.' Mandy gently took James's hand. He seemed almost in a dream as he followed her out. He watched as she pulled the door to, and handed the key to Mrs Bradshaw. Seamus and Lily rushed down the stairs, waiting at the front door, then waltzed out to the car.

'Do you have their seat belts?' said James. It was the first time he had shown any sign of knowing what was happening, thought Mandy.

'Of course.' She held them out for him to see. 'You get in the front, and I'll get the terrible two sorted out.'

He did as she said. When she climbed into the driver's seat beside him, he gave a wobbly smile. 'Anyone would think I was one of your animals in need of rescue,' he said.

Mandy cocked her eyebrow at him. 'Really? They don't need so much luggage, I can tell you that.'

James managed half a laugh, then his mouth quivered and he closed it tightly. 'Thanks, Mandy,' he whispered. When she looked back at him, his head had fallen to one side and he was asleep.

By the time he woke, they were passing under the Animal Ark sign. Mandy caught sight of his movement as he sat up. 'We're here,' she said. 'Mum and Dad are expecting us.' She had called them on the hands-free on the way over. As the car rolled round the corner, Emily and Adam appeared at the cottage door.

'Come in, James.' Adam ushered them inside. 'We've got the bed made up in the spare room.'

'There's plenty of milk for hot chocolate,' Emily said.

'That would be lovely.' It was little more than a whisper.

Emily smiled. 'I'll get it made, then,' she assured them. 'Take James upstairs,' she told Mandy. 'I know it's a warm night, but we put the electric blanket on to air the bed.'

'Thanks, Mum.' She could always rely on her parents not to make a fuss. 'Is it okay if the dogs come upstairs?'

'Of course. If you give your dad the keys, he can bring their beds up.'

Mandy handed them over. She had already brought in James's suitcase. Guiding him up the stairs, she opened it, laid his pyjamas and dressing gown on the bed, and dropped his slippers on the floor. James shook his head again, as if he couldn't quite believe what was happening.

'I'll give you a minute to get changed,' Mandy said. Making her way back to the kitchen, she waited while Emily sorted out hot chocolate and a plate of cookies. Hugging her mum, Mandy lifted the tray and carried it upstairs.

James was sitting up in bed. Handing over the hot chocolate, Mandy lifted her own cup. 'Mind if I sit down?' she asked.

'Just like the old days,' James said.

As Mandy lowered herself onto the foot of the bed, she thought of the many sleepovers and holidays they'd had together.

'I've been thinking about what you asked earlier.' James's voice jolted her out of her memories.

'What did I ask?' Mandy looked at him in confusion.

She had done a lot of ordering about, but had she asked anything?

'About me being one of the trustees for Hope Meadows.' Though his voice was still sad, he sounded as if he was starting to come back to reality. 'I would be honoured.'

'Thank you.' Mandy looked at him, at his thin face and darkened eyes. 'I don't know what I should say,' she began. 'I can't begin to imagine what you're going through, but you will get through it. If anyone deserves to find love again, it's you.'

'And what about you?' James asked.

She looked at him. 'What do you mean?' She was amazed to see he was looking at her with sympathy.

'There's something wrong, isn't there?'

Mandy closed her eyes then opened them again. James was gazing at her, still sorrowful. 'Simon asked me to marry him,' she admitted.

'You said no,' James said. It wasn't a question.

'I haven't given him an answer yet.'

James smoothed the duvet with one hand. 'When Paul proposed to me,' he said, 'I couldn't wait for him to get to the end of the sentence before I said yes. I knew at once it was right. I think you know in your heart that it isn't right with Simon.' His eyes were dark and very piercing. 'Don't you?'

Mandy felt her cheek muscles quivering. She pressed her lips together. 'Simon and I have had some great times together,' she whispered.

James gave a tiny shake of his head. 'That's not enough,' he said. 'It's not a foundation for forever.'

It was Mandy's turn to fall silent.

'I know we haven't seen each other much lately,' James went on, 'but it's easy to see how you've slotted back into Welford. It's as if you've never been away. You didn't plan for your rescue centre to move so fast, but it's developed a life of its own. It seems to me, it was meant to be. But there isn't any space for Simon. If he were different, if he could fit in around your plans, it might be possible, but he has his own plans and dreams. Doesn't he?'

Mandy sighed. How could James see so clearly, when it had taken her so long? James was watching her. How tired he looked. 'You should get some sleep,' she said. Moving up the bed, she hugged him. He lay down and she pulled up the sheets and tucked him in, just as Emily had done so many times over the years. 'Thank you,' she said. 'Who knew you were such a wise old bird?'

James was muttering something. She put her ear closer to him. 'Do you have a licence for rescuing owls?' he said.

'Not yet.' Mandy smiled. 'But maybe you can help me organise it.' She looked down. James had fallen asleep, his glasses halfway down his nose. Gently, she reached out, removed them and set them on the bedside table. 'Goodnight,' she whispered.

★ ★ ★

She was surprised to find James at the breakfast table when she went downstairs next morning. 'I thought you'd have a lie in,' she said.

'I wanted to help with the animals,' he said. Though he still looked sad, the dark rings round his eyes were less pronounced. He was tucking into pancakes, too. Emily seemed to have gone into mother-hen mode.

Mandy helped herself to pancakes, adding syrup and lemon juice. 'I should have friends over more often,' she said.

Out in the wildlife unit, Mandy showed James the black cat and her kittens. Two of the babies were black with green eyes like their mother. The third was a sleek grey. James watched as Mandy put them through their paces, calling them, waiting for them to come and sit before she fed them. Without needing to be asked, he pulled out the litter tray while they ate. He had never minded getting stuck in, Mandy thought. To her pleasure, when she opened Sky's door, the collie came straight out to sit in front of him and waited while he stroked her face.

'What a beautiful dog,' James said. Sky's brown eyes were fixed on Mandy as she moved around the room. 'She seems very attached to you.'

'I haven't had time to ask Mum and Dad yet,' Mandy admitted, 'but I want to keep her.'

'I can see that,' James said, watching as Sky stood up and followed Mandy. 'She really is very lovely. You've worked wonders. From what you told me when you got her, I wasn't sure if you'd be able to help.'

Together, they went to look at the Animal Ark in-patients. 'You haven't lost your touch,' she told James as she watched him wrangling one of the more difficult cats. Together they flushed out the intravenous catheter and set up a new drip. 'But even you will struggle with Percy,' she added as they approached the last cage.

'Who's Percy?' James pulled aside the towel that was draped over the front of the kennel.

'Percy wants a peanut.'

James's eyes widened when he heard the parrot's high-pitched voice.

'Watch yourself,' Mandy warned. 'Percy isn't keen on men. He nearly took Dad's nose off the first day he came in.' She lifted a pair of protective gauntlets that she had stowed in the neighbouring cage and handed them over.

'I'm sure he'll be okay,' James replied, pulling on the thick gloves. 'You know I have a way with birds.' Letting the towel fall back into place, he lifted the catch and drew the door towards him, standing in the gap in case Percy decided to make a flap for freedom.

When the space was big enough, he moved towards Percy with a wheedling tone. 'Come on, Percy. I'll find you a peanut.' To Mandy's surprise, despite a look of disgust, Percy made no attempt to bite. 'Come on, then.' James put out his arm. 'You and I are fine, aren't we, Percy?'

'Fuck off, freaky!'

For a moment, Mandy couldn't believe what she had

heard. When she looked at James, his face was astonished. Catching his eye, she found herself laughing, and then James was laughing too and they were holding onto one another while Percy, who had flapped back into his cage, shouted, 'Don't laugh at Percy.'

Sobering first, Mandy straightened up and pushed the cage door to. The last thing they needed was Percy escaping to unleash his profanity on their other patients.

James stood up at the same time, clutching his side. 'Oh,' he groaned. 'That's the first time I've found anything to laugh at since Paul . . .' He tailed off.

Mandy pulled him into her arms for a hug. 'Paul will always be with you,' she told him. 'Your memories will keep him alive.'

James hugged her back very tight. 'Thanks, Mandy,' he said. 'Thank you for everything.'

Chapter Thirty

She was going to have to visit Simon, Mandy thought. She had made up her mind. Now she needed to let him know. Heading back inside after James and she had finished with the in-patients, she went upstairs and changed. She needed to feel the best she could.

Returning, she found James in the kitchen, working on his laptop, which Mandy had popped into his suitcase at the last minute.

'Look at this,' he said, turning it so she could see the screen. 'There's loads of information here on how to set up a charity. I'm finding out as much as I can before we start the application.' His eyes were studying her face. 'What's wrong?'

'I have to go and sort things out with Simon,' she admitted.

James nodded. 'It's the right thing to do.' He gave a wry smile. He knew her so well, Mandy thought. Most people would have asked her what she was going to do, but James didn't have to. 'Good luck,' he said.

Mandy sighed. 'Thanks,' she said. She would have to ask Mum and Dad for yet more time off, too. Bracing herself for an inquisition, she found Adam in consulting room one. He was staring at the computer, muttering.

'What's up, Dad?'

'Another outbreak of measles,' he said, frowning at the screen. 'After a music festival. Luckily most of our clients trust us when we tell them vaccination is one of the safest methods of protection. It's no different for animals than humans. There was an outbreak of canine distemper in Wales a couple of years ago. I haven't seen a single case in my whole career, but I've read what it used to be like. People don't remember how bad these diseases were.'

Mandy knew it was one of Adam's bugbears when people refused to vaccinate their pets. Any puppies in the neighbourhood were put at risk when someone's unvaccinated pet came down with parvovirus. Animal Ark offered a progressive approach to vaccination, with blood testing if owners preferred, but for now, Mandy didn't want to get bogged down in the conversation.

'Dad?'

Hearing her tone, he looked up at her. 'Is everything okay?'

'Not really. I want to go down to Leeds to speak to Simon. I promise this is the last time I'll ask for time off.'

'You shouldn't make promises you can't be sure you'll keep.' Adam's voice was light, but he became serious as he continued to look at her. 'Of course you can go,' he said. 'Do you want to talk about it?'

Mandy shook her head. 'Not yet.'

'I'll let Mum know that you've gone.' Adam reached out and hugged her. 'Whatever it is, I know you'll make the right choice,' he said. 'And we're here for you.'

She was so lucky, Mandy thought as she stumbled out to the car. She had told her dad she would be back that evening. As she drove, she tried to think what she wanted to say, but it was so difficult. She had no idea how Simon would react. Their relationship had been the most stable thing in her life for a year. Then she had moved back to Welford, and it had turned into a roller-coaster.

It was approaching lunchtime when she reached Leeds. Not that she could have eaten anything. Her mouth was dry, but she kept swallowing. Her hands were not quite steady as she turned into the car park at Thurston's and pulled on the brake. What should she do now, she wondered. If she went bursting in, everyone would want to know why she was there. She couldn't face their greetings and questions. Pulling her phone out of her pocket, she called Simon's number. *Please answer, please answer.* Maybe he didn't have his phone on him. If he was consulting, he wouldn't be able to reply.

Mandy had pulled the phone away from her ear, was about to cut the call, when she heard his voice.

'Mandy? What can I do for you?' He sounded the same as always.

Mandy's fingers shook as she returned the mobile to

her ear. 'Are you at work?' she said. 'I'm parked outside. I want to talk to you.'

'What a lovely surprise,' he said. There was no trepidation in his voice. How could he be so confident all the time? 'I was about to go out for lunch with Samantha. She's had another paper published in the Veterinary Dentistry Journal. Would you like to join us?'

'No.' Mandy's reaction was too quick. She needed to slow down. 'I'd like to talk to you alone, if that's okay.' Better, she thought.

'Did you say you were in the car park?' Simon sounded puzzled, but not put out. 'Give me a minute to sort things. I'll be out as soon as I can.'

'Thanks.' Mandy ended the call and took some deep breaths. By the time Simon appeared in the rear-view mirror, she was calmer. When he climbed into the passenger seat and kissed her, she managed a smile. Starting the engine, she backed out of the parking space and turned left onto the road.

'Where are we going?' Simon asked.

'Roundhay Park,' Mandy replied. She had made up her mind while she was waiting. The park was beautiful all year round. It was almost like being in the country-side.

'Okay. We can have lunch in the café.' He sounded pleased. 'This is a lovely surprise,' he said again. Putting out a hand, he patted Mandy's knee. Once she would have been charmed, but now the movement seemed patronising. Why hadn't he asked why she had come?

She drove to the car park beside the café, but instead of going in, walked past the open door and headed for the path that led round the lake. Simon sauntered beside her, looking relaxed. It was a perfect August day. There were other couples walking hand-in-hand. The blue sky and the leaf-heavy trees were reflected in the calm surface of the water. Mandy had been planning her words, but now Simon and she were here, everything had gone from her head.

'I'm glad you came,' Simon began. 'I've got lots to tell you. I want you to know, I've been listening to what you said.'

Mandy felt her heart rise into her throat. Did he really believe he had been listening? Taking a deep breath, she spoke. 'I'm sorry, Simon,' she said. 'It's just . . .' she struggled to find the words. 'I think we need to split up. I . . . I appreciate you asking to marry me, I really do. But it's too late. It's all come too late for me.'

He had stopped on the path, was looking at her with a bewildered expression.

'How do you mean, it's too late?' he said. 'Everything is still in front of us. I've been looking at premises in York as you suggested. It's not going to be as straight-forward as Leeds, but I think it should be possible.'

Mandy clenched her fists. If he had said that two weeks ago, it might have all been very different. And yet she couldn't go back.

'It's over.' She said it as gently as she could. 'I'm so sorry,' she said again. She was finding it hard to breathe.

His blue eyes still held confusion. 'But . . .' he began, and stopped, almost imperceptibly shaking his head. 'We were going to get married,' he said.

Mandy turned towards him and grasped his hands. Both of them were shaking. 'We can't get married,' she said. 'We want different things. I want different things,' she amended. What did she want to say? That she felt he had been putting his own needs ahead of hers? There was no easy way to say it. 'It's seems to me,' she began, 'that since I've been back in Welford, we've been growing apart. I thought we'd agreed, before I went, that we would wait and discuss our future, but then you started looking in Leeds and . . .'

'Well, you started planning too.' Simon pulled his hands away and a petulant tone crept into his voice. 'You were the one who went and got architect's plans made.'

Mandy pressed her lips together. There was no way to deny that was true. 'I did,' she admitted. 'When I first moved, I thought, like you, that we would set up in Leeds. I wasn't sure we could manage it as quickly as you hoped. But I was willing to try, so long as we were working towards what we both wanted.' Her eyes drifted over to the water. There were tiny waves lapping against the walkway. 'It worried me,' she explained, turning her face back, finding his eyes again. 'You were looking at those expensive buildings and all that equipment. And when I tried to talk about my rescue centre . . . I just felt it was forgotten.' She paused for a moment, then went on. 'I felt like you were expecting me to put aside what I wanted. But that you intended to go ahead with your own dreams.'

The blue eyes had suddenly become cold. 'But the rescue centre was never going to make any money.' Simon shook his head, his mouth tight. 'It was obvious I was going to have to support your venture. There's no reason you shouldn't have done the same for me at the start. It was obvious I was going to be propping up your "business" for the rest of my life.'

Mandy felt a wave of shock run through her. Was that what he had thought? She had never wanted to make a fortune from her rehabilitation work, but she knew that she was going to work hard to make sure it supported itself.

He was speaking again. 'Samantha said it would happen.' How mean his mouth looked as he pronounced Samantha's name. 'She said once you went back to Welford that you wouldn't want to come back. That you'd be too comfortable with your parents.'

Mandy had the feeling she had experienced so often with Simon lately: that he was rushing onto a new subject without the last being resolved. And there was Samantha's name again. Mandy had always trusted Simon. She still trusted that he hadn't been two-timing her. But there was no way he should have been discussing *their* business with Samantha.

'Why were you talking about our plans with Samantha?' Mandy searched Simon's face, hoping somehow she would find the answer there.

Simon averted his head slightly. 'I needed someone to talk to,' he muttered. 'You were never available. You were always too busy looking after everyone else.'

Mandy thought about Emily's exhaustion. About Paul and about James and Robbie Grimshaw and she almost wanted to laugh. Was Simon jealous of her poor, poor friends?

'Anyway,' and now Simon was looking straight at her again, 'Samantha said that if you did back out, she would be very willing to set up in practice with me. She wouldn't be a drain on me, she said. There would always be plenty of dental work she could do.'

Mandy felt the breath go out of her. Had Samantha really said that? They had been friends, back when they had worked together. At least, she had thought they were. Had Samantha always had designs on Simon? And were they really only business designs?

Then she realised that she didn't really care. If Samantha did have designs on Simon, she, Mandy Hope, would not be standing in her way.

'I think we should go back to the car,' she said quietly.

Simon looked out of the side window all the way back to the clinic. Mandy kept her eyes on the road. He hadn't had any lunch, she thought, but there was no way she was going to stop. She pulled into the car park, into the same bay as before, and Simon took off his seat belt and looked at her.

'I have to get on,' he said. He closed the door and

Mandy watched him in the rear-view mirror as he walked back into the clinic. The door closed behind him.

She turned the key in the ignition, reversed out and began the slow trek through the city. She felt numb. Trying to turn left, she found her way blocked by signs. They were mending the road. Swinging the car round, she backtracked, turning right and then right again. It was a dead end. Stopping the car, she switched off the engine. She would have to consult the GPS on her phone. She would do it in a minute, she thought.

She had stopped in a residential street of terraced Victorian houses. They reminded her of Simon's. Her hands were shaking. She pressed her knuckles over her mouth, closed her eyes and held her breath until the spasm passed. James's face drifted into her mind. How could she feel sorry for herself? Simon was not dead. He wasn't her boyfriend any more, that was all. It had been the right decision, she knew.

Pulling up the GPS on her phone, Mandy checked the map, turned the car in the narrow roadway and set off for home.

Chapter Thirty-One

It was gone three o'clock when Mandy drove back under the Animal Ark sign. James was waiting for her in the kitchen. 'How did it go?' he asked as she bent to greet Seamus and Lily.

'As well as could be expected.' Mandy didn't want to go into any more detail. She was glad when James didn't press her.

'Helen was in a couple of minutes ago,' James said. 'There's been a call from Woodbridge Farm Park. A couple of the calves are scouring. They've isolated them, but they want them checked out as soon as possible.'

'Are Mum and Dad out?'

'They've both been out a couple of hours,' James said. 'Your mum's at a TT test, your dad's gone to a downer cow at the top of the valley. I told Helen I'd let her know when you came in.' He pushed the lid of his laptop closed and stood up. 'Would you mind if I came with you?' His head was on one side as he looked at her. 'I know we went out with your mum and dad when we were younger, but I've never been out on a call with you.'

Mandy managed a smile. It would be good to have company. 'That would be great,' she said. She thought for a moment. 'Would it be okay if we took Sky along as well? I've wanted to take her out with me for the last couple of weeks, but I've never been sure how she would react. If you were there, and she got frightened, you could stay with her . . . If that's all right with you, of course.'

'Of course it would be all right,' James assured her. 'If I end up staying with her, we can sit in the car and howl together.'

Mandy shook her head. 'I hope that won't be necessary,' she said. 'But if it is, I hope you won't mind if I join in, too.'

'Maybe we could have a sponsored howlathon,' James suggested. 'We could do it in aid of Born Free.'

Mandy sent him a mock glare. 'If there is any sponsorship on offer,' she told him, 'I expect all proceeds to go to Hope Meadows.' She made her way to the door.

'I'll just put these two upstairs.' James called to Seamus and Lily. 'They'll be fine for a couple of hours. I'll get Sky and meet you outside.'

Mandy waited until he had shut the door and then walked through to the clinic. She had to search for the nurse, who was in one of the consulting rooms, washing down the inside of the cupboards. Helen looked pleased to see her. She accompanied Mandy through to the waiting-room where the day book was kept. 'You're back,' she said. 'I wasn't sure how long you would be.'

'Is it just the one call?' Mandy asked.

'Yes. Two scouring calves at Woodbridge,' Helen confirmed.

'James and Sky are coming with me,' Mandy told her. She looked round as James opened the clinic door and Sky rushed in, pulling on her halter. 'We'd better go before Sky pulls James off his feet.'

'Bye!' Helen gave them a wave as they walked out.

Sky jumped straight into the back seat of the SUV. She sat very still as Mandy strapped her in. So far so good, Mandy thought. Her main concern was how Sky would behave when she was left alone in the car out on the farms. If she could relax and lie still, Mandy could take her on calls. If she became stressed, it would be far more complicated. She stroked the collie's ear, closed the door and went round to the driver's seat.

It was only a few minutes' drive to Woodbridge. Mrs Waterstone was waiting.

'Thanks for coming so quickly,' she said as Mandy and James climbed out of the car. 'You know how it is. We can't be too careful with children coming in to see the animals.' Woodbridge Farm was run as a tourist attraction, open to visitors to see how the animals were kept and where food came from.

'I know,' Mandy agreed. It was always a concern when lots of visitors came into contact with farm animals. Not only could the children pick up infections, but diseases could also be carried in. She knew how careful the Waterstones were. 'We'll have a look at the calves,' she said, 'and get some samples to be on the safe side.'

The calves were not too bad. Although they showed some signs of diarrhoea, there was no blood. Both of them looked bright-eyed and alert. Mandy placed the lid on the second sample pot and removed her gloves. 'I'll get these sent off first thing,' she said. 'The post will have gone today. In the meantime,' she rooted in the boot of her car and pulled out a pack of rehydration sachets, 'give them these twice a day for two days,' she said. 'Then if they're getting better, you can start to reintroduce milk for one meal a day. Give us a call if they get worse or if they don't improve.'

'Thanks.' Mrs Waterstone took the sachets. 'I'll get the first dosage done shortly.'

'If I haven't heard from you, I'll let you know as soon as we get the results,' Mandy said. 'Keep them isolated until then, you know the drill.'

Mrs Waterstone nodded. 'I should do, after all these years.'

They went back to the car. Mandy was delighted to see Sky curled up on the seat, her nose tucked under her tail. When they opened the doors, the collie stood up, wagging her tail to greet them. Reaching back, Mandy put out a hand to stroke her and Sky pushed her nose forward to snuffle in Mandy's ear.

'What do you say to going to visit your old home?' she asked the collie. Sky put her head on one side and wagged her tail harder. 'What do you think, James?' Mandy raised her eyebrows. 'Should we pop to Lamb's Wood Cottage for old times' sake?'

'Why not?' James agreed. 'I didn't get a chance to have a good look round last time. What's the cottage like inside?'

'Pretty grim,' Mandy admitted. 'It wouldn't do any harm to check the garden and farmyard again. It's not impossible some of the chickens might have turned up.' She started the engine. In no time at all, they were pulling up in the long grass beside the track outside the cottage.

'It looks as if nobody has been here in years,' James commented.

It was true. When Mandy had been coming here daily, there had been trampled pathways and signs of life. The animals had called out to her as she arrived. Now the only movement came from insects flickering through the tangled foliage. Mandy couldn't help thinking back to the day years ago when they had first met Robbie Grimshaw. The cottage had been cared for back then. It had been a home. House and outbuildings had been filled with the old man's much-loved animals.

'What do you think will happen to this old place?' Mandy said.

They had pushed their way through the jungle to the front door. The green-stained weatherboarding looked worse than ever. Mandy tried to imagine the cottage in a few years' time. Would the roof fall in? Perhaps a tree would grow where once the cat had suckled her kittens under the old stove.

'Auctioned off, I expect.' James, having tried the front

door and found it locked, had turned on the doorstep and was looking at the garden. 'There would be a lovely view into the valley if you cleared away some of those overgrown shrubs. I expect some rich second-homer from the city will come and rip everything out and start again.' He sounded as gloomy about the prospect as Mandy felt.

She peered through the vegetation. James was right about the view. The overgrown garden and the avenue of trees covering the roadway obscured the valley at the moment. But with some work, it might be possible to see down to the village.

James had stepped away and was looking up at the roof. 'They'll probably tear the cottage down,' he said. His shoulders drooped.

'Not if I can help it!' A wave of emotion surged through Mandy. James stared at her. 'I can't live with my parents forever. Sky could come home. It would be perfect.'

'What do you mean?' James was frowning, half confused, half hopeful. 'Are you thinking . . .'

'I want to buy Lamb's Wood Cottage,' Mandy declared. 'I can't afford to do everything immediately, but with a few repairs and a whole lot of cleaning, it should be habitable. Wouldn't it be wonderful to live up here?' She threw her arms wide, narrowly missing the waist-high nettles.

James grinned. 'You're mad,' he said, shaking his head, 'and completely brilliant. There's just one thing . . .'

'What? Out with it.'

James looked as if he was choosing his words carefully. He gazed up at the sky for a moment, then back at her. 'When you choose the colour schemes,' he said, 'please let me help you. I've seen the decor you chose for your bedroom at Animal Ark. Even with the tasteful pictures you bought from me . . . well . . .' He made a face and then laughed, reaching out his arms too, and Mandy fell into them and they hugged, standing there amongst the weeds and the tangled grass. Stumbling apart, they picked their way back to the car.

'Could you look up the number of the estate agent in Walton?' Mandy pushed her phone into James's hand as they drove down the track. 'I should call them as soon as possible. They're the most likely to know what's happening.'

'Here.' Within moments, James had found the details and handed the mobile back to her. Putting her foot on the brake, Mandy stopped halfway down the lane. Setting the phone on loudspeaker, she dialled the number.

The call rang twice before the voice came. 'Simpson and Forager Estate Agents.'

Mandy could hardly breathe. 'It's Mandy . . . Amanda Hope here from Welford,' she said. 'I was wondering if you had Lamb's Wood Cottage on your books?' Now she had started to imagine living there, it was almost unbearable to think it might not be possible. At the other end, she could hear the woman typing in the information. Mandy closed her eyes, willing her to get a move on.

'Oh, yes.' Her eyes snapped open as the voice came over the airwaves. 'We do have details for that one here. Lamb's Wood Cottage and outbuildings, Welford, is that right?'

'Yes.' There was another long pause.

'It's due up for auction a week on Friday,' the woman continued. 'Guide price £235,000. Would you like the details of the auction house?'

Mandy's free hand gripped the handbrake. She wasn't sure she could wait that long. Taking a deep breath, she asked, 'Is it possible I could call in to discuss it, please? Preferably tomorrow?'

'Yes, of course. I'll set you up an appointment with Mr Forager at ten o'clock. Would that do?'

'That would be perfect,' Mandy said. 'Thank you.' She looked at James, who grinned at her.

'Can I come with you?' he said.

Mandy nodded. 'I'd be glad to have you.' Shoving her phone into the pocket of her jeans, she released the handbrake.

When they opened the door to the clinic, Helen greeted them with a red face and wild eyes.

'Close the door quickly,' she shouted.

Mandy was astonished. Helen never looked flustered, but she did as the nurse asked. To her surprise, Helen got down on her hands and knees and started crawling behind the reception desk. There was a scuffling sound and a high-pitched 'Baaaaaa,' and a sturdy little goat came racing out from the other side of the desk. With his shaggy brown coat and the white tuft on his tail, he looked as if he had come to life from a cartoon.

He tossed his head as he passed Mandy and James, short legs pounding the tiled floor. He skidded to a standstill beside the line of potted bamboo that Mandy had introduced to separate dogs and cats in the waiting-room. The goat stared at the three of them with disapproving eyes, then as if overwhelmed with temptation, turned his back to nibble on one of the leaves.

'Where on earth did he come from?' James got the question out before Mandy had time to pull herself together. 'And what is he? He looks like a goat, only smaller.'

Helen, who had reappeared from behind the desk, put her hands on her hips. 'He's a pygmy goat,' she said. 'This woman appeared about ten minutes ago, muttering something about an unwanted present. She'd heard we had a rescue centre so "you can help right?"' Her impression of a simpering woman was so out of character, Mandy almost choked. 'He's called Rudolph, apparently. I think they thought he was a reindeer.'

'Well he does look a bit reindeer-like with his colouring,' Mandy said. There was something very cheeky about the goat's face. His jaunty horns waggled as he pulled another leaf from the plant. 'Why's he running around in here?'

'I can't catch him,' Helen confessed. 'I've been chasing him for the last half-hour. I've never seen a client beat such a hasty retreat. I didn't even get her name.'

'Welcome to Hope Meadows, Rudolph,' James said. 'Where we *hope* you don't get ill from eating the waiting-room decorations.'

Mandy laughed. 'He won't get ill, but if we don't get him caught, the bamboo might not survive.' Working together, they formed a line and when Rudolph tried to break through, Mandy grabbed him.

'If you two can put him in one of the kennels,' James suggested, 'I'll go out to the orchard. I should be able to make him a little paddock out of pallets. It shouldn't take long.'

'Hopefully he isn't as much of an escape artist as Houdini used to be,' said Mandy.

'Who's Houdini?' Helen asked.

'He was a goat who used to belong to Lydia Fawcett,' James explained. 'He could escape from anywhere. Don't worry, I'll make sure there are no holes.' He headed outside.

Half an hour later, James and Mandy stood beside the makeshift paddock. Rudolph sniffed around inside, examining every corner. 'He looks happy enough,' said Mandy. 'We could go back in now, start looking at the charity stuff and do the application.'

'Okay,' said James. 'Can you give me a minute on my own first? I want to sort a couple of things out before I show you.'

'No problem.'

It was a gorgeous day. Mandy decided it would do no harm to stay here for a few minutes while Rudolph settled in. Things had moved so fast in the past twenty-four hours. This time yesterday, she was just thinking she should phone James. He seemed much more cheerful already. And Simon. Poor Simon. She had never wanted to hurt him. But he'd be okay. He was born to rise to the top.

Mandy looked around at the field where, very soon, Hope Meadows was going to become a reality. She had the oddest sensation of swooping upwards like a bird. For months, she had been worrying about how she was going to share her plans with Simon. The surging tide that was carrying her forwards didn't fit with what he wanted. Now she could go wherever the current took her.

She should go and sort out the application with James, she thought. Pushing herself away from the apple tree she had been leaning on, she turned. But as she walked away, there came a thudding of hooves behind her and then silence. Swivelling, she was amazed to see Rudolph in mid-air, sailing over the fence James had so carefully built. Mandy burst out laughing. They should have known a goat named after Santa's reindeer would be able to fly.

As the short-legged creature thundered across the orchard, she gave chase, panting behind him as he headed towards the road. Running headlong, she cringed as Rudolph slipped through a tiny gap in the hedge and she heard the sound of a vehicle in the lane. Thankfully, there was no squealing of brakes. Just the sound of a car coming to a halt, then a door opening and closing.

Breathless, Mandy reached the hedge and began to squeeze through. She crossed her fingers that it was one of their farm clients, who would understand about escaping animals: not Rudolph's owner, coming back to see if they were looking after him properly. Arriving on the far side, her spirits lifted. Jimmy Marsh stood on the verge, hanging on to Rudolph as the goat bucked and twisted.

'I think I might have something of yours,' he said with a grin.

Mandy leaned forwards, hands on her thighs, catching her breath. 'Thanks,' she gasped. After a moment, she straightened up.

'I hear you're interested in Lamb's Wood Cottage.'

Mandy blinked. 'How on earth do you know that?'

'I was in the post office,' he said, 'when Mrs McFarlane came in. Her niece had been talking to her cousin's next-door neighbour, who was in the estate agent's when you rang up. Or something like that.' His eyes creased with amusement.

'You should be careful,' Mandy shot at him. 'You'll be turning into a village gossip next.'

Jimmy laughed. 'If that means I'm considered a local,' he said, 'I'll take it gladly.'

'No chance.' Mandy shook her head as she moved towards him. 'You have to be here at least thirty years before that happens.'

Between them, they began to guide Rudolph towards Animal Ark. They would have to put him in a kennel,

Mandy realised, until they could double the height of the fence.

'If you have to be here thirty years before you can become a local,' Jimmy said as they manoeuvred Rudolph back into the cage, 'does that mean you're still an outsider?'

'Not at all.' Mandy stood up, staring him straight in the eye. 'This is my home.' The thought of Lamb's Wood Cottage suddenly came into her head. 'I want to buy Lamb's Wood,' she said. 'I know it would be a whole load of work, but if I get the chance, I'm sure I could have it habitable in a couple of months.'

'Wow,' said Jimmy. 'That's quite a project.' He scuffed the lino floor with the toe of his boot. 'If you need any help with anything, patching the roof, that kind of thing, I'd be happy to lend a hand.'

Mandy pictured him up a ladder, confidently hammering boards to keep Robbie's animals safe until they could be moved. There wasn't anyone she'd trust more to build her new home.

'Thank you,' she said. 'I hope you don't regret making the offer!'

Jimmy reached down and touched Rudolph's nose through the wire of the cage. 'No chance,' he said quietly. He stood up. 'I'm really glad you're staying, Mandy,' he said. He suddenly seemed very close.

Mandy looked up at him. His green gaze burned into hers. 'I'm glad, too,' she said. For a moment, she wondered if he was going to kiss her. He reached out a hand, but only touched her shoulder before stepping back. 'I'm sorry,' he said. 'I have to go and collect the children.'

Mandy grinned at his rueful expression. 'You're sorry you're collecting the children?' she teased. 'That's not something I thought I would ever hear you apologising for.'

He laughed. 'You know I didn't mean it like that. But if I wasn't collecting them, I wouldn't be rushing away. That's for sure.' He reached out again, this time grasping her fingers for a moment. 'I'll see you very soon,' he promised, and with that, he turned, opened the door and disappeared.

For a breathless moment, Mandy leaned on the wall, the warmth from his hand still coursing through her. Only this morning, she had been with Simon. Over in Leeds, it had felt as if everything was ending. But here she was, back where she belonged in Animal Ark with Emily and Adam, with James and her friends and all the animals. Sky was waiting for her in the clinic. And now there was Jimmy, too.

It felt as if everything was only just beginning.